This book should be returned to any branch of the
Lancashire County Library on or before the date shown

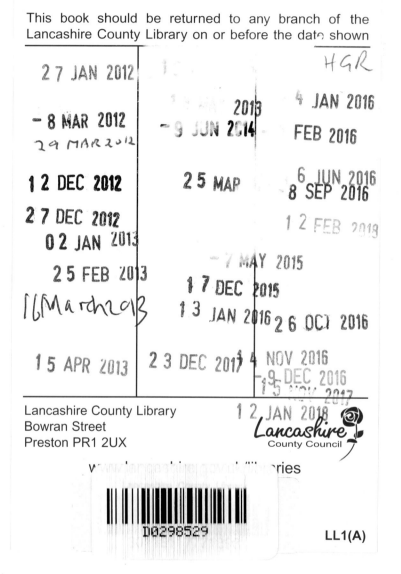

THE MAGIC OF CHRISTMAS

THE MAGIC OF CHRISTMAS

Trisha Ashley

WINDSOR
PARAGON

First published 2011
by HarperCollins*Publishers*
This Large Print edition published 2011
by AudioGO Ltd
by arrangement with
HarperCollins*Publishers*

Hardcover   ISBN: 978 1 445 85944 6
Softcover   ISBN: 978 1 445 85945 3

British Library Cataloguing in Publication Data available

11777189

Printed and bound in Great Britain by
MPG Books Group Limited

For my son, Robin Ashley, with love.

PROLOGUE: DECEMBER 2005, WINTER OF DISCONTENT

The venue for the last Middlemoss Christmas Pudding Circle meeting of the year (which was usually more of an excuse for a party) had been switched to Perseverance Cottage because Lizzy's thirteen-year-old son had come down with what she'd thought was flu and she wanted to keep an eye on him.

Later, looking back on the events of that day, it seemed to Lizzy that one minute she'd been sitting at the big pine table in her kitchen, wearing a paper hat and happily debating the rival merits of fondant icing over royal with the other four members of the CPC, and the next she was frantically snatching at the card listing the symptoms of meningitis, which she kept pinned to her notice board, and shouting to Annie, her best friend, to ring for an ambulance.

*   *   *

At the hospital, Jasper changed frighteningly fast from a big, gruff teenager to a pale, sick child, and Lizzy tried urgently to contact her husband, Tom, who was away on one of his alleged business trips. But as usual he didn't answer his mobile and was nowhere to be found, so all she could do was leave messages in the usual places . . . and several unusual ones.

The hospital radio was softly warbling on about decking the halls with boughs of holly, but Lizzy, filled with a volatile mixture of desperate maternal

1

fear and anger, wanted to deck her selfish, unreliable husband.

It was just as well that Annie was such a tower of strength in an emergency! During that first long day while Lizzy anxiously waited for the antibiotics to kick in, her friend popped in and out between jobs for the pet-sitting agency she ran, visited Perseverance Cottage to feed the poultry and let out Lizzy's dog, and reassured Tom's elderly relatives up at the Hall that she would keep them updated with every change in Jasper's condition.

Then in the evening she returned to the hospital and she and Lizzy spent the long night watches sitting together while Jasper slept, reminiscing in hushed voices about when they first met and became best friends at boarding school. Lizzy had begun spending the holidays with Annie's family in the vicarage at Middlemoss, where she was quickly absorbed into the Vane household, much to the relief of the elderly bachelor uncle who was her guardian—and it was also in Middlemoss that she'd met Tom and Nick Pharamond, cousins who were often farmed out with relatives up at the Hall in the school holidays.

Nick was the eldest: quiet, serious and appearing to prefer the company of the cook at Pharamond Hall to anyone else's. Tom, who was really only nominally a Pharamond, his mother having married into the family, was the opposite: mercurial, charming and gregarious, though he'd had a quick temper and a sharp tongue, even then . . .

Nick was the first to fly the nest. Having inherited the Pharamond cooking gene in spades, it wasn't a huge surprise to anyone except his staid stockbroker father when he took off around the world at eighteen, tastebuds and recipe notebook at the ready. Now he was chief cookery writer for a leading Sunday newspaper and author of numerous books and articles, while Tom, in contrast, had dropped out of university and gravitated down to the part of Cornwall where many of his more useless friends had also ended up.

When he set eyes on Lizzy again after a long interval, it was across a buffet table at a large party in London, where he was a guest, and where she and Annie, who'd done a French cookery course after school, were helping with the catering. He fell suddenly in love with her, a passion that also embraced her rose-tinted dreams of a self-sufficient existence in the country.

Somehow she'd forgotten about his dark good looks, his overwhelming charm and his quirky sense of humour . . . Before she'd had time to think—or to remember his quick temper, occasional sarcasms and how short-lived his enthusiasms had been in the past—he'd swept her off her feet, into a registry office and down to the isolated hovel he was renting in Cornwall.

'Marry in haste, repent at leisure,' she said to Annie, as Jasper stirred restlessly in his hospital bed. 'You tried your best to warn me not to rush into it.'

'You fell in love and so did Tom: there was no stopping you,' Annie said. 'Besides, you were addicted to all those books about living in Cornish cottages, with donkeys and daffodils and stuff.'

'True,' Lizzy agreed wryly, 'and it *was* blissful that first summer—until the reality of living in a dank, dilapidated cottage in winter with a newborn baby set in, especially after Tom started vanishing

3

for days on end without telling me when and where he was going.'

'He was worse after Jasper was born, wasn't he? I think he resented not being the centre of attention,' Annie said.

'He still does, though how you can be jealous of your own son, goodness knows! Anyway, it was like living with a handsome but unreliable tomcat . . . and nothing much has changed, has it?' Lizzy asked bitterly.

'Perhaps not, but at least *two* good things came out of your marriage,' Annie pointed out, being a resolutely glass-half-full person: 'Jasper and your books about life in Perseverance Cottage.'

'True, and it was thanks to your telling Roly how cold and damp the cottage was, after you visited us, that he offered us a house on the estate rent free, so that actually makes *three* good things.'

'Oh, yes—and it was *marvellous* when you came back to Middlemoss to live,' Annie agreed fervently. 'I'd missed you so much!'

Her voice had risen slightly and Jasper woke up and grumpily demanded why they were muttering over him like two witches. Then he complained that the dim light hurt his eyes, and a nurse appeared and firmly ushered them out of the room for a while.

*   *   *

The following morning it was clear that the antibiotics were working. Great-uncle Roly visited Jasper in the afternoon and by evening he was so obviously on the mend that Lizzy managed to persuade Annie, who'd brought sandwiches and a

4

flask of soup ready to share a second night's vigil with her, to go home instead and get some sleep.

Lizzy herself intended spending a second night there, of course: by Jasper's bedside when allowed, or in the stark waiting room, with its grey plastic-covered chairs and stained brown cord carpet.

It was in the latter room that Tom's cousin Nick Pharamond found her, having driven non-stop halfway across Europe since Roly had given him the news about Jasper. His brow was furrowed with added frown lines from tiredness, and the dark stubble and rumpled black hair didn't do much to lighten his usual taciturn expression. Lizzy always imagined that Jane Eyre's Mr Rochester would have been *exactly* like Nick, but she was still both delighted and relieved to see him because, unlike Tom, you could *always* rely on him to turn up in an emergency.

Although she wasn't normally a weepy sort of person, she instantly burst into tears all over his broad chest, while he patted her back in a strangely soothing way. Then he made her drink the hot soup Annie had left and eat a sandwich she didn't want: he was forceful as well as reliable.

The only downside to his presence during the rest of that long night was that Lizzy became so spaced out with shock and exhaustion that something unstoppable took over her mouth. She could hear her own voice droning on and on for hours, telling Nick a whole lot of really personal stuff about the last few years that she'd only previously confided to Annie, like how bad relations had become between her and Tom, especially since she found out about his latest affair.

'I don't know who this one is, but she's been

5

having a really bad influence on him. He's played away before, of course, but it was never *serious*. He says it's *my* fault anyway, for being so wrapped up in the cottage, the garden and Jasper—and perhaps it is.'

'That's totally ridiculous, Lizzy: of course it isn't your fault!' Nick said. 'He should grow up!'

Filled with gratitude at his understanding, she'd fished out a petrol receipt from the bottom of her handbag and on the back of it feverishly scribbled down her cherished recipe for mashed potato fudge, a creation she'd first invented while trying to cook up some comfort from limited ingredients down in Cornwall (and which was much later to be christened Spudge by Jasper).

In return Nick, who was normally pretty tight-lipped on anything personal, divulged that Leila (his wife) refused all his suggestions that they both cut down their working hours to spend more time together, so they seemed to be seeing less and less of each other. This was *really* letting his guard down, so the night-watch effect must have been getting to him, too.

'Do you think everything will be all right with me and Tom once Jasper's off to university in a few years and I'm not so tied to Middlemoss and the school run?' she asked Nick, optimistically. 'I could even go with him on some of his business trips to Cornwall.'

'I honestly don't know, Lizzy, but it won't be your fault if it isn't,' Nick said, and gave her a big, wonderfully comforting hug.

Then something made her look up and over his shoulder she caught sight of Tom standing in the doorway staring at them.

6

'Oh, Tom, where have you *been*?' she cried, releasing herself from Nick's arms. 'Still, never mind—you're here now, that's the main thing.'

Tom ignored her, instead demanding suspiciously of Nick, 'What are *you* doing here, that's what I want to know?'

He was still looking from one to the other of them as if he'd had an extremely odd idea, which it emerged later he had—one that would finally turn what had already become a very sour-sweet cocktail of a marriage into a poisoned chalice.

But at the time, all Lizzy registered was that his first words were not an urgent enquiry about his only child and, in one split second, not only did the last vestiges of her love for Tom entirely vanish, but they took even the exasperated tolerance of the previous years with them, so there was absolutely no hope of resuscitating their marriage.

If Tom had ever possessed the core of feckless sweetness she'd believed in, then some wicked Snow Queen had blown on his heart and frozen it to solid ice.

CHAPTER 1: OLD PRUNE

Here in Middlemoss Christmas preparations start very early—in mid-August, in fact, when the five members of the Christmas Pudding Circle bulk-order the ingredients for mincemeat and cakes from a nearby wholefood cooperative. Once that has arrived and been divided up between us, things slowly start to rev up again. It always reminds me of a bobsleigh race: one minute we're all pushing ideas to and fro to loosen the runners and then the next we've jumped on board and are hurtling, faster and faster, towards Christmas!
The Perseverance Chronicles: A Life in Recipes

The members of the Christmas Pudding Circle were sitting round my long, scrubbed-pine kitchen table for the first meeting of the year. It was a hot, mid-August morning, so the door was open onto the sunlit cobbled courtyard in order to let some cooling air (and the occasional brazen hen) into the room.

I poured iced home-made lemonade into tumblers, then passed round the dish of macaroons, thinking how lovely it was to have all my friends together again. Apart from my very best friend Annie Vane, there was Marian Potter who ran the Middlemoss Post Office, Faye Sykes from Old Barn Farm and Miss Pym, the infants' schoolteacher. The latter is a tall, upright woman with iron-grey hair in a neat chignon, who commands such respect that she's never addressed by her Christian name of

Geraldine, even by her friends.

'Oh, I do miss our CPC meetings after Christmas each year,' Annie said, beaming, her round freckled face framed in an unbecoming pudding-bowl bob of coppery hair. 'I know we see each other all the time, but it isn't the same.'

'I was just thinking the same thing,' I agreed. 'And it doesn't matter that it's midsummer either, because I still get a tingle down my spine at the thought that we've started counting down to Christmas.'

'I suppose we are in a way, but it's more advance planning, isn't it?' Faye said.

'Yes, and we'd better get on with it,' Marian said, flicking open a notebook and writing in the date, for she organises the CPC just as she, together with her husband Clive, run most of the events around Middlemoss. As usual, she was bristling with energy right down to the roots of her spiky silver hair. 'First up, are there any changes to the list of ingredients for Miss Pym to order?'

'I still have last year's list on my computer, so it will be easy to tweak it before I email it off,' Miss Pym said, helping herself to more lemonade. An ice-cube cracked with a noise like a miniature iceberg calving from a glacier.

But there was not much to tweak, for of course we mostly make the same things every year: mince pies, Christmas cakes and puddings. We need large quantities too, for as well as baking for our own families, we also make lots of small cakes for the local Senior Citizens Christmas Hampers, which are annually distributed by Marian and the rest of the Mosses Women's Institute.

'Who has got the six small cake tins for the

hamper Christmas cakes?' asked Annie.

'Me,' I said.

'I'll put you down to bake the first batch then,' Marian said, scribbling that down, then she handed out the CPC meetings rota. We're supposed to take it in turns to host it in our homes but I don't know why she bothers, because after the first one it always goes completely haywire for one reason or another.

The important business of the meeting concluded, I got out some coffee granita I'd made. It never tastes quite as perfect as I hope it will, but they were all very kind about it. Then the conversation turned to frozen desserts in general and we discussed the possibility of concocting a brandy butter ice cream to go with Christmas pudding. I think Faye started that one: she makes a lot of ice cream for her farm shop.

*   *   *

Writing the CPC meeting up later for the *Chronicles*, I added a note to include the recipe for the brandy butter ice cream to that chapter if one of us came up with something good, and then laid my pen down on the kitchen table with a sigh, thinking that it was just as well I had the Christmas Pudding Circle to write about.

Although my readers loved the mix of domestic disaster, horticultural endeavour and recipes in my *Perseverance Chronicle* books, I could hardly include bulletins on the way the last, frayed knots of my failed marriage were so speedily unravelling, which was the subject most on my mind of late. I had become not so much a wife, as landlady to a surly, sarcastic and antisocial lodger.

The first *Perseverance Chronicle* was written in a desperate bid to make some money soon after we were married, influenced by all the old cosy, self-sufficiency-in-a-Cornish-cottage books that I had loved before the reality set in. Mine were a little darker, including such unromantic elements as the joys of outside toilets when heavily pregnant in winter and having an Inconstant Gardener for a husband.

It was accepted by a publisher and when we moved back to Lancashire I simply renamed the new cottage after the old and carried on—and so, luckily, did those readers who had bought the first book.

My self-imposed quota of four daily handwritten pages completed (which Jasper would type up later on the laptop computer Unks bought him, for extra pocket money), I closed the fat A4 writing pad and turned to my postcard album, as to an old friend. This was an impressively weighty tome containing all the cards sent to me over the years by Nick stuck in picture-side down, since interesting recipes were scribbled onto every bit of space on the back in tiny, spiky handwriting.

He still sent them, though I hadn't seen very much of him in person, other than the occasional Sunday lunch up at Pharamond Hall, since the time Jasper was ill in hospital. And actually I was *profoundly* grateful about that, what with having poured my heart out to him in that embarrassing way, not to mention Tom suddenly getting the wrong idea when he arrived and found Nick comforting me . . .

And speak of the devil, just as I found the card I

wanted, a dark shape suddenly blocked the open doorway to the yard and Tom's voice said, 'Reading your love letters?'

He was quite mad—that or the demon weed and too much alcohol had pickled his brain over the years! The album was always on the kitchen bookshelf for anyone to read, so he knew there was nothing personal about the cards—unless he thought that addressing them to 'The Queen of Puddings' was lover-like, rather than a sarcastic reference to one of my major preoccupations.

Mind you, Tom was not much of a reader, though luckily that meant he had never, to my knowledge, even opened one of my *Perseverance Chronicles*.

'No, Tom, I'm looking for a particular marzipan *petit four* recipe for the Christmas Pudding Circle to try,' I said patiently. 'The only love letters I've got are a couple of short notes from you, and they're so old the ink's faded.'

'So you say, but I don't find you poring over them all the time, like you do over Nick's precious postcards,' he said, going to wash his hands at the kitchen sink.

I dished out some of the casserole that was simmering gently on the stove and put it on a tray, together with a chunk of home-made bread, since he now preferred to take all his meals alone in the sitting room in front of his giant TV. Jasper and I had the old set in the kitchen and tended to leave him in sole possession.

He picked up the bowl of stew now and stared into it like a sibylline oracle, but the only message he was likely to read was 'Eat this or go hungry.'

'What are these black things, decayed sheep's

13

eyeballs?'

'Prunes. It's Moroccan lamb tagine.'

From his expression you would have thought I'd offered him a dish of lightly seasoned bat entrails.

'And I suppose *Nick* gave you the recipe. What else has he given you lately?' he said, with a wealth of unpleasant innuendo. 'Don't think I haven't noticed that your son looks more like him every day!'

'Oh, for God's sake, don't start on that again!' I snapped, adding recklessly, 'You know very well why Jasper looks like Nick, just as *you* look like Great-uncle Roly: your mother must have been having an affair with Leo Pharamond while she was still married to her first husband! Why don't you ask her?'

It was certainly obvious to everyone else, since those slaty purple-grey eyes and raven-black hair marked out all the Pharamonds instantly. But Tom went livid and hissed like a Mafia villain in a bad film, 'Never *ever* malign my mother's name again like that—do you hear me?'

Then he followed this up by hurling the plate of hot casserole at the wall with enormous force, shattering it and sending fragments of bowl and spatters of food everywhere. He'd never been physically violent (I wouldn't have stood for it for one second) so I don't think he was particularly aiming at *me,* but a substantial chunk of green-glazed Denby pottery hit my cheekbone and fell at my feet.

It was a shock, though, and I stood there transfixed and staring at him, one hand to my face, in a silence broken only by the occasional slither and plop of a descending prune. Suddenly finding

14

myself released from thrall, I turned and walked out of the door, dabbing lamb tagine off my face with the hem of my pale green T-shirt as I went, then headed towards the village.

I must have looked a mess, but luckily it was early evening and few people were about, for the Pied Piper of TV dinners had called them all away, using the theme tune of the popular soap series *Cotton Common* as lure.

*   *   *

I didn't have far to go for refuge. Annie's father used to be the vicar here, but now that he and his wife are alleviating the boredom of retirement by doing VSO work in Africa, Annie has a tiny Victorian red-brick terraced cottage in the main street of Middlemoss.

'Lizzy!' she exclaimed, looking horrified at discovering me stained and spattered on her doorstep. 'Is that dried blood on your face and T-shirt? What on earth has happened?'

'I think it's only prune juice and gravy, actually,' I reassured her, touching my cheek cautiously. 'A bit of plate *did* hit me, but it must have had a round edge.'

'Plate?' she repeated blankly, drawing me in and closing the front door.

'Yes, one of those lovely green Denby soup bowls we had as a wedding present from your parents.'

'Look, come into the kitchen and I'll clean you up with warm water and lint while you tell me all about it,' she said soothingly.

The lint sounded very *Gone With the Wind*—but

then, she has all the Girl Guide badges and I don't suppose the First Aid one has changed for years. So I followed her in and sank down on the nearest rush-bottomed chair, my legs suddenly going wobbly. Trinity (Trinny, for short), Annie's three-legged mutt, regarded me lambently from her basket, tail thumping.

'There's nothing much to tell, really,' I said. 'Tom flew into one of his rages and lobbed his dinner at the wall.'

'Oh, Lizzy!'

'I said something that made him angry and he just totally lost it this time. I don't think he was actually aiming at me, though it's hard to tell since he's such a rotten shot and—ouch!' I added, as she dabbed my face with the warm, damp lint.

'The skin isn't cut, but I think you might get a bruise on your cheek,' she said, wringing the cloth out. 'I could put some arnica ointment on it.'

'I don't think I could live with that smell so close to my nose, Annie,' I said dubiously, but her next suggestion, that we break out the bottle of Remy Martin, which she keeps in stock because her father always swore by it in times of crisis, met with a better reception.

'I think you really ought to leave Tom right away, Lizzy,' Annie suggested worriedly. 'He's been so increasingly horrible to you that it's practically verbal abuse—and now *this*!'

'I'm just glad Jasper wasn't there,' I said, topping my glass up and feeling much better. 'He's gone straight from the archaeological dig to a friend's house, and won't be back till about ten.'

'His exam results should be here any time now, shouldn't they?'

'Yes, only a couple more days.' I sipped my brandy and sighed. 'Even though I'll miss him, it'll be such a relief to have him safely off to university in October, because I live in dread that Tom will suddenly tell him to his face that he doesn't think he's really his son. That would be even more hurtful than ignoring him, the way he's been doing the last couple of years.'

'I don't know what's got into Tom,' Annie said sadly. 'He always had so much charm . . . as long as he got his own way.'

'He still does charm everyone else. I'm sure no one would believe me if I told them what he's really like at home.'

'True, but he's so used to me being around, he's let the mask slip sometimes, so I've seen it for myself,' Annie said. 'He was all right with Jasper for the first few years, though, wasn't he?'

'Well, he didn't take a lot of notice of him, but he was OK. But he started to turn colder towards me even before he got this strange idea that I had a fling with Nick, so I think whoever he's been having an affair with since then has had a really bad effect on his character.'

'You *did* have a fling with Nick,' Annie pointed out fairly.

'Oh, come on, Annie! I was way too young and anyway, it only lasted about a fortnight before he told me he was going abroad for a year because he wasn't changing his life-plans for *my* sake. I didn't see him after that until the day I got married to Tom and he turned up then with Leila in tow—do you remember?'

'Gosh, yes. She was so scarily chic, in a Parisian sort of way, that she made me feel like a country bumpkin—she still does! But I thought it was nice of Nick to make the effort, even though he and Tom had grown apart over the years. They never had a lot in common, did they?'

'I think the main problem was that Tom always felt jealous of Nick, since Nick was a real Pharamond and Roly's grandson, whereas *he* was just a Pharamond because his mother had married one. Allegedly,' I added darkly.

'It's odd how things turn out,' mused Annie, putting away the bowl of water and tossing the lint into the kitchen bin. 'You always had much more in common with Nick than with Tom.'

'How on earth can you say that, when we argue all the time?' I demanded incredulously. 'The only thing Nick and I have ever had in common is a love of food, even if mine is much less *cordon bleu*.'

Though of course it is true that food has played an important part in both our families. The search for a good meal in the wrong part of a foreign city was the downfall of my diplomat parents and would be the downfall of my figure, too, were I ever to stop moving long enough for the fat to settle.

As to the Pharamonds, the gene for cooking was introduced into the family by a Victorian heir who married the plebeian but wealthy heiress Bessie Martin, only to die of a surfeit of home-cooked love some forty years later, with a fond smile on his lips and a biscuit empire to hand on to his offspring.

'You and Nick have both got short tempers and you love Middlemoss more than anywhere else on earth,' Annie said. 'And of course *I* know that Jasper *is* Tom's son, but it's unfortunate that he's looking more and more like Nick with every passing year.'

'Well, yes, that's what Tom said earlier, so I reminded him about the rumours that his mother had an affair with Leo Pharamond before her first husband was killed, and that's what started the argument off! He always flies into a complete rage if I say anything against his sainted mother.'

'It's quite a coincidence that Leo Pharamond and her first husband were both not only racing drivers but killed in car crashes,' Annie said, 'though there did seem to be a lot of fatal crashes in the early days.'

'Someone told me they called her the Black Widow after Leo died, so it's not surprising her third husband gave it up and whisked her off back to Argentina,' I said.

Tom's mother had started a whole new life out there, but her firstborn was packed off to boarding school and farmed out at Pharamond Hall in the holidays. That made us both orphans in a way, which had once seemed to make a bond . . .

Annie said, 'Tom's hardly seen his mother over the years, has he?'

'No, or his half-siblings. He blames it all on his stepfather, of course, and won't hear a word against her. Come to that, I've only met her a couple of times and we can't be said to have bonded.'

'You'd think she'd at least be interested in her grandson—Jasper's such a lovely boy,' Annie said fondly.

'I used to send her his school photos, but since I never got any response, I gave up. In fact, with all this rejection, it's wonderful that poor Jasper isn't bitter and twisted, too!'

'Oh, he's much too sensible and he knows *we* all love him: me, Roly, even Mimi.'

19

I considered Unks' unmarried sister, Mimi, who is not at all maternal and whose passions are reserved for the walled garden she tends behind the Hall. 'You're right, she *does* seem to like him, despite his not being any form of plant life.'

'And Nick is fond of him—Jasper and he get on well.'

'He only really sees him during our occasional Sunday lunch up at the Hall, when we're all on our best behaviour for Roly's sake, because Tom's made it abundantly clear he isn't welcome at Perseverance Cottage.'

'How difficult it all is!' Annie sighed, which was the understatement of the year. 'I always agreed with Mum and Dad that marriage should be for ever, but once Tom started having affairs and being really nasty to you and Jasper, I changed my mind. He's not at all the man you married.'

'Oh, I don't know,' I reflected. 'I think perhaps he is, it's just that his true nature was hidden underneath all that charm. His sarcastic tongue has suddenly become a lot more vicious, though, which I expect is because he really wants me out of the cottage now, but I mean to try and stick to my original plan and hang on until I've got Jasper settled at university. It doesn't do a lot for my self-confidence when Tom's constantly belittling me and telling me how useless I am, though.'

'You're not useless,' she said, 'you've been practically self-sufficient for years in fruit, vegetables and eggs, made a lovely home for him and Jasper, and written all those wonderful books.'

'I don't actually get paid very much for the *Chronicles*—they're a bit of a niche market—and I'm running late with the next, what with one thing

20

and another.'

'I suppose it's hard to think up funny anecdotes to go between the recipes and gardening stuff, what with all the worry about Tom. But if you want to leave him right now, you know you and Jasper can move in here any time you like, and stay as long as you want,' she offered generously.

'I *do* know, and it's very kind of you,' I said gratefully, not pointing out that her cottage isn't much bigger than a doll's house: two tiny rooms up and down, crammed so full of bric-a-brac you can hardly expand your lungs to full capacity without nudging something over. Jasper, when he visits, tends to stand in the corner with his arms folded so as not to damage anything.

'Once Jasper is at university I might have to take you up on that offer, but very temporarily. I'll still need to make a home for him to come back to. I'll have to get a job stacking supermarket shelves, so I can rent somewhere. I'm not really qualified to do anything else.'

'Then what about Posh Pet-sitters? Business is expanding hugely since I added general pet-feeding and care to the dog-walking, and I could do with an assistant.'

Annie set up Posh Pet-sitters several years ago with a loan from her parents, and business seemed to be building up nicely, due to the patronage of several of the actors from the long-running drama *Cotton Common*, set in a turn-of-the-century Lancashire factory town, who have suddenly 'discovered' the three villages that comprise the Mosses.

Where they led, other minor celebrities followed, since although off the beaten track, we're within

21

commuting distance of Manchester, Leeds, Liverpool and the M6, and in pretty countryside just where the last beacon-topped hills slowly subside into the fertile farmland that runs west to the coast.

Some of the actors live in the new walled and gated estate of swish detached houses in Mossrow, but others have snapped up whatever has appeared on the market, from flats in the former Pharamond's Butterflake Biscuit factory, to old cottages and farms.

'Did you go and see Ritch Rainford yesterday?' I asked, suddenly remembering how excited Annie had been at getting a call from the singer-turned-actor who plays Seth Steele, the ruggedly handsome mill owner in *Cotton Common*. (All that alliteration must have been too much for the producers of the series to resist!)

He's bought the old vicarage where Annie's family used to live, a large and rambling Victorian building with a brick-walled garden, in severe need of TLC and loads of cash. (The new vicar is now housed in an unpretentious bungalow next to the church.)

Annie's pleasantly homely face, framed in a glossy pudding-bowl bob of copper hair, took on an unusually rapt—almost holy—expression and her blue-grey eyes went misty. 'Oh, *yes*! He's . . .' She stopped, apparently lost for superlatives.

'Sexy as dark chocolate?' I suggested. 'Toothsomely rum truffle?'

'Just—wonderful,' she said simply. 'He has such charisma, it was as though a . . . a golden light was shining all around him.'

'Bloody hell! That sounds more like finding all

22

the silver charms in your slice of Christmas pudding at once!' I stared at her, but she was lost in a trance.

'Lizzy, he's so kind, too! When I explained that I used to live at the vicarage, he took me around and showed me all the improvements he's made, and told me what else he was going to do. Then he just handed me a set of keys to the house so he could call me up any time to go and exercise or feed his dog.'

'Well, if your clients didn't do that, you wouldn't be able to get in,' I said drily. 'What sort of dog does he have?'

'A white bull terrier bitch called Flo—very good-natured, though I might have to be careful around other dogs.'

'And what's the new vicar like?' I asked, but she hadn't noticed, being full of Ritch Rainford to the point where her bedazzled eyes couldn't really take in another man. However, a crush on a handsome actor was not likely to get her anywhere.

Annie was once engaged, but was jilted with her feet practically on the carpeted church aisle. Since then she had safely confined her affections to unsuitable—and unattainable—actors.

'I've heard he's single *and* has red hair,' I said encouragingly since, despite her own copper locks, she has a weakness for redheaded men.

'He hasn't got red hair, he's blond!' she protested indignantly, and I saw that she was still thinking of Ritch Rainford. Perhaps I ought to watch *Cotton Common* to see what all the excitement was about.

Eventually Annie ran me home, since I wanted to be there when Jasper returned. I was by then attired in one of her voluminous cardigans—a bilious green, with loosely attached knitted pink

23

roses—to hide the dried but dubious-looking stains on my T-shirt.

She said she was going to come in with me and give Tom a piece of her mind, which would not have gone down well, but luckily Tom, his van and some of his clothes had vanished. He'd also locked me out; but not only did Annie have our key on her ring, I kept one hidden under a flowerpot, so that wasn't a problem.

'Looks like he's gone away again,' I said gratefully. 'Thank goodness for that.'

Of course he hadn't thought to feed the hens, who had put themselves to bed in disgust, or the quail, so Annie helped me to shut everything up safely for the night.

As we walked back to the cottage Uncle Roly Pharamond's gamekeeper, Caz Naylor, sidled out of a small outbuilding and, with a brief salute, flitted away through the shadows towards the woods behind the cottage.

He's a foxy-looking young man, with dark auburn hair, evasive amber eyes and a tendency to address me, on the rare occasions when he speaks, as 'our Lizzy', thus acknowledging a distant relationship that all the Naylors in the area seemed to know about from the minute I set foot in the place for the first time at the age of eleven.

Annie looked startled: 'Wasn't that Caz? What's he doing here?'

'I let him have the use of the old chest freezer in there. Since I cut down on the amount of stuff I grow, I don't need it,' I said, for I'd been slowly running things down ready for the moment that I knew was fast approaching, when I must leave Perseverance Cottage. 'He comes and goes as he pleases.'

She shook her head. 'All the Naylors are strange
. . .'

'But some are stranger than others? My mother
was a Naylor too, don't forget! Descendant of some
distant ancestor who made good in Liverpool, in
the cargo shipping line—which at least explains why
I'm such a daughter of the soil and feel so firmly
rooted here.'

She smiled. 'I expect Roly told him to keep an
eye on things after that animal rights group started
targeting you.'

'More likely he's keeping an eye on his freezer,' I
said, though it was true that the only evidence of
ARG (as they are known locally) I'd spotted
around the place lately were the occasional bits of
gaffer tape where a banner had been ripped off my
car or the barn. 'Perhaps they just aren't bothering
with me that much. I mean, I can see why they
might target Unks and Caz, especially since no one
knows what Caz does with all those grey squirrels
he traps, but why me? I'm not battery farming
anything.'

All my fowl lived long, happy and mainly useless
lives, except for an excess of male quail and the
occasional unwanted cockerel, which Caz
dispatched for me with expert efficiency.

'I expect they just include you in with the
Pharamond estate, since your cottage is part of it,'
she agreed. 'It's not personal.'

We cleaned up the mess in the kitchen as well as
we could and then Annie left, since it was clear
enough that Tom wasn't coming back that night, at
least—and I thanked heaven for small mercies.

'What happened to your face, Mum?' Jasper asked, getting his first good look at me in the light of the kitchen, when a friend dropped him home later. 'That looks like a bruise coming up. And why are you wearing one of Auntie Annie's horrible cardigans?'

'Your father dropped a plate and a piece hit me,' I explained. 'Annie loaned me the cardigan to cover up the gravy stains on my T-shirt and I forgot to give it back when she went home.'

He looked at the dent and new marks on the plastered kitchen wall and said, 'He dropped a plate *horizontally*?' in that smart-lipped way teenage boys have.

'Yes, he was practising discus throwing,' I said, and he gave me a look but let the subject drop.

He didn't ask where his father was. But then, at that time, he never did.

CHAPTER 2: ALL FUDGE

We are in the middle of a hot spell and the air is fragrant with sweet peas and roses and full of the dull, drowsy drone of bees drunk on nectar. Yesterday I divided up the bigger clumps of chives and began drying herbs for winter, crumbling them up as soon as they were cool and storing them in cork-topped containers, though the bay leaves have simply been left in bunches hanging from the wooden rack in the kitchen. But soon they, too, will be packed in jars and put away in the cupboard until needed.

As I used up the final jar of last year's mincemeat for brownies, I wondered if mincemeat would also work as an ingredient in fudge—maybe even in Spudge, the mashed potato fudge I invented while we were living in Cornwall . . .

The Perseverance Chronicles: A Life in Recipes

Tom had been gone a couple of days when Jasper pointedly enquired after dinner one night if there was anything I wanted to discuss, but I just said we would have a little chat before he went to university and he gave me one of his looks.

I knew he was now an adult, and at some point I'd have to explain to him that I was going to leave his father and the cottage as soon as he'd gone off to university, but at that moment he was so happy that he'd got the exam grades he needed for his first choice, I didn't want to rain on his parade.

Next day, when I let out the hens, I found it was

27

one of those delicious late summer mornings that reminded me of the early honeymoon weeks of our marriage in Cornwall: dreamy swirls of mist with the warm sun tinting the edges golden, like pale yellow candyfloss wisps. You could easily imagine King Arthur and Queen Guinevere riding out of it in glorious Technicolor, all jingling bridles and hooded hawks, though if they had they would probably have been surprised to find themselves transported from the land of legend into a Lancashire backwater like Middlemoss.

The last remaining acres of darkly watchful ancient woodland that crowded up to the back of Perseverance Cottage would have looked normal enough to them, I suppose—apart from Caz Naylor, who as usual was camouflaged from headband to boots, Rambo-style. I spotted him flitting in and out of the trees only by the white glint of his eyeballs and the sweat glistening between the green and brown streaks on his naked chest. A blink and he was gone, back to wage war on the dangerous alien life form known to the uninitiated as the grey squirrel.

Still, even in Arthurian times they would probably have had some kind of shamanistic Green Man and so would be used to such goings-on, and the duckpond, chickens and vegetable patch out front would look reassuringly normal to them. But what would they have made of the huge, tumbledown old greenhouse, the remains of a previous tenant's abortive attempt at market gardening? Or my battered, once-white Citroën 2CV? A 2CV that, I now noticed, had its hood down, so the seats would be soaked with dew and very likely lightly spattered with hen crap. Or even, which was much, much worse, duck gloop.

It was also listing drunkenly on one seriously flat tyre.

Tossing the last of the feed to the hens, I stuck my head inside the cottage door.

'Jasper?' I called loudly up the steep stairs, expecting him to be still asleep. By nature, teenagers are intended to be nocturnal, so it felt cruel to have to drag him out of his lair under the eaves each morning.

Instead, he loomed out of the doorway next to me, making me jump. 'I'm here, Mum. What's up?'

'Flat tyre. You have your breakfast and get ready while I change it. I hope it's a mendable puncture—the spare's not that brilliant and if I have to buy a new one it'll be worth more than the rest of the car put together.'

One of the Leghorns had followed me into the flagged hallway (a Myrtle: all the white hens are called that; and the browns, Honey) and I shooed it out again. There's something terribly cement-like about hen droppings when they set hard.

'I'll change it,' he offered. 'Or I can cycle over.'

'No, I'll have it done by the time you've had breakfast, and you'll be late otherwise.'

The medieval dig he was working at was only a few miles away, but the lanes between the site and us were narrow and twisty, so I worried about his safety. Annie calls it 'mother hen with one chick' syndrome, but she is just as dotty about Trinity, her rescued dog. And if I hadn't been an anxious mother, then maybe I wouldn't have demanded the right treatment for Jasper's meningitis that time he was rushed into hospital, even before the tests came back positive . . . It didn't bear thinking about.

29

Jasper wandered out again a few minutes later holding a piece of toast at least an inch thick, not counting the bramble jelly and butter, removed the wheel brace from my hand (giving me the toast to hold in exchange), and unscrewed the last nut.

'Thanks, that was stiff. You'd think if I'd tightened it up in the first place, I'd be able to undo it easily, wouldn't you?'

'Dad not back yet?' Jasper asked, glancing across at the large, ramshackle wooden shed Tom used as his workshop, with the 'Board Rigid: Customised Surfboards' sign over it.

'No.'

'Well, remember that time you asked him to go and buy a couple of pints of milk, and you didn't hear from him for a week?' he said, clearly with the intention of comforting me should I need it. But actually, I was sure he shared my feeling that his father's increasing number of absences were a blessing, even though I was usually the one on the receiving end of Tom's viciously sarcastic outbursts.

He couldn't help but have noticed the way Tom had estranged himself from both of us, behaving more like a lodger than a husband and father.

Just let me get him safely off to university in October, then I can sort my life out—somehow, I prayed silently.

Jasper said nothing more, but retrieved his toast and went back into the house.

The first golden glow of the morning was fading, much as my love for Tom had quickly vanished once I'd grasped what kind of man I'd married: the mercurial type, an erratic moon orbiting my Mother Earth solidity. For years I'd thought that deep down he loved and needed me, and he'd always managed

30

to sweet-talk me into forgiving him for anything and everything, although my exasperation levels had slowly risen as my son matured and my husband remained as irresponsible as ever. Have you ever imagined what it would be like to be married to Peter Pan once the novelty wore off? A Peter Pan with a dark side he kept just for me . . . like a sweet chocolate soufflé with something hard at its centre on which you could break your teeth—or your heart.

His cousin Nick, whose Mercedes sports car was slowly bumping down the rutted track towards me, scattering hens, wasn't any kind of soufflé—more like one of his own devilishly hot curried dishes. He does cook like an angel, though, and he's an expert on all aspects of food and cooking, writes books and articles and has a page in a Sunday newspaper colour supplement.

The Pharamonds didn't seem to do marriage terribly well and he'd had a volatile, semidetached relationship with Leila for years. She's another chef, which was at least one too many cooks on the home front, by my reckoning. I was glad to see she wasn't with him that day, because Leila is a lemon tart. Or maybe, since she's French, that should be *tarte au citron*?

Miaou.

I resolved not to be catty about her, even if every time we met she contrived to make me feel like a lumbering great carthorse. She's an immaculately chic, petite, blue-eyed blonde, while I am tall and broad-shouldered, with green eyes flecked with hazel, fine light brown hair in a permanent tangle, and the sort of manicure you get from digging vegetable beds without gloves on.

31

Unks—Great-uncle Roly—didn't like her either. He said if it weren't for her refusing to stop working all hours in her restaurant in London and settle down, there would have been lots of little Pharamond heirs by then. But he couldn't have thought this through properly, because if they were a combination of the scarier bits of Nick and Leila, that would be quite alarming indeed.

Leila was married before and was fiercely independent, with her own swish apartment above her restaurant; while Nick had a small flat in Camden. And considering he spent at least half his time at Pharamond Hall, which Leila rarely visited, you'd wonder when they ever saw each other.

I certainly hadn't seen Nick for ages. He always phoned up for any eggs, fruit or vegetables he needed when staying at the Hall and working on recipes, but I just dropped them off with Unks' cook, Mrs Gumball.

Yet here he was, deigning to pay me a visit. As his Mercedes pulled up I removed the jack and then slung the punctured tyre in the back of the car, where Jasper's bike already reposed. You can get anything in a 2CV, if you don't mind being exposed to the weather.

Nick got out. He was wearing dark trousers and an open-necked soft white shirt with the sleeves rolled up, the glossy, thick black plumage of his hair spikily feathering his head. His strong face, with its impressively bumpy nose, can look very attractive when he smiles, though the last time he'd wasted any of his charm on me was in the hospital when Jasper had meningitis. And after the way I'd bared my soul to him in the night hours, I could only feel profoundly grateful that I hadn't seen much of him since then.

I distinctly remember telling him how I hoped that once Jasper was at university, things would get better between me and Tom—and instead, from that very moment they'd rapidly got worse and worse . . .

I became aware that Nick was waving his hands slowly in front of my face, like a baffled stage hypnotist.

'Planet Earth to Lizzy: are you receiving me?'

'Oh, hi, Nick—long time, no recipe,' I said, wiping my filthy hands up the sides of my jeans—they were work ones, so it wasn't going to make a lot of difference. I only hoped I hadn't run them through my hair first, though since I didn't remember brushing it this morning, a bit of grease would at least hold the tangles down.

He frowned down at me. 'I sent you a card from Jamaica.'

'That was ages ago, and a recipe for conch fritters isn't exactly the most useful thing to have in the middle of Lancashire—the fishmongers don't stock them. Anyway, what are you doing here at this time of the morning? Have you driven straight up from London?'

'Yes, I'm looking for Tom,' he said shortly, checking me over with eyes the dark grey-purple of wet Welsh slate, as though he wasn't sure quite what species I was, or what sauce to serve me with. 'What have you done to your face?'

I flushed and touched the bruise on my cheek with the tips of my fingers. 'This? Oh, a plate got dropped and one of the pieces bounced up and hit me,' I said lamely; it was *almost* the truth.

His brows knitted into a thick, black bar as he

33

tried to imagine a plate that explosive.

'It looks worse than it is, now it's gone all blue and yellow—it'll have vanished in a day or two. And Tom's away,' I added. *Thank goodness!*

From the way Nick was looking at me I thought I'd said that aloud for a minute, but finally he asked, 'Oh? Any idea when he'll be back?'

'No, but he's been gone since Monday, so I'll be surprised if he doesn't turn up today.'

He raised one dark eyebrow. 'And do you know *where* he's gone?'

'He didn't say and there is no point in ringing his mobile because he never answers or gets back to me.' I shrugged, casually. 'You know what he's like. He might be off delivering a surfboard. I'm pretty sure he's not doing a gig with the Mummers, they don't usually go that far from home.'

'A gig—with the *what*?'

'The Mummers of Invention: you know, that sort of folk-rock group he started with three local friends?'

'No,' he said shortly. 'I'm glad to say I don't.'

'You must do because one of them's that drippy female Unks rents an estate cottage to—she sells handmade smocks at historical re-enactment fairs. And if you ever came up for the Mystery Play any more, you *would* have seen them—they provide the musical interludes. Tom played Lazarus as well, last year. He stepped in at the last minute and the parish magazine review said he brought a whole new meaning to the role.'

'I can imagine—and I *do* intend being here for the next performance.'

'I thought Leila couldn't leave her restaurant over Christmas?'

'*She* can't; *I* can,' he snapped, and I wondered if their marriage was finally dragging its sorry carcass to the parting of the ways, like mine. 'So, you've no idea where Tom is, or when he'll be back?'

'Probably Cornwall, that's where he mostly ends up, and if so, he's likely to be staying with that friend of his Tom Collinge, the weird one who runs a wife and harem in one cottage.'

'I suppose he may be there by now, but he was in London on Monday night, Lizzy. I ran into him at Leila's restaurant, but he left in a hurry—without paying the bill.'

'He did?' I frowned. 'That's odd. I wonder what he was doing in London?'

'Well, it evidently wasn't me he'd gone to see, since he bolted as soon as I arrived.' He looked at me intently, as though he'd asked me a question.

'Oh?' I said slowly, trying to remember whether Tom had actually ever said which of his friends he stayed with when he was in London.

'Still, you know Tom,' I tried to laugh. 'He probably just found himself near the restaurant and dropped in.'

'Then just took it into his head to shoot off without paying when I turned up unexpectedly? Leila said she didn't want to charge him for the meal anyway, since he's a sort of relative.'

'That's kind of her,' I said, amazed, because it wouldn't surprise me if she gives even Nick a bill when he eats there!

'Yes, wasn't it just?' he said drily. 'And one of the staff let slip that he'd stayed in her apartment the previous night, too—the staff seemed to know him pretty well. But I told Leila, business is business and she'd never let sentiment of any kind come before making money before, so I would just drop the bill in on my way up to the Hall. Here it is.'

I looked at his closed, dark face again and suddenly wondered if he suspected that Tom and Leila had something going on. Surely not. It would be totally ridiculous! I knew that Tom had been having a serious affair for the last few years, of course, but not who it was with, although I assumed it was someone down in Cornwall where he spent so much time. It couldn't be Leila . . . could it?

My mind working furiously, I took the offered bill and glanced down at it, then gasped, distracted by the staggering sum. 'You must be absolutely rolling in it, charging these prices!'

'Not me—Leila. And the prices aren't anything out of the ordinary for a restaurant of that standard. She's just got a Michelin star.'

'Congratulations,' I said absently, staring at the bill, the total of which would have fed the average family of four for about a year. More, if they grew most of their food themselves, like I do. 'But I'm sorry, *I* don't have that kind of money on the proceeds of my produce sales—and in case you haven't noticed, I've scaled that side of things down drastically in the last eighteen months.'

'Come on, you must get good advances for your "how I tried to be self-sufficient and failed dismally" books. You can't plead poverty,' he looked distastefully down at the mess he was standing in, 'whatever it looks like here!'

'You should have looked before you got out of the car,' I said coldly. 'The ducks have been up. And one small book every two or three years doesn't exactly rake in the cash. I only get a couple

36

of thousand for them. I'm lucky to still have a publisher! My agent says it's only because my faithful band of readers can't wait to see what else goes pear-shaped every time. And they like all the recipes.'

'Ah yes, the Queen of Puddings!' He wrinkled his nose slightly.

'What?' I said indignantly. 'Just because it's wholesome, everyday stuff, it doesn't mean it isn't good food! At least *my* recipes don't need ninety-six exotic ingredients, four servile minions and a catering-sized oven to produce.'

He grinned, as though glad to have got a rise out of me, and I began to remember why our boy-girl romance never got off the ground: an interest in food is the only thing we've *ever* had in common, whatever Annie says, and he never tires of reminding me that mine is not gourmet, and it's largely focused on sweets and desserts.

'And this is not my bill, so you'll have to come back and speak to Tom about it later,' I added, sincerely hoping that that was *all* he wanted to talk to Tom about. Clearly he was harbouring suspicions . . . But no, whoever Tom was having an affair with, it couldn't be Leila, his own cousin's brittle little acid drop of a wife, however strange the circumstances might look!

'If I can catch him,' Nick said, the grin vanishing. He abruptly changed the subject. 'Jasper had his results yet?'

'Oh, yes!' I said, happily diverted. 'Yesterday and they were just what he needed for Liverpool University, to read Archaeology and History. He's having breakfast at the moment—why don't you come in and talk to him? He hasn't thanked you for that Roman cookery book you sent him, yet.'

Jasper's keenly interested in food and drink too, but only from a purely historical perspective. Delving about in medieval cesspits and middens, which was what he seemed to be spending his days doing at the dig, suited him down to the ground.

Nick looked at his watch. 'I haven't time today, so congratulate him for me, won't you? I'd better be off. I'm doing some articles on eating out in the North-West—out-of-the-way restaurants and hotels—so I need to drop my stuff off up at the Hall and get on with it. Breakfast awaits, then lunch and dinner . . .'

'Lucky you,' I said politely, though sitting in restaurants isn't my favourite thing. I'd rather pig out at home than eat prettily arranged tiny portions consisting of a splat, a dribble and a leaf, in public.

He was frowning down at me again. 'You know, Lizzy, two thousand is peanuts compared to what I get for my books. No wonder you're living in a hovel—especially with Tom spending his earnings as fast as he makes them.' He gestured at the giant satellite dish, incongruously attached to the side of the cottage.

'We don't need a huge amount of money and Perseverance Cottage is *not* a hovel,' I began crossly. 'Uncle Roly had all the mod cons installed before we moved in, and it's exactly how I like it. I've got everything I want.'

'Have you? Or perhaps you've got more than you bargained for,' he said drily, his eyes again resting speculatively on my bruised cheek.

I hoped he didn't think Tom had taken to physical violence—or that *I* would have stayed to be a punchbag if he had! I was just about to disabuse

38

his mind of any suspicions in that quarter when he turned round to survey my domain and remarked suavely: 'I wouldn't say the family have come a long way from the heady days of Pharamond's Butterflake Biscuits, but they have certainly diverged in their interests.'

Then, before I could point out that *he* at least was still vaguely in the bakery line, he got back into his car and reversed away in a cloud of dust. A lot of gritted chickens shot out from under it.

'Wasn't that Uncle Nick?' Jasper asked, coming out ready for the off.

'Yes, but he couldn't stay. He had an urgent appointment with breakfast, though he did send you his congratulations on the exam results. Get in. I'll just wash my hands and we'll go.'

'Can I drive?' he asked hopefully. He'd recently passed his test, lessons courtesy of a lucky win on the gees at Haydock by Great-uncle Roly.

'OK. Turn it round while I get ready.'

He'd left the cottage door open, and one of the hens had made a small deposit on the rag rug.

CHAPTER 3: BITTERSWEET

We are more than halfway through August, the time of year for eating fruits and salads as they come into season; but all too soon we will be bottling, brewing, jamming and preserving as if our lives depended on it and famine was sure to follow glut. And the minute the Christmas Pudding Circle receive their bulk order of dried fruits, peel, nuts and other ingredients, we will all be making our mincemeat too, for we use a marvellous Delia Smith recipe that keeps for ever.
The Perseverance Chronicles: A Life in Recipes

All the way to the dig, while the loud music chosen by Jasper drowned out even the possibility of conversation, I wondered whether it *could* possibly be Leila that Tom had been having an affair with for the last couple of years—or the *main* one, because I'm sure he still scattered his favours pretty widely.

Was Nick really hinting that he suspected that, or had I imagined it? But things certainly didn't sound too friendly between him and Leila, even by their semidetached, sweet-and-sour standards!

And what *would* I say to Tom when he returned? While saying nothing would probably be the most sensible option until my plans to leave were in place, I couldn't let what he'd done pass, even if I didn't really think he was trying to hurt me physically.

Maybe I should have left before, even if it did

mean disrupting Jasper's schooling? The situation had certainly been affecting him—he seemed practically to have given up going out with his friends in the evening when Tom was home. Instead, he lurked in his room with the laptop Unks bought him, only suddenly looming silently up between us whenever voices were raised.

So now was probably the moment to clear the air and tell Tom straight that I was not prepared to put up with his behaviour any more, so I was leaving him. I was convinced this was what he'd been angling for, so he could play the hurt innocent party to everyone and, perhaps, install someone else here in my place . . .

I found that a particularly horrid thought, but Perseverance Cottage belonged to his uncle Roly, so obviously if anyone were moving out it would have to be me. And I simply *wouldn't* ask Roly to help me, for not only did I not want to disillusion him about Tom, whom he had treated like another grandson, but he'd already been so kind and generous to us all these years by letting us have the cottage rent free.

I expected I could find new homes for the hens and quail, but finding a new home for *me* would be the major problem. While the recent influx of newcomers into the area (especially the *Cotton Common* crowd) might mean that Annie's Posh Pet-sitters could expand enough to employ me part-time, on the downside, it also meant property rentals had soared out of my reach.

It was all depressingly difficult! Oh, *why* couldn't Tom just vanish into thin air, never to be seen again, like those mysterious disappearances you read about in the newspapers?

41

In need of comfort, I stopped off at Annie's cottage on the way home from dropping Jasper at the dig. It was still early, but she'd already made a chicken casserole and popped it in the slow cooker for later.

She seemed to have learned a lot more practical stuff than I ever did on that French cookery course we did in London after we left school, where volatile Madame Fresnet screamed at us all day long in French, the language in which we were supposed to learn to cook, thus killing two birds with one stone. At the end of the six months we all emerged with shattered eardrums, shattered French and the ability to whip up *tartelettes au fromage* at the drop of a whisk.

Trinity skipped up to greet me, and Susannah, Annie's deaf white cat, regarded me with self-satisfied disinterest from the top of the Rayburn.

'All right?' Annie asked anxiously, scrutinising my face.

'Fine. Tom's not back yet and Jasper's at the dig—I just dropped him.'

'It's great he got his first choice university, isn't it?' she said, getting down another mug from the rack and pouring me some coffee. 'Do you want a chocolate croissant? They're hot from the oven and I don't think I can eat the last one, I've had two already.'

'Your eyes are bigger than your belly,' I said vulgarly, accepting the plate, and sat down at the kitchen table, keeping my eyes firmly away from Trinny's pleading dark ones, because the last thing a dog with three legs needs is to be overweight.

42

'I saw Nick this morning,' I told her, dunking the croissant into my coffee so the bittersweet dark chocolate began to melt into it. This makes a change, because I usually do it the other way round and dip my food into melted chocolate, especially strawberries. It's amazing what you *can* coat in chocolate—and I'm not talking about that revolting body paint, because I prefer to keep the two greatest pleasures life can hold completely and unmessily separate . . . or at any rate, I *did*. I think I have forgotten how to do one of them.

'That's really what I came to tell you about, Annie. He called in early on his way up to the Hall, and he said Tom was in London on Monday.'

I described my conversation with Nick. 'Don't you think that sounds like he suspects Tom and Leila might be having an affair?'

'Oh, no, surely not? Not with his own cousin's wife?' she exclaimed, looking horrified. Annie is just too nice for her own good, but I suppose being a vicar's daughter didn't exactly help to squash her natural inclination to think the best of everybody if she possibly could.

'I don't know, but I certainly hope not. I can't really see him and Leila getting it together, can you? She's quite scary, in a beady-eyed and elegantly chic way. And I always thought it must be someone local or down in Cornwall, so perhaps Nick has got the wrong end of the stick.'

'I'm sure he must have,' she agreed, and then her eye fell on the kitchen clock. 'Look at the time! I promised I'd put in a couple of hours at the RSPCA kennels. The flu's hit the staff and volunteers hard. There are no pet-sitting jobs that I can't handle myself this afternoon, but tomorrow will be busier.'

She looked slightly self-conscious: 'Ritch Rainford has asked me to go in at lunchtime and walk Flo, because he'll be at the studios in Manchester all day.'

'You'd better get off, then, if you're sure there's nothing you want me to do. I'll see you at the Mystery Play committee meeting later, when I'll *finally* get to meet the new vicar.'

'Oh, yes, he's . . . he seems nice,' she said vaguely, but I could see that her mind was still too taken up with the delights of Ritch Rainford to bother with lesser mortals.

'Oh, before you go, can I borrow that candyfloss maker you bought for the last Cubs and Brownies' bazaar? Some lusciously lemon morning mist has given me ideas.'

'Of course. Now, where did I put it?' She vanished into the pantry and came back with a large cardboard box. 'The instructions and everything are still in there. Do you need anything else? Sugar?'

'No, I'm OK for sugar,' I assured her.

I left her putting Trinny in the back of her car, and then drove down to the other end of the village to drop the punctured tyre off with Dave Naylor at the local garage, Deals on Wheels. (And I know it seems confusing at first that most of the indigent Mosses population who are not Pharamonds are either Naylors or Gumballs, but you quickly get used to it.)

Then I headed for home, passing the entire contingent of the Mosses Senior Citizens' Circle waiting to board a coach for the annual trip to Southport Flower Show . . . including Unks' alarmingly spry octogenarian sister, Mimi Pharamond. I slowed down, staring, and she waved at me gaily, the rainbow-coloured Rastafarian knitted hat Nick brought her back from Jamaica flapping over one eye.

Since Juno Carter, her long-suffering companion, was currently laid up after an accident, letting Mimi loose alone on the flower show seemed a recipe for disaster. I only hoped someone had been delegated to keep an eye on her. *And* a firm grip.

*   *   *

There was still no sign of Tom's van outside the cottage and you couldn't miss it because it had 'BOARD RIGID' in big fluorescent orange letters up the side and the logo of a stickman surfing. The workshop door was closed too, but in the bedroom I found his dirty clothes scattered on the rug as though washed up there by a high tide, so he'd either gone out again, or come back without his van.

Still, clearly he *had* returned from wherever it was he'd been. I gathered up Tom's clothes, added some of Jasper's and mine, and then went down to stuff them in the machine. There was no beating them on a rock for me, even in the first flush of self-sufficiency in Cornwall, though before I bought the washing machine out of my first *Perseverance Chronicle* sale, I used to do the laundry by trampling up and down on it in the bath. Then I would pass it through an old mangle in the yard, which was not fun in winter.

It hadn't taken me long to realise that most books on self-sufficiency were written by men in warm, comfortable rooms, while their wives were out there dealing with the raw realities of life. Or that Tom, while initially enthusiastic, soon lost interest and succumbed to the burgeoning surfing culture instead. Once you added a tiny baby into the equation, the offer of a cottage on the Pharamond estate up in Lancashire was one I was determined we wouldn't refuse.

As I pointed out to Tom at the time, if you have the contacts, you can customise surfboards *anywhere*, and besides, Middlemoss was as close to a home as I had ever got, and I longed to return there.

Tom's jeans crackled when I picked them up to stuff into the washer, but then I always had to empty his pockets of a strange assortment of objects, from board wax to fluffy sherbet lemons.

This time the haul was a dark blue paper napkin tastefully printed in the corner with the word 'Leila's' in gold, a teaspoon that probably came from the same place, since it was definitely classier than any of our mismatched assortment, a stub of billiard chalk, a red jelly baby with the head bitten off and a piece of pink paper folded tightly into the shape of a very small rose.

Tom had doodled in origami roses as long as I'd known him, which could be very irritating when it was my shopping list or the top page of a stack of book manuscript; but equally, it used to be rather endearing when it was an apology for forgetting to tell me he was going off somewhere. At least, it was until the novelty wore off, along with my patience.

I flattened this one out and found it was the last part of a letter, abjuring my husband to 'Tell old Charlie Dimmock you've found someone else and give her the push', and promising, if he did, to tie

46

him up—and maybe even *down* if he really begged her to. It was signed 'Your Dark Heart'.

Well, that didn't sound like Leila, did it? I could imagine she'd give anyone a good basting, but would she have time in her busy schedule for bondage?

A horrible image flashed before my eyes of a naked Tom, trussed and oven-ready, and I found I was sitting on the quarry tiles feeling sick and recalling the last time we made love, which was just before Jasper was taken ill.

I'd accused Tom of having yet another affair, but this time his attempt to sweet-talk me round hadn't entirely worked and he'd said I was so unresponsive he felt like he was practising necrophilia. And then *I'd* said that I felt much the same, since he might *look* like the man I married, but the part of him I'd loved seemed to be quite dead.

This threw him into the first of his really frighteningly violent rages during which he said that living with a cold bitch of a wife who thought food could cure anything was enough to send any man off the rails, and stormed out.

After this I began sleeping in the small boxroom off our bedroom, and things between us went downhill rapidly. He made no attempt to conceal his affairs, though this note was the first hard evidence that any of them were serious . . .

Feeling suddenly dizzy, I put my head on my knees and closed my eyes, wishing our old lurcher, Harriet, was still around to snuffle sympathetically in my ear.

When the feeling passed off I resolutely got up and washed my face in the kitchen sink with cold water, ate an entire packet of those chocolate

47

mini-flake cake decorations, then went out to the workshop, from where faint strains of Metallica now wafted through the Judas door.

CHAPTER 4: MUSHROOMING

I know a lot of people dry mushrooms, or freeze the button ones, but I either eat them freshly gathered from the nearby fields, or not at all.

But I do make marzipan mushrooms sometimes and give them as gifts in the sort of little paper-strip baskets we used to weave at infants' school for Easter eggs. The mushrooms are very easy: you simply make the cap from marzipan and place it upside down. Then press a disc of more marzipan onto it, coloured brown with a little cocoa powder, and make a ribbed effect with a fork. Add a marzipan stalk, and hey presto! Realer than real.

The Perseverance Chronicles: A Life in Recipes

Tom had his back to me when I went in, spray-stencilling some intricate, hand-cut Celtic design onto a surfboard. He was wearing a mask and baggy dungarees over his T-shirt and jeans, and his dark hair curled onto the nape of his neck in a familiar ducktail.

Where his cousin Nick was built on a large and rugged scale, Tom was a slight, wiry man and every slender bone of his body was beautiful. But despite (allegedly) not being a Pharamond other than in name, he did have the unmistakable look of one, so I was convinced that all the rumours about his mother were true.

I stood there for a minute, thrown by that familiar curl of hair, shaken by the stirring of a tenderness I had thought long dead. Then he must have felt my presence, for he turned cold grey stranger's eyes on me, pushing down the mask. The CD came to an end and there was silence.

His eyes flicked to the fading bruise on my cheek and away again. 'You're still here, then? Thought you might have cleared off.'

'Like where?' I demanded. 'And Jasper? The animals? Did you think I had an ark ready and waiting somewhere?'

'Ah, yes, I forgot: *my* great-uncle by marriage, *my* cottage. Poor little orphan Lizzy has nowhere to go, has she?'

'Don't think I intend staying with you any longer than I have to,' I told him coldly. 'The minute Jasper's off to university, that's it. And if you're interested, his results came and he got into Liverpool.'

'It's always *Jasper*, isn't it?' he said pettishly.

'You should be pleased because he's your son too, whatever mad ideas you've got in your head. But I'm not playing your games any more, Tom—you can believe what you like.'

'Oh, come on, Jasper's the spitting image of Nick, my dear old no-blood-relation cousin—and don't forget I caught you in each other's arms at the hospital when Jasper was ill.'

'I've told you repeatedly that he was just comforting me—and *you* could have been doing that, if I'd been able to get hold of you! But I conceived Jasper practically as soon as we'd got married and I never even looked at Nick in that way—or any other man! No, there's another obvious reason why both you and Jasper look like Pharamonds, only you'd rather believe ill of me than your mother!'

50

'We'll leave my mother out of this,' he said, that ugly look in his eyes. 'But the sooner you clear out, the better.' Turning back towards his board he said dismissively, 'Fetch me a beer out will you? There's some in the fridge.'

'Fetch it yourself. I didn't come out here to wait on you. Oh, and here's a restaurant bill from Leila. I only hope the meal was worth it!'

'What?' He swung round and snatched it from me, glanced at it and then looked up suspiciously. 'Where did you get this?'

'Nick called by early this morning. You left Leila's without paying the bill, and she wants her money.'

'Oh, I don't think this is Leila's idea,' he said, crumpling the bill into a ball and tossing it into a corner. 'I've already paid her—in kind. Bed and board. So now you know, and presumably Nick also knows.'

'Suspects, perhaps . . . but . . . Leila can't possibly be "Dark Heart"!' I blurted.

He took a menacing step towards me. 'What do you know about Dark Heart?'

'I found a bit of a note in your pocket when I was sorting the washing, but it didn't sound like Leila,' I said, standing my ground.

'It isn't,' he said shortly. 'It's someone else . . . someone more conveniently local, who's prepared to please me in ways you wouldn't have, even if I'd *asked*, dearest wife.'

'Is it someone I know, Tom? And Leila—was that a one-off? She isn't the woman you've been having an affair with since before Jasper was ill, is she?'

He didn't reply, just smiled rather unpleasantly. I

51

hoped he hadn't been running two of them in tandem even then. But someone local . . . who could it be?

Oh God, he hadn't got drunk and started an affair with that drippy girl who played the electric violin and sang in the Mummers, had he? I'd noticed she hadn't been able to look me in the eye for months, but thought she'd maybe been one of his one-night flings. Evidently, he wasn't going to tell me anyway.

I thought of something else. 'Where's your van?'

'It broke down in a lay-by about twenty miles away. I had to get the garage to bring it in—think the gearbox's had it. Now, any more questions? Only I need to finish this board because I'm off down to Cornwall at the weekend to deliver it, assuming the van's fixed by then.'

I stared at him, thinking how normal a monster could look.

'If you aren't leaving immediately, you could make yourself useful and fetch that beer,' he suggested.

'Fetch it yourself! I'm going for a walk in the woods to think all this over, and then later I've got a Mystery Play Committee meeting, the first of the year,' I said, and saw a flash of anger in his eyes.

As I left I heard the music restart, and the hissing of the spray.

*   *   *

Outside I practically fell over Polly Darke, our local purveyor of stirring Regency romances—and I use the term 'Regency' very loosely, since she never let historical facts come between her and the story. She

52

gave me one of them once and I noticed the words 'feisty' and 'lusty' appeared on practically every page to describe the heroine and hero.

And now I came to think of it, she never let facts come between her and a *modern* story either, since she was always snooping about under one pretext or another, and twisting things she saw and heard into malicious gossip. Divorced, she had lived in her hacienda-style bungalow between Middlemoss and Mossedge for several years, and I'm sure was convinced that she was accepted everywhere as a local.

While I didn't suppose she could have heard anything much through a wooden door, that wouldn't prevent her from spreading lurid rumours about me and Tom around the three villages by sundown.

She was looking her usual strange self, in a severely truncated purple Regency-style dress, and with her hair cropped and dyed a dense, dead black. She clutched a small blue plastic basket of field mushrooms to her artificially inflated bosom, which might or might not be a fashion statement—are plastic baskets currently a must-have accessory?

Apart from the kohl-edged eyes and puffy, fuchsia-pink lips (which reminded me, strikingly, of a baboon's bottom), her face was pale as death. Paler.

'Oh, Polly, are you all right?' I asked. 'You haven't been eating your own home-bottled tomatoes or anything like that, have you?'

From time to time she fancied herself as the Earth Mother type and tried her hand at jams, chutneys and bottled goods, which she then gave to all and sundry, in my case together with a generous dose of botulism or something equally foul. Just my luck to get *that* one!

'Oh, no, I haven't had time for any of that, Lizzy—I've got a book to finish, you know.'

'Yes, Senga does like you to keep them coming, doesn't she?'

Having fallen out with two agents and three publishers, Polly had been taken on by my own agent, Senga McDonald—and may the best woman win.

Her dark eyes slid curiously to the closed workshop door and back to my face. 'I thought I heard raised voices—is everything OK with you and Tom? Only sometimes lately you haven't seemed entirely happy, and you *know* you can always depend on me if you need a shoulder to cry on.'

Oh, yes, but only if I kneel down first, I thought, as she smiled at me in a horribly pseudo-sympathetic sort of way.

'I'm fine,' I said shortly. 'We were just discussing business. Were you looking for me?'

She gave a start. 'Oh, yes. I picked loads of mushrooms in the paddock this morning early and I thought you might like to swap them for some quail eggs? But if it's inconvenient, it doesn't matter.'

'No, not at all. I'm just off for a walk, but you know where they are in the small barn? Help yourself and leave the mushrooms there,' I told her, and walked off, not caring whether she thought me rude or not. When she first moved to Middlemoss she went all out to be my best friend, but we had absolutely nothing in common (apart from Senga). Anyway, I already have a best friend in Annie.

Nor, it occurred to me, was she the type to skip about the fields at dawn gathering mushrooms, which in any case looked suspiciously like shop-bought ones, small, clean and perfectly formed. My marzipan mushrooms looked earthier than those!

*   *   *

I headed for the woods, for I found their dark, cool depths wonderfully soothing, especially on a hot day. They restored a sense of my unimportance in the great scale of things, shrinking my problems down to a more manageable, acorn size.

Luckily I was wearing a pinky-red T-shirt, so Caz would spot me if I strayed onto the smaller paths he stalked so relentlessly. But if he was out there with his gun, he didn't make himself known. He's not much of a talker in any case; but then, most of his dealings are with squirrels, so he doesn't need to be.

After a while I found my thoughts turning away from more painful subjects onto the comforting one of food, wondering which member of the Christmas Pudding Circle would come up with the best recipe for brandy butter ice cream.

More than likely it would be Faye, since she's a farmer's wife who has diversified by opening a farm shop and café, where she sells her own home-made organic ice cream. She was already perfecting a Christmas-pudding-flavoured one.

*   *   *

Eventually, as the shadows lengthened, I reluctantly had to turn for home, even though I dreaded seeing Tom again. But there was no need: he wasn't there and, more to the point, neither was my car.

Come to that, even the punnet of mushrooms Polly Darke had presumably left had vanished into thin air, though possibly Caz had been around and fancied them. He knows he can help himself to anything edible he can find, though it seemed a bit greedy to take them all. (He keeps the freezer I gave him locked, so goodness knows what's in there. Better not to know, perhaps?)

I searched for a note saying where Tom and my car had gone to, but there was nothing. Unless he came back by the time I returned from the Mystery Play Committee meeting, Jasper was going to have to cycle home that evening, and I would be extremely annoyed.

I fed, watered and generally cared for everything that needed my attention, then changed and set off for the village hall—on foot.

CHAPTER 5: SWEET MYSTERIES

The Mystery Play Committee will reconvene on the 19th of August with rehearsals to start in September as usual. If any member of last year's cast cannot for any reason continue in their role, would they please inform Marian and Clive Potter at the Middlemoss Post Office.

Mosses Messenger

The members of the Middlemoss Mystery Play Committee were gathered around a trestle table in the village hall, which exhibited reminders of its many functions: the playgroup's brightly coloured toys poked out from behind a curtained alcove and their finger-painting decorated one wall, while the other bore posters of footprints illustrating the various new steps the Senior Citizens' Tuesday Tea Dance Club were trying to master.

Personally, I thought salsa might give one or two of them a bit of trouble, but I was sure they would all give it a go. Their line dancing ensemble at the last Christmas concert had been a big hit, and Mrs Gumball, the cook up at Pharamond Hall, had got so excited she fell off the end of the stage. But fortunately foam playmats were always stacked there after an incident a few years back, when one of Santa's little elves fell over, causing a domino effect along the line until the last one dropped off and broke a leg.

'I think we might as well start, Clive,' I suggested to the verger, opening the plastic box of Choconut Consolations I'd brought with me and setting it in the middle, so everyone could help themselves. 'I don't know where Annie's got to, but Uncle Roly's gone to the races. He said after all these years he could do the Voice of God in his sleep, so you could sort it all out without him.'

This year's committee was formed of the usual suspects; some of them also CPC members. There was Dr Patel, our semi-retired GP, Miss Pym the infants' schoolteacher, the new vicar—untried and untested and looking more than a little nervous—and Clive and Marian Potter, who between them ran the post office, the *Mosses Messenger* parish magazine and also pretty well everything else that happened round Middlemoss, including directing the annual Mysteries. Then there was my humble self, for Clive liked to have a token Pharamond on tap, since Uncle Roly was inclined to give his duties the go-by if something more interesting came along. Annie was presumably held up somewhere.

'Very well. I've convened this meeting earlier than usual for two reasons,' announced Clive, who is like a busy little ant, always running to and fro. Marian is the same, and I have a theory that they never sleep, just hang by their heels for the odd ten minutes to refresh themselves, like bats. Come to that, they're so in tune with one another they have probably leaped up the next rung of the evolutionary ladder and communicate in high-pitched squeaks us mere bog-standard humans can't hear.

'First off, I thought the vicar might need a bit more time to get to grips with the Mysteries, it all coming as a bit of a surprise to him, like.'

The vicar, a carrot-haired, blue-eyed man with a naturally startled expression, nodded earnestly:

58

'But I'm delighted, of course—absolutely delighted.'

I wondered if anyone had warned him that the last vicar was currently having a genteel nervous breakdown in a church nursing home near Morecambe. An elderly man, he'd been hoping for a quiet country living, I feared, where he could jog along towards his retirement, not the whirl of activity that is the Mosses parish. But at least the new one was younger *and* unmarried. I observed with interest the way he suddenly went the same shade as his hair when Annie, breathless and dishevelled, rushed into the room.

'Sorry I'm late,' she said, subsiding into the seat next to me. 'One of the dogs slipped its lead and was practically in Mossrow before I caught him.'

She smiled apologetically around at everyone and, apart from the vicar, who was still looking poleaxed, we smiled back, since Annie is Goodwill to all Mankind personified. Even though I'm her best friend, I have to admit that she is a plump, billowy person the approximate shape of a cottage loaf and, although her hair is a beautiful coppery colour, that pudding-bowl bob does not do her amiable round face any favours. She certainly doesn't normally cause men to go red and all self-conscious . . .

'We were only just starting,' I assured her. 'Clive's called the meeting to familiarise the vicar—'

'*Do* all call me Gareth,' he interrupted eagerly, finding his voice again, but I expect most of us will just carry on addressing him as 'Vicar' because we are nothing if not traditionalists in Middlemoss.

'And you must call me KP,' said Dr Patel

agreeably, 'like the nuts.'

'And I'm Lizzy,' I put in hastily, seeing Gareth's puzzled expression at KP's old joke. 'You've already met Annie, haven't you?'

'Oh, yes.' He swallowed, his Adam's apple bobbing. 'At church.'

He was *just* Annie's type and clearly smitten, but she didn't seem to notice!

'Perhaps we'd better get on?' suggested Clive. 'Only the Youth Club will be in here tonight for snooker, and I'll need to set the tables up. First, could you all please read this quote from a recently published book.'

He passed round a bundle of photocopies.

Although called the Middlemoss Mysteries, this surviving vestige of a medieval mystery play, annually performed in an obscure Lancashire village, is in reality a much debased form. At some point in its history it was reduced to a mere series of tableaux illustrating several key Biblical scenes, such as the Fall of Lucifer, Adam and Eve and the Nativity. Then, early last century what little dialogue remained was rendered into near-impenetrable ancient local dialect by Joe Wheelright, the Weaver Poet, and this is constantly reinterpreted by each generation of actors. The head of the leading local family, the Pharamonds, traditionally speaks the Voice of God.

We all read it in silence.

Then Annie said, 'Well, it's not so bad, is it, Clive? We can't hope to keep the Mysteries a total secret, so we always do get some strangers coming along, especially since the Mosses have suddenly become so terribly trendy to live in.'

'No, it's the *folksy* visitors who would want to take over and fix the whole thing like a fly in amber that we want to discourage,' I agreed. 'The Middlemoss Mystery Play is just for the locals, something we've always done, like that Twelfth Night celebration they have up at Little Mumming.'

'That's hardly comparable with our play, dear, since I'm told it's only a morris dance and a small miracle scene of George and the Dragon,' Marian said.

'That's right,' agreed Clive. 'But they keep it quiet: I've even heard that they block the road into the village with tractors on the day, to deter strangers.'

'I think the best thing about our Mysteries is the way each new generation of actors adds a little something to their parts, even if we do now stick more or less to the Wheelright version,' I said, though actually, while the acting itself is taken very seriously, I often suspect the Weaver Poet of having had a somewhat unholy sense of humour.

'I don't think "debased" is a very polite description,' Marian said, looking down at her photocopy again and bristling to the ends of her short, spiky silver hair. 'And what does he mean, "impenetrable dialect"? If the audience doesn't know the bible stories before they see it, then they should, so they'd know what was going on!'

'Er . . . yes,' said the vicar, with a gingerly glance at Dr Patel, who was sitting with his hands clasped over his immaculately suited round stomach, listening benignly.

'Oh, don't mind me,' the doctor said, catching his eye. 'I went to infants' school right here—my father was the senior partner at the practice—so I know all the bible stories. So did all the Lees from the Mysteries of the East Chinese takeaway in Mossedge, and there's usually at least one of that family taking part in the play.'

'We have many mysteries,' I said helpfully. 'Even the pub is called the New Mystery.'

'Little Ethan Lee made such a sweet baby Jesus last year,' Miss Pym said sentimentally. 'He simply couldn't take his eyes off the angels' haloes.'

'None of us could,' Annie said. 'We'd never had ones that lit up before.'

'Oh?' said Gareth, clearly groping to make sense of all this. 'Well, Clive has kindly loaned me the videos of last year's performance, which I've watched with . . . with interest.' He cleared his throat. 'While I've seen the Chester Mystery Plays and, er . . . although the format of scenes from the Old and New Testaments have similarities to that, otherwise they don't seem much alike . . .'

'They're not, Vicar,' Clive said. 'They might have been at one time—you'd have to ask Mr Roly Pharamond, he's got all the records. But when the Puritans took over and tried to ban it, the squire—another Roland, he was—he told the players to cut it right down, so it could be performed in one day up at the Hall, instead of here on the green.'

'Yes,' agreed Marian, 'and on Boxing Day instead of Midsummer Day, because fewer strangers would be travelling about then. Then, when it was safe to perform the Mysteries in public again—well, we'd got used to doing things *our* way.'

'So it's still performed up at the Hall on Boxing

Day?' Gareth asked.

Miss Pym nodded. 'In the coach house. The doors are opened wide and the audience stands in the courtyard, with lots of braziers about to keep them warm. The stables on either side are used as dressing rooms. It lasts about five hours, with breaks for refreshments, of course, and musical interludes.'

'Musical interludes? Indeed?' Gareth brightened. 'Hymns, perhaps? I'm hoping to breathe a little life back into the church choir.'

'No, actually a local group perform—the Mummers of Invention,' I told him. 'My husband sings with them and they're quite good. Sort of electric folk style.'

'Mummers of *Invention*?' he murmured, looking bemused.

'The last vicar had the strange idea that the play was blasphemous in some way,' Clive said, 'but you could see yourself from the video that it's the exact opposite, couldn't you? It's all bible stories, and the entire parish is involved right down to the infants' school. The children always play the procession of animals into the ark.'

'And they helped me to make the Virgin's bower last year with wire and tissue paper flowers,' Miss Pym said, 'though since it kept falling on Annie's head (your fifth and last appearance as Virgin, wasn't it, dear?) it could not have been called an unqualified success.'

Annie caught the vicar's eye, went pink, and looked hastily away—but at least now she *had* noticed him.

'And you run the Mysteries committee, Clive, and direct the play?' Gareth asked.

63

'Yes, that's right. In September we start giving out the parts and rehearsing. No one can play the same role for more than five years except God, so things change, and different people come forward or drop out.'

'Some of the new actors who've moved into the area lately have volunteered,' I said.

'Yes, like Ritch Rainford,' Annie murmured dreamily, and I gave her a look. I hope she's not going to get a serious crush on the man, since it's unlikely to lead anywhere.

'But most of them don't live here all the time, Annie, and you need people who do, especially when there are more rehearsals just before Christmas.'

'Yes, so the parts are usually played by local people and someone always volunteers if there's an emergency, like last year when Lazarus broke both ankles falling off his tractor,' Dr Patel said. 'He could have lain down, but there was no way short of a real miracle he was ever going to rise up and walk. So Lizzy's husband, Tom, stepped in at the last minute.'

'He made a very good Lazarus: I gave him four stars in the parish magazine review,' Clive broke in.

Gareth turned to me. 'So, your husband is Tom Pharamond, and he also plays in a band called the Mummers? I don't think I've met him yet, have I?'

'I shouldn't think so, he's not much of a churchgoer. And he said he wouldn't take part in the play again this year, it was a one-off, Clive—sorry. You'll need a new Lazarus.'

'Pity,' Clive said regretfully. He coughed and shuffled his papers together. 'So, we'll ask for nominations for the parts and rehearsals will start in the middle of September in two groups, one on Tuesdays and the other, Thursdays. As usual, I'll need a director's assistant for each scene. Lizzy, will you take on the Fall of Lucifer, the Creation, and Adam and Eve? You *are* still doing Eve this year, I hope?'

'Yes, my fifth and final go too, thank goodness—even a knitted bodystocking is perishingly cold in December. I had to keep warming myself over a chestnut brazier last year and a couple of my fig leaves got singed.'

'You could try thermal underwear?' suggested Miss Pym. 'Those thin silk ones for under ski suits.'

'That's an idea! Not so bulky.'

'Miss Pym will do Noah's Flood, of course, and Marian will oversee Moses. One of the tablets broke last time; someone will need to make a new one . . .' Clive made a note, and ticked off Moses.

'Vicar, if you could be in charge of the Nativity—Annunciation, Magi, Birth of Christ, Flight into Egypt?'

'Yes, of course,' Gareth agreed, though rather numbly, I thought. But unlike the last vicar, at least he hadn't started gibbering and lightly foaming at the mouth by this stage.

'Dr Patel has offered to do the Temptation of Christ, the Curing of the Lame Man, the Blind Man, and the Raising of Lazarus: all short scenes.'

'Seems appropriate,' agreed the doctor, adding generously, 'and the Water into Wine and Feeding of the Five Thousand too, if you like.'

'I'll see to the Last Supper, Judas, the Trial and Crucifixion myself this year—the Crucifixion's always tricky, but you might want to take that on next year, Vicar—and then that leaves just the

65

Resurrection, Ascension and Last Judgement.'

'I'll do those again,' offered Annie.

'We do the final dress rehearsals for the whole thing up at the Hall in a couple of sessions before Christmas,' Marian helpfully explained to the vicar. 'In random order, or it would be unlucky. But since at least two-thirds of the players will have done their parts before, it's just a question of making sure the new ones know their lines and where to stand, that's all.'

'Oh, good,' said poor Gareth weakly. He looked at his watch. 'I'd better get back—I've got a funeral to prepare.'

'Yes, our Moses—such a sad loss,' Miss Pym said. 'We will have to recast that part, too.'

Clive stuffed his papers and clipboard into a scuffed leather briefcase and then he and Marian started transforming the hall into a snooker parlour for the Youth Club, turning down my offer of help.

When I went out the vicar was already halfway across the green with Annie, heading in the direction of the church. I bet they were only talking about something totally mundane like Sunday school, though, and she hadn't noticed at all that he fancied her.

Miss Pym climbed into her little red Smart car and vanished with a *vroom*, and Dr Patel wished me good night and got into his BMW.

I wended my way home to Perseverance Cottage, where I did not find my husband or, more importantly, my car, but did find a telephone message on the machine from Unks, asking me to ring him back. When I did, he told me that Mimi, his elderly sister who lived at the Hall with her long-suffering companion Juno, had been arrested

66

by the police at the Southport Flower Show, having temporarily got away from Mrs Gumball, who'd volunteered to keep an eye on her. You can't blame her, though, since Mimi is very spry for an octogenarian while Mrs Gumball is the human equivalent of a mastodon, so moves slowly and majestically.

Unfortunately, Mimi is a plant kleptomaniac: no one's garden is safe from her little knife and plastic bags, and she really just can't understand why anyone should take exception to her habits. Still, the police had merely cautioned and released her this time and, since the coach had by then set out on the return journey, drove her and Mrs Gumball home in a police car.

Roly said she was under the impression they had done it to give her a treat, and was hoping next year's flower show would be as much fun.

Then he added, rather puzzlingly, 'And I hope Tom told you that you can stop worrying about ever losing Perseverance Cottage, my dear, because after I'm gone, it's yours and Tom's. I would have said before, if I'd known it was on your mind.'

'But I *wasn't* worried, Unks! In fact, the thought never even entered my head,' I assured him. Since I would have to leave soon, it was immaterial to me, but Tom had evidently used me as an excuse to find out how things had been left. How Machiavellian he's becoming!

After this, I unpacked Annie's candyfloss machine to distract myself from worrying until Jasper arrived safely home. The instructions absolutely forbade me to use any natural essences or colourings other than special granulated ones designed for the purpose, which was disappointing from the point of view of making Cornish Mist, until I discovered one of the tubs in the box was lemon.

Fascinating how the floss forms inside the bowl like ectoplasm, and you have to wind the near invisible threads onto wooden sticks. Fine, sugary filaments drifted everywhere, and the kitchen took on the hot, sweet, nostalgic smell of funfairs.

It was really messy but fun, which Jasper said was a good description of *me*, too, when he got home and saw what I'd been up to, though by then I was sitting among the debris, writing it all up for the *Chronicle*.

Maybe I'll have 'messy, but fun' as my epitaph.

CHAPTER 6: DRIVEN OFF

I wonder if plastic bags of fluffy white candyfloss labelled 'edible Santa beards' would go down well with children at Christmas? I expect they would try them on and get terribly sticky, though.
The Perseverance Chronicles: A Life in Recipes

There was still no sign of my car next morning and, in a furious temper, I rang all of Tom's friends that I knew about, or who I had mobile numbers for although trying to contact his surfing buddies down in Cornwall was always like waking the dead, and I got little sense out of them even when they did answer the phone.

The first time or two he went missing for a few days I also rang the local hospitals and the police, but after that I learned my lesson.

I woke Jasper early and saw him off by bike to the dig, then I called Annie to tell her I was without transport; but luckily she only wanted me to exercise the two Pekes and a Shitzu belonging to one of the more elderly members of the *Cotton Common* cast, Delphine Lake. She'd bought one of the expensive flats in part of the former Pharamond's Butterflake Biscuit factory in the village and I'd walked her dogs several times before.

Uncle Roly sold the Pharamond brand name out to a big conglomerate years ago for cash, shares and a seat on the board, which was both a smart and lucrative deal; so now the factory has been converted to apartments, a café-bar called

Butterflakes, and a museum of Mosses history.

Delphine's dogs may be little, but they loved their walks, so it was late morning before I got back to the cottage and found a female police officer awaiting me on the doorstep. An adolescent colleague sat biting his fingernails behind the wheel of a panda car.

I immediately thought the worst, as you do. *'Jasper?'* I cried. 'Has something happened to Jasper?'

'Mrs Elizabeth Pharamond?' she queried solemnly.

'Yes!'

'I'm Constable Perkins and I'm afraid I have some very bad news for you.'

She paused, and I was just about to take her by the throat and shake her when she added,

'About your husband.'

'Oh—thank *God*!' I gasped devoutly, then burst into tears of relief.

Wresting the keys from my nerveless fingers, she ushered me into my own home, where she broke the news that Tom had had a fatal accident. He'd driven off the road into a disused quarry, which was odd in itself, since there's only one place within a radius of about fifty miles where he could have managed to perform that feat, and it's up a little-used back lane.

While her colleague made me tea, she spoke to me with skilful sympathy, though my reactions clearly puzzled her. But all I was feeling was an overpowering sense of relief that it wasn't Jasper.

And then I got to thinking that this was all so blatantly unreal anyway, that it couldn't be true: it must be just some dreadful nightmare!

70

This was a very calming idea, since I knew I'd wake up *sometime,* so I agreed quite readily to go and identify Tom's body. My head seemed to be this helium-filled thing bobbing about on a string— or that's what it felt like, anyway—but there's no accounting for dreams.

And Tom, apart from his thin, handsome face being a whiter shade of pale, looked absolutely fine. He was always one to land butter-side up . . .

'Is this your husband?' the policewoman asked formally.

'Yes—Thomas Pharamond. Are you *sure* he's dead? Only he looks just like he did when he was playing Lazarus.'

She gave me a strange look, but assured me that Tom had broken his neck in a very final manner. Then she offered me yet another cup of tea, which I didn't want, and took me home again, sitting beside me in the back seat while the adolescent did the driving. He feasted on his fingernails at every red light and I don't know why, but it suddenly reminded me of the stewed apple with little sharp crescents of core snippings that they used to give us at school for pudding.

The policewoman whiled away the journey by telling me that they thought the car (*my* car, which was now a write-off) had been at the bottom of the quarry for a few hours before it was found, and he must have died instantly, but I expect they say that every time. There would have to be a post-mortem examination, and probably an inquest. I *think* she said there would be an inquest. I wasn't taking it all in, because of course it wasn't real.

When we got to Perseverance Cottage, she asked if there was someone who could stay with me.

'Oh, yes—I'll phone the family right now,' I assured her, suddenly desperate to get rid of her. 'Thank you for . . . for—well, thank you, Officer. I'll be fine.'

She looked a bit dubious, but drove off leaving me to it, and I thankfully closed the front door and leaned against it: that seemed solid enough. So did the cold quarry tiles beneath my feet when I kicked my sandals off . . .

It began slowly to dawn on me that this really was happening and Tom was actually dead! In which case, I could only be glad that Jasper was at his dig, since I'm sure he would have insisted on coming with me to identify Tom, though actually his face had looked peaceful enough, if vaguely surprised by the turn of events. I felt a sudden pang of guilt, remembering how glad I had been that it was Tom who had died and not Jasper.

But now I'd have to break the news to him about his father . . . and to Unks and Mimi and Tom's mother out in Argentina . . .

Stiffening my trembling legs I tottered into the sitting room and dialled the Hall, getting Uncle Roly.

I don't think I was the mistress of either tact or coherence by this stage, but he took the news well, if quietly, and offered to phone Tom's mother and stepfather in Argentina himself, which was a huge relief. Then he said he would also try and contact Nick, still off touring the eateries of the rural North-West.

'And Jasper?' he asked. 'I take it he is at the dig, and doesn't know?'

'Yes, and I think I'll just wait for him to come home before I tell him,' I decided, for why rush to

72

give him the bad news? 'Anyway, Tom was driving my car—his van broke down—so I haven't got any transport.'

When I phoned Annie she was out and the message I left was probably unintelligible.

*   *   *

Roly thoughtfully called in later in the Daimler to say Joe Gumball was driving him over to the dig to collect Jasper and he could break the news to him on the way home, if I wanted.

'Oh, Unks, you are kind!' I said, gratefully. 'But it must be just as hard for you. You don't have to do it.'

'My dear, having lived through the war, I'm inured to breaking bad news.'

I offered him some of the damson gin I'd been drinking to try to dispel that feeling of being underwater with my eardrums straining, but which had just seemed to make everything more unbelievably bizarre, and said anxiously, 'I can't believe Tom isn't going to walk back in through that door at any moment, the way he always turned up after he'd been missing for a few days.'

He patted my hand. 'There, there, my dear. Leave everything to me. I'll be back with Jasper in no time.'

*   *   *

Mimi phoned me up just after he'd left, but halfway through offering me her condolences in a graciously formal manner, she completely lost the thread and said she was too busy to talk to me just now. Then

73

she put the phone down.

But at least her call had jarred me into remembering to feed the poultry. It was a bit late, but when I called, 'Myrtle, Myrtle, Myrtle—Honey, Honey, Honey!' they all came running.

Round the side of the big greenhouse I came unexpectedly nose to bare (except for the camouflage paint) chest of Caz Naylor, who indicated with a nod of his head and a raised eyebrow that he would like to know what was happening.

'Tom's driven off the quarry road,' I said. 'In *my* car.'

'Dead?'

'So they say.'

'Car?'

'That's a write-off, too.'

He grunted non-committally, then handed me a small blue plastic basket containing one slightly decayed mushroom. 'Poison,' he said, prodding it with a slightly grimy finger.

'I know,' I began, recognising it, but he turned and flitted off back through the shadows until he'd completely vanished into the woods.

That was the longest conversation I'd had with him for ages . . . and what was the significance of the poisonous fungi in a punnet that looked suspiciously like the one Polly Darke had brought me full of field mushrooms . . . was that only yesterday? Perhaps she'd inadvertently picked a poisonous one? After my previous experience of Polly's way with foodstuffs, I should have been more cautious in accepting them anyway!

Or perhaps Caz had simply taken to giving brief nature lessons in his spare time.

*　　　　*　　　　*

Jasper was very quiet and pale when he came in, and though we shared a long hug, said he'd like to be alone for a bit and vanished up to his room. I thought it best to leave him to talk in his own time.

He did reappear when Annie arrived and seemed pretty composed by then, though he being the quiet stoical type it's hard to tell, even for me.

I thought I was quite composed too, but as soon as Annie walked through the door I burst into tears, as though her arrival was some kind of absolute proof that it really wasn't all a ghastly nightmare. I left a full set of grubby fingerprints up the back of her lavender Liberty cotton shirt.

She hugged Jasper too, something which he would normally go out of his way to avoid, even though he is fond of her. Then we all just sat around in a fuzzy cloud of disbelief and damson gin.

It was the sheer unreality: Tom had gone missing so many times, it was hard to believe he wouldn't just walk through that door at any minute with the TV remote control in his hand (he secreted it away somewhere in his workshop when away), and sit watching endless films on Sky, which he'd had installed soon after he got the giant TV.

He'd always been supremely selfish. Even the Tom I fell in love with, charming though he'd been, really only thought about himself for at least ninety-five per cent of the time, which is why he always did exactly what he wanted and apologised afterwards.

'Yes, I know,' Annie agreed when I shared this gem with her, together with the rest of the bottle of

75

gin, after Jasper had gone up to bed (or at least, back up to the Batcave). 'But when he was around he seemed to cast a spell of charm, so people didn't realise it until later. Or if they did, they didn't mind, because they thought he wasn't doing it intentionally to hurt anyone, it was just how he was.'

The gin might not have been such a good idea after all, for my past life seemed to take on a darkly ominous pattern. 'Why?' I demanded. 'What have I done to deserve this? Why do *I* have to lose everyone? I know I didn't love Tom any more, but I didn't want any harm to come to him either!'

'We all have to die,' Annie pointed out soothingly, passing me the plate of ginger parkin she'd found in the fridge while looking for something to blot up the alcohol. I must have sliced and buttered it earlier, on automatic pilot.

'Yes, but why don't my loved ones die naturally of old age? Look at my parents! OK, Daddy was a diplomat, but of all the British Consulates in all the world, why did they have to be sent to *that* one? And having got there, why did they have to immediately sit in the wrong restaurant and get blown up? Couldn't they have settled for baked beans on bagels at home, and then lived nice, peaceful lives and been more than a few faded snapshots and some stored furniture to their only daughter?'

'But you had nothing to do with it—you'd just arrived for your first term at St Mattie's,' she pointed out. 'You weren't even in the same country. Stop imagining you're some kind of Angel of Death! What would Daddy say if he could hear you?'

From past experience I could confidently predict that Annie's father would go wandering off into a scholarly monologue on angels of death, the existence and symbolism of, which would be soothing, but not precisely helpful.

Annie gave me a hug. 'It's not your fault that Tom was killed and you did your best to save your marriage. I know what it's been like the last few years, and you're a saint to have stayed with him.'

'I'm not a saint. I stayed for Jasper, really, and because we both loved living here.' A tear rolled down my cheek and landed onto the half-eaten slice of parkin I was holding, though I didn't remember taking a piece.

'I'm sure for the first few years Tom did love and need you, Lizzy. He wandered off, but he always came back again.'

'Perhaps, but there were always other women. I tried to shut my eyes to it, but it hurt, Annie.' I swallowed hard. 'But I think I'm grieving for the Tom I married, even if the man I thought he was never existed. And I still feel guilty for being so relieved that it was Tom, rather than Jasper.'

Annie comforted me as well as she could, and I have a vague recollection of her helping me up to bed, where I must have passed out.

When I staggered down next morning, feeling like Lady Lazarus, everything had been cleared and tidied and washed up.

There's probably a Girl Guide badge for coping with a friend's bereavement too, together with the Advanced Award for staying in control of your faculties while under the influence of damson gin.

CHAPTER 7: LOOSE NUTS

Candied citrus peel makes a good gift and although the traditional process is messy and time-consuming, there is a quick method, which I have used with some success. When candied, the pieces can be dipped in good dark chocolate for a tasty treat.
The Perseverance Chronicles: A Life in Recipes

'Oh, my husband was really selfish,' I said to PC Perkins, when she came back again later that day for what she called 'a little background detail'. This, oddly enough, seemed to consist of asking me what Tom had been like, but I expect she'd been on some kind of Dealing with the Victims of Bereavement course, or something.

I'd finished quick-candying the orange peel left from yesterday and today's breakfast juice, and was just writing the recipe up for the latest *Perseverance Chronicle*, so even the sitting room, when I led the way into it, still smelled enticingly of citrus and hot sugar.

I seemed to be going through the motions of normal life, but most of the time my brain was entirely absent, so I must have been doing it on automatic pilot.

Jasper, who had phoned up the dig earlier to explain his absence, followed us in and loomed about protectively. After the previous night's hair-down, damson-gin-fuelled wake with Annie, I had given up trying to hide things from him. I don't think it worked in the first place.

'Oh, really?' she said encouragingly, seating herself on the armchair Tom had favoured for his telly watching. I made a mental note to do something about that giant blank screen, which was like having a dead eye in the room . . .

I shuddered and she eyed me speculatively.

'You don't make your husband sound terribly attractive, Mrs Pharamond!'

'Actually, he could be very charming, and when I fell in love with him I thought the way he used to vanish for days without a word was endearingly absent-minded and eccentric. But really, he was just too wrapped up in himself to bother doing anything he didn't want to, a bit like a cat.'

'But you can still love a cat,' Jasper pointed out. 'Most cat owners seem to think their cats love them back, too.'

'He did seem fond of me, in his way, until the last few years—and of you, too, Jasper, when you were small,' I assured him, wiping a runny tear away. 'Some men just aren't good with children.'

'I expect we'd have got on better if I'd surfed, or was interested in weird folk-rock music and stuff—fitted into his interests,' Jasper agreed. 'History and archaeology bored him.'

'Yes, and he wasn't even interested in food, was he, except from the eating it point of view?'

The police officer, who'd been listening in a sort of fascinated silence, now broke in, notebook at the ready. She seemed to have an agenda of her own. 'Just a couple of questions, Mrs Pharamond—and I'm sure you have a few you would like to ask me.'

She gave me a reassuring smile, though it contained no warmth. Yesterday she'd seemed so kind and sympathetic, so maybe she could switch a façade on and off at will, like Tom. She also had coral-pink lipstick on her front teeth and it was *so* not her colour.

'Perhaps your son—Jasper, isn't it?—could make some tea,' she suggested.

'I think I'll stay here,' Jasper said thoughtfully, settling down on the sofa next to me.

'Can you tell me what time your husband left here on the Wednesday? You said you last saw him then, didn't you?'

'I don't know when he left, because I went for a walk in the late morning—a long walk in the woods—and when I got back my car had gone.'

'Did he often borrow your car?'

'No, practically never, because I usually made sure he couldn't find the keys. His van had broken down, that's why he took mine.'

'So you were surprised to find your car gone?'

'Yes, and annoyed when he didn't come back in time for me to go and collect Jasper from the dig . . . or at all. I *needed* my car.'

'He would probably have come back in good time if the accident hadn't happened, Mum. His mobile was in the workshop and I expect he'd have taken it with him if he hadn't just popped out for something,' Jasper said. 'Wonder where he was going. I checked it for messages, but he'd wiped them, so that was no help.'

'I don't know,' I said dubiously. 'He probably just forgot his phone.'

'Where do *you* think he might have been going, Mrs Pharamond?'

'I've no idea. But he told me earlier he had to finish a surfboard to deliver this weekend, so I was surprised when he didn't come back.'

'Finish a surfboard?'

'He customised surfboards for a living. You know—spray-painted designs on them? He was a keen surfer, too . . .' I stopped, having a sudden vision of Tom freewheeling into space off the quarry road and wondering if he found the sensation exhilarating? I wouldn't put it past him, and of course he'd never expect anything he did, however dangerous, to actually kill him.

'And you were here all evening?'

'Yes. After I got back from the Mystery Play Committee meeting in the village hall I was experimenting with candyfloss, so I was pretty busy.'

She gave me a strange look but didn't follow that one up. Instead she turned her attention to Jasper.

'And you were at this archaeological site all that day?'

He nodded. 'Occasionally I cycle there in the mornings, but Mum usually picks me up in the evening. The narrow roads round the site have become a bit of a rat run since everyone got satnav and she thinks I'll get knocked off the bike,' he said tolerantly. 'When I got home she'd been making lemon candyfloss. Yummy.'

'Right,' she said, scribbling away. I nearly asked her if she would like me to whip her up some Cornish Mist, but I could see she had no sense of humour.

'So, Mrs Pharamond, you must have been angry about your husband taking the car?'

'I was, and even more so when he didn't come back. But I knew if I didn't turn up at the dig, Jasper would cycle back, he really didn't mind.'

I was starting to feel strangely worried, despite

81

knowing I had nothing on my conscience other than guilt for that profound moment of relief I'd felt on hearing that it was Tom who'd had the accident and not Jasper.

'Jasper, perhaps tea *would* be a good idea? Or coffee. Would you mind?'

He gave me a look, but rose to a gangling six foot and, stooping under the low beam, went to the kitchen, though he left the door ajar. This is not a cottage where you can have private conversations . . . or indeed, private much of anything.

'Can you tell me how the accident happened yet? I thought he must have had a seizure, perhaps, or a heart attack, even though he seemed a bit young for that? Or perhaps the brakes failed, or something?'

'Actually, it looks as though one of the Citroën's wheels came off.' Her eyes were fixed on my face to gauge the full effect of this pronouncement.

'A *wheel* came off? But would that have caused him to veer off the road?'

'Not necessarily. It's usually possible to drive on three wheels to a safe halt.'

A sudden, rather nasty, thought struck me. 'Do you know which wheel came off?'

'The front driver's side.' She looked at me intently again, and I realised I must've turned pale. 'Why?'

'I had a flat tyre . . . it must have been that same morning, so I changed the wheel for the spare and took it in to be mended. Jasper undid the last nut—it was stiff—but *I* changed the wheel and put the nuts on again,' I said firmly. 'Jasper had gone back into the house by then. And what's more, it was absolutely fine on the drive to the dig and back!'

'Mrs Pharamond, I'm not accusing you of

82

anything!'

Wasn't she? It began to sound amazingly like it!

'Isn't it just possible you didn't tighten them up quite enough, so they slowly worked loose? Accidents do happen.'

'You mean I might have *accidentally* killed my husband?'

Now I saw which way she was heading with this, I thanked God it was me who had tightened the nuts and not Jasper!

'If they were a bit loose, then the tight bends of the quarry road could have completed the job,' she said. 'It's a possibility. We haven't found any of them yet.'

'But I'm sure they were tight, because I used a wheel br—' I stopped as Jasper came back in carrying a battered tin tray of mugs and an open carton of milk.

'Yes, they were,' he said, putting the tray down on the coffee table with a thump that slopped some coffee over the rims. 'I could hear what you were saying from the kitchen and Mum put the wheel back on and tightened the nuts. And then when she went in to wash her hands, *I* tightened them up even more.'

We gazed at him, though presumably not with the same mixed feelings of affection and exasperation.

'Oh, Jasper,' I said, 'I'm not being accused of anything except carelessness, so you really don't have to try and protect me!'

'I'm not, Mum, it's quite true. I left you putting the wheel back on, but I checked it was tight enough later, when you weren't about.'

I wondered how often he'd felt he needed to

check up on me, and from my expression he deduced that he ought to add something. 'It was fine—I thought it would be.'

'Of course it was! Any idiot can change a wheel,' I said indignantly.

PC Perkins had lost interest in the ins and outs of our dispute, and turned to Jasper, notebook at the ready. 'So you are quite sure that the wheel was in a safe condition?'

'Absolutely. And I often checked them and the tyre pressure since I passed my test, for the practice.'

'So, how do *you* account for the same wheel coming off?'

'I don't—that's your job, isn't it? But we don't know how long he'd been out, so he could have left the car standing about, and loosening the wheel nuts might have been someone's idea of a joke.' He shrugged. 'Mum's car was ancient, so who knows? Maybe the threads had gone or something, even?'

I stared at him, thinking that he certainly didn't get his coolness and sang-froid from me or Tom— but, of course, my father *was* in the diplomatic service.

She closed her notebook with a snap. 'Once the post-mortem has been completed, if everything is in order, an inquest will be opened and adjourned and an interim death certificate issued,' she said briskly, by which I presumed she meant unless they found I'd been feeding him Cyanide Chutney for months. (Or Polly Darke's poisonous tomatoes. Pity I hadn't thought of that one!)

'The funeral can then take place, and the inquest proper will open at a later date.'

'Must there be another inquest?'

'Yes, it's standard procedure in cases of this kind.'

'Which kind?' I demanded, when I heard the kitchen door suddenly burst open and crash back against the wall, rattling all the china on the dresser. Then Polly Darke stumbled over the sitting-room threshold like a dishevelled, shrink-wrapped Bacchae, all billowing green chiffon sleeves, stick-thin legs and enormous boobs.

'Well, stay me with flagons,' I said, surprised (damson gin for preference), for even Polly wasn't usually *this* avid to garner news.

Her slightly prominent eyes passed over the policewoman and fixed on me. 'Is it *true*?' she demanded thrillingly. 'Is Tom really dead? They're saying he had an accident—in *your* car!'

Presumably this was rhetorical, for with an anguished cry of, 'Tom! Tom!' she threw herself into the nearest chair and burst into hysterical sobs.

Jasper and I exchanged glances. Attention-seeking taken to extremes, combined with a raging desire to know what was happening was, I'm sure, our first thought.

'This is Polly Darke, Officer,' I explained resignedly. 'She's a novelist and lives near Mossrow.'

Polly looked up, her face like a drowned flower (a slightly withered pansy). 'I can't believe it. Only the night before last Tom was with me, and now he's gone. *Gone!*'

'Why was he with you?' asked Jasper, puzzled. 'I thought he'd finally finished those Celtic murals you asked him to do ages ago?'

'Because he loved me!' she exclaimed tragically and began to sob gustily again.

85

'He was with you the night before last?' I stared at her, my mind whirling faster than a tumble dryer. 'Good heavens, don't tell me that you, of all people, are Dark Heart? No, it can't possibly be you!'

'Yes it is! Why not?' she demanded belligerently, straightening from her pose of utter despondency. '*I* could give him what he needed—'

'Tie him up, tie him down?' I suggested a bit numbly. You know, I'd never even considered her as a possible suspect, because to me she was a rather pathetic and ludicrous creature, though perhaps men might see her differently? But not young men, apparently, for Jasper looked even more incredulous than I was.

'Dark Heart?' he queried.

'Yes, your father was having an affair with someone, but though I found a note in his pocket on the morning of the day he vanished, it was only signed "Dark Heart", so I didn't know who it was.'

'You mean, Dad was having an affair with *her*?'

'Evidently, but I certainly thought it would be someone younger.'

I'm quite sure Polly is *much* older than I am—well the other side of forty—even if she does try to hold back the years with every ancient and modern art at her disposal.

'What do you mean?' she demanded indignantly, glaring at me. 'I'm only thirty-five!'

'And the rest,' Jasper said drily.

I'd entirely forgotten the policewoman was there until she interjected into the sudden lull in the proceedings, 'So you knew your husband was having an affair, Mrs Pharamond?'

Her notebook was open again, I saw, pen poised.

I glanced uneasily at Jasper. 'He . . . well, he *had*

had lapses occasionally in the past, but they didn't mean anything. Then I found out about a more serious affair about five years ago, when my son was ill—and I'm so sorry, Jasper: I didn't want you to find out about your father's affairs, especially like this.'

'Oh, I knew all about the women, Mum,' he said calmly. 'I even caught him at it with that girl out of the Mummers once, when I walked in on them in the workshop.'

'You did?'

'That's a lie!' Polly yelled furiously, but Jasper just glanced coolly at her, one eyebrow raised, as though she were a failed soufflé. He looked terribly like Nick. I don't think Polly is any kind of soufflé, though, more of a synthetic Black Forest gateau with poisonous cherries.

'So you were not on good terms with your husband,' the policewoman suggested to me, 'although he'd had affairs in the past to which you hadn't objected?'

'Of course I objected!' I exclaimed. 'What do you take me for? And they were usually more in the nature of one-night stands than anything serious. For a long time I used to believe him when he said he loved me and they meant nothing.'

'Yes, but that was the old Dad, not the nastier model we've had to live with lately,' Jasper pointed out. 'Even I've overheard him, taunting you about some woman he's been seeing—and he's not coming across as a very admirable-sounding character, is he?'

The police officer said patiently, 'So this time he was having a serious affair, Mrs Pharamond? He would have left you?'

'No, it had to be the other way round, because this cottage belongs to his great-uncle by marriage, Roly Pharamond. So I intended leaving, once Jasper was at university and I'd found new homes for the livestock and sorted out somewhere to go, some sort of job . . .' I trailed off.

'That's *so* not true! I heard you arguing in his workshop that very morning and when I questioned him about it later, he told me he'd asked you to leave and you'd refused!' Polly cried. 'He was afraid Roly Pharamond would take your side and he'd lose the cottage and everything he'd worked for.'

'Obviously you didn't hear much, Polly!' I said, surprised. 'What I actually told him was that I'd had enough and was going to leave him as soon as I could. And if anyone worked around here and stood to lose everything, it was me!' I added incautiously, and the policewoman's pen skidded quickly across the page.

'Well, at least you don't have to do that now, Mum,' Jasper remarked, and a small silence ensued.

I sighed. 'We might still have to move, Jasper. It depends on Uncle Roly.'

'Unks won't put you out, Ma. He's really fond of you.'

'So,' said the officer to Polly, 'you overheard an argument, and what then?'

'*She* came out,' Polly said, with a venomous look at me. 'So I said I'd brought her some field mushrooms to exchange for eggs, and she said, "Help yourself, I'm going for a walk." She was really odd—she looked furious. When she'd gone I spoke to Tom briefly and he said he'd come over later, after he'd finished the board he was

88

painting—which he did. And that's the last time I saw him, because when I woke up early next morning he'd gone. He parks around the back of the house, out of sight, so I'd no idea he hadn't come in his own van,' she added. 'I just assumed he had.'

'No, it was still at the garage,' I told her. 'But if he hadn't taken my car, when he knew very well I wanted it later, it might have been me and Jasper who had the accident.'

'It *should* have been you!' she said venomously. Her reddened eyes and sharp nose made her look like a particularly unsavoury rodent.

Jasper stood up slowly and said in a tone of menace I'd never heard from him before, 'I think you've said—and done—quite enough. Why don't you clear off?'

She floundered hastily and inelegantly out of the chair and backed towards the door. PC Perkins jumped up and stood between them.

'If I could have your name and address, Ms Darke? I'll follow you over and ask you a few more questions in your own home, if I may?' She turned to me with a thin smile: 'Thank you for your assistance, Mrs Pharamond.'

I had a horrible feeling she suspected me of loosening the wheelnuts on purpose, then leaving the keys out where Tom was sure to find them. And goodness knew what Polly would tell her!

'Jasper,' I said when they'd gone, 'you were wonderful!'

'Don't worry, Mum, that cop may have a suspicious mind, but we know there's nothing to find, so they can't pin anything on you.'

'Thank you, darling,' I said weakly, then had a

thought. 'I wonder if Tom had anything to eat at Polly's? Only if he had an attack of food poisoning, that might account for why he lost control of the car when the wheel came off.'

'I don't think he went there to eat, Mum,' Jasper said, before vanishing back up to his Batcave.

In the kitchen I discovered that half the candied peel had vanished, presumably eaten by Jasper while waiting for the kettle to boil, but then, it's very moreish. But it didn't matter, I was only going to dip it in dark chocolate as a treat for later.

Meanwhile, there was a whole row of bolting lettuces (I'd planted too many, as usual) to toss to the hens, and fruit to pick: a fresh strawberry Pavlova would be wonderfully comforting.

CHAPTER 8: WELL BRACED

Once our bulk order for dried fruit, peel and all the other ingredients has arrived and been divided up among the five members of the Christmas Pudding Circle, you can tell where we all live by the rich aroma of cooking mincemeat wafting from the doors and windows. We tend to make it early and of course it's useful all year round, for making mincemeat brownies, stuffing baked apples and a host of other things—not least the famous Middlemoss Marchpane tart.

I'm going to make a bumper quantity this time, before I really get going on all the bottling, preserving and freezing of garden fruits and vegetables that starts to build up momentum at this time of year: the making of chutneys, jams, curds and relishes . . .

The Perseverance Chronicles: A Life in Recipes

On the Monday Jasper returned to his dig (by bike) and I went to the Christmas Pudding Circle meeting. I was glad of any distraction from the turmoil of mixed emotions caused by Tom's death and Polly's revelations, though it would have been impossible to describe what I felt. It wasn't even as if Tom had played a major part of our lives for the last few years, except in a negative, passing storm-cloud sort of way, but still, grief of some kind was an element and Jasper, I was sure, felt much the same. And also, I was increasingly uneasy at the direction the police enquiries seemed to be taking . . .

Marian's carefully drawn-up CPC meetings rota had already gone to pot. This one was held at Faye's farm instead of Annie's cottage, because our ingredients had arrived and she had more room in her kitchen than anyone else for dividing everything up.

Annie picked me up and ran me there and was concerned to know how Jasper was doing.

'Still confused, poor boy,' I said. 'Tom had been so horrible to him lately—but he was still his dad, after all.'

'I expect he feels all angry and sad and muddled up,' she agreed. 'And you, too!'

When we got to Faye's, the others were already there and expressed their condolences, before we got down to the business of the meeting: dividing up our purchases of flour, dried fruit and peel, flaked almonds and all the rest of it. Faye's cavernous farmhouse kitchen slowly became redolent with the spicy fruity smell of Christmas and I found that strangely comforting.

So too was the tea Faye laid on afterwards, with strawberry jam and clotted cream to spread on the freshly baked scones. It was no wonder her little tearoom was perpetually packed out, so that she had to take on extra staff!

I felt so much better after spending an hour or two in the undemanding company of my friends. And then the making and bottling of my mincemeat over the following days, along with producing some jam and chutney from a basket of ripe apricots given to me by Marian, proved a pretty good distraction.

*   *   *

Due to Unks ringing an old number instead of that of Nick's BlackBerry, it was Wednesday before he tracked him down to give him the bad tidings, and by then I'd already received a postcard of Morecambe Bay he'd posted a couple of days ago. It bore a scribbled recipe for spiced potted shrimps, which I found immensely comforting.

Unks said Nick sent his love and would call me when he got back, because, of course, being a true professional, he will complete his assignment and send in his copy first. This was more than I seemed able to manage, for the end of August deadline for sending in my newest *Perseverance Chronicle* was fast approaching.

I rarely mentioned Tom in the books—though when I did I referred to him only as 'the Inconstant Gardener'—but I couldn't entirely ignore what had happened to him, so bringing the latest one to a close on any kind of upbeat note would be *impossible*. Unless, that was, I ended it just *before* Tom's demise. Then I could include it in a foreword at the start of the book after that, which would come out when a decent interval had passed, the misery blunted by time.

I could even end my current *Chronicle* with an apocryphal near-death by mushrooms instead. It's the sort of thing my readers seemed to enjoy and I often embroidered the truth to make a good story. Saved by Caz Naylor in the nick of time . . . assuming he *had* found the poisonous fungi in the basket of mushrooms Polly left me, which I don't think was ever clearly established. He could have been giving me a hint about Polly and Tom. I'm sure Caz must often have been flitting about the

93

place in the evenings like a shade, so may well have seen and heard some of what had been going on.

But I should have known better than to accept anything edible from Polly's hands, even if the mushrooms had looked suspiciously like supermarket ones, brought as an excuse to snoop around Perseverance Cottage—or maybe, now I know about her affair with Tom, in order to see him without my suspecting anything.

I had a sudden horrible thought. If I'd cooked the mushrooms without spotting the poisonous one, *Jasper* might have been made ill too! (But not Tom, who didn't like them.) That put me right off mushrooms, whereas before I loved them.

*　　　*　　　*

A lovely letter of condolence came from the Vanes this morning. They must have posted it practically the minute Annie told them about Tom. Of course, they only really knew the old, charming Tom and not the monster I'd been living with lately, but it was very kind and comforting all the same.

The latest issue of the *Mosses Messenger* was in the letter box too, and carried a Mystery Play notice, which I found a bit poignant.

IMPORTANT NOTICE!
Everyone wanting to take part in the next Mystery Play should put their name forward immediately to Clive and Marian Potter at the Middlemoss Post Office, including any of last year's performers intending to reprise their roles. (Applicants must be residents of Middlemoss, Mossedge or Mossrow and able

to devote one night a week to rehearsals.) Sadly, due to bereavement, the important roles of Moses and Lazarus need to be recast and, as always, we need a new baby Jesus. Rehearsals will start in mid-September.

I'm sure I will never be able to watch the Raising of Lazarus scene again without thinking of Tom, though actually when Lazarus's mother says to Jesus, 'Our Lazarus hath popped his clogs, and he were my only child,' my eyes tend to well up anyway.

Of course, Jesus immediately tells Lazarus to stop larking about, because his mother is in a proper state about him, and up he jumps with a cheery, 'Hello, our ma. Is summat up?'

But there will be no miracle this time for Tom, who hath well and truly popped his clogs.

*   *   *

'Hi, Lizzy, I hear fate caught up with Tom before I did,' was Nick's bluntly uncompromising opening gambit later that day when he did finally phone. 'Roly told me what happened.'

I gripped the receiver tightly. 'Oh, Nick! Did Unks tell you it was *my* car? The wheel came off, and it was the one I'd just changed the tyre on, so I'm sure the police think I did it on purpose!'

'Don't be so bloody stupid, of course they don't think that! Why would you tamper with the wheel on your own frigging car?' he snapped, and I stopped wilting over the receiver and glared at it, as though Nick could see me.

'That's true, I wouldn't—but his van was at the

95

garage and for once I'd left my keys out somewhere where he could find them. *And* we'd just had an argument, which Polly Darke overheard—she told the police. Nick, she was the one Tom was having the affair with, but I don't think anyone except the police and Jasper know about that yet.'

'Well, I certainly didn't, but it doesn't surprise me, because apart from you, he always did have crap taste in women.'

That was as close to a compliment as I'd ever got from Nick—and he can't include his own wife in that statement either, can he? So he mustn't *really* think Tom and Leila were having an affair, after all. The idea of Leila as Tom's lover is even more ludicrous than Polly, so I expect Tom was simply after free bed and board in London and lied to me to spur me into finally leaving him.

'I had to go and identify Tom,' I said abruptly, my thoughts taking a sudden, darker turn. 'It was all right until we actually went in, because I thought it was a nightmare, so it didn't matter. But then there he was and . . . I kept expecting his eyes to open. I couldn't believe he was really dead, even though they said his neck was broken. Now I keep thinking about him, so white and . . . gone.'

'*Don't* think about it, then,' he said sensibly. 'It's a pity I wasn't home to identify him for you. Anyway, it wasn't your fault and I think he's given you a rough time the last year or two. I've kept my nose out, but I've heard things.'

Tears pricked behind my eyes. 'Well, it's over now and they're releasing the body. They've done the post-mortem and adjourned the inquest,' I said, shivering. 'The inquest will reopen again later, but not for ages probably, so the funeral can go ahead on Tuesday.'

'Then they *don't* suspect you of anything, you stupid bat,' he said, with what sounded suspiciously like relief. Surely Nick didn't secretly think I'd bumped Tom off, too? 'I'm heading down to London tomorrow,' he added, 'but I'll be back in a couple of days, if you need any help with the arrangements.'

'Thanks, but I've got Annie—and the rest of my friends in the CPC have volunteered to help. The new vicar seems very pleasant and helpful too. In fact, everyone has been so kind. Roly offered to have the bunfight after the funeral up at the Hall, but I wanted it here. I'm going to do everything just the way the Tom I married would have wanted it— the fun one with a sense of humour.'

'Let's hope it's a nice day then, because you won't get more than six people standing up in your sitting room.'

'I'm going to use the old greenhouse: that's certainly big enough. I was going to get rid of it, so it's fortunate I haven't got round to it yet.'

'It'll still have to be a fine day, because it leaks like a sieve,' he objected.

'Caz Naylor asked me if he could do anything, and he's out there now mending the cracked panes with gaffer tape.'

Saying Caz had volunteered to help was a slight exaggeration, since his precise words had been a questioning, 'Do owt, our Lizzy?'

'You're honoured,' Nick said drily. 'Whenever Roly or I ask him to do anything, he vanishes. How's Jasper taking all this?'

'Stoical and quiet, but much the same as me: in some ways it's a relief to know Tom's not coming back, but then we feel guilty for even thinking that, and sad at the same time and . . .' I broke off, my voice wobbling.

'Do you want me to come straight back now?' he asked abruptly.

'No, of course not! What could you do?' I said, braced by his tone.

'Nothing, I suppose. Where's Jasper now?'

'He's been back at the dig since Monday. He thought he might as well, rather than mope around the house.'

'Very sensible. Has he sorted out his university accommodation yet? Or is he going to live at home?'

'I wanted him to live in the hall of residence for the first year at least, because that's what university is all about, isn't it—getting away from your parents and making your own life? Only now he says he might share a house with one of his friends and some other students instead.'

'He's very level-headed for his age. I'd let him do whatever he wants.'

'Yes, I suppose so, and at least Liverpool is close enough for him to come home for the weekend, or for me to drive over, if he gets homesick or anything.'

'I expect he'll quickly have other distractions.'

'I should think the course will be distraction enough. I'm so proud of him, getting onto it. And he should get the full student loan now too, I think, because it'll be based on my income and I've hardly got any, because I don't suppose barter counts. Unks told Jasper yesterday that he was going to make him an allowance. He's so kind, and really, we have no claim on him.'

'Roly thinks of you as family. And speaking of family, have you heard from Tom's mother and stepfather? You'd think they would offer to help!'

'Oh, they have, and it was *dreadful*! *He* phoned and said Tom's mother was too upset to speak to me and probably wouldn't be well enough to travel all this way for the funeral, but he would pay for it all! I told him I didn't want his money and I haven't heard anything since.'

'Well, burn all your boats at once, why don't you?' he said sarkily.

'You're such a comfort to me!' I snapped, but beginning to feel much more like the real Lizzy Pharamond under all this bracing common sense.

'Fellow feeling, darling. Leila and I are going to split, though I hope not in *quite* so final a manner as you and Tom.'

'You are? I'm so sorry!'

'Are you? Then don't be! Things haven't been good between us for a long time, though she's always refused to discuss divorce.'

'Well, she's Catholic,' I pointed out. 'That's probably it.'

'Only nominally, and she's going to have to get used to the idea, so the sooner the better. That's why I'm going straight down there now, to tell her.'

'You mean she doesn't know yet?'

'She knows how I feel: our marriage is dead in the water, and it's time to call it quits. And I want to spend much more time in Middlemoss: I feel more creative there.'

'Lawrence Durrell's "spirit of place",' I agreed. 'Middlemoss gets your creative juices flowing. Mine, too—this is my real home and I'm not sure I could write anywhere else.'

'If you can call your stream-of-consciousness burblings *writing*, any more than you can describe your recipes as *cookery*,' he said. 'We can only be grateful you do your ghastly *Chronicles* under your maiden name and disguise anything that might give away the location!'

'At least anyone can make my recipes, you don't need a thousand pounds worth of equipment and three underlings to help you!' I shot back rather unfairly, since I know very well he whips up his recipes in his own kitchen, or the one at the Hall: personally tried and tested before being unleashed in his Sunday newspaper cookery page, or in his books. They're mostly straightforward recipes too, not *nouvelle cuisine* or anything, though some are still a little fancy for my taste. I like to keep things simple.

'Plebeian', he once called me, when he found me devising a recipe for strawberries and custard bread-and-butter pudding. But then, as I recall, he ended up eating two plates of it . . . and now I come to think of it, I haven't made that for quite a while and it's yummy . . . *real* comfort food.

'I think we're digressing,' he said, sounding pleased as always to have got a rise out of me. 'I'm going to London to tell Leila that I'm instructing my solicitor to start divorce proceedings, whether she wants it or not. After that, I'll be back at the Hall, so I'll be around if you want me. Don't tell anyone about the divorce yet. I'll break the news to Roly later. I'm not sure how he'll take it, and I don't want to give him any more shocks.'

Actually, I thought Roly would be pleased rather than shocked, but I didn't say so. 'No, I won't mention it to anyone and—' I broke off as a thought struck me. 'Nick, I don't think Leila knows about *Tom* yet! How awful, I forgot to tell her!'

'I'll tell her and I'll be back before the funeral,' he said, and put the phone down.

If he'd been here in person, I wondered if he would have given me a big, comforting hug like he had in hospital that time, when Jasper was ill . . . and looked at me with that same startled expression in his slate-coloured eyes, as though surprised to find himself doing it?

He *does* have a softer side and, although he can be a bit taciturn, he's all bark and no bite.

*   *   *

In the event, Nick wasn't back before the funeral, calling from London to explain briefly that Leila insisted on being present at it and was refusing to discuss anything about the divorce until afterwards, so he'd be driving her up on that morning.

There wasn't anything for him to do, anyway—I was pretty well organised, Annie having taken over the finer details. When you've been Leader of the Pack (Brownies) for years, these things come naturally to you.

The funeral being on a Tuesday, the preceding Monday's CPC meeting had been cancelled and instead my friends all brought to Perseverance Cottage food for the buffet and then stayed to help get everything ready. Annie must have spent half the night making little sausage rolls, Faye had baked both sweet and savoury scones, Marian brought the makings of three different kinds of sandwich and Miss Pym had assembled two huge platters of cold meats.

So by late Monday afternoon the preparations for the Feeding of the Five Thousand—or however many turned up to be fed and watered after the ceremony—was complete. Every surface in the kitchen and larder groaned under the weight of plates and bowls and platters. The fridge door kept trying to spring open, and plastic bags of yellow candyfloss swung from the rack above the kitchen table. The very air could have been sliced up and served with whipped cream, it was so loaded with mingled aromas.

Annie came back later, and she and I sat in the tiny sitting room, drowning our sorrows in elderberry wine and eating some of the mincemeat brownies intended for tomorrow, while Jasper was out the back, immolating Tom's favourite surfboard on the garden bonfire. He was accompanied by the strange, small dog (rather like a hairy haggis with legs) which Annie had brought with her, along with Trinny, and it had immediately attached itself to Jasper.

He came in from his bonfire with the creature under one arm and vanished up to his Batcave in the attic to bludgeon his emotions with loud music.

'Annie, that dog—' I began.

'Jasper's agreed to foster it until he goes to university,' she interrupted brightly. 'The kennel was full, and no one seems to want to adopt it.'

'You surprise me,' I said tartly. 'It nipped my ankles when it came in and it sheds so much hair it leaves a trail behind it across the carpet.'

'I expect Jasper will give it a good brushing. You've still got all Harriet's stuff, haven't you?'

'Yes, but I don't want another dog at the moment, and what if Jasper gets attached to it? He can't take it to university with him. You'll have to take it away with you right now!'

Putting my glass down I went upstairs, determined to oust the creature before things went too far. Jasper's door was open just a crack and through it I saw him sitting on his bed, his face buried in the hairy haggis and his shoulders shaking.

Silently I backed away and tiptoed downstairs.

'It can stay for a couple of weeks,' I conceded to Annie, 'but that's it. You'll have to keep looking for a permanent home for it.'

'OK,' she agreed. 'Unless you find you want to keep her, after all.'

'I doubt it. I've got puncture marks in my ankle.'

Annie went home soon after that. She was going to come here straight after the church service the next day, instead of attending the interment, and organise the Women's Institute volunteers who are manning the buffet at the funeral feast in the greenhouse.

*　　　*　　　*

Around three in the morning, entirely unable to sleep, I went downstairs and whipped up a batch of strawberries and custard bread-and-butter pudding *à la* Lizzy Pharamond, and then Mimi wandered in out of the night, dressed in wellies and with a man's Burberry overcoat over her nightie.

'Hello, dear, I've come for tea,' she said brightly, sitting down at the kitchen table. 'And to tell you that Tom's dead.'

'I know,' I said, handing her a portion of bread-and-butter pudding and the cup of cocoa I was just

103

about to drink myself.

She seemed very taken with the words, and was still repeating softly: 'Tom's dead, Tom's dead!' all the time I was walking her back up the dark drive to the Hall later, which was a little trying.

When we got there, Juno had just discovered her absence and was frothing gently at the mouth. But there was no harm done, though the sooner her leg is healed so she can keep tabs on Mimi again, the better.

CHAPTER 9: SOUL FOOD

I had one of those confused moments standing at the edge of the grave, where I couldn't remember where I was—or even *who* I was—let alone who was six feet below me, tastefully attired in sustainable Norwegian pine. The coffin was crowned with a home-made wreath of dried hops (Tom had been a great devotee of real ale), bearing the handwritten epitaph: 'For the Tom we loved, from Lizzy and Jasper'. We had refrained from adding 'if he ever existed'.

The circle of eyes fringing the grave reminded me of a stargazy pie, except that they were not blank and dead, but expectant—and fixed on me. What could they want?

There was Nick's tall, broad-shouldered figure, his purple-grey eyes dark and brooding, possibly because his chic French wife was hanging tightly on to his arm, as she did to all her possessions.

Next to him was his father, Nigel, in whom the strong Pharamond genes had surprisingly been subjugated by the more nondescript ones of his mother, his expensive suiting trying to turn a sow's ear into a silk purse.

Dr Patel, Marian and Clive Potter and Faye, wearing a borrowed-looking black hat jammed over her dark curls and with her squarely-built, rosy-cheeked husband in tow. Miss Pym, nodding encouragingly at me, as if I were a recalcitrant four-year-old. A ragbag of Tom's old surfing chums, looking shifty. Polly Darke, wearing a short and inappropriate black chiffon garment cut low over

105

the twin pink Zeppelins of her bosom, hovering uninvited and unwanted on the fringes of the crowd. Gareth, the new vicar, with his pale, interestingly knobbly face, bright red hair blowing in the slight breeze like a fiery halo . . .

Jasper nudged me with a bony elbow. *'Mum?'*

As though his action had opened the sluice gate, a scummy dark tide of realisation rushed into my head: I was Lizzy Pharamond, widow, mother of the willowy youth next to me, and now expected to toss earth onto my late husband's remains like a cat tidying up after itself.

The husband who had once had a quirky sense of humour, until something dark, angry and increasingly nasty had slipped in to inhabit that space instead. I'd been mourning the loss of the old Tom for a long time, but now these last rites seemed to form an epilogue to our life together and a full stop.

'Mum?' Jasper said again, more questioningly, draping a sinewy arm across my shoulders. For a teenage boy this was touchingly demonstrative and, for the first time that day, I felt painful tears at the back of my eyes, though earlier I'd struggled to suppress grossly unbecoming giggles during the vicar's eulogy, when he tried to reconcile wildly conflicting descriptions of Tom's character by using surfing as a metaphor for his journey through life and on into the great ocean that was Death.

I remembered what was expected of me. Slowly I reached into my large, gaily embroidered shoulder bag and took out Tom's mobile phone and the TV remote control, then tossed them with a clatter into the open grave on top of the coffin. Grave goods: the things most dear to him—apart from his favourite surfboard, immolated by Jasper of course. But even *that* was here in spirit, for as I turned and left amid stunned silence, I stumbled over its effigy worked in wired flowers, with a card attached reading, 'Yo, dude! Catch a big one.'

From behind me came the light patter of earth as the mourners hastened to cover up the evidence of my eccentricity, though I fear Tom will be gone but not *entirely* forgotten until the battery on his mobile runs out. He was always popular with his drinking companions.

At the end of the gravelled path stood Tom's white van, which had done duty today as his hearse, and I suddenly recalled how the six mismatched surfers and Mummers of Invention had earlier tried to shoulder the coffin before carrying it into the church.

A hysterical bubble of laughter attempted to force its way up my throat, though I managed to stop it escaping by clamping my lips together. But two painful tears squeezed out and ran down my cheeks, compounded of laughter and sorrow, inextricably mixed together with an over-heavy seasoning of the guilt that seems to be an inescapable accompaniment to death.

'Ow-do, missis,' Dave Naylor said. The proprietor of Deals on Wheels had driven Tom's van to the funeral and was now leaning against it, rolling a cigarette between scrubbed but darkly cracked fingers.

Another Naylor, you note—and also, on less official days, likely to address me as 'our Lizzy'. I really must do a bit of family research some time!

'Bear up, lass. It's all sorted now and a great send-off it were, too. Them Mummers singing

"Amazing Grace"?' He shook his head in slow wonderment. 'By heck, we'll never hear the likes of *that* again.'

'Oh, I do hope not,' I agreed fervently. 'And thanks for driving the van, Dave. You are coming back to the cottage, aren't you?'

'Aye, but I'll let the fancy cars go first. I'll take the van back to the garage with me afterwards and drop your new car off in the morning.'

'That's fine—see you later,' I said gratefully, and carried on to where Roly Pharamond awaited me in his long black Daimler on the main pathway, having sensibly eschewed the interment in favour of a sit-down and a swift nip of brandy. His sister, Mimi, seemed to have eschewed the funeral altogether.

Joe Gumball, husband of Roly's cook and jack of all trades up at the Hall, got out of the driver's seat and opened the door for me. He was wearing the hat and jacket of a chauffeur over faded blue dungarees and wellington boots.

Jasper, who was silently following me, got in the front and I slid onto the leather back seat, where Roly patted my hand with his thin, dry one and said gently, 'All done and dusted, my dear?'

'All done and soon to *be* dust,' I agreed numbly. 'It seems so surreal—and the way everything keeps undulating slightly isn't helping,' I added. This underwater rippling feeling had been going on ever since I got the news of the accident, and nothing, not even the best elderberry wine, could entirely make it go away.

He shook his head sadly. 'I never thought to outlive Tom—but there, anyone can have an accident. Well, better get the bun fight over with, I suppose. Mimi should be along later with Juno.'

Joe pulled out and headed for the cottage where, with the help of Annie and two ladies from the WI, the big, ramshackle greenhouse would have been turned by now into a venue for the funeral baked meats. Trestle tables and folding chairs had arrived this morning, borrowed from the village hall, along with tea and coffee urns.

We'd moved what plants there were towards the far end, but an aroma of tomatoes and moist earth scented the air. Still, I'd judged that better than holding it in Tom's wooden workshop, with its stale smell of dope, and the spray paint he used to customise the surfboards, several of which were propped in various stages of completion around the walls.

'You know, I *still* expect to open his workshop door and find him there,' I said, following this train of thought. 'Just like all the other times when he vanished for a few days and turned up as though he'd never been away.'

Jasper turned around and looked anxiously at me, and I summoned a smile from somewhere. Luckily he couldn't hear us, because the sliding glass partition was shut and Joe was playing muted country-and-western music.

We drove over the hump-backed bridge crossing the stream, scattering the gaggle of five vicious geese, which had taken up residence there among all the innocently stupid ducks.

'Must get something done about those creatures,' Roly said absently. 'The children are all too frightened to go to the playground, and I'm told you can't feed the ducks without being attacked.'

'That local animal rights group, ARG, might have something to say about that,' I said. 'But the geese *are* getting more and more aggressive, and they leave such a mess behind them, too. Someone is bound to skid on it eventually and then there will be hell to pay, though I don't know who you can sue if no one owns them?'

'Perhaps, since I own the green and the stream, *I* own them, too—or at any rate, the right to deal with them,' Roly suggested. 'I'll ask my solicitor—Smithers will know. Or perhaps I'll just get Caz Naylor to quietly round them up one night and move them somewhere else.'

'How's he doing with the squirrels?'

'Very well. Constantly patrols the exclusion zone, of course, but that's what you have to do, to keep the grey buggers out. Only way. Reds, that's what we have at Pharamond Hall. Always have, always will. On the coat of arms, even.'

I thought this showed a touchingly Canute-like optimism, since the tide of grey squirrels seemed to have swept over most of Britain. But then, the reds *had* got Caz on their side.

'I think the signs Caz has put up on the main pathways might have caused some talk,' I suggested. '"Red or Dead!" is a bit ambiguous and that new one just inside the gate that says, "Warning! Keep to Path!! Trespassers May Be Unexpectedly Terminated!!!" is a bit over the top.'

'Only to outsiders—and what are *they* doing wandering all over my estate, that's what I want to know? Locals—yes. They know the score: keep to the public footpaths, don't wear grey.'

'Are you still being targeted by ARG?' I asked. 'I don't seem to be bothered by them so much now, but I suspect that's because Caz's keeping an eye on the place.'

'Well, family, aren't you?' Roly said vaguely. 'And they've eased up on the estate a bit since I put that piece in the parish magazine saying Caz uses humane live traps to catch the grey squirrels. Ingenious things: the reds can get out again, but the grey's too big.'

'Mmm,' I said, because of course the question not to ask is: what does Caz do with the grey squirrels after he's caught them?

We passed between the impressively pineapple-finialed gateposts of Pharamond Hall, then turned sharp right onto the track that led down to Perseverance Cottage, which is just inside the estate boundary wall. I'd stuck a sign up earlier deflecting the mourners away from the Hall, but the ravening and curious horde would be hard on our heels, probably expecting an abundance of finger food and alcohol in a suitably sombre setting. Instead, they would find themselves in a huge glasshouse, eating home-made scones spread with jam and cream, strawberries and custard bread-and-butter pudding and other, even less usual, comestibles (I got a bit carried away yesterday), all washed down with tea or coffee.

I'd noted the police presence at the funeral (PC Perkins and Little Boy Blue), but somehow their car had managed to arrive at the cottage first. As I got out, so did they, and Perkins came over and said they'd come to offer their condolences. But there was an underlying implication that she thought I was a merrier widow than I let on, and she'd been expecting me to cast myself onto the coffin with a last-minute confession. But perhaps I was becoming paranoid.

'Do stay for refreshments in the greenhouse,' I

said politely and, after a small, uncertain pause, she said they would follow us over. At least her colleague would have something to eat other than his fingernails.

'How the wheel came off is destined to be one of life's great mysteries,' I mused aloud, as we walked across the cobbled yard. '*And* why he didn't stop the car from going over the edge. Still, at least I know who Dark Heart is now, so that's one puzzle solved.'

'Dark Heart?' Roly said. I'd quite forgotten he didn't know about Tom's affair.

'Dark Heart's how the woman Dad was having an affair with signed herself,' Jasper explained helpfully. Roly was leaning on his arm as he picked his way over the smooth, slightly slippery stones. 'It's that novelist woman—Polly Darke. Would you believe it? She's got to be even older than Mum, and a complete hag.'

'Thank you, darling,' I said. 'I think she is fashionably haggard, rather than a hag, really. And I'm sorry, Roly, I didn't mean to tell you about her. It just slipped out.'

'Boy must have been mad!' Unks exclaimed, patting my arm. 'Wondered why she turned up to the funeral. Wearing a black see-through nightdress, too. Woman's got more bones than a picked chicken carcass!'

'Was she in church? I didn't actually take in most of who was and who wasn't.'

'She was there, Mum, but I thought Uncle Nick was going to throw her out when she tried to sit in one of the front pews. And it was a black chiffon dress, Unks—but she's, like, fifty years too old to wear it.'

I think that might have been a slight exaggeration, but I didn't feel I was a winner in the sartorial stakes either. I didn't have any black, so was wearing a floaty, dark, paisley-patterned Indian dress over a long pink crinkle-cotton skirt, both borrowed from Annie. I'd belted it severely in around my waist, but I still looked like Widow Twankey.

'Woman's got a nerve turning up at all, if she was carrying on with Tom! Well, well, it just goes to show you that the boy wasn't himself the last few years.' Roly shook his head.

'His character *had* changed . . .' I began cautiously, and then broke off as the nose of Tom's white van appeared, followed by a cortège of assorted vehicles. 'Here they come! Dave must have got tired of waiting and decided to lead the way instead.'

'Let's have a drink before battle commences, shall we?' Roly suggested.

'It's only tea or coffee, Unks, unless you want Jasper to fetch you a glass of elderberry wine? I've hidden a few bottles under the table in the corner, just in case. I didn't want this to turn into some kind of drunken revel and go on for hours.'

'Quite right, but I've got some brandy in my cane,' he said. 'Ah, Annie, my dear . . .!'

We established him in the greenhouse, on one of the chairs grouped before a veritable thicket of tomato plants and rampant bell peppers, and he unscrewed the top of his cane and poured a generous slug of brandy into his tea while I went and peeped out of the entrance.

As the cars arrived, people milled about in front of the cottage, so Jasper went out to usher them in

113

the right direction and I retreated back to Unks. I expect I should have stood in the doorway and accepted their condolences as they came in, but I couldn't face it.

The mourners massed in the entrance like worried sheep, nearly balked and broke away, then came slowly in a surge towards me. At the last minute most of them sheered off and spread out to range up and down the trestle tables, probably looking for alcohol.

I accepted a slug of brandy in my teacup from Roly and sat down.

'That's it: let them come to you and do the polite,' Unks said. 'The ones with manners, anyway. Half of this lot weren't at the funeral—probably just after food and drink. Freeloaders!'

'Weren't they? The church did seem to be full, though, and I thought the new vicar made a brave job of it.'

'Not bad. Bit much to expect him to do a complete stranger's funeral two seconds after he arrives. Let's hope he lasts longer than the last vicar. Ah, here's Nigel.'

Roly's portly retired stockbroker son was indeed forging towards us, though there was no sign of his wife. Still, I hadn't expected even Nigel, who didn't seem to care much for the North—or indeed Tom, for that matter, whom he considered a cuckoo in the nest—to make the effort to come today.

'My son and heir,' Roly said drily in my ear. 'And unless Nick and that French woman get a move on, nearly the last in the line.' He nudged me with a sharp elbow. 'What do you think, Lizzy—is she past it?'

Leila, chic in a vintage Chanel suit, bold red

114

lipstick and with her hair drawn sleekly back like a bleached Paloma Picasso lookalike, stood poised in the doorway looking capable of anything, though the curl of her lip said exactly what she thought of her current location. Just wait till she saw the catering!

Nick, wearing his best sardonic Mr Rochester expression, loomed behind her.

'I wouldn't get your hopes up, Unks,' I said.

CHAPTER 10: CORNISH MIST

I found myself mentally writing the recipe for a funeral feast, as though it was something I could put into one of the *Chronicles*.

Recipe for a Fine Funeral Feast

Step 1: In a large greenhouse mix together approximately sixty assorted mourners, half of them uninvited, several wearing wildly inappropriate surfer garments, and some that you're certain you've never met before in your entire life hovering furtively around the edges.

Step 2: Add two police officers steeped in dark suspicions, a mad historical novelist dressed like the porno version of a Poldark widow, and a depleted folk/rock group all wearing identical black 'Gaia Rocks!' T-shirts.

Step 3: Gently fold in your best friend, trying valiantly to suppress her natural expression of cheerfulness; a mourning, lightly intoxicated nonagenarian great-uncle by marriage; a tall, dark and glowering chef and his acidulated and tangy French wife (soon to be ex and who might, or might not, have been having a fling with your late husband), and the man from the garage who'd volunteered to drive Tom to the funeral in his own white van with the 'Board Rigid' logo up the side.

Step 4: Throw in a pompous stockbroker, the entire Mystery Play committee, including a nervous but well-meaning vicar and a furtive-looking youngish man in a strangely mossy green suit, who has forgotten to remove his Rambo-style headband.

Step 5: Sprinkle with borrowed WI tea and coffee urns and crockery, garnish with triangular sandwiches, halved scones spread with clotted cream and home-made blackcurrant jam, trays of cubed chocolate Spudge on cocktail sticks, wedges of bread-and-butter pudding and bowls of Cornish Mist.

Step 6: Stir well before it coagulates into clumps or—even worse—curdles.

Step 7: Garnish with assorted hens, a three-legged whippet, and one yapping haggis-sized hairball that someone, probably Jasper, has let out of the cottage.

Step 8: Stand back, since once warm the mixture could go up like a rocket—and down like the stick . . .

But now the Pharamond family (and one or two of the bolder hens) began slowly to converge on me from all directions. Nigel reached me first, but once he'd kissed my cheek and said he was very sorry he wandered off again, probably in search of non-existent sherry.

Great-aunt Mimi was pushing Juno in a wheelchair, though she'd told me last night she was hoping Dr Patel (not KP, but his daughter) was going to let her start walking again by the end of the week. The expression on her face was grimly stoical, at odds with the gaily frivolous arch of tissue-paper flowers Mimi'd attached to the back of the chair.

'Isn't that the bower from the Adam and Eve

temptation scene that the Infants' School made last year—the one that kept falling on the snake?' Annie asked.

'Yes. Thought it would brighten things up,' Mimi agreed. 'Damned gloomy things, funerals,' she added. 'Better if he'd gone ages ago, because he was nowhere near as much fun, the last few years.'

'Mimi!' protested Juno. 'What a thing to say!'

I focused slightly (for the shot of brandy had been generous, on an empty stomach; I hadn't been able to eat anything before the funeral). 'Oh, did you notice that too, Mimi?'

She leaned over Juno's chair towards me. 'Possessed!' she hissed. 'The devil was looking out of his eyes!'

Juno twisted her head upwards. 'Mimi, you haven't taken your pill today, have you? Where have you hidden it?'

Mimi backed off, looking guilty and slightly agitated. 'I didn't need it—why do I need it? Lizzy doesn't need one, and she's seen the devil looking out, too!'

'She's quite right, I did,' I assured Juno. 'And Mimi seems fine to me. I'll get her a glass of elderberry wine, that'll do her good. I've hidden it under the end table, so the surfers and Mummers don't get drunk and silly. *Sillier*,' I added, for they seemed to have joined forces behind the tomato plants, together with some flagons and bottles *I* certainly hadn't supplied.

As well as the wine I collected a plate of food, since I was suddenly ravenous. One or two people spoke to me (including one of the WI ladies, who complimented me on the garnish of golden quail eggs, an effect I achieved by boiling them wrapped

118

in onion skins), but I was glad I'd decided to dispense with the moving-about-graciously-thanking-everyone-for-coming thing, because I didn't feel at all thankful to most of them.

The Mummers of Invention—or what was left of them—now struck up a lively tune at one end of the greenhouse. The drippy girl (and I can only assume Tom was *desperate* when he slept with her) stuck one finger in her ear and started to drone a song. She'd have to do her own harmonising without Tom, but since she talks to herself worriedly all the time just like Alice's white rabbit, that shouldn't cause her any great problem.

I gave Mimi her glass of wine and then sat next to Unks, eating steadily, as is my usual wont when stressed, unhappy, worried . . . *or* happy, cheerful and optimistic. Let's face it, I eat. That morning's fast was simply an aberration.

Leila seemed to have the same thought. 'If you didn't do all that digging and outdoor work, you would be as fat as a pig,' she commented, coming to a halt in her stilettos in front of us, Nick right behind her like an attendant thundercloud. Then she kissed the air about an inch from Unks' cheek and said, 'Well Roland, how are you?'

'Fine, Leila,' he said cautiously. 'Nick, you haven't heard how the two thirty at Haydock went, have you? Only I had a sure thing running. Happy Wave out of Surfer's Paradise—couldn't go wrong with that pedigree, could it?'

'On a day like today, you can have no interest in horse racing!' Leila exclaimed, scandalised, and Roly looked slightly abashed.

'Joe's probably listening to it on the car radio, Unks,' I said. 'I'll go and ask him in a minute. In

119

fact,' I added slightly worriedly, 'I ought to go and see where Jasper is.'

'It's all right, I saw him sitting on the Daimler running board talking to Joe when I came in,' Nick said. 'That's a weird-looking dog he's got! I thought you'd go for another lurcher, like Harriet.'

I pulled a face. 'It's one of Annie's strays. We're only supposed to be fostering it, so it wasn't put down, but she and Jasper have taken a shine to each other. I'm going to end up looking after it when he goes to university, I can see.'

One more responsibility, when it came to leaving Perseverance Cottage and forging a new life on my own, too . . .

Leila seemed to be thinking along the same lines, for after looking me over in her usual critical way, as though she found me wanting in all aspects (which she probably did), she said in her strongly Parisian-accented English, 'So, Lizzy, I expect you will be moving on, now? Those books are your only real source of income, are they not? And those you can write anywhere.'

'But they are the *Perseverance Chronicles*,' Juno pointed out, 'about her life here in *Perseverance* Cottage—that's the whole point! All Lizzy's daily struggles—that's what her readers like.'

'They'll certainly love the next volume, then, even though I'm ending on a happier note, before the tragedy. After that,' I shrugged, 'who knows?'

'But you *must* keep writing them and including the wonderful recipes,' Juno enthused, her square, rather weather-beaten face animated. I hadn't realised she was a fan.

'Oh God,' groaned Nick, temporarily distracted from silent thundercloud mode, 'don't remind me!

120

Why anyone should find Lizzy's sugary, fatty recipes for nursery puddings and inedible bakes of any interest at all entirely beats me. And what's more, wasn't that bowl of yellow, lemon-flavoured stuff someone just offered me *candyfloss*?'

'Cornish Mist,' I said automatically, and Leila snorted.

Roly, who'd been sitting looking quietly baffled, suddenly put in, 'What did you mean, Leila, that Lizzy would be moving on? Moving on *where*?'

'I suppose Leila meant that I would be looking for somewhere else to live, Unks.' I smiled at him affectionately. 'It's been wonderfully kind of you to let us have Perseverance Cottage all these years, when you might have rented it out for a decent amount, but I realise you'll have other plans for it now.'

'That's right,' agreed Nigel belligerently. He'd suddenly reappeared behind his father and was swaying slightly, like a pot-bellied palm tree in a breeze. I couldn't imagine him hobnobbing with the Mummers and surfers, so he must have found the elderberry wine the way pigs find truffles. 'Told you it was stupid, not charging them rent all this time, Father—and Tom not even a real Pharamond! Besides, the place is too big for Lizzy on her own. I'd do it up and sell it—get a fortune for it, the way house prices are rising round here.'

'Would you?' Unks said coldly. 'Perhaps you'd sell off the rest of the estate for housing too, while you were at it?'

'Probably wouldn't get planning permission. Sodding red squirrels and trees are more important than people,' he slurred. 'But you could divide the Hall up into apartments—executive ones—and keep the best for yourself. Make a huge profit!' His eyes lit up with the fire of greed.

'So, that's what you would do to the Pharamond estate, Nigel, is it?' Unks said. '*If* you inherited it, of course.'

'But he is the heir, is he not?' Leila said. 'And his ideas, they are eminently practical!'

'Nigel shouldn't count his chickens before they are hatched. The entail on the estate was broken long ago, don't forget, so it is mine to leave to whoever I wish.'

Roly turned his head and smiled at me: 'I told Tom that I was making Perseverance Cottage over to him and Lizzy, but now it will be Lizzy's home for as long as she needs it—and Jasper's, of course.'

'Oh, thank you, Unks! That is *so* sweet of you!' I said, tears coming to my eyes, and kissed the top of his head.

'It's been a pleasure having you living so close, my dear. And the boy's a Pharamond—he should grow up here and regard it as his home.'

'But he isn't really a Pharamond, Father,' Nigel pointed out, swiftly sobered by the possibility of disinheritance.

'Course he is,' Mimi said, leaning on the wheelchair and waving her empty glass emphatically, and Juno twisted her head round and gave her another anxious look. She would be getting a crick in it at this rate. 'Only have to look at him to know that. The boy's the spit of Nick.'

There was a small silence, which Unks broke by saying drily, 'Before anyone lets their imagination run riot, when Tom's mother asked me to take Tom on, she confessed to me that she was having an affair with Leo before her first husband died, and

122

she was pretty sure Tom was his. I promised not to say anything, but I feel current circumstances absolve me from that now.'

'His mother said that? Oh, I *wish* she'd told him!' I said indignantly. 'He always had a chip on his shoulder about not really being a Pharamond, but he wouldn't hear a word against *her*. Instead, he pretty well accused *me* of—'

I broke off hastily, meeting Nick's eyes, and went pink. 'Well, I just wish he'd known, that's all.'

'I think you, Roland, are just saying this to cover up the truth! Jasper is *Nick's* child—Tom told me this himself,' Leila exclaimed unguardedly. 'They had an affair when they were very young, and then they picked it up again after she married Tom.'

'Rubbish!' Unks said firmly. 'Boy-and-girl affair one summer and fought like cat and dog—and then Nick went off on his travels and that was that. Dare say they hardly even saw each other for years, and Lizzy was mad about Tom when they married, anyone could see that!'

'Of course it isn't true,' I said hotly. 'Jasper is Tom's child. But I'm glad to have the truth I suspected come out at last, even if it is a bit late in the day.'

Nick was glaring at his wife. 'You mean, Tom told you *that* and you believed it? *When* did he tell you?'

'Oh, years ago.'

'It *can't* have been that many years ago. He only got that stupid idea after Jasper had meningitis,' I said.

'I think we all know you've had a difficult time with him lately,' Roly remarked, to my surprise. 'I hear things—know more than you think.'

123

'Yes, but I'm afraid it had got to the stage where I was going to leave him, Unks,' I confessed. 'I couldn't take any more. I was just waiting for Jasper to be settled at university.'

'Well, now you don't have to,' Mimi said brightly. 'You can stay here and dear Jasper can come home in the holidays. Such a clever boy!' She took a bowl of Cornish Mist from a passing tray and dug in her pastry fork. 'Mmm!'

Then, yellow-moustached, she looked up again at our rather silently thoughtful tableau. 'Where's Tom? He's missing all this lovely food and he is *so* fond of his stodgy puds.'

'He's gone, Mimi,' Juno said shortly. 'I'll explain later.'

Mimi's brain had clearly done one of its little loops and shunted Tom's death into a siding. I wished mine would.

'Oh, will you? Good,' she said, her eyes wandering around the very motley crowd. 'Look, that woman's wearing a black baby-doll nightdress! Should I have come in fancy dress too, Lizzy?'

'Good grief, it's that Polly Darke woman! As if it wasn't bad enough her coming to the funeral, without turning up in your home, Lizzy!' Annie exclaimed, scandalised, appearing beside me suddenly with her bob of coppery hair attractively ruffled and her cheeks flushed—but then, it was getting slightly steamy in the greenhouse, in more ways than one.

Polly had staggered backwards through the concealing tomato plants, where she'd presumably been drowning her sorrows with the surfers and Mummers. She regained her balance with an effort, turned, and then fixed her dark-ringed, sunken eyes on me. 'Lizzy! Not so much the grieving widow, I see! Maybe you're even celebrating, because it wouldn't surprise me if you loosened that wheel on purpose, and then *told* Tom to borrow your car!'

'Polly, that's entirely stupid. And you watched me walk off into the woods that morning, don't forget! When would I have done it?'

'You could have come back. You were probably hiding, waiting for me to leave.'

'Do you all know Polly Darke?' I said resignedly. 'You can probably spot without my telling you that she's a novelist of the raunchier kind, but she was also Tom's mistress.'

'Good grief!' Juno exclaimed incredulously. 'Was she really?'

'More, much more, than that, Tom *loved* me! He had to get Lizzy to move out, so the split looked like her fault, and then Roly would leave him the cottage; but after that we were going to get married,' Polly cried, looking about her wildly, as though expecting a sympathy vote and not getting it.

'You are quite mad—a fantasist!' Leila said, looking her up and down disgustedly. 'He would not have even a tiny affair with a woman such as you.'

'I'm afraid he did have a mistress, but I've only just found out that it was Polly,' I told her. 'It was a shock to me, too!'

'And me,' Unks said drily. 'Revelations, indeed!'

Leila narrowed her eyes at Polly, like a snake. 'What could *you* possibly have to offer him?'

'You'd be surprised,' I said darkly. '*I* certainly was.'

'This is fun, isn't it?' Mimi said brightly, but no

125

one took any notice.

Leila drew herself up. 'She is lying. It is true that Tom had a lover, yes—but it was *me*!'

Nick's hand closed in a vice-like grip on her arm. 'But you swore you'd never been more than friends with him! *And* you wouldn't agree to a divorce.'

She shrugged. 'He planned to move in with me eventually, but it is as this woman says: he wanted to keep in with his great-uncle, who is fond of Lizzy, and inherit the cottage, so he was forcing her out. She deserved it; she was still having an affair with you! Tom said even in hospital when Jasper was so ill, you couldn't keep your hands off each other.'

'That is *so* not true,' I said hotly.

'No, Lizzy isn't like that in the least,' Annie agreed loyally, 'and neither is Nick.'

Polly, who'd been quiet, rallied again: 'Oh, I knew he had an *old* mistress who wouldn't accept that their affair was over. But it was me he loved— and me he spent his last night with!'

'I don't believe you. He was with me only a few days before he died, and he swore he loved me and soon we would be together always,' Leila declared.

'Presumably after I had obligingly died, and he had inherited the cottage?' queried Roly mildly.

'You *are* ninety-two, Roland,' Leila said defensively. 'In France we are more practical about these things.'

'Not practical enough, my dear. I was leaving the cottage to him for life only, then to Jasper after him, not outright.'

'And you were going to tell me all this when, exactly?' Nick demanded of his wife in a voice that reverberated through the greenhouse like thunder. 'And why refuse me a divorce?'

126

'I knew that you would try and take half my restaurant that I've worked for so hard—half my money. Why should I give you what is mine? I thought once Lizzy was free, you might be more reasonable about it, and I would wait. And I will fight you through the courts for every penny!'

'I don't want your money—I don't want anything of yours, just my freedom!' Nick said furiously. 'I'll sign a statement to that effect any time you choose—would have done before, if I'd known what was worrying your mercenary little heart. You and Tom seem to have been made for each other!'

'No they weren't. She's a lying cow and it's *me* he loved and wanted to spend his life with!' Polly said, quivering with rage. Then she entirely lost it and lobbed her plate of food at her rival. Half a scone daubed with cream and red jam clung to the side of Leila's face like some exotic wart, before sliding slowly down her cheek and dropping off, smearing her expensive suit on the way.

Mimi giggled, but Leila gave a scream of rage and lunged at Polly with her long, sharp red nails. I was just thinking that I'd put my money on Leila, when Nick seized her arms from behind and two of the surfers, who must have followed Polly through the tomato plants, leaped forward and grabbed her too.

'Put them out!' Unks snapped. 'You!' he said to Polly. 'Whatever the truth of the matter, you should have had the decency to stay away. If you don't go now, I'll have you removed.'

Polly went limp and started sobbing, and the two surfers let go of her arms. She stumbled towards the door on her extremely high heels and, as the crowd parted to let her through, I realised we had unwittingly been providing entertainment for everyone within ear- and eyeshot—which, in a greenhouse, is pretty well everyone who could cram in.

The only good thing was that the police and the vicar seemed to have left before the floorshow.

Nick, still grasping Leila's arms, snapped in my direction, 'Excuse us! Back later, Roly—hope your horse won.' And he marched her off. I would have liked to have been a fly in the car on the way back to London: Nick's invective can be quite inventive when he's in a rage.

Unks looked pleased. 'Well, she was always a bitch,' he remarked happily. 'Don't know why he took up with her, except she was beautiful, I suppose, and they had the cooking stuff in common. Once he's over her, he can start again—with a sensible Lancashire lass this time, perhaps?'

'They're both lying old bags!' quavered the small, pathetic voice of the drippy girl from the Mummers right next to me, and it was quite lucky from her viewpoint that neither of them was there to hear that description, because it would have been tantamount to staking a kid to attract tigresses. 'He loved *me*—and what's more, I'm having his baby!'

White as a sheet and naturally rather pop-eyed, Ophelia Locke seemed an unlikely candidate for Tom's attentions, so I was probably the only person who believed her. Still, it was another reason to be glad the other two had gone. There was clearly a general feeling among the onlookers that this was a scene too far and we were into the farce; but then, before anyone could rally enough to say so, Ophelia fainted backwards.

Caz Naylor stepped forward and caught her

128

neatly, then slung her over his shoulder, where she dangled limp as a shot rabbit. 'Not right in't head, Mr Pharamond,' he said tersely.

'Evidently, poor girl,' agreed Unks, looking rather taken aback.

Hanging upside down must have sent the blood rushing to Ophelia's head, for she revived enough to beat weakly on Caz's back and whimper, 'Put me down, you big bully!'

Caz ignored her and carried her off, the crowd parting to let them through. There was a spontaneous spatter of applause.

Unks unscrewed the top of his cane. 'Anybody want a shot of brandy? I certainly do! And wasn't that the girl I let an estate cottage to—makes handicrafts, or some such stuff?'

'Barbola work?' suggested Mimi. 'And is Caz walking out with her?'

'Smocks,' I said. 'Yes, Unks, that's the girl.'

'Nobody does barbola work these days,' Juno said. 'And I shouldn't think she's Caz's type.'

'Oh? Well, that was all just like a play!' Mimi said, still clapping her hands. 'Was it a play, Juno? Is that the end?'

'Yes, time for us to go home,' she agreed. 'Come on, that gardening programme you like will be on by the time we get there.'

Mimi whirled the chair about with no more ado. 'Lovely party—thank you for having me!' she called politely over her shoulder. The remains of Polly's jam scone squidged under the wheels.

The excitement clearly over, some of the remaining guests followed them out, though the last two Mummers were still obliviously droning on in the background and I could see one of Tom's surfing chums stretched out under the trestle tables, snoring.

'Jasper,' I said, as he finally came in, closely followed, nose to heel, by the little dog, 'Unks says we can live at Perseverance Cottage for as long as we want to. Isn't that kind?'

'Really? Thanks, Unks. I was worrying what would happen to Mum when I went off to university, but now I won't need to any more.'

'You don't have to worry about me at all!' I said indignantly. 'I'm perfectly capable of taking care of myself.'

Jasper eyed me uncertainly. 'Are you all right, Mum? Only you look a bit strange.'

'Strange? Why on earth should I look strange?' I demanded, though I could feel hysteria trying to tweak my mouth into an idiot's grin.

'I think we're all tired and a bit overwrought,' Annie said quickly. 'What an exhausting day! All these scenes and revelations.'

'What scenes and revelations?' asked Jasper, looking from one to the other of us.

'I'll tell you later,' I promised, which I would have to, even if only the edited lowlights. 'I wonder how we can get rid of the last of the guests.'

'I'll send Joe back to turf out the stragglers,' promised Unks, hoisting himself to his feet with Jasper's help. 'But most of them will go when they see me leaving.'

He advised me, before Joe drove him away, not to dwell on recent events, but instead remember Tom as he once was. He looked frail and tired, so I hoped it all hadn't taken too much out of him.

I was fine—too numb and full of elderberry wine and brandy to feel anything except a desire for

130

oblivion.

*　　　*　　　*

It was early evening before Joe Gumball loaded the last drunken surfer into the back of the taxi called to take them to their B&B in Mossedge, and finally persuaded the two Mummers to go away. They had been too drunk to notice the scene with Ophelia, or even question where she had vanished to. (And what *had* Caz done with her?)

The urns and crockery had long been efficiently removed by the WI ladies, with my grateful thanks, and Marian and Clive Potter had supervised the local Cubs and Brownies in carrying the trestles and chairs back to the village hall, so that was that.

Annie saw to the poultry, and then cooked us a meal we none of us really felt like, except the dogs, before going home.

Finally alone with Jasper I felt almost too exhausted for the effort of explanation, but when I told him that he really *was* Unks' great-great-nephew he just said, 'Yes, I know. Unks told me ages ago, when I asked him why I looked more like Uncle Nick than Dad.'

'You did?' I stared at him. Then I sighed tiredly, and decided to tell him about the other pretenders to the throne of love and get it all over with at once. 'Did you also know that your father was having an affair with Leila as well as Polly? They nearly came to blows this afternoon.'

'Oh, so that's what she and Nick were arguing about when they left! He pushed her into his car and roared off, and then Polly came out and drove away too, though she didn't look fit to be behind

131

the wheel. And another thing,' he added thoughtfully, 'why was Caz giving that Mummer girl a fireman's lift? She didn't seem to appreciate it.'

'She fainted—right after declaring that it was really *her* your father loved, not the other two. And, Jasper, she says she's pregnant!'

His eyebrows rose. 'She does?'

'I hope it isn't true, because goodness knows, things are complicated enough without that.'

'Well, look on the bright side,' Jasper said, with the breezy insouciance of youth. 'At least there's no chance the baby's mine!'

CHAPTER 11: POPPED CORKS

Ginger Beer

Let me give you a few words of wisdom culled from many years of making the stuff. (And you will find the recipe for making a ginger beer culture in Book 1 of The Perseverance Chronicles.*)*

1. Ignore the Quatermass-experiment effect once the yeast starts working—whatever it may look like, the ginger culture will not take over the world . . . yet. And isn't it amazing that water and a bit of yeast and ginger scum can turn into something so delicious?

2. Ask everyone to save their screw-top plastic pop and water bottles for you, because if you go the traditional route of glass bottles and corks, expect your house to explode at frequent intervals.

3. Even with screw-top bottles, it is not a good idea to transport large quantities of ginger beer about, especially in a car. Nor should you be tempted to celebrate any special event by shaking the bottle before opening.

The Perseverance Chronicles: A Life in Recipes

I was woken early next morning by a thirteen-gun salute, which proved to be half my remaining stock of ginger beer exploding.

After cleaning the sticky mess up and loosening the rest of the caps so I wouldn't lose all of it (Jasper and I are very partial to ginger beer), I went out to see to the poultry.

133

There appeared to be fewer quail. Presumably Caz had taken the opportunity the previous day to cull the male ones again, though I wasn't sure how he found the time, unless he'd popped back after taking Ophelia to . . . well, where *had* he been heading? So long as it wasn't to his giant freezer, I didn't suppose it really mattered. Perhaps he had just put her in a Mummer's car and left her to it. Or carried her home to her estate cottage, which is not far from his, protesting all the way? (Though I didn't think most local girls would protest if he wanted to carry them off, the foxy sheikh of the western Lancashire world.)

I hadn't really thought of him in the knight-errant role before, even if he appeared to have been protecting me against the ARG activists. Perhaps he'd got something going with Ophelia. But then, that did seem a bit unlikely too, since he was definitely carnivore and I remembered Tom telling me once that all the other Mummers were vegan and wouldn't even wear leather shoes.

The quail, in their little pens, all made identical cheeping sounds. I'd never managed to tell one from the other, which was lucky since I didn't actually get attached to them, like I did to all the Honeys and Myrtles, and even the ducks. But sometimes even they were so nasty and vicious to each other that I stared to feel maybe their real destiny was to be on a plate with stuffing and gravy, or orange sauce. Nature is red in beak and feather, as well as tooth and claw—someone should tell ARG that.

But after wrapping a couple of dozen quail eggs in onion skins during the sleepless night watches before the funeral, I really didn't care if I never ate

134

another one, let alone a quail itself . . . so I thought I'd get rid of them; find them another home.

The duck population was here before me and was pretty self-sufficient, but the hens could just naturally reduce as they died of old age—so long as I found the eggs before they hatched. After all, it was just going to be me here at Perseverance Cottage most of the time, and if I didn't produce much more food than I could eat, with the bit extra for barter, then I'd have time to throw myself into helping Annie expand Posh Pet-sitters, and earn some money. Barter worked well up to a point, but not with electricity bills and the Inland Revenue.

Yes, even the enormous, aluminium-framed glasshouse—relic of a doomed attempt at market gardening by a previous tenant—could go. There was a small one behind the cottage that did well enough for my needs. I decided to get Jasper to put it on Freecycle, where you can advertise anything you want to get rid of—but also get things you need, for free. I expect someone will want it. But what I was to do with Tom's workshop contents I couldn't imagine . . .

Back at the cottage I was surprised to find Jasper up and getting ready to go to the dig, which on the whole I thought a good idea (though possibly not in the Diesel jeans that had cost me a fortune). I think we both had that spaced-out, anticlimactic feeling, and the alternative was sitting about thinking unproductive thoughts.

'Do you know how many eggs I had to sell to buy those jeans?' I demanded, but he took the question as rhetorical and carried on cutting multilayered doorstep sandwiches.

I couldn't drive him there, since, even if the van

hadn't been down at the garage, now it had done duty as a hearse neither of us fancied ever getting in it again. But Dave Naylor was coming that morning with the ancient but, he assured me, very practical Land Rover I had in a rash moment agreed to swap it for.

So Jasper cycled off to the dig with the furball (now called Ginny, short for Guinevere, though anything less like a Guinevere I never saw) in the carrier, together with a bowl and a big bottle of water. He said there was plenty of shade to tie her up in and he could walk her at lunchtime, though from what I could make out of her shape beneath the fuzz, rolling her about a bit would probably do just as well.

Dave brought my new old car about an hour later, after I'd drafted the advert for the quail. His son Gary, who played Jesus in the Mystery Play for the first time last year, followed him down the track in Tom's van, to save him the quarter-mile trek back. That damned van with the horribly apposite 'Board Rigid' logo seemed to be a recurring motif, and I'd be glad when it was resprayed and sold on, preferably away from the area. I'd managed to find the paperwork for the van, which I expected would soon reappear for sale on the garage forecourt after a quick makeover.

The Land Rover had obviously had a hard life, being battered, dented and with high mileage, but Dave assured me they lasted for ever and, as soon as I had mastered the rather unyielding clutch pedal, I would be fine.

Jasper thought the vehicle swap was a good idea and was looking forward to driving the Land Rover. It was fortunate I have a son who prefers antiquities. I tootled it around the yard and up the track, and it certainly felt more solid than my 2CV ever did. Later I steered it cautiously down to the post office and handed Marian the quail advert for the parish magazine. She said I was just in time for the next issue, which would be out at the end of the week, but that was sheer luck, since their publication dates are erratic and entirely depend on how Clive feels about it.

*   *   *

In the late morning one of Tom's surfer friends, who'd been a bearer at the funeral, phoned up and asked if he and his mate Jimbo could drop in.

'That's nice of you, Freddie,' I said, assuming they wanted to say goodbye before setting off back down to Cornwall. It was amazingly thoughtful of them and, I would have previously said, totally out of character.

'Well, we wanted to say goodbye, Lizzy, but we've also got a proposition.'

'A *proposition*?'

'Yes, we thought we might take on Tom's business and wanted to discuss it with you. If you've no other plans for it, of course.'

'No, I haven't really had time to think of it. But of course you can come down and we can talk about it,' I said, for it would be a relief. I had no idea what to do with all his equipment and half-finished boards and stuff, and it would be rather nice if his friends carried on with Board Rigid.

So far as I could gather from male-bonding rituals, Freddie and Jimbo had been two of Tom's best friends. They'd all been at Rugby School together, dropped out of university and then washed up in Cornwall, bumming around on family money. But I suppose even that and the patience of your family is finite, and when a man is heading rapidly for his forties it's time to stop being the playboy of the western UK, and earn your own bread and wetsuits.

I went into the workshop and opened the big front door to the sunshine for the first time since the accident, instead of the little Judas door.

Things looked dusty already and there was that familiar smell of paint, varnish and dope (both kinds). Tom's wetsuit swung from a hook like the spent chrysalis of some strange creature: which I suppose it was, when I came to think about it.

One or two boards that were obviously commissions were almost finished, and there were several of the ones he bought in and painted to sell on through shops. I had a rough idea what they were worth and the people who had ordered boards had their names and phone numbers taped to the back: Tom's idea of paperwork. Mind you, the system seemed to work, which is more than could be said for his tax returns: I only hoped the Inland Revenue was not now going to fall on *me* like a ton of bricks.

Tom's friends turned up so quickly they must have phoned from a mobile up the lane and were very kind, kissing my cheek and hugging me as if they had always liked me, which they didn't. I was the wrong sort of girl: Tom should have married someone sea-sporty, acquiescent, well connected and, above all, rich.

Jimbo has a long body, stumpy legs and a big nose, but he didn't get his nickname from his appearance: his name is James Bow. Freddie is tall and skinny, with grey-blond hair fuzzing over a head like a bleached coconut. They must have to get their wetsuits made specially.

After looking over the workshop as though it was a dubious garage sale, they um-ed and ah-ed a bit, then said they would take the worry of it off my hands for three hundred pounds, what did I say?

'What, for the whole lot?' I gasped, thinking I hadn't heard right.

'Well, let's say four hundred, to be fair. There's not much here, and we'd have to finish off the old orders and deliver them, of course,' Freddie pointed out, as if this would be a big favour.

'But Tom's almost finished them, and he hasn't been paid yet. And the other boards that belong to him are worth more than that alone!' I protested, stunned.

They exchanged quick looks and I realised they hadn't expected me to know anything about the business or the value of it, and be too upset to think straight. I'd fallen among thieves.

'Oh, no, Lizzy, they're not top-quality boards, you see,' Jimbo said quickly, 'and several are half-finished—you'd never sell them like that. Besides, you don't have the contacts, do you? But *we* do.'

I looked at them: these were supposedly Tom's closest friends. He'd been to school with them, hung out with them over the years, and they were well off by *my* standards, even if they did look like bums most of the time. And now they wanted to make a quick profit by cheating his widow!

They were also cunning beach bums, for Freddie now produced a neatly printed agreement. I read it through a couple of times, noting the words 'sale to

139

include everything pertaining to the business of Board Rigid', but my brain wasn't really up to coping with possible pitfalls.

'Trust us—we're doing you a favour, Lizzy,' Jimbo said persuasively. 'I mean, who else would be interested?'

'Take it all off your hands—one less thing to worry about,' agreed Freddie, shiftily avoiding my eyes.

But when I looked around the workshop again I discovered I didn't have any fight left in me. I really didn't care that much—and Tom wouldn't have seen it as anything other than a smart move by his friends.

So, reluctantly, I signed. They paid me cash from a wad of notes: I *said* they were rich. 'Do you want a pint or two of my blood as well?' I asked bitterly. 'Or a kidney, perhaps?'

'Poor Lizzy,' Jimbo said sadly, 'I can see Tom's death was a huge shock to you. You're doing the best thing, putting all this behind you.'

'Yes . . .' Freddie agreed, looking around again with more of a proprietorial air, 'once it's gone, you'll feel much happier, you'll see.'

'Might as well load it up and take it all now,' Jimbo suggested. 'Where's the van parked, Lizzy?'

'The van?' I repeated blankly.

'Tom's van—the one we've just bought,' Jimbo said patiently.

'But you didn't mention any van!'

'Well, not as *such*, perhaps, but you did agree to sell us *everything* pertaining to the business, lock, stock and barrel.'

'*Two* smoking barrels!' I said, woken out of apathy into indignation. 'Look, you've already

140

screwed me over this deal, you can't possibly have expected to get Tom's van for *four times* that much!'

'Lizzy, you don't know how big a favour we're doing you. Of course we only offered you that much money because of the van. It's worth more than the stuff in the shed,' Freddie began.

'I know, because I bought it myself, out of the advance for the third of *The Perseverance Chronicles*! And anyway, you're too late: I've already disposed of it.'

They stared at me, aghast. *'Disposed!'* they exclaimed as one.

'If you're interested, it's down at Deals on Wheels.'

'Deals on Wheels?' echoed Freddie.

'The garage in the village. I swapped it for a Land Rover this morning, so the van is now the property of Dave Naylor. I suggest you go and talk to him, if you're still interested in it.'

They were not happy, but the van *was* legally my property and they couldn't do anything about my having already disposed of it, which certainly made me feel better. Eventually they stopped trying to browbeat me into getting it back and giving it to them, and went off to talk to Dave at the garage, saying they would be back later to empty the workshop.

'Fine.'

'Perhaps you could give us the key, so we don't have to disturb you again?'

'Not until I've removed his personal things. The CD player and stuff like that.'

But when it came to it, there wasn't actually much in there that I cared to take, so when they came back again in Tom's van, which I'd hoped never to see again, I left them to it. I bet Dave struck a hard bargain, and serve them right, too.

Later, I went to collect Jasper and Ginny in the Land Rover and when we got back the workshop doors swung open, and it was empty of life except for some curious hens, one of whom had laid an egg on the old easy chair among the burst stuffing.

Jasper and I have decided to sell Tom's insanely huge TV and buy a small one that he can take to university with him, along with his laptop—and I am going to put the money I got for Tom's workshop contents towards a computer and printer of my own.

'Then you can bring me up to speed on using the internet and emailing before you go,' I suggested.

'Good idea,' he agreed, 'your skills do need honing a bit. It's a pity we still only have dial-up connection, though, because it's really slow. Middlemoss must be the last area in Lancashire that hasn't got broadband yet.'

'Miss Pym says we will get it by the New Year and anyway, slow suits me fine to start with,' I said, reflecting how much I had changed from the first days of my marriage when I hadn't even wanted a TV, to now carrying a mobile phone everywhere (even if I forgot to switch it on half the time) and accepting that a computer was going to have to be part of my everyday life.

Still, adapt and survive . . .

*   *   *

When it began to get dark I went out to shut everything up for the night and while coming back noticed that the light was on in the empty workshop.

My heart stopped dead for a moment, until reality set in and I thought it might be Freddie and Jimbo, returned in a fit of pique to make a thorough job of it. There were still the tattered old sofa and chairs, the ancient upright piano and the kettle, for instance. No resurrected Board Rigid van stood outside to load anything into, it was true, but I wouldn't have put it past them to have parked it on the road and sneaked in through the side gate.

Then again, it could be Caz, curiosity stirred by the unlocked door; or ARG, setting dynamite charges. Even Mimi on the loose . . .

I crept up to the open door and peeped in to find, to my astonishment, that the workshop was infested with Mummers. They weren't *doing* anything, just hanging about with an air of aimless expectancy, but when they saw me they drew together into a defensive, sheep-like huddle.

Ophelia was mumbling to herself as usual and I thought her pale froggy eyes were going to pop out altogether. 'Oh God! Oh God! It's *her*—she'll kill me—she'll kill me! Oh *God*!'

I looked dispassionately at her. She was as limp and wet as seaweed and I was still finding it hard to square what Jasper had said about finding her and Tom *in flagrante*, with the reality of what she actually looked like. In fact, she has all the allure of a white blancmange, so it must have been simply availability allied with drink, or the demon weed. After the Leila/Polly revelations it didn't seem of much moment anyway, unless she really *was* pregnant by him? Hard to tell, when she dresses in her own smocked garments most of the time.

'Ophelia didn't mean what she said, yesterday,'

Mick said hastily, his fingers fiddling with the blue feather in his hat. The three of them edged even closer together.

'No, no-no-no!' whimpered Ophelia, while nodding rapidly.

'She's *not* pregnant?'

'No, she meant that bit.'

'Tom loved me!' Ophelia said, but rather uncertainly.

'Nah, we keep telling you—he just wanted a quick shag,' Jojo said brutally.

'So the baby *could* be Tom's?' I asked him.

'It could be anyone's—Caz Naylor's even.' They stared accusingly at her. 'Sleeping with the enemy!'

'The enemy? Caz's your *enemy*?' I frowned over that one, but I suppose gamekeepers and rabid vegans *are* oil and water and shouldn't mix, though clearly at some point two of them had.

'Well, come to that, it could be mine—or even yours,' Mick pointed out fair-mindedly to his friend.

'Ooh!' moaned Ophelia, chewing her lip frantically like a mad albino rabbit, huge pink eyelids fluttering.

'You've got around a bit,' I said to her, though feeling a bit sorry for her now Mick and Jojo were being so horrible. But Ophelia's having slept around was quite a good thing in a way from my point of view, because it seriously lessened the chances of the baby being Tom's. I supposed I would just have to await the outcome, and so would she.

'Mr Pharamond's bound to put her out of her cottage, after what she said at the funeral,' Jojo suggested helpfully.

Ophelia wrung her hands and stared at me with

the eyes of a mad martyr embracing her doom. 'Yes, yes, it's all my own fault and I deserve to be punished!'

Oh, good heavens, she wasn't another kinky one, was she? But then I sighed resignedly, for if there was any chance she was pregnant with Tom's child, I couldn't let her be turned out.

'You two stop trying to stir things up,' I said severely to the men. 'Of course Roly won't give you notice, Ophelia—or at least not until after the baby's born. I'll speak to him about it, but I'm sure Mick and Jojo are quite wrong.'

'Don't think he could do it, anyway,' Mick said belligerently. 'She's got her rights!'

'Possibly not, but I don't think the question will arise. Anyway, what are you all doing here?'

They shifted uneasily again, looking around the near-empty workshop as though expecting something—or someone—to materialise out of the dark shadows.

'He's not coming back, if that's what you're all waiting for,' I said evenly. 'Tom's played his last gig and you'll have to get a new singer: not that I thought he was much good, anyway.'

'His voice harmonised with mine very well,' Ophelia blurted, then blushed as she caught my eye, like she usually did—as well she might. 'Oh God!'

'And he wrote most of the lyrics to my tunes,' said Jojo, slowly turning the gold hoop in his ear as though tuning what remained of his brain.

'No, actually, that was me,' I said incautiously and they stared. 'He used to hammer them out on the old piano and I'd try to fit words to them—just give you a base to work it up from, you know? I

145

mean, they weren't really mine when you'd finished with them, because they evolved into something else—something better, usually.'

For at their best (after a pint or two of Mossbrown Ale), the Mummers sometimes acquired a near-Pentangle unity that was quite hypnotic. 'But the last couple of years, he didn't ask me to help him with them any more.'

'*Thought* they'd gone off,' Mick, the one who looked like an escapee from *The Clan of the Cave Bear*, said. 'Can you sing, too?' he asked hopefully.

'No.'

'But—'

'Absolutely not,' I said firmly. 'Look, I don't mind if you want to come and keep using the workshop to practise in, as long as you don't bother me. But you'll have to find a new Mummer.' A thought struck me: 'Annie—you know Annie Vane, don't you?'

They nodded.

'She pet-sits for an ex-pop singer who bought the old vicarage. Ritch Rainford, he's called and he's an actor now, playing a Victorian mill owner in that *Cotton Common* soap.'

'Not Ritch Rainford from Climaxxx?' Miss Drippy said breathlessly. 'I thought that was just a story, that he'd bought the place. He's famous . . . but old,' she added belatedly.

'Nah, he can't be much more than forty-five, at most,' Jojo said, giving her a dirty look and adjusting his bandanna over his bald spot to the point where it almost became a headscarf. It'd have to be the pirate look next, low down on the forehead. 'And he might want to keep his hand in, do a couple of gigs with us—worth asking . . . Good

146

to talk to him, you know?'

'You do that,' I agreed.

'But would the Mysteries Committee let us play for them, if one of us wasn't from the Mosses?' said the girl. 'You know how stuffy they are about second-homers. I shouldn't think he lives here all the time.'

'I don't know, Ophelia, but you could ask. It's not like you're performing in the plays and have to go to all the rehearsals, is it? Just incidental music and filling in between scenes.'

'Olivia,' she corrected me.

'What?'

'My name's Olivia, not Ophelia.'

'Oh?' That was a surprise, but I fear due to her water-dipped appearance she will forever remain Ophelia in my mind. It seemed to strike a chord with the other two as well.

'Suits you,' Jojo said, and Mick agreed.

'Why not change your name—new name, new start?'

'Yeah! Ophelia Locke—cool,' she agreed, brightening slightly. 'I'll do it! Ophelia . . . Ophelia . . . *Ophelia*.'

Loopy Locke, more like.

'Looks different in here, somehow, without Tom,' Jojo remarked intelligently.

'That's because I've sold the surfboard business and all the stuff's gone,' I said patiently. 'Look, Jojo, here's a key to the workshop—I've got a spare. It'll save you asking for it if it's locked, and you can leave equipment here safely if you want to.'

'Thanks,' he said and, giving my arm an earnest squeeze, added, 'And, you know, anything you want—do anything we can . . .' He trailed off, made earnest eye contact and let me go.

'Ophelia Locke . . .' whispered Miss Drippy in an ecstatic undertone. There were brown rabbits stencilled on the pockets of her smock.

Watership Down has a lot to answer for.

CHAPTER 12: JUST DESSERTS

As you will see in the preface, life took a sad turn here at Perseverance Cottage with the sudden loss of the Inconstant Gardener. However, my friends are all rallying round to divert my mind from unhappy thoughts, especially my fellow members of the Christmas Pudding Circle.
The Perseverance Chronicles: A Life in Recipes

Less than a week had passed since the funeral, yet with disconcerting rapidity summer had slid into September and what passed for normal life resumed. Even when Tom had been home he'd never played much part in the family rounds, so his absence was not really missed, insofar as you would miss a ticking time bomb.

Jasper seems to be feeling much the same, though it didn't help that half the time Mimi forgot what had happened and we had to explain it to her all over again.

We made an expedition to buy the laptop and printer Jasper thought I should have and then he set me up a little workstation in the window of the sitting room, which provided at least a temporary distraction for his thoughts.

Still, at least Jasper could escape to the dig every day and I had way too much to do to brood, for the garden had taken advantage of my lack of attention to burgeon forth into a burst of flowerings and fruitings like a butterfly dancing along the edge of winter. I was harvesting and bartering the excess, bottling tomato chutney and pickling shallots.

This morning the members of the CPC all went to Faye's farm again for the meeting, since she wanted us to taste the Christmas ice creams she was developing—and it turned out she had also managed to produce the perfect brandy-butter one, too! I think it will be a lovely change with the Christmas pudding and we have all ordered a tub each.

'Thank you all for helping me with the buffet for the funeral too,' I said, when we had settled down to the coffee and gossip part of things. 'I don't know how I would have managed without you.'

'That's all right—what are friends for, if not to help each other?' Marian said, and the others murmured agreement.

'There were certainly a few eye-opening revelations about Tom, weren't there?' Miss Pym said forthrightly. 'Neither that French wife of Nick Pharamond's nor Polly Darke appear to have any moral code whatsoever!'

'Or Ophelia Locke,' Faye pointed out.

'I don't think you can entirely blame Ophelia—she's obviously a sandwich short of a picnic,' Annie said generously.

'No, and I do feel a bit sorry for her, even if she is exasperatingly silly,' I agreed. 'I've persuaded Unks not to evict her from her estate cottage.'

'It's a pity it's not in his power to evict Polly Darke from *her* house though, isn't it?' Marian suggested. 'She's been seen everywhere, dressed in weirdest widow's black, playing for the sympathy vote.'

'Well, she won't get it from any of us,' Annie said. 'In fact, she's not at all liked locally.'

'She asks me every year if she can take part in the Mystery Play,' Marian said, 'and I turn her down. She's just attention-seeking.'

'I'm glad my part is small,' Faye said, who was currently playing Mary Magdalen. 'I hate getting up in front of all those people.'

'Me too,' I agreed. 'I saw Gary Naylor the other day and he said he was going to be Jesus again.'

'Oh yes,' Marian said. 'He made quite a good job of it last year, once we'd persuaded him out of wearing black during his scenes, especially those big boots with all the metal studs.'

'Jasper says he's an Emo,' I explained.

'What's an Emo?' asked Faye.

'Sort of a gloomier Goth, I think.'

'Only a year older than Jasper, isn't he?' Miss Pym said. 'Expect he will grow out of it soon. He was a good boy at school . . . and speaking of which, term starts again next week, so I will soon be rehearsing the little animals for the Noah scene.'

Miss Pym must be long past official retirement age and they are too afraid to tell her, but though she now only works part-time, she is still very much in control of the small infants' school and, I suspect, always will be.

*   *   *

Jasper and I agreed that there was nothing to beat a supper of globe artichokes with a little pot of melted butter for dipping, and fresh bread and cheese, with blackberry fluff and cream to follow.

151

One afternoon I was out in the garden waging a Canute-like attempt to assert my authority over Nature, when the vicar visited me.

While Gareth ostensibly came to see how I was going on and offer comfort and a shoulder to cry on, should I need it, I quickly discerned that he really wanted to talk about Annie. So I told him all about our long friendship, dating back to our schooldays at St Mattie's, where she was hockey captain and my best subject was Nature Studies, and the French cookery course we did afterwards in London.

'Neither of us was academic, you see. After the course we worked for a party catering firm for a couple of months, until I married Tom and she came home to live in Middlemoss.'

'And now she has her own pet-minding business?'

'Yes, and it's very successful,' I said, and told him what a lovely, trusting person Annie was, even after being jilted practically at the altar several years ago, when her fiancé ran off with one of the prospective bridesmaids. Then I pointed out her many activities within the parish.

'Of course,' I added casually, tossing a handful of weeds into the wheelbarrow, 'the way to Annie's heart is through her love of dogs. She even puts in several hours a week as a voluntary helper at the RSPCA kennels.'

Gareth left carrying bags of salad vegetables and runner beans, and looking thoughtful, so I hoped I'd planted some idea of how to win her affections: now the ball was in his court.

He was very nice in a serious and *terribly* good way, so I thought they would be very well suited. I couldn't give my best friend in marriage to just *any* old eligible bachelor, he had to be Mr Right. Or, in this case, Mr Bright.

This could be just the right moment for him to make his move, too, for I'd got the impression lately that Annie was finding Ritch Rainford disconcerting, now her initial bedazzlement was wearing off. She'd never had one of her fantasy men become flesh before.

If Gareth played his cards right, she could very well rebound quite happily into his arms.

*   *   *

Annie had managed all the Posh Pet-sitting stuff herself since the funeral, but I told her I could cope now if she needed help. So the following morning I walked Delphine Lake's three little dogs, who were very glad to see me, because Delphine's idea of a walk is from the car into the house.

Then I went to collect a cat from the vet's surgery and returned it to the owner—or rather, the owner's au pair, who didn't seem very pleased to have it back. But I expect once it had got over its indignant rage at being confined in a carrying box it would soon calm down. How weirdly vocal Siamese cats are!

On the way home I popped in at Annie's little terraced cottage again to see if anything else needed doing, and found her making a chart of her Posh Pet-sitting for the next fortnight, with different coloured stars for the regular customers and fluorescent spots for the one-offs—very

153

organised. Even the keys for houses where she lets herself in were starred and spotted to match.

'I see Ritch Rainford's bagged all the gold stars,' I commented, having made us each a cup of coffee.

'Well, he is our major celebrity so far,' she said defensively. 'And he seems to be turning into a regular customer, though he doesn't give me much notice. He's terribly casual—handed out the keys and the code for the burglar alarm to me and his new cleaning lady before he really knew us at all.'

'Who has he got cleaning for him?'

'Dora Tombs. She's a Naylor—niece or great-niece of Ted, the gardener up at the Hall.'

'We Naylors get everywhere, like Mile-a-Minute.'

'I think you're more of a rambling rose than a Russian Vine,' she said kindly.

A brazen strand of hair fell into her eyes, and she pushed it back and clamped it down with a white Scottie dog hairslide. She has no taste: even the smock she was wearing over her cord trousers and T-shirt had dogs stencilled around the bottom and made her look like a pregnant bun loaf.

'What on earth are you wearing?' I demanded. 'Isn't that one of Ophelia Locke's little creations?'

'Yes. The big pockets are really useful and it wasn't expensive. She sells most of them at those historical re-enactment fairs, but she printed one with dogs as a special order for me.'

'It does nothing for your figure,' I told her frankly.

'I haven't got a figure.'

'Yes, you have, an hourglass one with a very small waist. But that thing doesn't go in in the middle at all. You look entirely globular. Take it

154

from me, it's a mistake.'

'It's very practical, which is why I wanted it,' she said defensively. 'Anyway, no one is interested in my figure.' Then she blushed underneath all the little freckles.

'Come clean, obviously someone's interested! Tell Auntie Lizzy,' I said encouragingly. Had Gareth actually made his move already?

'They're—he—he's not really, it's just that he can't seem to take his eyes off my bust when I'm wearing a T-shirt,' she confessed. 'So I feel happier covered up.'

'What, the *vicar*?' I exclaimed.

She looked at me as if I'd run mad. 'The *vicar*? Of course not, Lizzy! No, I meant Ritch Rainford. I thought he was lovely at first, so charming and amazingly handsome. Only there's something in his eyes when he's talking to me and everything he says seems to have some kind of innuendo in it . . . and . . . well, I'm simply not used to that kind of thing. It makes me feel very gauche and uncomfortable, though I'm sure he doesn't mean anything by his manner, it's just his way.'

'Oh? So he's turned out to be mad, bad and dangerous to know?'

'It's just me being silly and not knowing what to say back, I expect. For instance, when I was bending over patting Flo the other day he walked into the kitchen and stared at my chest, then said, "You don't get many of *those* to the pound!" I simply didn't know where to put myself.'

I choked. 'Oh dear! That was *very* rude and un-PC of him.'

'Yes, but *you* would have known what to say to him, wouldn't you?'

'Probably. Or socked him one.'

'I find I just—just don't want to go there any more in case he's in, although Flo is a very nice dog.'

'Then don't go! I'll do his pet-sitting instead. He knows you've got an assistant, doesn't he?'

'Oh, yes. But, Lizzy, he might be even worse with you, because you're so pretty!'

'I'm not pretty at all, you daft lump,' I said, surprised. 'My hair is a really boring light brown colour and I'm way too tall! So don't worry, I can deal with him, no problem. Some of Tom's friends were rather oddball too, don't forget. So hand over his keys and pass on any requests for pet-sitting— *I'll* sort him.'

'Well, actually, Lizzy, he wants me to go in to walk and feed Flo tonight, because he's out at some party until late. But then Gareth—the vicar— suddenly asked me to dinner and I said yes without thinking, so now I don't know what to do.'

'He has? There, I knew he fancied you. I could tell at the Mystery Play Committee meeting, and he made a beeline for you at the funeral feast!'

'No, of course he doesn't fancy me,' she protested, blushing again. 'I can't imagine how you got that idea!'

'So, why has he invited you to dinner, then?'

'We just sort of got chatting earlier. He was admiring Trinny and said he would love another dog—his last one died of old age just before he moved here. Isn't that sad? Only he's out such a lot he doesn't feel it would be fair just at the moment. So I told him about the kennels and the rescue dogs and how they always needed people to walk them, and he said he would come with me whenever he has time. So *then* he asked me if I would have dinner with him and help him understand what he's supposed to be doing with the Mystery Play and village things like that. There's a lot for him to take in, coming into somewhere like Middlemoss.'

'There certainly is,' I agreed, 'especially pitchforked straight into a stranger's funeral, poor man. But he's quite right; who better than the former vicar's daughter to help him make sense of it? But *don't* wear the smock.'

'Of course not!' she protested, then added thoughtfully, 'He's very good-looking, isn't he?'

While I was glad to see she'd stopped mooning over Ritch Rainford and transferred her interest to Gareth, I couldn't help but feel that calling him good-looking was pushing it a bit, unless you particularly fancied knobbly, flame-haired, blue-eyed, lanky men who didn't seem to be fully in control of their limbs.

If something comes of this, their children will all be gingernuts (though perhaps they will raise a family of rescue dogs instead).

'He's delightful,' I agreed, hastily banishing my mental picture of their possible progeny. 'And don't worry about Mr Rainford: *I'm* not afraid of the big bad wolf.'

*   *   *

When I got home the latest *Mosses Messenger* with my advert in it had been pushed through the door, and there were two messages on the answering machine. I seemed very popular, suddenly.

The first was from Nick, saying he was finally returning from London, though why he thought I

157

would be interested in his movements I don't know. *Or* what he thought I would do with the postcard of Camden Lock, with 'Sorry!' and a recipe for jellied eels scrawled on the back, which arrived the other day. I couldn't possibly eat eels—they're too snaky. And what was *he* sorry about? Leila and the permanently absent Tom are the ones who should be sorry!

'Hi, Lizzy, I'm on my way back,' Nick's deep voice said. 'Things took longer than I expected because I couldn't persuade Leila I really *didn't* want any of her precious assets, even after her solicitor drew up an agreement for me to sign, until I stuck his ebony paperknife in my thumb and signed in blood. A bit melodramatic, perhaps, but it seemed to do the trick.'

There was a pause, then his voice resumed with just a hint of rueful laughter in it, 'OK, *very* melodramatic. And the solicitor didn't seem to want the knife back—said I could keep it as a souvenir. Anyway, the divorce is on its way, a clean split, and no claims on each other's property or earnings. We never shared anything anyway, so that makes it easier. Oh, and it's all given me an idea for a recipe. Got any raspberries, or am I too late?' The message clicked off.

Raspberries?

The second message, from my agent, Senga McDonald, was short and to the point. After drumming her fingers and humming a brief snatch of 'Will ye no' come back again?' she said, 'Lizzy? Can you send me the new *Chronicle*, pronto? Only Crange and Snicket want it right now, and your sales figures aren't so good that you can afford to miss your deadlines. You did say you'd finished it and it just needed a polish, so slap it into the post right this minute!'

Well, don't stop the carnival on *my* account, even if I have only been widowed for five minutes! I thought.

Still, it was as finished as it would ever be. I only needed to read through it and make final corrections before it went off. But I was starting to wonder if I would ever finish another *Chronicle*, because I was not exactly hitting my target of four pages a day any more and said as much to Senga when she rang me back later to make sure I'd got her message, and was obeying orders.

'Oh, don't worry your wee head about that one just now. I've had a brainwave and sold Crange and Snicket on the idea of a collected book of your recipes and hints, with the odd anecdote thrown in. They think it's a great idea—they're going to call it *Just Desserts*. Shouldn't take you too long to do, should it? Toss in some new recipes to liven it up.'

I stared at the receiver as if it had bitten me, while her voice rolled inexorably on.

'What? When? I mean, when do they want it?' I broke in urgently, when she stopped for breath.

'Oh, not until early next year—January, say. Loads of time. Now, have you put that manuscript in the post?'

'Tomorrow,' I promised. 'I'm just making final corrections and I might have to reprint a few pages later.'

'See you do—I'll be expecting it. Send a copy directly to Crange and Snicket, too.'

'I've got my own computer now and I'm getting going with it, so I'll be able to email the next book to you, instead of posting it,' I told her, because

159

she'd made it pretty plain that she and the publishers would prefer my books that way, rather than printed out and posted. I'd simply have to move with the times if I want to stay published.

'Well, welcome to the twenty-first century at last!' she said sarcastically and rang off.

It was just as well I *would* be able to print my own pages off, too, because I'd just remembered that Jasper wasn't going to be home until late. He was going straight to Liverpool with a friend after he finished work at the dig.

Not, of course, that he'd ever objected to my using his laptop and printer; it had just seemed like a personal intrusion to use them when he wasn't there.

I wandered rather aimlessly round the kitchen for a few minutes, then dolloped clotted cream and raspberry jam onto some meringue halves I made yesterday with leftover egg whites.

They were so yummy I ate six, and I think I'll put them in the latest *Chronicle* and *Just Desserts* as an alternative to scone cream teas.

*   *   *

I did try to read through the manuscript, but I just couldn't concentrate and found myself staring blankly at the same page. Eventually I gave up temporarily and went to do a bit of gardening instead. I picked loads of strawberries and even a few raspberries—everything was still burgeoning forth like nobody's business. I wished someone would tell my garden it was time to start winding down into autumn and taking it easy.

As I worked I thought about Ophelia Locke, also

burgeoning forth with a baby that might just possibly be Tom's. But whoever the father proved to be, the poor little thing was trying to grow on a vegan diet and I wasn't sure Ophelia was capable of seeing it got enough of the right nutrients.

With a resigned sigh I fetched a big wicker basket from the outbuilding, and began to pack it with fresh fruit and salad vegetables, a bunch of baby carrots, eggs and ripe tomatoes. Then I set off up through the woods to Ophelia's estate cottage.

Like me, she lives right next to the boundary wall of the estate, so it would have been quicker to walk up the road, but not as pretty as the woodland paths, or as cool. The sky was a brazen blue and it was Indian summer hot.

Ophelia had attached a nameplate to her front door that said 'Whitesmocks', but whether she meant that as a name or a description of her way of making a living, was unclear. There was unlikely to be any passing trade interested in purchasing antique-style clothing down here anyway, since her only next-door neighbour was the old and very deaf gardener who was Mimi's sparring partner and occasional accomplice in plant larceny, and I couldn't see Ted taking to smocks. Caz's cottage was quite nearby, only set further back in the woods in isolation, on the other side of a small stream bridged by mossy, ancient slabs of stone.

'Oh God!' Ophelia said predictably, opening the door and staring at me, 'Oh, no, oh God!' and fell to chewing her lower lip.

Oh, my ears and whiskers!

'Hello, Ophelia,' I said bracingly. 'Can I come in? Only I've brought you some spare fruit, vegetables and salad stuff, which will do you good.

And eggs, though I wasn't sure if you ate those.'

She fell back rather reluctantly and I stepped straight down the one worn step into the tiny living room. It smelled of unbleached calico and herbal tea. A sewing machine was set up by the window, and white material was festooned everywhere. A clothes rack on castors crammed with the finished product swayed slightly in the breeze from the open door.

'That's kind—that's *so* kind!' she said, and for a horrible moment I thought she was going to burst into tears or embrace me, or something equally embarrassing. Instead, she wrung her hands and stared at me despairingly. 'But Ted, the old gardener next door, he says that Mr Pharamond *will* give me notice to quit the cottage because I was . . . well, he won't want me here.'

'No, didn't you get my message? I've spoken to him and he's no intention of throwing you out, so you don't need to worry about that. We'll see what happens after the baby arrives—which will be when, do you think?'

'I don't know really—January, maybe?' she said vaguely. 'I didn't realise I was pregnant for ages and then I thought I'd just sort of wait and see . . .'

I frowned. 'Wait and see what? Have you visited your doctor?'

'Oh, no! I believe nature should take its course. One of my friends will come for the birthing.'

'The *birthing*? Come on, Ophelia, this isn't the Dark Ages! You need to see a doctor and have the baby in hospital. Nature's way may turn out to be pre-eclampsia, or something like that.'

She stopped chewing her lower lip and looked stubborn.

162

'I hope you're eating well, anyway? Couldn't you give up the vegan stuff for the duration?'

'Vegan is healthy. There are lots of vegan mothers.'

'Then make sure you vary your diet as much as you can. I'll keep leaving you fresh fruit and vegetables on your doorstep every week, a bit like one of those organic delivery services.'

'You don't have to,' she began, blinking nervously. Her big pink eyelids reminded me of those festooned blinds.

'No, but I want to. Whatever you did isn't the baby's fault, is it?'

'Noooo . . .' she muttered, walking backwards until she was half-enveloped among the hanging smocks. 'No, no, no!'

'There you are then, that's settled,' I said soothingly, following her and thrusting the basket into her arms.

'I'll—I'll unload this, so you can have it back!' she gasped and, fighting her way out of the folds of material, escaped into the lean-to kitchen.

I looked in from the doorway. Although basic, it was at least clean and tidy, though yet more eternal rabbits had been stencilled everywhere. On the little gate-leg table lay a roll of familiar-looking recycled yellow paper, a big black felt-tip pen and a coil of silvery gaffer tape—and something clicked in my head.

'Ophelia, when Jojo and Mick said you'd been sleeping with the *enemy*, meaning Caz Naylor, did they mean because you three are all members of ARG?'

She dropped the bunch of baby carrots. 'No, no no . . . not me. Not us. No, I—'

163

'You're a terrible liar,' I said dispassionately. 'I recognise the paper on the table from the posters you put on my barn and my car—and even over my front door!'

'No, no, no!' she jabbered, backing away, her prominent eyes starting. It is a pity she didn't say 'no' more often when men were around; it would have saved her a lot of trouble.

'Yes, yes, yes,' I said firmly, quite certain now. 'So, Ophelia, let's get this straight: you're living here on the Pharamond estate and, as a member of ARG, targeting not only the owner of that estate but also his gamekeeper, with whom you've been having an affair?'

'Oh, no! He—we didn't! Or only *once*, when Caz caught me putting up a banner on the Hall gates and . . . and I don't know what came over me! But I said I wouldn't go with him again, because he was evil and persecuted the poor woodland creatures!' she whimpered.

'Once?'

'Or . . . maybe twice . . . three times,' she conceded, which reminded me of the joke about only being unfaithful once, with the Household Cavalry. 'And Caz's not really murdering the grey squirrels, he catches them and takes them away!' she said earnestly. 'I still have to put the posters up, though, because the Pharamonds are on the ARG hit list, but Caz takes them straight back down again, like he was doing with the ones at your place.'

'I suppose you might have some kind of case for targeting Caz and the estate, though it's a pretty shaky one to my way of thinking, but none at all for me. I mean, there are battery hen farmers and goodness knows what else in the area. Why?'

'S-someone said that you were cruelly exploiting your hens and the poor little quail, but when I said I wouldn't do it unless ARG told me to, this person *made* me do it . . .'

I frowned, while she stood there wringing the feathery stems of the carrots between her hands. I'm not entirely sure I'd trust her with a small baby when she's overwrought. 'So someone *made* you target me? Who? And how? Do they know something about you?'

'No—yes, oh God!' Ophelia went white. 'If ARG find out I've been targeting someone not on the hit list, I'll be expelled from the organisation!'

'Jolly good idea, especially in your condition. Who exactly is this person with a spite against me?'

She pressed her lips together firmly and said nothing.

'You know,' I said to her severely, 'there are better and perfectly legal ways of campaigning for animal rights, aimed at the people who really *do* abuse animals . . .'

Then I remembered something I'd read in the local paper. 'Ophelia, were you involved in that big raid at the end of last year, on the lab rat farm over near Skem?'

If possible, she went even paler. 'Nooo . . .' she moaned. 'I wasn't there—she didn't see me—there wasn't any proof!'

'Ah, I see. So it's a *she*, and she knows you were involved in that raid?'

She moaned again. 'I was the last into the back of the van and her headlights caught me.'

'Don't you all wear masks, or something?'

'I forgot my balaclava and the scarf slipped,' she

165

said rather sulkily. 'But now Caz says I don't have to do anything she says any more, because *he's* got something on *her*, so she can't make me—and now I know the truth about her, I wouldn't anyway!'

'So Caz knows all about it, and who this person threatening you is?' I said, trying to disentangle her sometimes cryptic and convoluted utterances. I had a growing suspicion that *I* knew who it was now, too.

'He already knew most of it, he'd been watching me . . . following me! He made me tell him everything,' she said, blushing.

I didn't ask how. 'At least Caz seems willing to take some responsibility for you.'

She went pink and looked away. 'He's not so bad really—not now I know what he does with the squirrels.'

'What *does* he do with the squirrels?' I asked, then added quickly: 'No, don't tell me, I don't really want to know!'

She snivelled. 'I thought Tom loved me, I really did, but I see now it's just like Jojo and Mick said: I was a handy bonk.'

'At least you seem to have grasped the realities of the situation,' I agreed. 'I suppose it's none of my business, but since Caz rescued you the other day after the funeral, he must care about you.'

'He's furious with me for making a scene and saying that about . . . about Tom,' she whispered, twisting a strand of dishwater-blond hair around her fingers. 'Only I was so angry, hearing those two going on as if they meant something to him, when *I* was the one who was pregnant!'

'And did Tom really say he loved you?' I asked curiously.

'He said I knew how he felt about me, and so I *thought* he meant he loved me. But he wasn't any different to me afterwards—and sometimes he could be very cruel, even though he didn't really mean it!'

'Yes, I know.' I wondered how many times Jojo, Mick and Caz had . . . No, even *I* couldn't ask that, though it seemed that the odds on it being Tom's baby were at least three to one. We would just have to await the birth and guess. Or do DNA tests, or something. If it were Caz's, I suspect the entire Naylor clan would instantly know it anyway, in a very Midwich cuckoo way, just like they recognised me the second they saw me.

I walked home, thoughtfully swinging the basket. Someone had been angry or jealous enough of me to force Ophelia to include Perseverance Cottage in the ARG campaign, which was an act of petty spitefulness. And when it came down to it, I could only think of one likely person.

I'd love to know what Caz has got on her, but I don't suppose he would tell me even if I asked.

CHAPTER 13: RASPBERRIES

September means the last of the late-fruiting raspberries and picking blackberries for jams, crumbles and wines, and the making of damson gin by Miss Pym, one of the CPC members, to a secret family recipe. It is so delicious that the barter rate is very high!
The Perseverance Chronicles: A Life in Recipes

When I got home Nick's car was there and he was just walking out of one of the outbuildings, brushing light-coloured feathers off his sleeve. When he saw me he stopped dead and looked slightly taken aback, though goodness knows why: it was my house, after all.

'Oh, hi, Lizzy! I was just talking to Caz.'

I expect he meant that literally, since he was unlikely to get a complete sentence in exchange, let alone a conversation. Caz often makes me feel like a Shakespearean actor embarking on a long monologue, although of course he does nod, shake his head or scratch his nose from time to time.

'It was kind of you to let him have that big freezer to store stuff in,' he added, carefully closing the door behind him.

'Well, why not? I wasn't using it any more now I don't grow so much. The other one in the larder is quite enough.' I turned to lead the way to the cottage, since I was hot and thirsty after my walk. 'God knows what he puts in it, but I've a horrible feeling it might be all those grey squirrels from the humane traps.'

'Oh, no, not squirrels,' he assured me, so I assume Caz had let him see into it, which was quite a relief, really. I expect it is just rabbits and stuff, for the pot. (And I thought again what a strange mismatch it was that vegan, animal rights Ophelia and carnivore Caz should ever have come together!)

'I've been downsizing the fruit and vegetable production for nearly two years, ever since I realised I was going to have to leave Perseverance Cottage. Only now, of course, I don't have to. Unks is so kind.'

He followed me into the kitchen and leaned against the fridge, arms folded and glowering darkly, like Mr Rochester in a strop. 'I hadn't realised things were quite so bad between you. You should have told me. Caz says when he's been down here in the evenings he's heard Tom being really abusive.'

That accounts for the feeling I often got that our arguments had an audience—and also why Unks was not surprised that I had intended to leave Tom, because Caz must have given him a hint. I really should draw the downstairs curtains more, though you tend to forget when other houses don't overlook you. But who knows when Caz might be flitting past on his nocturnal activities?

'I was suspicious when you had that bruise on your face and were so evasive about how you got it,' Nick said.

'That wasn't intentional! He was never physically violent—what sort of doormat do you take me for? I'd have left immediately with Jasper if he'd tried anything like that,' I said indignantly.

'No, sorry, I expect you would. But I also thought

169

you might have told me what was going on.'

'It was none of your business. What could you have done?'

'Probably made things worse,' he admitted ruefully. 'It was pretty clear that Tom didn't want me around here the last few years, so I thought you both might patch things up if I gave you a wide berth.'

'No, things just steadily got worse. Do you want some ginger beer?' I offered, as a peace-making gesture. The top came off and it fizzed gently into glasses. I simply *love* the sensation when the bubbles get up the back of your nose and ginger explodes in your head.

'I still think you could have told me things were so bad that you were going to leave him, Lizzy.'

'Like when?' I demanded. 'I could hardly have bellowed out the information while we were all sitting round the dining table up at the Hall over a Sunday lunch, with Tom turning on the charm for Roly's benefit, and you in and out of the kitchen worrying over the roast beef and whether the horseradish sauce was just a trifle too "piquant". Maybe I should have sent *you* a postcard?'

He ran a hand through his black hair so that it stood up like a cockatoo's crest and said more reasonably, 'After what you said at the hospital, I thought it was best to distance myself a bit—especially after Tom accused me of having had an affair with you.'

'He did? I hadn't realised . . . But did you also know he suspected Jasper was yours?'

'Yes, but I told him he was mad, so I hoped he'd quickly come to his senses.'

'Well, you might have told *me* that you knew.'

170

'I wasn't sure how much he'd said to you, so I thought it better not. And, of course, I didn't know then that my wife was having an affair with him,' Nick added. 'But when I found him in Leila's restaurant that night it all sort of clicked into place, even though she denied it.' He looked sombrely at me. 'Perhaps he only started the affair in the first place to get revenge on me for something he imagined I'd done—and I'm sorry she made that scene at the funeral, Lizzy.'

'Well, it wasn't your fault, was it?'

'No, but I brought her, and I knew she was still lying when she insisted there was nothing between them, although I didn't know then why she wouldn't agree to the divorce.'

'And then it turns out she was sharing Tom with Polly Darke, and Ophelia Locke was the slightly wilted side salad! Oh—you did hear about Ophelia's revelations—the pregnancy?'

He nodded. 'Roly says she's deranged and invented it.'

'No, but she deluded herself into thinking a quickie meant something deeper. She seems very naive for her age. There's a good chance the baby isn't Tom's, though. We'll have to wait and see.'

'She's spread her favours a bit?'

'I don't think she's capable of saying no. But at least Ophelia is just credulous and silly, while with Polly and Leila it all boils down to greed and self-interest, doesn't it?' I said sadly. 'And the ironic thing is that Tom thought Unks was going to leave him the cottage outright when he died, and even I could have told him that he would never have split the estate up like that!'

'No, and I'm afraid my poor father scuppered his

chances of inheriting by giving us his plans for turning Pharamond Hall into apartments,' Nick said ruefully.

'I expect Unks will leave it to you, because you wouldn't do that to it, would you?'

'No, of course not! I love it the way it is. And actually, Roly says he *is* leaving it to me, though keep that to yourself. Which means that I do have every right to worry about your welfare, if only because you live on the estate,' he added. 'And that, I suppose, puts Jasper in line as next heir, by rights, since it's not entailed.'

I stared at him. 'Don't you dare put that idea into his head! You'll remarry, probably to some young, skinny model type like that photographer who came to the Hall last year for that feature on you—Lydia, was it?—and have a multitude of children.'

'I don't think so,' he said shortly.

'Famous last words. Well, *I'm* certainly not getting married again. It's the single life for me from now on. Pretty much as before, really, only without the threat of intermittent verbal abuse hanging over me.'

'And I married a woman who was so territorially defensive she insisted on keeping her own flat on and pencilled me into her schedule if I wanted to see her! But now Leila and I are divorcing, I'll be spending most of my time up here in Middlemoss. I might even sell my London flat, because Roly never uses it, he prefers his club. I send most of my work in by email these days, so I can base myself anywhere.'

Nick picked up his glass and absently drank his ginger beer down in one go, which made his eyes

172

water because it's good, strong, peppery stuff. 'My God, you are just *so* Enid Blyton at times, Lizzy! Aren't you going to offer me a sticky bun and an adventure, too?'

'No, but there are Choconut Consolations in that tin, if you want one?'

'No, thanks, you know I don't like sugary stuff much.' He finally sat down, uninvited, on a spindly old kitchen chair that groaned slightly. 'Lizzy, didn't it occur to you that Unks would have been sympathetic if you'd told him what was going on? He would certainly have helped you and Jasper to find somewhere else to live, for instance.'

'Since Tom was always his old, charming self to me whenever Unks or anyone else was around, I wasn't sure he would believe me! And I didn't want to tell him about the affair, especially since I had no idea who it was . . . and—Oh, Nick, I'm so sorry!' I exclaimed. 'I keep forgetting it was Leila.'

'Among others. And I don't really care any more, except on your account. I've been trying to get her to agree to a divorce for ages, so one good thing has come out of all this.'

'The last couple of years with Tom have been fairly hellish, but all's well that ends well . . . though I suppose I shouldn't say that when it is Tom's death that's made everything come right. It makes me feel so mixed up—guilty and relieved and sad, all at once . . .' I sniffed and took a gulp of ginger beer.

Being Nick, he didn't rush to comfort me, but instead said bracingly, 'Time to move on, for both of us. And since I'm going to be around a whole lot more from now on, if you want any help with anything, you only have to ask.'

'Thank you, that's very kind. But I do most of the work here myself and, as I said, I've scaled things down. In fact, Jasper's put the details of the big greenhouse up on the Freecycle website to see if anyone will dismantle it and take it away, and I've put an advert in the parish magazine about the quail. I'm selling that enormous TV of Tom's, too.'

'Didn't you throw the TV controller into Tom's grave?'

'Yes, but Jasper had one of those universal ones all the time, so he could watch the History Channel on the big screen when Tom was away.'

I took another sip of ginger beer and reached for the biscuit tin. 'At least I got rid of the goats years ago, when they learned how to climb trees.'

He gave me a scathing look. 'Goats can't climb trees, Lizzy!'

'You obviously don't know much about goats. And you wouldn't believe how strong they are! If a goat sets its mind on going somewhere, there's not a lot you can do to stop it. Anyway, I never did get used to goat-flavoured milk and yoghurt and I thought the cheese tasted like brown soap.'

'What are you going to do with Tom's business?'

'That's already sorted,' I said, taking a crunchy bite of Choconut Consolation. 'The day after the funeral two of Tom's friends, Jimbo and Freddie—do you remember them?—came and made me an offer for everything, and I accepted it. I could have got much more, but I wanted to . . . well, I wanted to just get rid of it all! They got a really good deal, but the funny thing is that they assumed Tom's van was included, only I'd already swapped it with Dave Naylor for that Land Rover in the yard, so they had to go and buy it back!'

'Really, Lizzy, you should have left all that to me. I'd have got you a good price for everything!' he said, not seeming at all amused.

'It's none of your business,' I said tartly as a few faint, plangent notes wafted across the courtyard and through the open kitchen door.

'What the hell's that?' he demanded, startled. 'It seems to be coming from the workshop!'

'It's just the Mummers of Invention, Nick. I let them carry on using the workshop to practise in. I wasn't using it.'

He gazed blankly at me. 'But Ophelia Locke is—'

'Pregnant with Tom's child? Chances are it isn't his, but I think she was more sinned against than sinning because she's so very easy and persuadable. Gullible, even. I've just been up to her cottage to take her some spare fruit and veg to build her up a bit, but if I'd known she was coming down here tonight she could have taken it back with her.'

'You're crackers!'

This didn't seem to be the moment to tell him she was also one of the members of ARG who'd been targeting my cottage and the estate. Anyway, she'd said she'd stopped now and I expect Caz would make sure she did.

'Strangely enough, I suspect Ophelia's half in love with Caz, only she doesn't want to admit it,' I said, following that train of thought.

'Is she? Well, they do say that opposites attract! Maybe *we* could have made a go of it all those years ago, if you hadn't suddenly decided to marry Tom on the rebound after we split up.'

'I did *not* marry Tom on the rebound. We fell in love months afterwards!' I said hotly. 'And we only

175

split up because you decided to go off on a world recipe-finding mission for a year, don't forget.'

'You should have understood—and waited. I wrote to you.'

'No you didn't, you only sent me recipes on postcards!'

'That's the same thing.'

His eyes, the purple-grey of wet Welsh slate, were baffled.

'Well, whatever,' I said. 'It's pointless having post-mortems at this stage, isn't it? We married other people and moved on.'

There was a tap on the door and a shadow darkened the threshold. 'Hello!' called a deep and attractive male voice. 'Mrs Pharamond?'

The man, who was tall with curling blond hair and a ruggedly attractive face, stopped halfway through the door. 'Oh, sorry if I'm disturbing you,' he said, with a charmingly apologetic smile. 'I'm Ritch, you know—Ritch Rainford?'

As my eyes met his incredibly blue ones, it struck me that Annie's description of his charms had been *wildly* understated. A force field could not have held me faster at that moment and I fear I might even have been drooling—but then, he did make me think of slabs of golden-brown Honeycomb Crunch . . .

His gaze released mine and he looked enquiringly at Nick, who was sitting there with his arms crossed like a terribly gloomy wooden Indian.

'You're not interrupting anything,' I said, managing to get my voice back. 'This is my late husband's cousin, Nick Pharamond.'

'Hi,' Ritch said in a friendly manner, but the two men seemed to me to be eyeing each other in a very

176

sizing-up-for-battle way. It reminded me of a film I once saw of bull elephants fighting, probably a territorial thing. They were both big, fit men, so I wouldn't know which one to put my money on.

'I just wanted to say how kind it was of you to let the group continue practising in the workshop, Mrs Pharamond, and to let you know I'll be up here jamming with them sometimes. So if you see a stranger around the place, it's me.'

'Do call me Lizzy,' I said. 'And actually, I'll be the stranger round at *your* place tonight, if you still want Posh Pet-sitters to come, because I'm Annie's assistant and I'll be seeing to Flo.'

He gave me another warm—*very* warm—smile, his blue eyes crinkling at the corners, and I could see what Annie meant, because there was just something about his expression that made you feel hot under the collar (or the smock, in her case).

'Great, I can see she'll be in good hands. Well, better get back to the gang, I suppose. Not my sort of music, really, but it's good to keep my hand in!'

Another one-hundred-and-fifty-watt smile and he was gone. I sighed involuntarily, watching his retreating, lithe figure until it vanished into the workshop. Ophelia might think he was old, but I bet that was before she saw him in the flesh.

'Well, you do seem to be managing everything very well without *my* help,' Nick said, abruptly getting up and banging his head on the ceiling light, which swayed alarmingly. 'Bloody hell!'

'Jasper's started doing that too, now he's over six foot. I must shorten the chain, or something. Thanks for coming though, Nick. Jasper will be sorry to have missed you.'

'He's at the dig?'

'Yes, and then his friend was going to pick him up and they were going over to talk to the owner of the student house his friend's brother rents with a couple of others. Jasper's taking that dog that Annie dumped on us, and thinks he can sweet-talk the landlady into letting him keep it in the house, even though it's supposed to be no pets. He'll be home late. But it's probably just as well, because I need to read through my new book tonight—if I can bring myself to concentrate on it for long enough to spot any mistakes!'

He gestured at the dog-eared heap at the end of the table. 'Is that what all this stuff is? Yet another glorious *Perseverance Chronicle*?'

'Yes, and possibly the last. I'm not sure I'll be able to finish the next, because I'm only managing to write about a paragraph most days instead of four pages. And I tried to go through the manuscript earlier, but my brain got stuck and I read the same page over and over,' I said despairingly. 'My agent will kill me if it isn't in the post tomorrow.'

'I'll read it for you,' he offered, to my surprise.

'What—*you*?'

'Why not? I'm literate and I've nothing in particular to do for the rest of the day. It's not that big a manuscript, so it won't take me long. I'll red-pen any mistakes and drop it back later.'

It was amazingly kind of Nick, but perhaps he just wanted to do something to help, so I pushed it all into a manila folder and handed it to him thankfully. 'That is such a weight off my mind! I'll be out around seven to see to Mr Rainford's dog, but you know where the key is if I'm out, don't you?'

'Raspberries,' he said.

'What?'

'I left you a message earlier. *Do* you have any?'

'Oh yes, there's a September-fruiting bush behind the greenhouse, but there aren't an awful lot of them. I put them aside for you in the small barn.'

'That's OK. I bought some supermarket ones too, just in case, though they don't have the same flavour. I can mix them together.'

'What are you making?'

'A variation on liquorice ice cream, with a raspberry coulis.'

I looked at him doubtfully, but he seemed to be serious. Then he stunned me by stooping and swiftly kissing me on the mouth, which he absolutely *never* does, and left with my manuscript under his arm.

My lips tingled. I supposed we *were* kissing cousins, if only by marriage . . . but I wouldn't have described that as an affectionate peck on the cheek! Also, since he was the sort of man who gets a five o'clock shadow five minutes after he'd shaved, I got a free exfoliation into the bargain.

Staring after his car as he drove off (and it was very nearly pressed duck for dinner), I realised what I hadn't admitted to myself before: that in recent years I'd really, really missed our invigorating exchanges of opinion. Every life, especially one so literally down to earth as mine, needs just a little vinegar in the mix.

But Ritch Rainford, now—he was more of a sweet treat . . .

Going back in, I slightly loosened all the caps on the ginger beer bottles, just in case, then looked out

179

the Honeycomb Crunch recipe. It is much the same as cinder toffee, really—sugar, white vinegar, water and bicarbonate of soda, only with added butter and golden syrup. It's the mixture of bicarb and vinegar that makes them go all bubbly.

I added that thought to the current chapter of the next *Chronicle*, before the inspiration bubbles went flat again.

CHAPTER 14: SLIGHTLY CURDLED

After making Honeycomb Crunch, it occurred to me that if you crumbled it up, it would make a wonderful topping for home-made vanilla ice cream. You could wrap a chunk in a plastic bag and hit it with a rolling pin—that would do the trick.
The Perseverance Chronicles: A Life in Recipes

Jasper phoned to tell me his new landlady had agreed that Ginny could take up residence in the rented house with him and his friends at the end of the month, so that was sorted. I would have preferred him to live in a student hall of residence for the first year, but the whole point of your children going away to university is so they can live their lives, not yours, so I would just have to go along with his decision.

The thought of my little boy exposed to all the big city temptations of drugs, unprotected sex and being knifed in the street . . . well, I had to swallow hard before I could say brightly, 'Oh good, I'm so glad, darling. That will be great, living with your friends and having Ginny with you. What time will you be back tonight?'

'Chris's mum is going to drop me off, probably about eleven. She doesn't like him driving late at night—she's nearly as bad as you are for fussing.'

'Jasper, I don't fuss! How can you say I fuss?' I demanded indignantly. But then, despite my best intentions, asked, after a moment's pause, 'What are you doing tonight?'

'Sex, drugs, tattooing our arms with old syringes off the street, that kind of thing,' he said good-naturedly.

'*Jasper!*'

'Watching DVDs, making popcorn, drinking beer,' he amended.

'I'm going into the village in a minute, to pet-sit an actor's dog—Ritch Rainford. He used to be some kind of pop star in the eighties.'

'Never heard of him,' he said, unimpressed. Had it been a bosomy model from one of the boys' magazines I expected he would have been much keener, but the only creature with artificially inflated breasts in the Mosses is Polly Darke, and I knew he classed her with the pensioners.

How can silicone be sexy? Isn't it peculiar that many men find artificial breasts just as much of a turn-on as real ones? Another one of life's strange mysteries to ponder when you are examining your marrows.

*   *   *

I ate a generous portion of my own version of Lancashire hotpot—good and peppery, with rich gravy and a shortcrust topping—and read the rest of the latest issue of the *Mosses Messenger*, before going out.

According to 'The Verger's Village Round-up', Caz Naylor had 'kindly volunteered to resolve the goose situation in Middlemoss, because children and the elderly were being terrorised, and the mess they left was proving a danger to life and limb. Caz has therefore now caught and rehomed them to somewhere more suitable, a solution we know will be acceptable to all interested parties.'

There was also a notice that rehearsals for the Mystery Play would be starting in the village hall on the fourteenth, Tuesdays (generally acts 1–9) and Thursdays (acts 10–22). Luckily, we've filled the vacancies for Moses and Lazarus without any trouble, and Miss Pym, who is a dab hand with papier-mâché after a lifetime spent teaching infants, is making a new Thou Shalt Not Commit Adultery commandment tablet.

I set off for the old vicarage just before seven, since it's only a short walk, but first I changed into a pair of decent, clean jeans and a pale green T-shirt with pretty old buttons sewn in a border all round the neck, an idea I got from one of Annie's magazines. I sewed them onto my best Indian leather toe-post sandals too, though they kept getting ripped off.

When I rigorously brushed all the knots out of my hair it went into a ripply light-brown mass round my head like something Rossetti would have painted, though thankfully *sans* the sulky Pre-Raphaelite trout-pout.

The T-shirt brought out the green in my eyes, and my face looked glowingly healthy for a recent widow. I wondered about applying a bit of make-up (I often *think* about make-up, but rarely bother to do anything about it), but then suddenly thought, what the hell am I doing, getting all duded up to walk Ritch Rainford's dog? Am I crackers? Do I think Flo is going to give her master my marks out of ten for effort and appearance when he staggers home from his party?

But it was too late to change, so I set off as I was. As I passed the vicarage bungalow, I wondered how

Annie and Gareth were getting on. It seemed very daring of him to invite a single lady to dine with him alone. Well, I assumed they were alone (apart from Trinny), unless he's invited half the village round for support?

The old vicarage now sported the new name of Vicar's End. I unlocked the front door with the key Annie had given me and stepped inside. It was always unlocked when Annie's father was vicar, so that seemed odd in itself. And somehow, I still expected the cool, tiled hall to smell of lavender, floor polish and beeswax, just like it used to, rather than of some exotic artificial household fragrance mixed with slightly acrid cigarette smoke.

The old hallstand had been replaced by a glass-topped console table bearing an indecent bronze sculpture and a severely tailored arrangement of decayed-looking black orchids among spiky foliage. I was just touching them to see if they were real (they were), when, with a clatter of claws, Flo hurtled down the hall to meet me, velvet coat rippling and tail thrashing about. Annie had said she would be delighted to see me, even though I was a total stranger, and she was quite right. In fact, had I been a burglar, I expect she would have been equally pleased.

'Good girl, Flo!' I said, patting her. 'Good girl!'

My instructions were to let her into the garden and feed her, then hand her a chewy rawhide bone and shut her in the kitchen on departing. I thought I would feed her first, since she didn't seem particularly interested in going out.

What happy, smiley faces white bull terriers have! 'Come on then, Flo, din-dins,' I said, and had just started towards the door at the back of the hall that led into the kitchen, when a deep, instantly recognisable masculine voice from above called out, 'Tobe, is that you? I'm on my way!'

He was, too: leaping athletically down the stairs two steps at a time, Ritch Rainford landed in the hall almost at my feet, though an advance wave of expensively intrusive aftershave just beat him to it.

'Yark!' I squawked inelegantly.

He looked equally surprised for a moment, then smiled. 'Sorry, thought you were my lift! Did I startle you, Lizzy?'

'Well, yes,' I said, swallowing. 'I thought you'd have been long gone.' Despite myself I was answering that effulgent smile, drowning dizzily in the depths of his cerulean-blue eyes . . .

'I'm *so* glad I wasn't,' he said, to which I couldn't think of a thing to say.

Was he flirting? *My* flirting abilities were not great, even in my youth, and by now had atrophied to the point of no return. I looked at him doubtfully, but decided it was just his usual manner and got a grip on myself. I even started breathing again: in, out—it was quite easy now I'd remembered how to do it.

'No . . . well, since you are still here, you won't need me to see to Flo, will you? You can do it before you go,' I suggested.

A horn sounded: 'No time—that's Toby. You know Toby Little, plays Rufus Grace in *Cotton Common*?'

'No, I'm afraid not, I haven't seen it,' I confessed. 'I don't watch much TV. I quite like gardening and cookery programmes, but anything else just doesn't seem to hold my concentration, probably because it isn't real. Life's much more interesting, isn't it?'

'Is it?' he said, looking at me curiously. The horn hooted again, impatiently. 'Look, Lizzy, why don't I tell Tobe to hang on a couple of minutes while we sort Flo, and then you could come with me, meet some of the cast, come on to the party?' he suggested.

'What—*me*? Oh, no, thanks, I couldn't! Jasper—my son—is coming home later . . .' I began, automatically stammering out excuses, though secretly a little bit of me was rather tempted by the idea in a fascinated-by-a-snake kind of way.

'Isn't he grown up? I don't suppose he needs his mum on the doorstep, waiting for him,' Ritch said, with another dangerously beguiling smile.

How did he know that? Did he know all about me?

He turned serious again, blue eyes concerned and sincere. 'But I'm sorry—you were very recently widowed—what *was* I thinking of? Of course you don't want to go to parties yet!'

'No,' I agreed, having entirely forgotten about Tom until that point. 'And his cousin, Nick—you met him earlier—is coming back this evening too. He kindly offered to correct the manuscript of my next book, which needs to be posted off tomorrow, so it would be very rude of me not to be there. Sorry.'

'Your book? Are you another novelist, like Polly Darke?'

'Ah, yes, our Trollope of the North,' I said sourly. 'No, I write sort of autobiographical books with recipes. Do you know Polly?'

'Met her around a few times,' he said vaguely. 'She had a fling with a friend of mine. Apparently she's pretty fit—does some weird yoga stuff.

186

Muscles like knots on string, he said.'

'Really? I've never seen her arms, she always wears long sleeves. I thought she might be on drugs or something.'

He shrugged, then his eyes flicked over me and he gave me a slow, sexy smile. 'I prefer natural, curvy women to skinny ones with monster boob jobs, every time.'

'That must make you fairly unique,' I said tartly, and he grinned.

The front door was thrust open and a voice bellowed: 'Ritch, what the hell are you doing, you bastard? Are you coming or what?'

'On my way out!' Ritch called back. Then he turned to me, 'Well, see you later, then. Be good, Flo.' And off he went.

Was he actually flirting with me, Lizzy Pharamond, mature (even overripe) Middlemoss tomboy, or was he like that with all women? I could quite see why he'd disconcerted Annie, though, because I felt slightly and interestingly singed around the edges. The words 'moth' and 'flame' came vividly to mind.

Sizzle, sizzle.

If he comes across on the TV like that, no wonder *Cotton Common*'s ratings have risen drastically since he joined the cast—he's trouble at t'mill!

I spent almost an hour with Flo, who is a delightful dog and will fetch a thrown rubber ball indefinitely, though she seemed quite sanguine about swapping my company for a chewy bone when I left.

*   *   *

187

Halfway home, while sauntering past the eerily quiet, goose-free green, I suddenly remembered about Nick and broke into a guilty run.

He'd obviously been at the cottage for some time, since he'd let himself in and there was an empty coffee cup on the kitchen table.

'Oh, sorry, Nick—have you been here long?' I said, panting slightly. 'I was playing with the dog and didn't notice the time.'

He rose to his feet, heavy brows practically meeting across his impressive nose, and snapped, 'You look pretty smart for dog-sitting. Going somewhere?'

'No,' I snapped right back, flushing. 'I don't spend all day, every day, in gardening clothes, you know!'

He took me in with his slaty, sardonic eyes, from gold sandals to waving, if now dishevelled, hair. 'You always did scrub up well. Hope your client appreciated it.'

'How did you know Ritch was still there?' I gasped, startled, then felt myself going pink again.

'You just told me!'

'Well, he was, though on his way out. And don't call him a *client* in that tone of voice, like I was a hooker!'

'Sorry!' he said, but didn't sound it. 'I'll be on my way. Didn't find too much wrong with your manuscript, except a bit of tailoring of the truth.'

'I have to. Nobody would believe the real things that happen. They're much too incredible, and anyway, it would be too depressing. My misfortunes are supposed to be funny.'

'Yes, your formula for success with your readers

188

does seem to be a series of pratfalls linked with nursery-pudding suggestions,' he said unkindly.

'You offered to read through it, I didn't make you!' I said indignantly.

'I wanted to help.' He ran a hand through his black hair, which stood up on end. 'Look, seeing you're all gussied up, why don't you come out somewhere quiet for a drink with me? I'll even give you some pudding ideas for your new recipe book.'

The poet Wendy Cope puts it so well about men being like buses: there isn't one for ages and then two come along at once, flashing their signals. (Not that that necessarily means they're going to stop.) And I didn't even want to catch one!

'That's kind of you, Nick, but I really don't feel like going out tonight and I need to make those alterations to the manuscript and pack it up. Anyway, we'd only argue like we usually do.'

'Not necessarily, but please yourself,' he said, and walked out.

I stared after him, which was well worthwhile, because his rear view was just as good, if not better, than Ritch's.

I *thought* he was just trying to be kind to me in his way, but Nick's kindness moves in mysterious ways, its wonders to perform.

*   *   *

It was still just about light when Clive Potter cycled up for some tomatoes and to tell me that Adam (as played by a local farmer) had given himself a hernia while lifting bales, and had to drop out of the Mystery Play.

'We'll have to audition for a new one, I'm afraid,

189

Lizzy, unless anyone comes forward.'

I had a sudden mental vision of playing my Eve to Ritch Rainford's Adam, but firmly suppressed it: an innocent in the Garden of Eden he certainly was not. More like the snake.

He displayed even more snake-like tendencies later, when he phoned from somewhere noisy to invite me to his housewarming party at Vicar's End on Friday night!

'Just a few people—you could come to that, couldn't you?' he said persuasively, and I won't say I wasn't tempted for a minute, before common sense reasserted itself and I politely declined.

It got me thinking about Honeycomb Crunch all over again, though, and I decided to try using it in a variation of Eton Mess. I called it Cinder Cream and I thought I was on to a winner.

While I worked away putting in the corrections to the manuscript that Nick had marked, I thought how odd it seemed in the cottage without Jasper there . . . but I supposed it was a foretaste of what was to come and I'd just have to get used to it.

CHAPTER 15: DRINK ME

I was up early, picking sound, firm apples for storing. I don't know the names of the varieties of all the old trees that were already here when we came, but by now do know by trial and error which will keep and which are best eaten or cooked straight away. I thought I might do baked apples filled with mincemeat and drizzled with cream for dessert that night, always a favourite.

The Perseverance Chronicles: A Life in Recipes

Next day Annie relayed a request from Ritch that I take Flo to the Mossedge canine beautician for nail clipping and a bit of pampering.

She'd been quite right about the Posh Pet-sitting taking off, because I was already down to look after two cats in a converted barn over at Mossrow for two days, plus a couple more one-off jobs. I'd be so busy that weeds would soon outnumber vegetables in my garden and the finished crops would remain uncleared.

I managed to fit in a visit to the cats while Flo was being done, and then returned her to Vicar's End, where Ritch was flirting with his cleaning lady, Dora Tombs, whom he called 'Dorable'.

'Get away with you!' was her standard response to each sally.

'Morning, our Lizzy!' she said, as I went in (being a Naylor, and so distantly related). 'Keep that dog off my clean floor until it's dried—and the same goes for *you*,' she added, jabbing at Ritch's feet with her mop.

Ritch took a step back and gave me a lazy, glinting smile that took me in from top to bottom, lingering thoughtfully on the way.

'Flo's clean as a whistle, Mrs T,' I assured her. Flo skittered and slid over to her bowl and started wolfing biscuits as though she was famished.

'They said at Doggy Heaven that she was good as gold,' I told Ritch, adding severely, 'and you could have taken her yourself, if you're not going to work, and saved some money!'

'Ah, but then I wouldn't have had two beautiful women at my beck and call, would I?'

'Get away with you, you daft bugger!' Dora said. 'You're all mouth and trousers, you!'

'Don't you *ever* work?' I asked, unimpressed.

'Actually yes, and I'm on my way. Just waiting for the car.'

'You don't drive?'

'Lost my licence and I've got another twelve months before I get it back again,' he said ruefully, but I didn't feel sympathetic because I expect it was drink driving, which in my opinion is a criminally stupid thing to do.

'Tough luck,' I said, but when he smiled at me I found myself smiling back. He's clearly as self-centred as most of the male race, besides being unable to resist flirting with any female who comes within range, but I must admit he is extremely attractive.

'I could use a part-time chauffeur?' he suggested, raising a questioning eyebrow.

'I've got enough to do. My garden will be an impenetrable jungle if I don't spend more time at home.'

A horn beeped outside. 'Pity—and there's my car. See you later, girls!'

After he'd gone, seeming to take the sun with him, Mrs T put the kettle on and we had tea, toast and gossip.

She's also Polly Darke's cleaner, which was fascinating: apparently she had a whole room devoted to some weird kind of yoga, and worked out in there twice a day.

'Fit as a flea and strong as an ox,' Mrs T averred, crunching toast. 'Wouldn't think it to look at her, would you? And I'm that sorry about your troubles,' she added, which is as close as anyone's got to mentioning the goings-on at the funeral feast. 'I could tell sometimes she'd had a man in the house, but if I'd known who it was, I'd have told you.'

'Oh, thanks,' I said. 'But it's all water under the bridge now, and I'm trying to move on and put it all behind me.'

'That's right—and I'm sure Mr Nick will help you sort everything out. He's a proper man.'

'A proper man as compared to *what*?' I asked curiously.

She gave me a Mona Lisa smile. 'Eva Gumball says he's divorcing that foreign woman and going to be living up there at the Hall most of the time, now. His granddad's that made up about it!'

Information in the Mosses travels as fast as thought. 'I'm glad for Uncle Roly's sake that Nick will be spending more time in Middlemoss, but I certainly don't need anyone to help me sort things out,' I said firmly.

'That Polly Darke's turned a whole bedroom into a walk-in wardrobe, too,' Mrs T said, changing the subject back.

                    *   *   *

On Friday night I felt restless, especially after I'd
popped into Delphine Lake's earlier to walk her
dogs, and she'd said she was going to Ritch's party.

'For cocktails at eight, dear. But us old ones will
clear off early and then I expect it will go on until
the small hours!'

I don't actually like parties, except family ones,
so I can't imagine why I felt left out . . . All right,
perhaps I did, because my mind kept presenting me
with scenarios involving Ritch that were quite
unbecoming to a widow of such recent date.

                    *   *   *

I had an unsettled night and then, when I went
downstairs early next morning, I found Mimi fast
asleep on the sofa in the sitting room.

Why do I even bother locking my front door
when absolutely everyone seems to know where I
hide the spare key?

Juno, who was now allowed on her feet again,
arrived in search almost immediately, limping
gamely. 'I wish you'd stay in your bed at nights!' she
scolded Mimi, who simply gazed blandly at her like
a comfortable cat.

'Stay to breakfast?' I invited. 'Jasper's getting
up—he's going to the dig.' Thuds and yapping from
above were evidence that Ginny was doing her best
to help. The ceiling light swayed gently and small
flakes of plaster drifted down, like the grey-white
feathers Nick had been brushing off his sleeve when
he came out of the small barn the other day . . .

If Caz hadn't fitted a padlock to his freezer, I'd have had a quick snoop by now!

'No, thanks, we must get back. Mrs Gumball always cooks enough for twelve, and think of the waste!' Juno said, propelling the reluctant Mimi away.

I didn't think Mimi would be terribly hungry anyway, because when I opened the fridge to get the milk, I discovered that half a bowl of experimental Cinder Cream had been eaten, and it's surprisingly filling.

'Come up to the Hall later—around eleven!' Mimi said, clinging to the doorframe with both hands and smiling at me. 'Nick's invited us all to try out some ice cream he's making—yummy!'

'He invited me, too?' I asked doubtfully.

'Especially,' Mimi confirmed, still beaming but losing her grip on the gloss paint, and then was borne away until her cracked soprano singing, 'Hokey pokey, a penny a lump!' faded into the distance.

'You've just missed Mimi and Juno,' I told Jasper when he finally came down. Ginny shot past my ankles and scattered the chickens in the yard, but unintentionally, I think. She probably couldn't see them for all the hair in her eyes.

'I know, I heard. Mimi sounded happy.'

'She mostly does. Oh, there's the phone.'

I should have said, rather, 'where's' the phone, since I couldn't find it until I traced the long flex from the kitchen into the sitting room. Mimi seemed to have built a nest for it with all the cushions.

By the time I got to it, it had stopped ringing, but the caller had left a message: Ritch, sounding very gin-and-cigarettes gravelly. 'Lizzy? If you get this, come round and sort Flo out right away, will you? I'm feeling a bit rough this morning and she keeps yapping . . . I don't think Dora's coming until this afternoon . . . just let yourself in.'

I could hear faint barking, and then Ritch groaned (rather sexily, it has to be said) and put the phone down.

Well, he might at least have let the poor dog out, even if he did have a hangover! It would be nearly an hour until I could get there, since I wanted to drop Jasper off at the dig first, so by that time he would probably have given in and done it himself. And didn't he have to go to work every day? I know nothing about these things; perhaps they record the shows in batches or something? Or not on Saturdays?

The phone rang again while I was carrying it back into the kitchen, but it was just a man who had spotted the greenhouse last night on Freecycle and asked me for my phone number, wanting to arrange to come and look at it.

'You're very popular this morning, Mum,' Jasper commented. 'And a bit pink,' he added, but I ignored that. I'd already let the hens out and fed them, collected the eggs, watered the garden and greenhouse, put a load of washing in the machine, made an especially nice packed lunch for Jasper and cooked bacon and eggs. Who wouldn't look flushed?

*   *   *

When I cautiously let myself into Vicar's End, there was no sign of life other than a muffled barking

196

from the kitchen.

Poor Flo had been unable to keep all four legs crossed and left a puddle by the door, about which she seemed to feel apologetic, though it was not her fault, as I told her while I let her out before finding the mop and disinfectant and cleaning it up.

Then I filled her bowl with fresh water and put a few crunchy dog biscuits down to keep her going for a while. I didn't know what Ritch wanted me to do, but I was quite sure he could afford the Posh Pet-sitter prices, so after that I took Flo for a nice long walk. It had rained in the night, so she wasn't such a clean, white and glossy creature on our return, though she was a very much happier one.

I hadn't even started out clean and glossy, being back to gardening jeans and old T-shirts, Nick's remarks having rankled slightly.

While I was still rubbing Flo with a tartan towel helpfully inscribed 'DOG' that I found hanging in the scullery next to her lead, Ritch wandered into the kitchen, obviously fresh from the shower, in gilt-edged designer stubble and a very short white towelling robe. Clearly he's a natural blond, because the hair on his legs was golden right up to the hem. He was carrying a glass beaker of straw-coloured liquid, which he set down on the counter.

'Morning. I could do with a rub down too,' he said with a wicked if rueful smile. Then, opening the fridge, he bent over and rummaged around. I looked away hastily.

'Thanks for coming,' he said, emerging with an opened carton of milk. 'Don't know what we were drinking last night—that's the trouble with cocktails, and after a couple you don't care any more—but today I feel like hell.' He picked up the glass beaker again. 'I'll just finish this, and then make some coffee: want some?'

'What is it?' I asked cautiously.

He grinned. 'I meant, do you want some coffee! I don't think you'd want any of this, though I could be wrong—it's pee.'

He drained the last drops and put the glass in the dishwasher. Did he say *pee*? Eeeugh!

'Er, no,' I said, backing away slightly. 'Did you say you were drinking . . .?'

'My own urine? Yeah, every morning—everyone's doing it. It's good for you.'

After last night I should think his pee was at least forty per cent proof. 'I . . . hadn't heard about that,' I said, wondering if he was quite mad. 'How interesting!'

He gave me a wicked smile, but it wasn't working any more. 'It cures anything. That and frequent sex are all a man needs to keep healthy.'

'Really?' I felt as if some miraculously attractive bubble had burst and taken all the rainbows with it, but managed with an effort to gather my wits together: 'I've taken Flo for a walk and changed her water, so she's OK. I'd better go now—I've got things to do.'

'Sure you can't stay awhile?' He switched on one of those espresso machines that look as if you need a whole generator and a degree in engineering to make them work.

'No, really.' I wasn't drinking any more coffee out of any of *his* cups, now I knew about his habits. 'Shall I settle up with you now, or do you want to send me a bill?'

'Oh, Annie will send you one at the end of the month, if that's OK? I put it all down on her chart and she does the bookwork. Bye, Flo.'

I bent to fondle her smooth, velvety head and, when I rose to go, Ritch followed close behind me up the hall and reached out a long arm to open the front door, brushing casually against me as he did so.

'Oh—thanks,' I said, unnerved by the proximity of all that naked male flesh, and shuffled past into the sunlight just as Annie, towed by four large hounds, was passing the end of the drive. Unable to wave, she began to smile, then caught sight of Ritch lounging in the doorway in his mini-robe. The smile wavered, she went pink and hurried on.

I dashed after her, calling out: 'Hey, Annie, wait for me!'

She turned reluctantly. '*Lizzy!*'

'That was *not* what it looked like,' I said severely. 'Honestly! You should know me better by now! He phoned me this morning and asked me to go and sort Flo out, because he had a hangover.'

Actually, in that bathrobe it was almost a hang *under*, so it's just as well it was only Annie who spotted us, because she's probably the only one who would have believed me. I took two of the dog leads.

'He simply couldn't be bothered to let Flo out this morning, which is terribly selfish, and has put me right off him.'

'I should think so, too,' she said indignantly. 'The dog must have been desperate!'

'She'd made a puddle, but as close to the back door as she could, poor thing. But speaking of pee, Annie, you'll *never* believe what Ritch does with *his*!'

And I was right: she didn't believe me and

insisted he must have been joking, though I'm sure he wasn't. It's not a fad likely to catch on in Middlemoss.

'So, how did you and Gareth get on the other night?' I asked, changing the subject. 'You never really said.'

She blushed under her freckles. 'Fine . . . he is *so* nice. But he can't cook, so it was just reheated ready-meals. I told him about the French cookery course we did after we left school and I'm going to get him a slow cooker like mine and show him how to use it.'

'You should invite him back to dinner at your place, only early enough so he can help you cook it,' I suggested. Cooking together is, I think, a very intimate thing to do.

'That's a good idea. Something simple but nice, like that chicken in white wine thing you do, or a risotto.'

'And a stodgy pud. Bet he likes those—most men do.' Even Nick, though he pretends he doesn't, just to wind me up.

'Yes, he'd bought a chocolate gateau,' she agreed, 'and he ate quite a bit of it. Oh, well, must go and take these dogs back. I'll put the extra Ritch pet-sitting on the chart for you when I get home . . . and Lizzy,' she added anxiously, 'you aren't falling for him, are you?'

'No, though he's very attractive—or *was*, until I got grossed out by his habits! But even were I looking for another man, one who thinks pee and hot, casual sex will cure anything is obviously operating on a different wavelength from mine.'

'Gosh, yes!' she agreed, innocent blue-grey eyes open wide. Ritch is not the only one in Middlemoss operating on a different wavelength from me, but I love her anyway.

'I've served my time in the prison of love, though I might get another dog later, once Jasper's taken Ginny off to university with him.'

'Tell me when, and I'll find you a nice stray,' she promised, beaming. '*Is* Ginny going to university with Jasper?'

'Yes, he's persuaded the landlady of a student house to let him keep her with him, but don't ask me how.'

'Oh, he can be just as charming as Tom was, when he wants to be,' she said. 'Only of course, he is much more solid, reliable and kind.'

The church clock struck eleven, galvanising my memory. 'Oh, must fly, Annie! I'm supposed to be up at the Hall tasting some ice cream Nick's made, and Mimi said he invited me especially, so he'll be cross if I don't go.'

Thrusting the dog leads back into her hands, I rushed off.

*   *   *

In fact, Nick seemed totally surprised, but not displeased, to see me. He was wearing a blue-striped apron, a smudge of sugar and a streak of raspberry, and looked good enough to eat . . . *if* you liked that kind of thing, of course.

I looked at Mimi suspiciously and she waved her spoon at me and called gaily, 'Just in time!'

'Hello, my dear,' Unks said. 'I didn't know you were coming. This is going to be a treat, isn't it?'

He, Mimi, Juno, Mrs Gumball and even Caz Naylor, half-concealed by the shadow of the inglenook, were all sitting round the kitchen table, spoons poised.

'Here, have mine, Lizzy, and I'll get some more,' Nick said, and I took the proffered bowl and sat down, looking at it dubiously. The ice cream was sort of grey, like town snow turned to slush, and the blood-red raspberry coulis swirling over it contrasted strangely.

'It tastes better than it looks,' Mimi remarked. 'I love liquorice! Yum!'

She was right. Nick sat down again next to me, long legs brushing mine. 'What do you think?'

'It looks horrible in a sophisticated sort of way, but tastes great.' I turned to see what Caz was making of it, but he'd quietly stolen away, leaving only an empty dish behind, which was tribute enough, I suppose. 'It's the opposite of coffee granita, which I always *expect* to be delicious, but never quite comes up to expectations.'

'Oh? I'll have to see what I can do about that.' His eyes gleamed.

'Nothing I haven't already tried!' I snapped.

'You want to take a bet on that?'

I might have been tempted to rub ice cream into that superior smile, if I hadn't already eaten it all.

Mrs Gumball was still daintily spooning hers in. 'What that boy will think of next!' she said, shaking her head so that all the silvery-grey curls, tied up on top of her head in a skittish whale spout effect, quivered.

'Great,' Juno said, laying down her spoon. 'Mimi, don't lick the bowl!'

'Why not, when we're just family?' she demanded indignantly.

'It's still not polite.'

'Roly eats roast duck with his fingers and then licks them.'

'Would you like to go for a drive?' Juno asked, in an attempted diversion. 'I think my leg's up to it now, if we don't go too far.'

Mimi clapped her hands. 'Martin Mere to feed the ducks!'

'Oh good, good,' Unks said. 'Bit of fresh air will do you both good.' He got up. 'Must go and study the form a bit—got a horse racing on Saturday. Snowy Sunday.'

'Not in September, surely?' I said, puzzled.

'Name of the horse. Snowy Sunday out of Weekend Blizzard.'

Unks has shares in three racehorses, but they usually seem to fall over, or go backwards, or do something that doesn't involve getting past the post.

'Cold lunch in the dining room at one,' Mrs Gumball said, heaving herself to her feet. 'I'm just off to see to my Joe's dinner. Mind my kitchen's clean and tidy again when I get back, Nick Pharamond!'

'Don't I always clear up after my cooking?' he demanded indignantly.

'I'll load the dishwasher myself,' I promised her.

One by one they went, and Nick and I quickly sorted out the kitchen in fairly amicable silence.

'That's that,' I said finally, looking round to see if we'd missed anything. Nick is a very messy cook and it was surprising how many pots and pans he had used just to produce ice cream and sauce. 'I'll have to go, I've got someone coming to look at the greenhouse and he said around lunchtime.'

'You have? Someone you know?'

'No, a stranger who saw the ad on the Freecycle website.'

He frowned. 'I'd better come and deal with him for you. You should get me to do this sort of thing. Anyone might turn up on your doorstep.'

'I can handle it! I mean, I'm only selling an old greenhouse, not the crown jewels,' I said firmly. I'm used to doing everything myself, so why would I suddenly need a man to do it for me?

'I'll walk down with you anyway, just make sure—' he began to insist, as though I were some frail little flower; then his BlackBerry went off and while he answered it I slid quietly away home.

*   *   *

The man was waiting for me in the yard outside the cottage, leaning against an old pick-up truck and smoking a roll-up, and I instantly rather regretted refusing Nick's offer so hastily, because there was just *something* about him I didn't like, even apart from the aroma of stale alcohol.

'Had a bit of trouble finding you,' he said, straightening with a leer and running bloodshot eyes over me as though I were a dubious filly. 'Lonely down here, isn't it?'

'Not really, people go past on the main road all the time and my family live up the drive,' I said briskly. 'So, Mr . . .'

'Roach,' he slurred.

'So, you're interested in having the greenhouse?'

'Well I was, but I took the liberty of having a look at it while I was waiting, and it's in pretty poor condition.'

'The supports are fine and it should dismantle

204

easily. Anyway, what were you expecting for nothing?'

'It'll cost you a fortune to pay someone to take it away for you,' he said. 'But I don't suppose a lady like you would know about that. Recent widow, aren't you? Bet you miss having a man about the place.'

He came a bit closer, flicking his cigarette onto the cobbles.

'Look, are you interested or not?' I demanded, ignoring the innuendo but backing off slightly. The yard brush was leaning against the wall behind me and I reckoned that if desperate, I could always beat him into submission with it: it was a good, sturdy one.

'Perhaps I might be,' he said, with what was *definitely* a leer. 'Maybe you'd like to discuss it somewhere more comfortable? I wouldn't say no if you invited me in.'

'Oh, Nick!' I exclaimed thankfully, as his tall, broad-shouldered figure appeared round the end of the barn. He looked from one to the other of us from under dark brows and I took his arm and squeezed it meaningfully. 'This is Mr Roach. He came to look at the greenhouse.'

'Loach,' the man corrected me, backing off warily. 'But I've had second thoughts. It's not quite what I wanted. Doubt it's what *anyone* wants,' he added. 'Well, see you!'

He climbed back into the cab of his pick-up and drove off with a bit of unnecessarily macho revving and tyre screeching.

Nick looked at me with one raised eyebrow, but nobly refrained from saying, 'I told you so.'

Realising I was still clinging to his arm, I hastily

let go and moved away.

'Do you want to come in?' I asked. 'Or go back for lunch? I'm going to have ham and split-pea soup and home-made bread.'

'I'll stay, but only if you promise to let me handle anything else you want to get rid of. I'm sure Roly will back me on this one—and the cottage *is* part of the estate.'

'Oh, all right!' I agreed. 'But don't think I couldn't have handled that horrible man without you, because I could! I've already had much nastier people chasing me up for money they say Tom owed them, when they don't seem to have the least bit of proof.'

'You haven't paid them, have you?'

'Despite what you think, I'm not *entirely* stupid,' I said with dignity. 'I asked Unks' advice, and he told me to pass them all on to his solicitor, Smithers, and he would deal with them for me and let me know which were the genuine ones that had to be settled.'

'I don't think you're stupid,' he said, following me into the cottage. 'You just take independence a little too far sometimes, that's all.'

'Did you come down just to lecture me, or did you want something?' I asked pointedly.

He smiled innocently and said, 'I just wanted to know what recipe you'd already tried for the coffee granita?'

'One *you* sent me from Italy on a postcard of the Leaning Tower of Pisa,' I said with satisfaction. I hauled out the postcard album to look for it and he seemed amazed that I'd not only kept them all, but also carefully put them into a book. However, show me anyone interested in cooking who *wouldn't* have

206

hoarded the recipes.

We ended up looking through the album for almost a whole hour without arguing, which must be a record. Maybe he was mellowing.

'I'll see you at the first Mystery Play rehearsal on Tuesday night,' were his surprise parting words before striding off whistling, the sun glinting on his blue-black hair.

What *could* he mean? Had he volunteered to help Clive?

*　　　*　　　*

Ritch phoned and invited me for a quiet drink at the café-bar in the former Pharamond's Biscuit factory on Tuesday night, so he could 'get to know me better'! He said he was tied up until then, which gave me a bad moment because I remembered that note from Polly Darke I found in Tom's pocket just before he died . . .

I told him I couldn't go, since I had a Mystery Play meeting and the cast tended to go to the village pub afterwards, but he said that was OK, he would meet me and come along too, and I simply couldn't think of a way of telling him not to on the spot.

I looked long and hard in the mirror and was at a loss to understand why, unless he was currently desperately short of another woman for his frequent, healthy sex rota.

He probably wouldn't bother after all, but if he did, I'd just have to hide behind the crowd and hope avid *Cotton Common* fans mobbed him, which seemed quite likely.

I tried out two varieties of coffee granita on

Jasper, later, but although he said they were delicious I still felt they lacked that little extra something . . .

On the other hand, some mincemeat fudge turned out really well.

CHAPTER 16: UNREHEARSED ENTRANCES

I tried out my mincemeat fudge on the members of the Christmas Pudding Circle yesterday and it went down a treat, as did Marian's variation on gingerbread biscuits for hanging on the Christmas tree. She had cut out an inner star and placed a crushed boiled sweet in the middle, which melted during the baking process to form a stained-glass effect. I used to do something similar for Jasper when he was little—traffic light biscuits. We are all busy cooking for the annual Autumn Fête next Saturday too, where there will be much friendly rivalry for the various prizes. Annie has asked me to make some bags of candyfloss and will collect them on Friday . . .

The Perseverance Chronicles: A Life in Recipes

I was a little late setting off for the first Mystery Play rehearsal on the Tuesday evening, because I'd spent the afternoon making a start on my Christmas cake—and not just my own, but the six small ones that each member of the CPC makes for the local Senior Citizens Christmas Hampers, to be distributed by Marian and the rest of the Mosses Women's Institute.

I like to soak the fruit in dark rum for about five days—no faffing around pouring alcohol into holes in the base for me!—so, after an afternoon of chopping and mixing, I had three enormous covered bowls sitting in the larder gently marinating, and an aching arm.

When I got to the village hall the actors were standing about in groups, chatting. Acts 1 to 9 of the Mystery Play rehearsal would be supervised by me, the vicar, Miss Pym and Marian, whose husband, Clive, was, as usual, overall director. Roly, Voice of God in perpetuity, never put in an appearance until the final performance, since having played the role for so many years he could do it in his sleep. On the actual day he sits in a corner of the courtyard in a little striped canvas pavilion like something from a jousting field, well wrapped up and with a warm brazier, and speaks his lines into a mike connected to the speaker just inside the barn door.

Clive was putting cardboard signs up in the parts of the room where the different acts were to gather and I found Marian filling the boiler in the kitchen area behind the hatch, ready for its long, slow journey towards the tea break.

I was just handing her my offering of treacle flapjacks, to go with what was left of her experimental gingerbread biscuits, when Nick loomed up beside me.

'Hi, Lizzy: should *I* have brought something to eat, too?'

I nearly dropped the box: he moved disconcertingly quietly for such a big man. 'Oh, hello Nick!'

'No, that's all right. These of Lizzy's are just extras, because I always bring a tin of Teatime Assortment with me,' Marian said, 'though the current one's down to them pink wafer things, which no one seems to go for. But nice of you to offer, Nick—and that lamb recipe of yours in the Sunday supplement was a right cracker! I'd never

210

have thought of doing that with olives.'

'Oh, thanks, Mrs Potter,' Nick said modestly with one of his most charming smiles, and she blushed. I was quite sure he knew the devastating effect these had, like silvery sunshine breaking out from behind lowering, purplish storm clouds.

Clive, clipboard in hand, bustled up. 'Ah, Nick, you've told Lizzy you've volunteered?' he beamed.

'To help out?' I asked. 'Continuity man? Props?'

'To be Adam to your Eve,' Nick told me blandly. 'Delving while you spin. Giving in to your temptations. Eating the apple from your hand.' He looked down at me quite seriously, though one eyebrow was quizzically raised. 'Passing you the fig leaves.'

'*You?*'

'I'm sure we're all delighted,' Clive said. 'I hadn't thought to ask him before, because he's been here so infrequently in recent years, but now he'll be able to make most of the rehearsals, so that's all right. And it's only one fairly short scene, isn't it?'

'Er—yes,' I agreed, still taken aback.

'If I do miss any rehearsals, Lizzy can put me through my paces at home,' Nick suggested. 'I'll be based up at the Hall from now on.'

'I'm sure we're all very glad to hear that,' Marian said warmly.

'Oh, there's Annie,' I exclaimed, spotting her walking in. 'I thought she'd be going to the other rehearsals on Thursdays?'

'She's very kindly going to assist the vicar, too, since he hasn't done this before,' Clive said, then clapped his hands and announced into the resultant silence, 'To your places, please!'

Everyone separated to his or her group. Mine

211

was small, since I was in charge of only the Fall of Satan, the Creation and my own scene in the Garden of Eden.

We began with the Fall of Satan, which is basically just the Voice of God (which I read, in Roly's absence) and Lucifer, plus nine entirely silent angels.

As always, God has the last word: 'I am reet disappointed in thee, Lucifer, thou art too sharp for thine own good. I loved thee like a son, yet thou art naught but a foul fiend, fit only for t'pit of damnation. Get thee gone!'

After this, Lucifer vanishes in a puff of yellow smoke, signifying the sulphurous fumes of Hell, with a receding wail—or in some years a shriek, depending on the interpretation of the role. At any rate, he vanishes. We ran through it a couple of times, then I released the angels to go over to the vicar's corner, where they were required during the Nativity to join with the shepherds and Three Wise Men in a stirring rendition of 'Silent Neet, 'Oly Neet' around the manger.

The Creation is a monologue by the Voice of God, with sound effects off, and after I'd read through that I handed over the directing to Lucifer while I put Nick through his paces as Adam. He refused a script and had evidently been studying the video of last year's Mystery, because he was word perfect and you couldn't fault his Lancashire accent.

It went smoothly right up to the point where he asked, 'What are thou eating, Eve?'

I replied: ''Tis a fruit the snake told me were reet tasty—and see, yonder birds peck at it and come to no ill. Dost thou want a bite, flower?'

I offered him an imaginary apple and he said warmly, 'From you, darling, *anything*!'

'That's not in the script,' Lucifer objected.

'I thought we could change the script if we liked?' Nick said innocently.

'Only if it's an improvement—this is *serious*,' I said severely. 'Stop messing about.'

'I was serious,' he protested, and Lucifer grinned. I was just glad I'd sent the angels away, reducing the audience by nine in one stroke.

'And don't think me coy, but on the night, how do we preserve our modesty, Lizzy? I've forgotten.'

'In my case, with a very long wig and a bodystocking. The last Adam wore a pair of beige swimming trunks and carried a strategically placed leather bucket. Apparently, in the old days Adam and Eve used to speak their lines standing behind boards painted to look like bushes.'

'I'll see what I can do,' he said gravely. 'Is it a *big* bucket?'

I gave him a stern look: we seemed to be rapidly reverting to the innuendo and sparring of our teenage years, and this was a Nick I'd pretty well forgotten ever existed. Perhaps the euphoria of pending divorce had brought it out in him again?

'Thou hath tasted t'fruit of knowledge that wor forbidden thee and found it sweet—yet shall it be bitter henceforth on thy tongue!' read Lucifer, in his temporary role as Voice of God, though still grinning. We stopped for refreshments after that, before I ran everyone through their lines again: I would work on the movements and check the props and costumes during later rehearsals.

'That'll do for tonight,' I said finally, and went to see how Annie and Gareth were getting on with the

213

Nativity cycle.

Dave Naylor from the garage, as Joseph, was wheeling Mary to Bethlehem on the back of an old-fashioned butcher's boy bike. On the night of the performance a star lantern is hauled slowly across the stage on a wire, a very pretty effect.

'Not far to go now, luv. Bethlehem's on t'horizon, ower yonder.'

Mary, who was inspecting her fuchsia-painted fingernails, replied absently, 'The sooner the better, chuck, for my time's close—but will we find a place t'lay our heads?'

'I'll find thee a roof ower thy head this night, flower,' Joseph promised, 'no matter what, don't thee worry thi'sen.'

'So,' the vicar said to Annie, 'the bike represents the donkey. But there *is* a real donkey on the night, is there?'

'Not any more. We stick to the bike for the performance, too.'

Gareth looked baffled.

'We used to have a donkey,' I chipped in, 'but it was more trouble than it was worth, and when it died of old age someone suggested the bike. The rack on the front is really handy for carrying baby Jesus on the flight into Egypt later, too.'

'Er . . . yes,' he agreed. 'I suppose it would be.'

I looked critically at Mary, who worked at the hairdresser's in Mossedge. 'I hope Kylie's going to lose the false fingernails and not chew gum on the actual night.'

'Yes, she's really taking it very seriously,' Annie assured me. 'She said she was going to put that cushion up her T-shirt tonight even though it's not a costume rehearsal, so she'd get the right posture for sitting on the bike.'

'That's the spirit,' Nick said, having followed me over.

Clive clapped his hands again, thanked everyone for coming and said he would see them every Tuesday until Christmas.

'Now we all go and unwind in the pub,' Annie informed Gareth.

'Oh, *do* we?' He was looking a little dazed, as well he might, but his eyes when they rested on Annie were almost dog-like in their devotion, which was bound to appeal to her.

'Where's Jasper tonight?' Nick asked me as we left.

'At home. One of his friends is staying over and I left them pizza ready to heat up, and some strawberries dipped in chocolate as a treat.'

'You're a good—if weird—mother,' he commented, as we all trooped out of the door onto the green, where Ritch Rainford stood leaning against a tree, smoking.

Marlboro man.

Until that moment I'd entirely forgotten what he'd said about turning up—not that I'd really thought he'd meant it in the first place. I stopped dead and Nick practically fell over me.

Ritch ground the cigarette out under his heel and walked over rather beautifully, as if the cameras were on him. 'Hi Lizzy, good rehearsal?'

He glanced around at the others, smiling generally, like warm sunshine. 'Lizzy said she thought you wouldn't mind if I tagged on tonight to the pub?'

'No, I didn't!' I muttered half under my breath, though clearly Nick thought it was an assignation

215

because he gave me a dirty look. I couldn't see what it'd got to do with him anyway, though, even if I had been making assignations with Ritch, except, I suppose, that it was a bit early for his cousin's widow to be involved with another man.

But I wasn't involved, and I was sure Ritch couldn't be seriously interested in me, so perhaps he just wanted to get out and meet the locals.

'I'm Ritch Rainford, you know,' he told everyone. 'I've just moved into the village.'

Fortunately, most of them did know who he was and swept him along with us. Some of the locals were certainly glad to meet him: Kylie was hanging on to his every word, and she's terribly pretty despite two nose rings and shocking pink hair, so I might well be worrying needlessly.

At the pub, which was rather full, I managed to slide onto a bench seat next to Annie. She had Gareth on her other side and he was looking about him as if he'd never been in such a place before, which for all I know he hadn't, an innocent abroad. But he was in safe hands.

Ritch's arrival had caused a minor sensation and, even if he'd wanted to sit by me, which I dare say he didn't, by the time he'd disentangled himself from his admirers Nick had got there first.

He rang the bell on the wall behind my head. 'This has got to be one of the few pubs left where you can ring for service and have your drinks brought over,' he said with satisfaction. 'That way, you don't lose your seat when you get up.'

Ritch pulled up a chair opposite and, leaning over, said in his warm, intimate, liquid-chocolate voice, 'So . . . rehearsals go well, Lizzy? What part are you playing?'

216

'Eve, and yes, we made a good start.'

'And Nick is playing Adam, Annie tells me, now the original actor has had to drop out,' Gareth said. 'Keeping it in the Pharamond family!' He smiled around genially.

'Really? I wish I'd known about it because *I'd* have loved to have played Adam to Lizzy's Eve!' Ritch said. 'She could tempt me to anything!'

'I'm sure you'd have been brilliant, but the actors need to be local people, because of the commitment,' Annie explained diplomatically. 'I expect you're much too busy to give up all that time!'

When our drinks came, the barmaid also apologetically handed me a folded paper. 'Landlord says he's sorry to bother you, Mrs Pharamond, but if you could see your way to settling up this bill, he'd be very grateful.'

I unfolded it and glanced at the total, which was pretty huge. Nick leaned over and took it from my hand, though I tried to snatch it back. 'Tom's bar tab? I'll take it back with me to add to the rest, for Roly to settle.'

'I wish you'd give it back! I don't see why Roly should have to settle all Tom's bills—and for goodness' sake, how many more are there?' I added despairingly.

'Oh, I should think that's about the last,' he said, tucking it into his jeans pocket, from where I certainly wasn't going to try to retrieve it.

I glowered at him, but he smiled blandly and turned to talk to Marian Potter. Kylie had cornered Ritch's attention again—he was either giving her his autograph or his phone number, or possibly both. On my other side, Annie and Gareth were totally engrossed in their own conversation.

The noise level in the packed bar was now so high it was hard to hear what anyone who wasn't right next to you was saying, though I nodded and smiled at friends who seemed to be mouthing in my direction. After a while, feeling I'd had enough, I nudged Nick in the ribs with my elbow.

He grunted and turned.

'Do you think you could let me out? I'd like to go home.'

Ritch caught my eye and, leaning forward until his golden head practically touched mine, said, 'Are you going, Lizzy? I'll walk you home.'

'No need,' Nick said, draining his pint and slamming down the empty tankard, 'I'm going the same way.'

'But I'd *like* to,' Ritch said stubbornly, half-rising to his feet.

'Do stay, Ritch!' I said hastily. 'Nick has to walk right past my cottage to get to the Hall anyway, so we might as well go together.'

Better the devil you know, after all.

Ritch looked at me, eyes bluer than cornflowers and, I'm sure, as sincere as a quagmire. 'Right . . . well, I'll ring you, then.'

'Ring you about what?' Nick demanded as soon as we were outside in the blessedly cool, quiet evening.

'Pet-sitting Flo, his bull terrier—and I'm so sorry to drag you away from your long and clearly engrossing conversation with Marian.'

'I wanted the secret ingredient in her Lancashire hotpot recipe,' he said simply.

'Oh.'

There was a silence as we walked up the quiet

218

village street and along the lane. Then, as we turned through the stone gateposts of the Hall, I said, following my somewhat tortuous train of thought, 'What do you think about drinking your own pee?'

He stopped dead, though it was a bit too dark to make out his expression. '*What?* You do say the damnedest things! Do you mean like on the *Bounty*, when they ran out of water and there was nothing else? At least, I *think* it was the *Bounty*.'

'No, it's some health thing—supposed to be good for you.'

'I do vaguely remember reading about it, now I come to think about it,' he said slowly, 'but I don't think it's likely to take off, Lizzy! You aren't thinking of trying it, are you?'

'God no!' I shuddered. 'Horrible thought.'

'Why are we talking about it, then?' he asked reasonably.

'I know someone who does it and I just wondered. It seems very odd to me.'

'It seems very odd to me, too,' he agreed. 'Lizzy—'

'What?'

'Nothing!' he snapped abruptly and, abandoning me outside the cottage, turned and strode off into the darkness, back towards the drive.

*   *   *

'Hi, Mum, nice night?' Jasper asked as I staggered wearily in. He was collecting Cokes and an indigestible assortment of snacks out of the fridge.

'Don't ask!'

He grinned. 'We're playing computer games in

my room. OK if we drop Stu home on the way to the dig in the morning? It's not far out of the way.'

'If you can get him up that early,' I agreed. '*And* me. I'm off to bed, I'm shattered!'

I did look for the chocolate strawberries first, though, but they'd all gone. I ate a slice of cold cheese and onion pizza instead, followed by a frozen banana dipped in maple syrup and chopped nuts.

It's no wonder I had bad dreams.

CHAPTER 17: TART

Most villages have a summer fête but in Middlemoss, for reasons long forgotten, we have ours in mid-September. Despite this, the weather is always Indian summer good, which is generally thought to be a reward from on high for performing our local Mystery Play so faithfully every year.
The Perseverance Chronicles: A Life in Recipes

Annie and the vicar were also helping with the second Mystery Play rehearsal and I popped down under the pretext of dropping off the bags of candyfloss she'd asked me to make for the fête, though really I was simply curious to see how the other scenes were going.

I arrived just as Satan was tempting Jesus. 'Si'thee, Jesus, tha's been biding here in t'wilderness some time now,' he said. 'Art though not famished? Would thee not like a bite of Hovis and a sup of brew?'

'Nay, gi'ower—there's nowt thou can tempt me wi', for thy beautiful face hides a foul heart,' responded Dave Naylor's son Gary, bringing an interesting touch of Goth gloom to the part. 'Man can't live b'bread alone and I want none of thy offerings—get thee gone!'

'I don't remember anyone mentioning Hovis before,' I commented to Annie, handing her the bags of candyfloss.

'No, I think that's a touch of Gary's own,' she agreed. 'I only hope he doesn't turn the water into

Alcopop during the Miracles!'

Then the actors were called for the Resurrection and I left before Marian could rope me in for anything.

Most of the indigent population spent the week before the fête polishing their marrows, arranging flowers, baking, or labelling jars of preserves and pickles, for the various prizes were always strongly contested. Annie and I were no exceptions: her cheese scones always swept the board and her fruit tea bread was legendary.

I enter only a few categories (but usually win them), among them Best Plate Apple Pie and Best Middlemoss Marchpane, the latter being a local delicacy consisting of an open mincemeat tart in an almond pastry case, the top water-iced and criss-crossed with marzipan strips. Yummy.

*   *   *

As expected, on Saturday morning the warm sun shone down on the small field next to the village hall where two marquees had been erected. They were the same ones used to keep the local sheep dry during lambing and they are also hired out for wedding receptions, so we've all come to associate the smell of damp wool with celebrations.

The fête is always run with military precision by Marian and Clive, who I'm sure would both spontaneously combust from sheer, pent-up excess energy if they did not have the entire management of every activity that goes on in the Mosses.

One or two of the minor celebrities now living amongst us had probably half-expected to be asked to open the fête, but Mimi always does it, having assumed the role as of right on the death of Unks' wife years ago. It would certainly be more than the Potters' lives were worth to attempt to change something so fixed in her head.

Wearing a drab cotton safari skirt suit sporting many pockets, slightly muddy Gertrude Jekyll boots and incongruously lacy cotton gloves, Mimi briskly admonished the gathered throng to spend lots of money, because the church roof had seen better days and, with no more ado, declared the fête open.

Then she leaped from the podium with surprising agility and trotted over to the plant stall, which she appeared to think was some kind of free lucky dip for gardeners, snatching up anything that took her fancy and leaving poor Juno to pay for (and carry) it all, like a royal lady-in-waiting.

Ted, the old gardener who helps her up at the Hall, hovered at her elbow, offering unwanted advice in an agonised bleat: 'You don't want that, Miss Mimi! *That* won't do well, Miss Mimi, not in our soil it won't—and who's going t'plant all of 'em, that's wor *I'd* like t'know?'

He gloomed away unheeded until Juno suggested he help carry everything to the Daimler, at which point he switched to the subject of his bad back and melted away into the crowd, so I gave her a hand instead.

I thought I might as well, since I felt at rather a loose end: Jasper was at his dig, which meant that this was the first year I'd come here alone, and it felt odd . . . but it was something I was quickly going to have to get used to. In fact, he'd probably just been good-naturedly humouring me the last year or two by coming with me!

The sudden realisation that life wasn't ever going

to be the Lizzy and Jasper Show again was almost unbearably poignant. How thin and near-transparent the folds of time are! I could almost step through them into another dimension, where the child Jasper would put his hot, sticky small hand in mine, dragging me towards the swingboats, or to ride his favourite giraffe on the little roundabout . . . I could see him excitedly dipping into the bran tub, or clutching some cheap, hideous, furry toy I'd spent pounds winning for him.

I'm a sentimental idiot: even the smell of the toffee apples made the tears come to my eyes.

When I'd helped load Mimi's haul into the Daimler I did a stint behind the counter of the hoopla stall, where the bags of candyfloss I'd made were hung up as prizes. (I'd given the borrowed candyfloss maker back to Annie, because it was such fun I'd splashed out on one of my own.)

Annie usually got roped into organising the children's races, where she was very popular, since she could always be guaranteed to have pockets bulging with little prizes for any disconsolate losers—sherbet dabs, jelly worms and flying saucers.

I had quite a good view of the goings-on from the hoopla stall, but there was no sign of Nick, who is so tall that his dark head can usually be spotted above any crowd. And Ritch must have been working, for once, for otherwise I was sure he wouldn't have been able to resist treating the peasantry to the sight of his golden magnificence.

But Polly, brazen as ever, was there with a group of rowdy friends, though I noticed she avoided me—*and* Caz, when he emerged from the shadows of the beer tent to perform his part, with silent and ferocious concentration, among the morris dancers.

The Mosses morris team eschew the traditional white clothes, hats and streamers in favour of all-black outfits, including leather waistcoats, and you really wouldn't want to try to tie a bell on any of them.

After this, Caz applied his skills to the coconut shy, awarding the resultant pink teddy bear to Ophelia, who seemed to be constantly near him while looking as if she didn't know quite why. She also suddenly appeared *very* pregnant, even under the bunny smock.

I noticed the way Annie and the vicar gravitated together between their various duties like those magnetic ladybirds—so it must be love, love, love! But if so, it's a strange, old-fashioned, Jane Austen-ish love, with no declarations or physical contact whatsoever.

While I'm sure they think their passion is a big secret (and it certainly seems to be a secret from each other), I expect the whole parish is indulgently watching the progress of their romance with almost the same avidity they confer on the twice-weekly episodes of *Cotton Common*.

Annie's cookery lessons now seemed to take place most evenings when Gareth wasn't otherwise engaged, and they'd been seen together walking rescue dogs up near the RSPCA kennels. But they had *not* been observed holding hands, or engaging in any other lover-like activities.

In the absence of her parents, I could see I'd soon have to ask him if his intentions were honourable, or this state of affairs could go on indefinitely. And if they married, that would be yet another change: for though of course Annie and I

225

would always be best friends, since she had fallen in love with Gareth I already saw much less of her than I used to.

Ever felt totally isolated in a crowd? I was just wallowing in a murky trough of self-pity when I was distracted by spotting something that made me doubt the evidence of my own eyes. So when Jojo and Mick came to try their hands at the hoopla (they were useless, but I gave them a bag of candyfloss each anyway), I said curiously, 'I didn't just see Caz and Ophelia sharing a *hot dog*, did I?'

'Caz told her there wasn't any meat in hot dogs,' Jojo said, 'and the stupid bat believed him, so God knows what she thinks they make them out of. ARG's thrown her out. I shopped her—living with a gamekeeper on the hit list!' He looked around furtively to see if anyone could overhear.

'Your secrets are safe with me, Jojo,' I assured him. 'I'm glad ARG's thrown Ophelia out and I hope you two aren't going to do any more silly things. Can't you just join the Green Party, and Friends of the Earth and that kind of thing, and lobby peacefully for what you want?'

Mick gave me a pitying look but didn't deign to answer this question. 'I expect it's just the pregnancy that's made her go weird,' he suggested. 'She might be all right afterwards.'

'Doesn't that depend on how you define "weird"?'

'Nah,' Jojo said, 'she'll be shacked up with him by then. He's already got her twisted round his little finger. He even hangs around your cottage on the nights when we're practising, so he can take her home.'

I could see there was a bit of jealousy going on,

but you could hardly blame Caz for keeping tabs on a girl who so notoriously found it difficult to say no to other men. Somebody needed to.

'He hangs around my cottage anyway,' I said. 'He has the use of the freezer in one of the outbuildings, and also it's part of the estate, so he keeps an eye on things.'

'He's certainly keeping an eye on Ophelia,' Mick said.

'Are they really going to move in together?'

'They pretty nearly are already—matter of time,' said Jojo disgustedly.

'Mum's the word about ARG,' Mick said, tapping his nose as they moved away.

'*Mummer's* the word,' I amended, watching them shamble off. At least, unlike Tom's avaricious surfer friends, they were mostly harmless. I didn't feel any need to shop them to anyone, including Nick, because I was sure they'd given up targeting the estate for the moment, and targeting *me* had been all Ophelia's doing.

'We're going home,' Juno said, suddenly bobbing up next to me out of the throng, Mimi in tow carrying bags of popcorn, candyfloss and a half-eaten hot dog. 'Forgot to mention, Nick said to tell you he was coming, but he'd be late.'

'If he doesn't come soon it'll all be over,' I said. 'And I can't see why he thought it mattered to me whether he was coming or not. *I* don't care.'

'Don't care was made to care,' Mimi chanted. 'My governess used to say that.'

'Well, come along—you're overexcited,' Juno said firmly. 'Tears before bedtime!'

'She used to say that, too,' Mimi said, being borne away in the direction of the car. I would have said 'sick before bedtime' was more likely than tears.

The flaps of the marquees had been firmly closed while the vicar and two other local worthies judged the exhibits, but were now thrown back. I felt fairly complacent about the outcome. After several years of walking off with golds in two or three categories, I was already counting my book tokens and debating whether to give them to Jasper, or blow them on myself for a change.

So, when I was relieved of duty on the stall, I strolled over there, prepared to be gracious and modest as I collected my prizes. And I had won Best Fruit Chutney and Best Middlemoss Marchpane—but Nick, a surprise late entry, had beaten me into second place for Best Plate Apple Pie.

I stared at the gilt-edged card with his name on, feeling surprisingly infuriated, as though he had performed a mean and underhand trick. Several local ladies were looking secretly pleased to see me pipped for gold this time, and there was some nudging and whispering as Nick, doing his silently materialising trick, reached past me and collected his prize.

'Congratulations,' I said through gritted teeth, while fanning myself slightly ostentatiously with my own handful of cards. 'Was that Mrs Gumball's recipe?'

'No, a variation of my own,' he said, smiling modestly, then was engulfed in a tide of congratulatory and admiring women. I stalked out of the tent.

Next year he wouldn't find it so easy, as I told him when he walked home with me. Not that I wanted him to walk home with me: I pretended not to hear him when he called out, 'Wait for me, Lizzy!'

Catching up, he demanded, 'Are you sulking?'

'Why on earth should I sulk? And anyway, I never sulk!'

'Oh, no? Isn't this the cold shoulder because I won the pie prize? Do you have to be the queen of *all* the puddings?'

'Don't be silly,' I said, striding briskly off again.

'You show me yours and I'll show you mine?' he said suggestively.

'*What?*' I exclaimed, coming to a stop and turning to stare at him.

'Apple pie recipe,' he explained innocently.

'No way!' I snapped.

* * *

Apart from popping out to do a couple of pet-sitting jobs for Annie, I spent most of that Sunday making Christmas cakes: one big one for us and the little ones for the Senior Citizens' hampers. I knew I would need to pass on the small cake tins to someone else at the CPC next day, since we were all to make six each.

My arm certainly ached after all that stirring, but the cottage smelled totally delicious, and Jasper scraped the mixing bowls out with a teaspoon, just the way he'd always done.

* * *

'What gift is the WI giving the Senior Citizens along with the hampers this year?' I asked Marian

229

at the CPC meeting.

'It's some kind of fleecy blanket with arms to snuggle into while watching the telly, called a Slanket.'

'I like the sound of that, I wouldn't mind one myself,' Annie said.

'I never seem to sit down long enough to make it worthwhile,' I said.

'Me neither,' agreed Faye. 'Coming to the CPC meetings is the only time off I ever seem to get.'

'If I feel at all chilly when I sit down with my bedtime tot of whisky to watch the news at ten, then I wrap myself in my pashmina,' Miss Pym said. 'It is light, but warm.'

I certainly couldn't imagine her wrapped in anything going by such an inelegant name as a Slanket!

I handed over the little cake tins to Faye, who was next on the rota, and then we discussed what extra treats to make for the hampers—rum truffles, peppermint creams, *petits fours* and things like that. I already make most of those anyway, for ourselves and for gifts, so it would be no trouble to make extra.

Afterwards, when everyone had gone, I rang Unks to remind him to get his solicitor, Smithers, to tell me how much Tom's debts came to once he had wound up his affairs, but he said it would be a while yet, and not to worry about it.

Tom really didn't have any affairs to wind up, so I suspected Roly was going to take care of it and not tell me at all, but he was vague about it and hard to pin down.

Still, after many delays, the insurance company had disbursed a paltry sum to compensate me for my lost 2CV—barely enough to buy a decent bicycle, let alone another car. Just as well I had had Tom's van to swap for the Land Rover.

But I used some of the money to order knitted silk long johns and a vest at off-season prices—quite a bargain. They were white and so I would have to tint them flesh pink when they arrived, so they wouldn't look too obvious from a distance under my Eve bodystocking, wig and figleaves. This year, I would be a *very* well-padded Eve.

They'd be useful afterwards in winter for gardening too, though not sexy, but since I wasn't intending to show my underwear to anyone, sexy was entirely irrelevant. Anyway, I wouldn't have the time or energy, since suddenly we were into the peak season of mellow fruitfulness so for the foreseeable future I'd be jamming, freezing, salting, chutneying, bottling and cordial making as though Famine were just outside waiting to knock on the door. Dried apple rings were already hanging in festoons above the stove; wine bubbled in every corner and bunches of onions, lavender and bay leaves dangled from the wooden rack above the kitchen table.

I always felt much happier—sort of safer—once the cottage was full to bursting with a huge store of food and drink. I must naturally have a siege mentality.

I dashed out between jobs to see to Ritch's dog. He wasn't there, but I had seen him once or twice on the evenings when he'd turned up to jam with the Mummers in Tom's old workshop. He'd taken to calling into the cottage kitchen afterwards, where I plied him with food and drink while I worked, just like everyone else who dropped by.

I rather liked the company. Jasper was out much more in the evenings, another foretaste of my solitary existence soon to come—and I didn't mind the flirting now I knew it was just his manner, nothing personal. Besides, he was decorative to have around *and* he said it would be impossible to make a better apple pie than mine, it was perfect.

While I was seeing to Flo, Dora Tombs told me Kylie had been spotted sneaking out of Ritch's house at the crack of dawn, and said he'd better watch out when her soldier fiancé comes home on leave.

'And she's not the only one!' she added darkly. 'A regular harem, he seems to be running. He's a charmer—like honey to humming birds, he is.'

'That's terribly poetic, Mrs T!'

'Saw them when I went over to Canada, to see our Sara,' she explained. 'Vancouver Island—wings whizzing round like bike wheels.'

'Ritch reminded me of Honeycomb Crunch the very first time I saw him. You know, a bit like cinder toffee?'

She gave me a sharp look. 'And what does Mr Nick remind you of, then?'

'Nick?' I said, surprised. 'Oh, hot spicy curry every time!'

'Better for you than toffee,' she remarked cryptically. 'Honey or not.'

*   *   *

Clive and Marian Potter had got to hear the rumour about Kylie, and confided to me at the second Mystery Play rehearsal that they thought it conduct unbecoming, considering her role.

232

'Just look at her over there, playing the Virgin Mary,' Marian said, scandalised. 'Butter wouldn't melt!'

'Mary, thou art chosen as the mother of the Son of God, so think thisen lucky,' the Angel Gabriel was telling her.

'By heck, then, thee'd better have words with my Joseph smartish and explain t'matter,' she riposted forthrightly, 'or t'wedding's off!'

'It's probably just gossip,' I told Marian and Clive, but when Ritch, who was waiting for us outside again, swooped down and kissed me a smacker right on the lips, they exchanged meaningful glances as if to say, 'What, you too, Eve?'

Actually, I thought the way he and Kylie avoided each other in public was much more obvious than if they'd been entwined for the whole evening. I was sure they had an assignation set up for later, because although Ritch sat next to me and flirted outrageously, when I got up to go he didn't offer to walk me home this time—I went alone.

Nick had already left, much earlier. Maybe he'd got the Lancashire hotpot recipe out of Marian? Mission accomplished.

*   *   *

Jasper was home when I got there, eating cheese on toast with Ginny snuffling hopefully round his feet for crumbs. He said Nick had phoned to say he'd found a taker for the big greenhouse, and it was to be dismantled tomorrow morning and removed on a lorry.

'I don't see why he didn't tell me that earlier!'

233

'He said even with your clothes on he found you so distracting as Eve that he forgot, and goodness knows what he would be like at the actual performance.'

'He *did*? What kind of thing is that to say to my son?' I demanded, scandalised.

Jasper grinned.

'And he doesn't mean it either,' I said snappily. 'He's just being sarcastic and horrible.'

'No, he's not: he likes you, Mum.'

'I think I know your uncle Nick by now *and* all his little ways,' I said firmly.

*   *   *

After dropping Jasper and Ginny off bright and early at the dig next morning, I went home and changed into my oldest jeans, ready to help dismantle the greenhouse.

But the new owner proved to be one of those men who doesn't recognise any woman's existence in a business deal and so addressed himself totally to Nick, who was hanging around looking taciturn. I returned to the kitchen and my jam making.

When they had gone and I went out, I found my little domain totally changed, with the last plants that had been inside it pathetically huddling together in the open, as if for warmth.

It was another thing sorted out, though—and the huge TV has already gone, after I put a card in the post office window. On the proceeds, Jasper had chosen a small one with an integral DVD player to take to university with him. I only hoped he was going to work and not spend his entire student loan on films, drink and stuff.

I'd begun to notice that if Jasper was home when Ritch called by, he seemed to be in and out of the kitchen all the time, and having six foot of sardonic teenage youth critically observing him rather cramped Ritch's flirting. I didn't know why Jasper disliked him, unless he had joined the ranks of those trying to pair me up with Nick (I was not blind to all the hints various people, including Juno and Mimi, had been dropping), though I could tell them right then that this was only wishful thinking and not a horse that was *ever* going to run.

But clearly everyone saw Ritch as some kind of threat, to either my heart or my virtue (or both), for when Jasper wasn't there, Caz seemed to be hanging about the yard until Ritch left, instead.

And I was forever finding Nick wandering about the place, as if he owned it . . . which I supposed he sort of did, come to think of it, though he didn't own *me*.

In fact, my cottage seemed suddenly to have become one of the most popular spots in the Mosses.

I invented a recipe for potato and nut biscuits, which came out so well I tried making chocolate flapjacks with mash, too.

However, Jasper said they were more like 'mudflaps', so a little more experimentation was clearly in order.

CHAPTER 18: SIMMERING GENTLY

I've been potting hyacinth bulbs and putting them away in a dark cupboard today—pink, blue and white. It seems indulgent to take the time, when there's so much to do in the garden and the blackberries still cluster thickly on the brambles, begging to be picked and turned into wine, jelly and jam. But when they flower, they'll be like a breathy promise of spring to come.

And we might need it, for a heavy crop of berries on all the bushes means a hard winter, according to old country lore.

The Perseverance Chronicles: A Life in Recipes

The skiing underwear I'd ordered was sitting in a neat brown parcel on my doorstep when I got back from dropping Jasper at the dig one morning, so I went straight upstairs to try it on.

It fitted tightly, but I had quite a job getting the old, stewed-tea-coloured bodystocking on over it (one of us was losing our stretch with age—or maybe *both* of us).

When I looked in the mirror I saw that I presented a strangely padded and seamed appearance, like an unsuccessful home-made Cabbage Patch doll, especially once I got the totally unrealistic flaxen wig out of its storage box and completed the ensemble.

Sexy it was not, and when I heard someone walk into the hall downstairs I nearly *died*: my heart certainly stopped and I went still as a mouse. There was no way I was going to let anyone see me like this!

'Lizzy?' called a familiar voice.

'Oh, thank God!' I muttered devoutly. I'd quite forgotten I'd arranged for Annie to come over and help me sort out Tom's clothes and personal stuff, a task I'd been cravenly putting off.

'Come up—I'm in the bedroom,' I called.

She clumped upstairs and I turned to face the door, striking a soulful pose and twiddling one long gold ringlet round my fingers.

'Have you already started?' she was saying as she walked in. 'I'm a bit late, I—'

Her jaw dropped and her stunned expression sent me into near hysteria. After a dumbstruck minute she started to giggle too and soon we were both entirely incoherent.

'So,' I said finally, trying to wipe the tears from my face with a long tress and finding that nylon wasn't very absorbent, 'you *don't* think I should play the Eve part for laughs, then?'

'Oh, Lizzy, can you *imagine* Nick's face if he walked on and saw you like that?' she said, sitting down on the bed, limp with laughter.

'I could—but I'd rather freeze to death first!'

'Well, you can't possibly, anyway. But perhaps if you bought a new Spandex bodystocking it might be warmer than that old one?'

'It hardly seems worth the expense when this is the last year I'll play Eve.'

'Never mind, you looked stunning, even in the old outfit, last year,' she said loyally, 'though quite indecent from a distance!'

'Speaking of indecent, I don't know what Nick intends wearing, if anything. Do you?'

'I asked him, in case he hadn't given it any

237

thought,' Annie said innocently. 'He said he'd ordered footless tights from a ballet-clothing place and would wear his cricket box under them to protect his modesty.'

That conjured up quite a vision . . . which I hastily dispelled, though not without some difficulty. 'He'll freeze,' I said with conviction. 'We *both* will!'

'I expect he'll be all right, because it's only a few minutes, the Garden scene, isn't it? Then you can rush into one of the loose boxes and put your warm clothes back on.'

'Still, that does it—if he's going to be half-naked, then I'm not going out there padded up like Michelin woman! A new Spandex outfit it is. I've still got some car insurance money.'

I thought I might even go completely mad and get myself a pretty frock, too, for Christmas dinner, which we always had up at Pharamond Hall. I couldn't remember when I'd last bought myself something new to wear that wasn't vital, like jeans.

I changed back into ordinary clothes and then we got down to sorting out Tom's stuff, which I'd collected up and pushed into his wardrobe or drawers out of sight.

'Jasper's taken a couple of things—cufflinks, mostly—but the rest can go to the charity shop, or in the recycling bin.'

'I'll take it all down to the Animal Shelter shop,' she offered. 'I brought the car up rather than walk, in case.'

Tom didn't have a huge wardrobe of clothes, so it didn't take long. I was so glad I wasn't doing it alone, though, because memories, mostly painful, tended to tumble out of every open door and drawer.

'How are you and Gareth getting on, Annie? You're seen almost everywhere together, like Siamese twins,' I teased, once we'd loaded her car and retired to the kitchen for a well-earned cup of coffee and a restorative plate of chocolate slab cake. 'And the cookery lessons too! Is he teaching you anything in return?'

'No,' she said, her face clouding over. 'Lizzy, I enjoy being with him, but I think he's just being friendly. I'm that type of girl, aren't I? Men don't think of me romantically at all, so I expect I'm exactly like a sister to him!'

'You daft bat!' I said, regarding her incredulously. 'He's absolutely dotty about you! When he looks at you he has that soppy sheep expression in his eyes, and every time he speaks to you he goes red as a beetroot. *And* he told me he thought you were very pretty!'

'He didn't!' Annie went pink with pleasure.

'He did.'

She looked at me doubtfully. 'Then why . . .? I mean, you must be wrong, Lizzy!'

'Oh, I'm sure he's just shy. Encourage him a bit.'

'I couldn't possibly! What if he only wants to be friends? Think how embarrassing it would be if I'd made a fool of myself and we had to go on meeting as if nothing had happened . . .'

'But you do fancy him, don't you, Annie? I mean, this *is* love's young dream and all that?'

'More love's not-so-young dream,' she said ruefully.

'Rubbish, we're still thirty-somethings, and that's a very good age for love.'

'It might be, but I daren't risk destroying my

239

friendship with Gareth to find out.'

'You won't. You wait and see.'

'You aren't going to do anything, are you?' Her soft, blue-grey eyes looked at me anxiously.

'No, of course not,' I reassured her quite untruthfully. 'I'll await events to prove me right and then I expect to be matron of honour at the wedding, in a mid-calf-length puce taffeta dress with those puffed shoulders that make you look five feet wide.'

'Not puce,' she said seriously. 'The church carpet and hassocks are scarlet, so it would clash.' Then she sighed, her eyes refocusing, as though abandoning a beautiful dream. 'Anyway, enough of *my* boring affairs, Lizzy—what about you? The whole village is talking about the way Ritch Rainford flirts with you!'

'Oh, come on, you must have realised I'm just a smokescreen for the women he *is* having affairs with, Kylie among others. But I do like him, and I enjoy flirting with him. At least he makes me feel I'm still attractive.'

'Perhaps, but it's making Nick jealous, haven't you noticed?'

I stared at her. 'Well, yes, but not jealous of me *personally*—he simply doesn't like Ritch paying attentions to his cousin's widow. Come to that, he just doesn't seem to like Ritch. But I'm sure his attitude's mainly a territorial thing.'

'I think you're wrong, and he's fond of you,' she said earnestly.

'Annie! It's bad enough Juno and Mimi—and now even Jasper—trying to matchmake, without you joining in!'

'Do they? I hadn't realised. But there, you

see—even the family think it would be a good thing if you got together!'

'Annie, it's not going to happen—and it would certainly be a marriage made in hell, not heaven.'

'I don't think Nick would agree with you,' she persisted stubbornly.

I considered it seriously for a minute, remembering the way he'd kissed me once or twice in a most uncousinly manner, and how he'd referred back to our short-lived romance as if he couldn't understand why it hadn't worked out . . . But apart from that, there wasn't anything to suggest he was harbouring an undying passion for me.

'No,' I said firmly, 'we bicker more than we agree, and drive each other mad: too many cooks again. He might still *fancy* me—I don't know—but he isn't in *love* with me.'

'So you're just friends—like Gareth and me?'

'Well, not quite. More sparring partners. The family—and probably the whole village, going by the hints Dora Tombs has been letting fall—just wants a neat and tidy ending: you in the parsonage, me in the Hall, all's well that ends well. Only life isn't like that.'

'I suppose not.'

She sighed sadly, but I was determined that at least her romance would turn out right. All Gareth needed was a bit of encouragement.

*   *   *

That evening Ophelia came round, driven by Caz in his ancient Land Rover (even more ancient than mine and painted with camouflage, just like him sometimes), and to my astonishment asked me if she could buy the quail!

'You haven't anywhere to keep them,' I pointed out, 'and anyway, what would you do with them? You won't eat them or the eggs, so you'll be overrun with male quail in no time.'

'No she won't, then,' Caz drawled, leaning against the bonnet, his khaki hat tipped over his nose.

Really, he's getting almost loquacious! It must be love. Anyone would think it was spring, the way Cupid's fiery darts are flying in all directions.

'There's the old piggery behind my cottage—I can keep them in that for now,' Ophelia said, rabbited at her lower lip a bit and added, 'I've decided to become vegetarian while I'm pregnant, *and* eat fish and eggs.'

'Good idea!'

She gave Caz a half-defiant look: 'But not flesh of *any* kind!'

What does she think fish are made of?

'Right, I'll start including more eggs in your basket of fruit and vegetables. I wasn't sure if you were eating them or not.'

'No, no, no, you shouldn't! It's too kind and . . . and I don't see why you *should* be kind,' she muttered, her bulging eyes taking on that sainted martyr look. 'I don't deserve it.'

'You may not, but we have to think of the baby. It needs good wholesome food to grow properly.'

'But you carry it all the way up to my cottage and it must be really heavy!' She wrung her hands in an anguished sort of way. Let's hope she is never holding a quail—or, indeed, the baby—when she's in one of these states. 'Don't—please don't do it

242

any more. Caz says he'll fetch it.'

'OK—that will be good. I'll leave the basket near the eggs in the outbuilding on Monday mornings, how about that?'

I couldn't really see Caz in the Little Red Riding Hood role with a basket, but that was his problem. Maybe he'd bring a backpack.

She nodded like a car mascot and then added, after another of her lip-chewing ruminations, 'Thank you for the bottled tomatoes.'

'I didn't give you any bottled tomatoes!'

She blinked slowly. 'Yes, you did. They were on the doorstep last night, with that yellow checked material tied over the lid, like all your jars of stuff.'

'Gingham? I bought a whole roll of it years ago, and never got to the end of it. But I didn't leave any jars of anything on your doorstep.'

'But . . . it must be you. I don't know anyone else who bottles tomatoes.'

I had a sudden horrible thought. 'I know someone who *tried* to,' I said grimly. 'Polly Darke! And they gave me botulism or something equally ghastly.'

'But she's not . . . she isn't . . . she wouldn't . . .' Ophelia trailed off, and then wrung her skinny hands together again distractedly, her eyelids frantically fluttering.

'Look, I guessed she was the one who made you do the ARG stuff to me, out of sheer spiteful jealousy. There was no one else it could have been.'

'But Caz made her stop, so perhaps she's sorry now, and this is a present?' Ophelia suggested. 'But I don't want her peace offering!'

'If it *is* a peace offering. We know she's spiteful enough to do something nasty. I'd throw it away,

243

just in case, if I were you.'

'I'll do that,' Caz said, the stony expression on his face boding ill for Polly—though would she have tried something that might have harmed Ophelia's baby? I thought back to what I knew of her, which, due to my avoiding her as much as possible, was not a lot.

'I could be quite wrong about her, but it is odd that I was the only one who got the dodgy jar of tomatoes when she was handing them out to half the village that time,' I said slowly. 'And another thing: although I've only been to her house once for a book launch party, I was horribly sick afterwards, though I didn't hear of anyone else being taken ill.'

'Toadstool,' Caz said meaningfully.

'*Toadstool?*' For a minute I thought he'd run mad, then I remembered: 'You mean that poisonous one you showed me—was it in the basket of field mushrooms Polly brought me to swap for eggs?'

He nodded grimly.

'And wasn't it the kind you only get in woods, not open fields?'

He nodded again.

'Could she be that jealous and vindictive? It's so downright nasty!'

Caz shrugged.

'Well, if it is true, let's hope she doesn't present any more little gifts to other people disguised as my offerings! I'd better tell Marian Potter tomorrow that someone is maliciously leaving tainted jars of food that look just like mine on doorsteps and she will spread the word. And I'll stop covering the jars with anything except Cellophane from now on, even if they don't look as pretty!'

244

Ophelia had lost interest by now and wandered off to commune with the quail by means of little cheeping noises. She seemed to be frighteningly at one with them mentally, which didn't bode well for the intellect of her future offspring.

I followed over. 'So, what are you going to do with the quail?'

'Give them a happy life and I can sell the eggs, too. I think that's all right,' she said earnestly.

'OK, they're yours,' I agreed.

She was totally impractical, but I expected Caz would just quietly go in and do what had to be done with the birds when she wasn't looking.

They seemed to be settling down into a pair, though an odd couple they made. Maybe knowing secrets about each other forms a bond, for he was aware she was in ARG, and he'd told her what he did with the grey squirrels he caught. And Ophelia seemed very malleable, apart from a bit of occasional stubbornness, so I expected he'd slowly bend her into the shape he wanted over time.

Why did that make me think of brandy snaps?

Caz found some cardboard boxes, which he punched holes into, and loaded the quail up then and there, dismantling the pens and taking those, too, since I would have no further use for them.

What with the big bare space where the greenhouse used to be, and the lack of cheeping, moving feathers in the barn, things were looking quite deserted, apart from the hens and ducks. They'd all sheered off while Caz and Ophelia were there, but now came back looking for any pickings.

With a sigh, I went back into the cottage and looked out my recipe for brandy snaps, even though trying to wind them round the handle of a wooden spoon is such a pain that I couldn't usually be bothered.

*   *   *

Next day when I was on my way back from a spot of pet-sitting duty, I spotted Caz and Nick in the woods near the drive. Caz seemed to be talking, or at least, replying, which was amazing! Then they shook hands . . .

What was that all about? Had some kind of deal been done?

*   *   *

On Sunday we were invited up to lunch at the Hall. Actually, we had an open invitation, but sometimes I was too busy, or wanted to go out with Jasper for the day while I'd still got him.

Nick was cooking, as he often did because he said it gave Mrs Gumball a rest. Though she protested at having her kitchen taken over, I think she was quite pleased really: she was no spring chicken any more, after all.

He was in and out of the kitchen when I got there and spurned my offer of help, though he accepted Jasper's even though he only knows the theory of cooking and not the practicalities. So I left him to stew in his own *jus* and sat down at the dining table with the others.

Unks smiled at me fondly, then went back to reading the sports section of the Sunday paper.

'We're going on a garden tour by coach,' Mimi informed me chattily.

I stared at Juno. 'Is that a good idea?'

'Don't see why not—I'm fully fit again. I'll frisk her for knives, scissors and plastic bags before we set off, and I won't take my eyes off her for a minute within fifty paces of anything green. It's a late-booking bargain.'

Mimi smiled innocently.

'I don't think *you* will get a lot out of it, Juno,' I said. 'You could do with a more restful holiday, after your accident.'

'There are entertainments in the evenings at the various hotels,' Mimi said. 'It'll be fun. But Juno and me have got to share a room. People will think we're an odd couple.' She giggled.

'Pity, I was hoping to pick up a toyboy,' Juno said, 'preferably a rich one who could whisk me away from this madhouse.'

'She doesn't mean it,' Mimi confided to me. 'Her heart belongs to Sean Connery.'

'I've never been one of those romantics,' agreed Juno, 'but I like a man to be a man.'

'Do you think Nick is a macho man, Lizzy?' Mimi asked, with one of her disconcertingly clear looks, just as the man himself strode into the room carrying the soup tureen, with Jasper following up behind with a silver basket of bread.

'If macho is big, male and overbearingly bossy, yes,' I said sweetly.

Nick gave me one of his slaty looks, the purple-edged sort.

It was good soup, followed by roast beef and perfect Yorkshire puddings, and he'd made one of his apple pies for dessert, which I have to admit was delicious, though I certainly wasn't going to tell *him* so. Instead, I said the pastry was a little dry and asked for more cream.

247

Jasper and Nick were talking quietly in the kitchen when I carried through the dessert plates, and I hoped it was serious male stuff, because my attempt to discuss Safe Sex and STDs with Jasper certainly hadn't gone down too well.

Nick seems to be Confidant of the Moment—but not mine. Been there, done that, and once was enough!

I was stuffed to bursting point after the coffee, but then Nick practically dragged me back into the kitchen and made me taste three different coffee granitas before I left. When I said I didn't think any of them had that extra something, he went very sulky, even though (unlike what I said about the apple pie) it was quite true.

On the way home Jasper said I'd hurt Nick's feelings and I should have pretended one of the granitas was great, and I said, astonished, 'Why should I, when he's always so rude about *my* cooking?'

'But you know he doesn't mean it. He's just joking—it's affectionate.'

'I'm not so sure about that,' I said darkly.

Anyway, I'm never again going to tell a man something is wonderful when it's not. It's my un-New Year resolution.

CHAPTER 19: STIRRING

We're heading towards October and I'm catching up with the garden: clearing away the finished crops and storing layers of carrots in boxes for the winter. At the Christmas Pudding Circle the small cake tins changed hands yet again and soon we will have enough for all the Senior Citizens' hampers. When Marian first suggested we bake the cakes we also offered to make individual Christmas puddings; but it turned out that when the WI asked them for likes and dislikes, they all preferred bought microwavable puddings and cartons of ready-made custard.

The Perseverance Chronicles: A Life in Recipes

I passed on the warning about gifts of possibly tainted bottled goods being left on doorsteps by the simple method of mentioning it one morning at the Christmas Pudding Circle meeting. Marian especially is permanently plugged into the local grapevine via the post office, so by afternoon everyone within a five-mile radius would know, like dropping a pebble into a pond and watching the ripples spread.

After that I hadn't intended to give the matter much further thought. In fact, I was half inclined to think Ophelia's jar of tomatoes had been a gift from some well-meaning villager, who'd simply reused a gingham circle from something of mine. Goodness knows, I've supplied enough preserves and pickles to village fairs, fêtes and bazaars over the years!

But then Leila phoned me out of the blue in mid-afternoon while I was making a carrot cake and, to my complete astonishment, apologised for what she'd said at the funeral.

'Of course, much of it was true, but it was not the time or place for such matters. I had come simply to pay my last respects.'

'Quite . . . and . . . thank you,' I replied cautiously, though not sure quite what I was thanking her for.

'I see clearly now I was deceived by Tom and also, perhaps, by Nick. But that is life, so now I am resolved to stay single. Nick says he will still review my restaurant in his articles; it will not make a difference, our divorce,' she added, sounding surprised and slightly scornful of his magnanimity. 'So, we should all bury the hatchet and move on, yes?'

'Er, yes . . . and it's nice of you to phone me,' I said doubtfully, wondering if there was a catch, for example, exactly *where* she meant to bury the hatchet.

'I could do no less, after you sent me the peace offering, though a pot of blackberry jam, that is not sensible to put in the post, even packed so well.'

'Jam?'

'It says "Blackberry Jam: Middlemoss Autumn Fête" on the label, so I knew it must come from you.'

I'd provided some to be raffled off for charity, so it must be one of those. 'You haven't eaten any, have you?' I demanded urgently.

'No. I do not eat jam, it is not in my diet regime.'

'Then don't! I didn't send it, someone else did—

and I'm afraid it might be . . . tainted.'

'Tainted? You mean poisoned? Someone is trying to *kill* me? But that is ridiculous!' she said witheringly.

'No, I'm sure she doesn't intend to kill you, just make you sick and pin the blame onto me. She's tried the same thing with Ophelia Locke, but I wasn't sure—' I broke off. 'Oh, you don't know Ophelia, do you?'

'I know *of* her. I have been told she claims to be carrying Tom's child, but she sounds a type most hysterical and neurotic.'

'I suppose she is a bit,' I agreed, wondering who Leila's spy in the village was. 'But she is pregnant and there's a possibility it could be Tom's—about one in four, if you want the odds. But anyway, she found some bottled tomatoes on her doorstep the other day and assumed they were from me, and they weren't. And then I remembered once having a bad experience with bottled tomatoes someone gave me, and I got suspicious. Only it seemed so incredible that then I thought I must be imagining it.'

'But you are confusing me with all this talk of bottled tomatoes! Who—and why? And . . .' There was a pause. 'It is Tom's other woman doing this, that weird person, Polly something?'

'I think so,' I admitted. 'I can't imagine who else it could be, and there are a few too many coincidences. She's been blackmailing the local animal rights campaigners into targeting me, too, so I wouldn't put it past her.'

'I will set the police on to her!'

'There isn't any proof, so I don't think they could do anything, but I'm going to let her know that

251

she's found out, so she'll think twice before trying anything else!'

Leila still maintained that the police should be involved, but I was wary: what if they thought I'd done it myself, as a sort of double-blind?

But in the end she agreed she would do nothing for the present, and rang off, after adding that if I was ever in the vicinity of her restaurant there would always be a table free for me, an offer I thanked her for but was unlikely to take up.

*　　　*　　　*

When I next popped into Annie's cottage on the way to see to Flo, I told her exactly who I'd meant when I'd warned them at the CPC meeting that someone was leaving poisoned preserves on doorsteps. Then I retailed my conversation with Leila.

'Poor, poor woman!' she said sadly.

'There's nothing poor about Leila!'

'No, I meant Polly, to be so consumed with spite and jealousy that she could do such awful things!'

'Well, that's one way of looking at it,' I said. 'Trust you to feel sorry for her! And it's all very well playing these pranks on me and Leila, but Ophelia's pregnant and it might have made her really ill or harmed the baby! Goodness knows what she put in those tomatoes.'

'That's true, and she might do something else! Perhaps I ought to tell Gareth so he could go and reason with her?' she suggested doubtfully.

'Absolutely not! There's no way she's going to cast herself upon his bosom and weep tears of repentance, and it would be like sending Daniel

252

into the lioness's den.'

'What are we going to do, then?'

'I'm going to speak to Polly, preferably in a public spot with other people about. I'll tell her I know about her tricks, and if she does anything else I'll report her to the police. That should stop her.'

'Oh, I hope so,' Annie said earnestly. 'Perhaps it will shock her into realising how badly she's been behaving, so she can move on.'

'I wish she would move *away*,' I said, getting up. 'Well, must go and see to Flo on my way home. Ritch isn't going to be back until late and she's probably got all four paws crossed by now.'

'You really aren't falling for him, are you, Lizzy?' she asked anxiously.

'No, of course not, though if celibate widowhood ever palls on me, it's nice to know my options for random sex are still open.'

'Lizzy! You wouldn't!'

'Probably not—especially if he continues with *all* his dubious habits.'

*   *   *

In the afternoon Nick rang and *demanded* I go up to the Hall and taste his newest version of coffee granita, but I declined, since I was in the middle of a huge quince jelly-making operation by then and could hardly down tools at his bidding.

He slammed the phone down, but strode into my kitchen not ten minutes later, carrying an insulated box cradled in his arms like a baby.

'This one's perfect!' he said, the light of battle in his eyes and his dark hair sticking up in an angry crest. 'I defy you to find fault with it!'

'Look, I'm up to the elbows in this, I can't sit down and eat,' I protested, so he followed after me around the kitchen, feeding me teaspoons of granita as if I were a stubborn toddler. Much though I would have liked to find fault, however, I couldn't. The colour, taste and texture were all pure perfection.

When I said as much he tossed the spoon into the Belfast sink with a clatter, grabbed me and planted a triumphantly emphatic kiss on my lips before I could fend him off with the ladle.

'Mmm . . . you taste of the perfect coffee granita!' he murmured, half-closing his eyes.

'I don't know what else you'd expect, when you've been force-feeding me the stuff for the last ten minutes,' I snapped, taking a step back. We unpeeled rather stickily.

'You're a very messy jam maker,' he said severely.

'And you are a very messy cook, full stop. I've never seen anyone use so much equipment to make even the simplest dish.'

'Like my apple pie?' he said, a gleam in his eyes. 'Come on, Lizzy, you know there was nothing wrong with it last Sunday.'

'It wasn't bad,' I conceded, then I smiled at him innocently and asked, 'That granita . . . just what did you add to make it taste like that?'

'Wouldn't you like to know!' he said tantalisingly. 'Well, see you at the play rehearsal later, Eve!' Then, picking up his cold box, he walked out.

*　　　*　　　*

He was still being exasperating at the

rehearsal—and so were the Nine Angels, who kept gurning at each other when they thought I wasn't looking.

I didn't go to the pub afterwards, because I simply wasn't in the mood, but sneaked out of the side door and dashed home. Anyway, the kitchen was still a sticky mess and I wanted to clear that up and then, while still in quince mode, make some wine.

*   *   *

Friday was Jasper's last day at the dig and he returned smelling of real ale and with some kind of excavation certificate, with which he was highly pleased. I knew he'd been feeding Ginny pork scratchings at the pub after the dig, because she threw most of them up behind the kitchen door.

Jasper went straight off after dinner to stay for a couple of days with his friend Stu, whose family lived in Ormskirk, and although I wanted to spend every precious moment left with him before the start of his first university term, I didn't try to persuade him not to go. Instead, I drove him there and dropped him off myself, hoping Stu's mum was expecting Ginny, too—and thank heaven she came ready-house-trained.

I also hoped Jasper would behave himself, though frankly there are not many dens of iniquity in the lovely old market town of Ormskirk. But before he left home Unks gave him a *huge* amount of spending money. He must have had a win on the horses, to have so much cash about him.

'You'll be sensible, won't you, Jasper?' I said, hugging him before he got out of the Land Rover,

255

which he suffered me to do in a resigned sort of way.

'It's not *me* who needs to be sensible, when that Rainford man's forever dropping in and hanging out with you, or chatting you up in pubs,' he protested. 'Not to mention phoning you up and asking you to go round to his house all the time!'

'He's just being friendly, Jasper, and I only go round to his house to look after the dog.'

'I don't see why he can't look after his own dog.'

'Well, neither do I, really—or get one of his many girlfriends to do it.'

'So you *do* know about all the girls he takes back there, then?' He sounded relieved.

'Honestly, Jasper! I'd have to be deaf, dumb and blind not to, even if Dora Tombs didn't tell me. The whole village is talking about him, which at least means they've moved on from going over what your dad got up to with Leila and Polly, and taking bets on who the father of Ophelia's baby is,' I said tartly. 'Now, you stop worrying about me, because anyone would think I was some naive innocent out of a Victorian melodrama, about to be taken advantage of by the villain of the piece!'

'He does do that all the time in *Cotton Common*.'

'But not in real life,' I said firmly. 'And I'm not interested in Ritch that way—or any other man. I just want to be left alone with my hens, my garden and my recipes.'

Especially the search for the perfect apple pie and coffee granita . . .

'Try not to fall out with Uncle Nick while I'm away,' was his final admonishment as he removed his holdall and slammed the door. He must have been reading my mind—and bossiness seems to run

256

in the Pharamond blood, just like cooking.

*　　　*　　　*

I didn't get a chance to fall out with Nick, since it turned out that he had left for London and was then going on to Cornwall in search of fish recipes for some forthcoming article.

I felt a bit . . . piqued, I think is the word. I'd sort of got used to having him around again, annoying though he is, because he's someone to bounce food ideas off and argue with. Annie's interested in food, but I wouldn't call her a creative cook, and she's so even-tempered I couldn't pick a quarrel with her even if I tried.

Mind you, since every second word she utters these days is 'Gareth', exasperation might eventually lead me to smother her to death, probably with a hassock.

Ritch was off in London too, shooting some cameo role for a film, so Dora Tombs and I were taking care of Flo between us. On Sunday I joined the depleted party up at the Hall for lunch and Mimi and Juno were full of talk of their holiday and deep in planning the installation of a water feature in the walled garden, while Unks was happily doing his own thing, as usual, mainly involving studying racing form.

I was still extremely busy myself, perpetually preserving, storing, gardening and pet-sitting, but it gave me a foretaste of what it was going to be like once Jasper went off to university . . .

I suspected Nick wouldn't give up his flat in London after all, but go back to dividing his time between there and the Hall. Eventually, once the divorce was finalised, he'd marry someone young and beautiful and start a family. I was quite convinced this would happen, because even I had to admit he was wildly attractive, except when he was annoying me . . . so it was just as well he annoyed me most of the time, wasn't it? And clearly he had no great interest in me, whatever my misguided relatives thought, since he couldn't even be bothered sending me postcards any more!

Anyway, I liked being on my own, and Jasper wouldn't be a million miles away, so I couldn't imagine why I was feeling suddenly so depressed.

* * *

But of course I wasn't totally alone, for I still had my friends in the Christmas Pudding Circle, and at the next Monday meeting Miss Pym gave us all a surprise gift of candied angelica. Marian had brought me her giant round two-part metal Christmas pudding mould, too, so the following afternoon I abandoned everything else and made a huge spiced fruit cannonball instead. The smell of the ingredients took me right back to happy times at the vicarage with Annie's family, and was *very* comforting.

Stirring, I made a wish.

CHAPTER 20: FRESHLY MINTED

I have been preserving apples in wine and making green tomato chutney, before clearing away the tomato plants. I'm not sure what I'll do with the bare patch where the huge glasshouse used to stand, but I'm very tempted to turn it into a little apple orchard, with several unusual old kinds.
The Perseverance Chronicles: A Life in Recipes

The most *dreadful* thing! Gareth called to tell me that Tom's mother and stepfather had just arrived in the UK and were on their way down to pay their respects at Tom's grave!

'What? But why didn't they call me?' I asked, stunned. 'I haven't heard a word since the funeral— and it's *years* since they saw Jasper, too, and he's away at the moment. If only they'd let me know they were coming!'

'I don't know, but I thought I'd check to see if you knew about it, because they didn't mention you and you ought to be there. I gave Mr Barillos directions to the graveyard. They've hired a car and were only about an hour away when he rang.'

I ran a distracted hand through my tangled hair. 'Well, thanks for telling me, Gareth. They're such odd people that I suppose them behaving like this shouldn't surprise me, but you're right and I'd better meet you at the graveyard.'

I hoped they wouldn't be too disappointed that the stone has not yet been erected. It's ordered, but these things do take time.

Quickly I changed into something clean, though equally unsuitable for the occasion, and set off, collecting Annie on the way for moral support.

Gareth was standing by the grave, which did indeed look forlorn, especially on such a grey, cold October day as this one: a grassy mound in the Pharamond corner. I intended planting spring bulbs there, once it had its stone, and possibly a bit of lavender. I don't much like cut flowers left dying on graves, or in those little stone urns.

I wasn't sure I would have recognised the Barilloses if I'd met them in the street, but on a gravel path in an old country graveyard, they stood out like sore thumbs. For a start, there was something glossily expensive about their clothes and, although it was not a sunny day, they both wore huge, wraparound reflective sunglasses.

The skin visible on Tom's mother's face looked stretched, smooth and peachily tinted, while her skittish curls were a rich brassy blond. Her husband looked positively withered and prune-like in comparison, apart from having a head of hair like black Astroturf.

Gareth stepped forward and clasped their hands in turn, murmuring a few earnest words. Then, since they were pointedly ignoring me, he gestured and said, 'And here's your daughter-in-law, Lizzy, come to meet you and her friend, Annie Vane, whom I don't think you've met.'

'Well, Elizabeth, I didn't expect to see *you* here,' Jacqueline Barillos said coolly.

'My wife did not wish to see her—you should not have told her we were coming,' argued her husband.

'But she's Tom's widow,' began poor Gareth,

baffled. 'Who better to offer comfort and—'

'But we know she did not care about him and was a bad wife,' interrupted Jaime Barillos. 'We have had many beautiful letters from the woman he *did* love, whom he wanted to marry. We know how grieved he was when he found out about his wife's affair and realised that even his own son was fathered by his cousin!'

'Now, just a minute!' I broke in angrily. 'I think I can guess who's been telling you this pack of lies, but it most definitely is *not* true!'

'Certainly not!' Annie defended me stoutly. 'It was Tom who was the unfaithful one, not Lizzy, and Jasper *is* Tom's son.'

'And you, of all people, must know why my son looks so like a Pharamond!' I added pointedly to Mrs Barillos.

She gave me a dirty look, then threw a dramatic hand towards the grassy mound and cried, 'Here's the proof—does *this* look like the tomb of a loved husband?' Clearly she'd missed her calling and should have been on the stage.

'The stone is ordered. These things take time,' I explained.

'Not even any flowers . . .' she sobbed, turning to her husband, who put his arm around her and glared at me.

'Please,' began Gareth, '*please* don't distress yourself, Mrs Barillos! Look, why don't we all go back to the vicarage and talk this through? I fear you're letting the natural grief of a mother lead you to unwarranted conclusions—'

'No!' she declared, lifting her head and turning her dark lenses in my direction like an inimical ant. 'I would like you all to go away so I can pay my respects to my son—*alone.*'

'Then afterwards, perhaps . . .' suggested Gareth tentatively.

'No. Leave us in peace,' she said implacably.

I turned and walked off before I could say something I would regret, and Annie followed me, though Gareth paused to speak to them before catching us up.

'This has been a bit of a shock, Lizzy. Why don't you come back to the vicarage for a cup of tea anyway?' he suggested kindly, but I insisted I was fine and, despite their protests, set off for home. I didn't even want Annie's company just then.

That ugly little scene had seemed too melodramatic to be true at the time, especially with the Barilloses resembling nothing so much as a pair of Thunderbirds puppets, but now, suddenly, my legs began to feel trembly and I realised it had affected me more than I'd thought.

So when a sleek dark red sports car slid to a purring stop next to me and Ritch offered to run me home, it was a relief to get in. I didn't have to talk, either, because he was full of what he'd been doing.

In fact, it's sometimes pleasantly relaxing being with a man who notices nothing much other than himself, though it was kind of him to take me home when he'd just driven all the way up from London.

When we got to Perseverance Cottage I pulled myself together and thanked him for the lift, then added firmly that I knew he wouldn't mind if I didn't ask him in, since I had lots to do before the Mystery Play rehearsal.

'That's OK. I'll see you later, after it,' he said, and I managed to smile at him before climbing out of the car and waving him off.

Turning, I spotted Caz through the open door of the barn, doing chin-ups on a crossbeam, like a very strange clockwork toy. Hadn't he got a beam of his own to swing from?

*   *   *

Without Nick, that night's rehearsals were a bit . . . flat, I suppose is the only word to describe them.

The only highlight was when I overheard the new Moses, in answer to God telling him that he'd written down Ten Commandments on tablets of stone, reply testily, 'Could thee not find something lighter? I'm no spring chicken, tha knows! Just as well I hadn't t'carry 'em up t'mountain as well as down!'

I felt hugely tired and unusually down, which was probably reaction from that horrible scene in the graveyard, so I might have just sneaked straight home again rather than on to the pub with the others, except that home was empty without Jasper.

There wasn't any sign of Ritch after the rehearsals, but he was already in the pub, the centre of an admiring circle. I expect he was telling *them* all about his cameo film role, too. I sat quietly in the corner with Gareth and Annie for a while, then left early and fairly abruptly when I spotted Polly coming in, wearing a wrapover dress that made her breasts look like a giant pair of loosely packaged white puddings.

I pounced on her near the door, grabbing her sinewy arm. 'I want to talk to you! I know what you've done, Polly.'

She went the colour of clotted cream and stared

263

at me through a spidery inch of clogged mascara. 'I don't know what you mean!'

'Those tricks you've been playing—the jars of jam and tomatoes made to look like mine, the ARG harassment, the poisonous fungi in the mushrooms, even the lies you've been telling the Barilloses! And I'm warning you, if there's any more of it, I'll go to the police.'

Her colour came back in a rush. 'Tell them, then, and see if they believe you!' she hissed, then wrenched her arm away with surprising strength and shoved her way through the crowd towards the bar.

There was no point in following her, but Ritch caught me up outside.

'Wait for me! I said I'd run you home tonight—you look exhausted.'

'It's been quite a day,' I agreed wearily, though it just goes to show that you shouldn't misjudge people: he might have seemed totally self-absorbed in the pub, but he'd still noticed I wasn't exactly a sparkling little star in the firmament tonight.

So when we pulled up outside Perseverance Cottage I didn't resist when he put his arm around me and kissed me: apart from suddenly feeling too exhausted to move, I needed comfort.

He tasted only of minty mouthwash. Now, that *was* a relief.

After a couple of minutes he must have detected a certain lack of enthusiastic cooperation because he sat back again. 'OK, I know when I'm flogging a dead horse. You don't really fancy me, do you?'

'I wouldn't exactly say that,' I replied honestly, 'but . . . well, to be frank, I find the thought of your morning pee-drinking sessions a bit off-putting!'

264

'Really? You know, you're the second woman to say that—though it's perfectly natural, you know—everyone is doing it.'

'Not round here they're not!'

'Well anyway, I've given it up, now. I get crates of Elyxr delivered instead.'

'What kind of elixir?' I asked curiously.

'Oh, Elyxr is the name they've given to a *very* special and expensive ionised mineral water. It comes from a secret source high in the Himalayas, where everyone's over a hundred and the local men all father children into their nineties and beyond. What do you think?'

'I think you've got more money than sense. What's ionised water?'

'I've no idea,' he confessed. 'But anyway, now you know I've given the other thing up, does that make a difference?' he asked hopefully.

'Not really, because it's pointless—I'm simply not harem material.'

'You can be chief concubine,' he offered, cheekily.

'Thanks, but no thanks. And you'd better watch your step with Kylie, too. Did you know she has a very tough boyfriend, in the army?'

He grinned unrepentantly. 'In the army *and* in another country, though. Anyway, she's not serious and neither am I; it's just a bit of fun. But you and I could be serious . . .'

'No we couldn't, don't be daft! There isn't a serious bone in your body,' I said severely, fending him off, then gasped as a spectrally pale face appeared at the window.

'*What* the hell . . .?' began Ritch explosively, letting me go just as the door on my side was pulled

265

open.

'Hens,' Caz Naylor said succinctly, with a jerk of his head.

'Oh God!' I scrambled hastily out. 'I entirely forgot to lock them up for the night before I left, and there's been a fox about. Good night, Ritch, thanks for the lift!'

'But, Lizzy—' he began to protest, though when I ignored him and started across the yard towards the henhouse he gave up and drove off.

'I've done 'em,' Caz said from behind me, stopping me in my tracks, and then he turned and loped silently off into the darkness.

Men.

CHAPTER 21: SLIGHTLY STEWED

There is already an autumnal feel to the air, along with the nostalgic hint of dead leaves and wood smoke. I put grease bands around my cherry and apple trees, and cleaned out the small greenhouse behind the cottage, before lining it with bubble wrap to conserve warmth through the winter to come—and perhaps it will be another hard one, in which case I will soon be cooking up my home-made version of fat balls to help the birds get through.
The Perseverance Chronicles: A Life in Recipes

Nick was still away, but very early one morning a postcard of Penzance arrived, with a recipe scrawled on the back for a dessert consisting mostly of Cornish clotted cream. It appeared to have travelled the length of the country before coming home to roost, possibly because the front was tacky so it had stuck to other mail. I had to sponge and dry it before adding it to the album. I expect he wrote it in a restaurant over a lush dinner, probably in the company of some equally lush Poldarkian beauty.

I was about to embark on my daily larder-filling (Lizzy the human squirrel), gardening and pet-sitting activities, though guiltily feeling that I should instead make a proper start on the *Just Desserts* book, when—speak of the devil—Senga rang me.

'I thought you might like to know that Polly Darke and I have parted company,' she told me crisply. 'She rang me up hysterically demanding I drop you as my client, or she would leave me. So I told her to take her business elsewhere.'

I nearly dropped the telephone. 'But, Senga, she earns *much* more than I do!'

'Perhaps, but she's ten times the trouble and I'm not having one of my authors telling me who else I can or can't represent. Anyway, if she carries on like she's doing, pestering her publishers and doing a prima donna act all over the place, they will drop her, too.'

While I was grateful that Senga decided to keep me and ditch Polly, it does give Polly one more thing to hate me for. But now she knows that I know she did all those spiteful things, surely she wouldn't be stupid enough to try anything else?

'Crange and Snicket want to know how *Just Desserts* is coming along,' Senga said. 'And so do I.'

'I'm collecting recipes,' I assured her hastily.

'Don't forget that you can use old stuff from all the *Chronicles*, though you need at least fifty per cent new material or your readers will feel cheated.'

'I will, and I'm picking Nick Pharamond's brains, too, only his recipes tend to be pretty sophisticated and I have to dumb them down to my level.'

'I'd forgotten he was some kind of relation of your husband's—that's lucky. And he's really attractive as well, isn't he?'

'Lots of women seem to think so. He's in the middle of getting divorced—shall I put in a good word for you?'

'God, yes!' she said enthusiastically.

*   *   *

In the afternoon Jasper returned and I needn't have worried about what he was going to spend Unks' holiday money on, because he came back laden with stuff to take to university with him: his own kettle, mugs and crockery, plus tons of archaeology books because he'd struck a rich vein in a second-hand bookshop.

He also sported a strange haircut and lots of new clothes, including some oddly worded T-shirts that probably meant something a mother shouldn't know about: I didn't ask for a translation.

Ginny sported a new collar. Jasper tried to persuade me that she was pleased to see me on her return, citing the fact that she hadn't yet nipped my ankles as evidence, but I wasn't convinced. I think she is a one-man bitch.

*   *   *

I went out early next morning to clean out the cage of a rather vicious African Grey parrot, leaving Jasper getting his stuff ready to go to university the following day.

When I got back he said Nick had phoned. 'He wanted to wish me good luck for university.'

'That was kind. Where is he?'

'Back in London, but he's coming home soon. He has to do something about the divorce first—go to the solicitor's maybe, and sign something? He said he and Leila were getting on better now they were divorcing than they ever had while they were married,' he added.

'How lovely. I'm *so* happy for them.'

Jasper grinned. 'He said he was sorry to miss you, and had you managed to make a decent apple

269

pie yet.'

'Ha, ha!' I said sourly. My shortcrust pastry is so light it practically floats off the plate, so I still can't see why the judges at the fête gave Nick the gold prize!

After a quick lunch we set off to the museum and botanical gardens near Southport, which was one of Jasper's favourite trips out as a small boy. He seemed to enjoy the outing as much as I did, though I expect he was just humouring his old mum again. I did let him drive the Land Rover, though, so that might have had something to do with it.

When we got home he brought down all his boxes and bags of stuff, and stacked them in the hall, while I cooked his favourite dinner of roast chicken with crinkly, thick-cut chips, followed by little pots of rich, dark chocolate mousse.

It had been a lovely day and, even if I was sad to see Jasper leave home, I was also happy for him too, because this was how it should be.

*   *   *

So there I was next day, about to leave my beloved offspring, bag and baggage, marooned in a strange place to start a part of his life that I would only peripherally be involved in.

Not that Jasper was entirely among strangers, of course, since not only was Ginny present, but also his friend Stu and another friend's elder brother were among the students sharing the terraced house.

Jasper's bedroom was on the ground floor in what had once been the morning room, so at least if there was a fire he could get out fast . . . And even

270

after half an hour I was still sitting quivering on the bed from the effect of having driven through the Liverpool traffic system, trying to find the place.

Jasper had somehow managed to fit all his stuff in the Land Rover, but now it had exploded to four times its original bulk, like popcorn in a microwave.

'When I went to London to do my cookery course with Annie,' I remarked, looking at it all with amazement, 'we had—'

'Just one rucksack and a sleeping bag each,' he finished for me, ripping the tape off a cardboard box and delving inside for coffee and mugs. He had his own little sink in the corner of the room, which was handy. 'I know, Mum, you've told me.'

'*And* I had a guitar.'

He frowned. 'I don't think you ever mentioned the guitar. And you can't play a guitar.'

'No, so I swapped it with someone in the first week for that glass pig with the three little pigs inside it.'

'Oh, yeah, cannibal pig.' He plugged in his brand-new kettle and switched it on. I was ready for a cup of coffee by then.

'You don't have to stay any longer, you know, Mum,' he said kindly, looking up. 'It'll be dark before you get home if you don't get off soon. Besides, no one's going to come in here while my mother's hanging about. I can hear them talking in the kitchen, so I'll go and take my food and stuff through in a minute when you've gone.'

'It'll be dark anyway by the time I get home,' I pointed out, feeling slightly hurt. 'But perhaps I had better go and leave you to get on with it. I only hope I can find my way back out of Liverpool again.'

271

'It'll be easier finding your way home than getting here, because you'll know where you are once you're out of the city. Come on, I'll see you off.'

'I'll phone you tonight, just to make sure everything's all right, shall I?'

'Well, I might be out somewhere too noisy to hear it,' he said dubiously, 'but you could leave a message.'

'No, that's OK—you call me when you feel like a chat,' I suggested, with a brightness I certainly didn't feel. 'I'd love to know how you're getting on.'

Out on the pavement I gave him a hug, which he suffered with saintly resignation, then got into my now empty Land Rover.

He leaned in at the open passenger door and said, 'Now, Mum, remember what I said, and don't try changing any plugs!'

'I only melted one once!' I replied indignantly.

'And switch the light off *before* you change a light bulb. Don't mess about with the timer on the boiler—and if the flame goes out again, ask Unks to send Joe down to do it, or Uncle Nick.'

'Now look here, Jasper, I'm not completely helpless, you know! I may not have an affinity with anything electric but—'

'Actually, you're the kiss of death to anything electric,' he interrupted firmly. 'Anyway, I expect I'll come home for the odd weekend before Christmas, so you can save anything that wants doing until then, if you like.'

Hold on, I thought, shouldn't this be *me* giving out the instructions? And not about electricity either, but drugs, safe sex and eating properly (though the eating bit wasn't so pressing since I'd

272

packed enough food and drink to last him for about ten years).

'I expect I'll survive,' I said, then looked at him—tall, skinny, his dark hair whipping about in the brisk breeze—and swallowed hard.

'Goodbye then, darling. Hope you settle in quickly,' I said slightly huskily, though I did manage a smile, before starting the engine and heading in the direction I hoped would take me home.

The sun was sinking in a clear sky, but just like the song, it was raining, raining in my heart.

* * *

Annie had kindly been to the cottage to shut up all the Myrtles and Honeys, and left me a pineapple upside-down cake with a nice note telling me to ring her if I wanted to, though ten to one Gareth was there, or she was out doing something godly and good with him.

The cottage looked desolate and empty, which was exactly how *I* felt. Jasper had been the centre of my universe for over eighteen years: what was I going to revolve around now?

Then Unks called to ask me how Jasper had settled in and I told him how he'd turned the tables on me in the good advice stakes, which made him laugh.

After that I turned to food and drink (last year's apple wine and flapjacks) for comfort until bedtime, when I fell into a state of comatose indigestion.

* * *

I wasn't feeling much happier in the morning, especially since I also had a hangover. It was lucky I didn't have any pet-sitting jobs to do, for I kept bursting into tears, which was quite unlike me.

I stripped Jasper's bed so that it would be made up all nice and fresh if he was homesick and popped back for a night or two. But I didn't linger in there, with the bare surfaces where his computer had been and the gaps on the bookshelves. It was too poignant.

While the bedding was going through the wash and dry cycle, I gave the cottage the sort of thorough cleaning it only gets when I'm trying to distract myself from something. It didn't quite work, though, because I kept finding things of Jasper's that set me off again.

In fact, Nick walked in on me just before lunch and discovered me slumped in a sobbing heap in the old wicker basket chair in the kitchen.

'Lizzy? What on earth's the matter?' he demanded, coming to a sudden startled stop and staring at me. 'I don't think I've *ever* seen you cry, except that once at the hospital!'

I snuffled back the tears and held out the large black Snoopy sock with a hole in the heel that I'd found down the back of the radiator. 'It's J-jasper's!' I wailed.

Looking relieved, he bent down and hauled me to my feet, then gave me a little shake. 'Oh, is *that* it? Come on, Lizzy, stop wallowing in pathos! He's only a few miles away at university, not the other side of the world. You can go and see him any time you want.'

I sniffled and tried to pull away, but he didn't let go. 'No I can't! He's got to make his own life there,

274

so I couldn't possibly keep popping in and fussing. But it's such a long time until Christmas!'

'I expect he'll come back for a weekend before then. Look, there's no point in sitting here moping like a wet weekday,' he added, 'so get your jacket and let's go.'

'Go? Go where?' I said indignantly, though at least I'd stopped feeling weepy.

'I'll take you out for lunch. You look quite decent—no need to change. Come on.'

Considering I was dressed in my oldest jeans and a washed-out sweatshirt, he had to be joking.

'I don't think I want to go out, thank you, Nick,' I began, but he wasn't taking no for an answer, so in the end it was easier to give in, though I insisted on changing, bathing my face in cold water and brushing my hair first.

Lunch was fish and chips, well laced with salt and vinegar, eaten out of newspaper on the seafront at Southport, with the expanse of beach stretching away under a cold blue sky scudding with clouds.

But that was *after* he'd made me walk for miles, so by then I was starving and, I admit, feeling much more optimistic.

*   *   *

After he dropped me back at the empty nest, Annie came around with someone else's Maltese terrier, so I didn't have time to start moping again and, anyway, all that fresh air and exercise seemed to have numbed the pain a little.

I even resisted the urge to call Jasper and see what he was doing, but instead got hot and sweaty stuffing his duvet back into its clean cover, a task

275

somewhat like giving birth in reverse, but without the excruciating agony followed by a stranger trying out their embroidery skills on your private parts.

The good thing about being pregnant (possibly the *only* good thing apart from the eventual baby) is that at least you know where your child is and have a pretty good idea what it's doing. Now we were only joined by the frail umbilical cord of Jasper's new mobile phone.

*   *   *

Mimi and Juno's Glorious Autumn Garden Colour luxury coach tour set off just after seven in the morning and, since I'm always up early, I volunteered to drive them to the pick-up point outside the New Mystery pub.

Mimi was highly excited, but I was sure Juno had thoroughly searched both her luggage and her person for any sharp implements with which she might attempt to steal cuttings from the various stately homes they were to visit, so provided she kept her eye on her I was hopeful they would have an enjoyable holiday.

While Juno was seeing to the luggage being stowed away, Mimi dashed into the corner newsagent's shop to buy cough candy and Uncle Joe's Mint Balls for the journey, and came back carrying several little paper bags, her cheeks bulging like a hamster's.

As the bus pulled away I looked up at Mimi, who was seated in the window, a sweetly angelic little old lady in a pink velvet Alice band and matching pearly beads. She waved benignly at me and I could have *sworn* something glinted in her hand . . .

But I must have imagined it, or she was wearing a ring . . . though I'd never known her to wear one, since they got in the way of her gardening.

The coach vanished down the high street and I turned the car for home, calling at Annie's cottage on the way as much from the hope of hot croissants as to see if any more pet-sitting jobs had come up.

It was a Danish pastry day, which was nearly as good, and she was bubbling with suppressed gossip.

'Gosh, Lizzy,' she said excitedly, 'there were ructions last night in the village! Kylie's boyfriend got leave from the army and came home a couple of days ago, and, of course, someone told him all about what Kylie's been up to with Ritch. So he went round to Ritch's and there were loud voices, then they had a fight! Or Kylie's boyfriend hit Ritch, at any rate, and the police got called.'

'Well, I did warn Ritch about the boyfriend, so it's entirely his own fault.'

'*And* Kylie's,' Annie pointed out fairly.

'That's true, but I bet she put all the blame onto Ritch.'

'Ritch's just phoned me up. He tried you first, but there was no answer. He wants one of us to go round and take Flo out, because he isn't feeling well.'

'Meaning battered and bruised? I'd better go on my way home and I'll ring you later and tell you what he says—if I can catch you,' I added. 'You're always out these days.'

Mainly with Gareth, whom I still hadn't had that quiet word with. What *was* holding him back? Perhaps I ought to give him the birds-and-bees talk I gave Jasper before he went to university?

Except that that wasn't such a great success,

277

come to think of it: Jasper said he was sure he already knew much more about it than I did.

*   *   *

Ritch took his sunglasses off to show me his black eye, but he seemed to have escaped relatively unscathed otherwise.

Tigger certainly hadn't lost any of his bounce. 'Kiss it better?' he suggested hopefully.

'No chance!' I told him severely. 'And I did warn you.'

He shrugged. 'It was just a bit of fun on both sides, nothing serious. I don't know what Kylie told him, but he swung a punch at me as soon as I opened the door and took me by surprise, then we had a bit of a scuffle until the police came and broke us up. I didn't press charges.'

'Magnanimous of you!'

'It is really, because Make-up are going to have their work cut out disguising this shiner for a couple of weeks, unless they can work it into the storyline . . . That's an idea,' he added thoughtfully, heading for the phone.

*   *   *

As you can imagine, the fight was the main topic of conversation at the Christmas Pudding Circle on Monday, when we were all crammed into Annie's tiny cottage. But once we'd exhaustively thrashed that out, we got down to deciding which sweets we would make for the WI hampers and then divided up the big packet of Cellophane circles we'd ordered, from which we would make little cone-shaped bags, to tie up with shiny ribbon. Rum truffles fell to my lot this year, but I also volunteered to make sugar-free Fruit and Nut Munchies for our one diabetic Senior Citizen.

*   *   *

Kylie was much subdued at the Mystery rehearsal, though at the same time strangely triumphant: I expect that's the glow from having two men fighting over your charms. She didn't look a bit embarrassed during the Annunciation scene, but I'd have curled up and died.

Afterwards her fiancé, a stocky and pugnacious-looking young man, collected her and whisked her away, though he didn't have to worry about Ritch tonight, because he wasn't anywhere to be seen.

Nick, who seemed to be in a foul mood, said sourly, 'Looking for Casanova? I hear Kylie's boyfriend's sorted him out big-time.'

'Actually, there's hardly a mark on him except a black eye, and I think he only got that because he was taken by surprise,' I said coldly.

'Oh? And did you kiss it better?' he asked sarcastically, so clearly his mind ran along similar lines to Ritch's. Must be a man thing.

'No,' I said shortly, going slightly pink. 'We're not on kissing terms.'

He raised an eyebrow. 'That's not what Caz says.'

'Caz? You've been discussing me with *Caz*? And I haven't—' Then I broke off, recalling that actually I *had* shared a kiss with Ritch.

'Slipped your memory?'

'Not that it's any of your business, but Ritch did give me a kiss—for comfort. Tom's parents showed

279

up while you were away. They didn't tell me they were coming, but Gareth let me know and I went to meet them at the churchyard. Only Polly's been writing lies to them and turned them against me, so there was a horrible scene. It really upset me. Ritch picked me up on the way home and he was very kind.'

'I bet he was,' Nick said nastily.

Up to this point I'd been automatically ambling in the direction of the pub, but I stopped dead and demanded, 'What *is* the matter with you tonight? You were really nice to me the other day too, when I was upset about Jasper leaving home, and now you're being horrible!'

'I hadn't had a chance to speak to Caz then.'

I glared at him: 'Have you told Caz to spy on me?'

'To watch over you, after he told me about the mysterious jar of tomatoes and the mushrooms— which, by the way, you might have mentioned to me yourself!'

'I dealt with it,' I said shortly. 'And it did sound a bit unlikely—The Case of the Poisonous Mushrooms—so I thought you might not believe me anyway.'

'True, I can't say it really convinced me until Leila told me about getting that pot of jam in the post. She had a friend run some tests on it.'

'She did? And was it poisoned?'

'It contained a strong emetic.'

'Well, *I* didn't send it.'

'I didn't think you had, but there doesn't seem to be any real proof that Polly did either, does there? Still, I wasn't taking any chances, so I asked Caz to watch out for you while I was away.'

'There's no need, I can look after myself. And what's more, whatever I get up to is my own private business!'

'Pardon me for caring!' he snapped.

'Look, Nick, I don't know why you're needling me like this tonight, but I've had enough, so good *night*!' I said, and walked off. Though I felt his eyes boring between my shoulder blades, he didn't follow me, so I expect he had other fish to fry.

*   *   *

In the morning I found an old envelope on the doormat, with Marian Potter's secret Lancashire hotpot recipe scribbled on it in Nick's spiky handwriting, so I suppose it was an apology of sorts for his foul mood.

Then when I opened the front door a parcel fell on my feet: *The Perseverance Chronicles* copy-edits had arrived with amazing speed. There was also a rough proof of the book cover, which was too twee for words: why did they always turn my solid northern sandstone cottage into something thatched, gabled and timbered to within an inch of its Anne Hathaway life?

CHAPTER 22: GIVEN THE BIRD

This morning I made some sugar-free sweets, suitable for diabetics: a sort of sugar plum, without the sugar! I tried various blends of chopped dried fruit and nuts: apricot, almond, brazils, raisins, with a little orange juice to bind the mixture together. I rolled some into little log shapes and others into balls, and left them on a sheet of baking parchment to dry out for a couple of hours. I think they would keep very well in the fridge, but they were so delicious they didn't last long.

The Perseverance Chronicles: A Life in Recipes

'Gareth found three large frozen geese on the vicarage doorstep this morning,' Annie said.

'Frozen geese?' I questioned, putting a mug of tea and a plate containing three small wedges of apple pie in front of her, each marked with a different coloured cocktail stick flag. 'I know we've had some night frost, but it hasn't been *that* cold yet!'

'Plucked, cleaned, oven-ready, with an anonymous note saying they were for the Senior Citizens' Christmas dinner. Gareth called me right away, to ask my advice.'

'That was a pretty generous donation,' I said thoughtfully. 'Frozen . . .?'

'Yes, they were in those big, see-through roasting bags, but there were no supermarket labels on them or anything like that.' She looked down at her plate. *'Three* pieces of pie?'

'Little pieces. I want you to taste them and tell

me which one you think is best. Here, have some cream.'

'*All* your apple pies taste wonderful.'

'But Nick's obviously taste better, or he wouldn't have won the gold at the fête.'

'Yes, but you won practically everything else, including Best Middlemoss Marchpane, Lizzy, so you might let him have that one small triumph.'

'Not if I can help it.' I watched her drizzle cream over the pie and asked, 'So, what did you and Gareth do with the frozen geese?'

'We took them up to the Hall. I thought we might as well, since Mrs Gumball cooks the Senior Citizens' dinner anyway—with your help, of course—and there are huge freezers in the cellar she can store them in.'

She tried another forkful of pie and chewed thoughtfully. 'Nick was there, and he said this year he was going to help cook the dinner.'

'He *is*? Then Mrs Gumball won't need me as well, will she?'

'I think she will, because I overheard Nick telling Gareth that you would *both* be helping her,' Annie said. 'And when we ran into Clive Potter on the way back, Gareth told him about the geese and how Nick and you were going to help Mrs Gumball to cook them for the Senior Citizens, so I expect it'll be in the next *Mosses Messenger*.'

'Then it can come straight back out again,' I said sourly. 'I have no intention of being the Demon Chef's whipping boy. He can find another one.'

'Whipping girl—and you're very crabby today,' she observed, then looked down at her empty plate as if surprised that she'd cleared it down to the last pastry flake. The coloured sticks lay round the edge like the hours on a clock.

'Which slice did you like best?'

'To be honest, I couldn't really taste much difference,' she confessed. 'They were all delicious!'

I sighed. 'Maybe he uses Dark Arts and says a spell over his cooking pots?'

'You'll be able to watch him cooking the Christmas dinner and find out,' she teased. 'Has he done something to annoy you?'

'When does he *not* do something to annoy me? But yes, he has excelled himself, because he set Caz on to watch me while he was away!'

'But Caz already does watch you. I mean, he keeps an eye on the place because it's part of the estate—and probably also because he thinks of you as family, however remote the connection.'

'Yes, I know that, but Ritch kissed me the other night when he drove me home and Caz not only interrupted us, but he reported it to Nick!' And I repeated to her what Nick had said, about not being sure it was Polly playing the nasty tricks and even thinking I'd imagined them at first.

'Of course, I haven't told him about Ophelia being in ARG, and I don't suppose Caz has either. I'm not sure how he would take it and he might feel he has to tell Unks.'

'He'd probably find it funny, Lizzy!'

'I wouldn't put it past him. He seems to find most things I do funny—except the bits involving Ritch. And that was a perfectly innocent kiss, even if it was any of his business who I kiss, which it isn't.'

'It *was*?'

I grinned. 'Well, it was a perfectly *enjoyable* one, at any rate, but just between friends. Ritch knows I don't want a relationship with him—or anyone else,' I stated firmly. 'I'm getting quite tired of Unks, Mimi, Juno and now even Jasper trying to throw Nick and me together, when it must be clear it's a complete non-starter.'

'But, Lizzy, it's very evident even to me that he's concerned about you, *and* jealous!'

'Do you really think so?' I considered the matter carefully, then dismissed it. 'I've noticed he's a bit jealous, but I'm sure it's not of me personally, but some dog-in-the-mangerish male thing to do with property. I'm part of his family and living on his land, as it were . . . except it's still Unks' land, of course.'

'No, you're wrong, Lizzy: you think I don't notice these things, but I've seen the way he looks at you and I'm sure he's in love with you.'

'No *way*,' I said positively. 'Just because you're in love, you think everyone else should be!'

She went slightly pink under the freckles, but carried on doggedly, 'And you missed him when he was away, so I don't think it's all one-sided, either.'

'No I didn't,' I lied, 'which is just as well, because that's what he always does, isn't it? He goes *away*. We split up the first time because he wasn't going to let a little thing like our romance come between him and his globetrotting, recipe-collecting expedition. I'm only surprised he's stayed around Middlemoss so long now, because he's obviously getting itchy feet.'

'Now, Lizzy, you know if it weren't for Tom, he'd have spent much more time here in the last few years. He's quite sincere about loving the place.'

'He may love the place, but he's only passionate about his cooking.'

285

'Well, he's using it to try and impress you,' she insisted stubbornly. 'He knows the way to your heart is through food.'

'He's certainly not going to do that by snatching my gold prizes away. Though if he has got any designs on my virtue, I'd probably do almost anything he asked, for that coffee granita recipe.'

'Lizzy!' she exclaimed, shocked.

'Just joking,' I said hastily. 'But you've got it all wrong, because *I'm* not interested and *he's* not interested. After all, if he cared about me that way, what's to stop him from telling me?'

'But you were only widowed in August and his divorce isn't through yet, so that might be holding him back, don't you think?'

'Yes . . . I suppose it might *if* he felt about me like that, which he doesn't. And I don't really feel newly widowed, now I'm over the shock, since Tom and I were so estranged.'

'If Nick was a dog, he'd be a big, dark, Irish wolfhound,' she said inconsequentially. 'Ritch is a bit of a tomcat.'

'I don't like the way your mind's working,' I said severely. 'Gareth has been a demoralising influence on you. I'm afraid poor Juno's feeling a bit demoralised too, because she rang Unks and told him she had to explain precisely what Mimi was doing to someone's stately garden with nail scissors. You know, I thought I saw her holding something metal up when the coach pulled away the morning they left. She must have got them in the corner shop when she was buying sweets.'

After she'd gone I got out the copy-edits of my book and went through them for errors for the second time, before parcelling them up and taking them down to the post office. The cover I pinned to the kitchen notice board in the hope it would grow on me, but it hasn't yet. Nor do all the flowers depicted in the cottage garden bloom at the same time anywhere other than in the artist's demented imagination—or not in this hemisphere, anyway.

*   *   *

Jasper seemed to be settling in well, and I sent off a box of chocolate-coated candied peel. I hoped he was eating properly and not pickling his liver with spirits, like many students do.

I'd decided Annie was right about my apple pies and you couldn't improve on perfection, so Nick winning first prize must have been a fluke. The final one I tried that night, though, using dark Barbados sugar to sweeten the apples, had an interesting slight toffee-apple flavour, which made a nice change.

A policeman who sounded like that boy who favoured finger food called to say that one of the 2CV's wheel nuts had been handed in by a metal-detecting member of the public and added, in a seemingly casual aside, that it appeared to be in a perfectly good state of repair, the thread undamaged. Then he informed me the inquest was set for the end of January, and rang off.

The light was fading fast. I put on a warm coat and went to lock up the hens and, as I did so, Caz emerged slowly from the shadow of the barn. Since my slight contretemps with Nick I had entirely ignored Caz when he was around, which hadn't seemed to bother him in the least—if he'd even noticed.

Now I ran my hand distractedly through my tangled hair and said, 'Oh, Caz, the police have found one of the missing wheel nuts—or rather, I think someone found it and handed it in—and the thread on it looks fine. I'm sure they still think I loosened them on purpose and encouraged Tom to take my car!'

Caz glanced at me in his usual obliquely wary yet not unfriendly way, then said, 'Don't you fret, our Lizzy, it'll all come out in t'wash,' and loped off towards the woods, his gun under his arm.

I stared after him: if he continued getting so garrulous, we might soon be able to hold an entire conversation.

He'd probably be back later, too, because the Mummers would be coming round to the workshop to practise. I hoped Ritch came too and popped in as usual for coffee and chat afterwards. I felt like some company.

*   *   *

Ritch not only stopped by, he took me out to the café-bar in the former Pharamond's Butterflake Biscuit factory, which was very pleasant now I had firmly established my unavailability for his healthy sex rota.

Or at least, I think I have . . .

Of course this didn't stop him flirting with me, but actually I found that quite enjoyable now that Nick had suddenly gone even more morose and distant than usual. And also, of course, now I knew Ritch had stopped his more dubious habits he had regained a little more of his previous attraction!

'You look great tonight—that top really shows

288

off your curves,' he said, leaning forwards towards me across the table. 'I'll butter your pie dish any time you give me the word!'

I grinned. 'Hanging round my kitchen has given you a whole new vocabulary!'

'And a whole new taste for real home-baking,' he agreed.

Afterwards Ritch dropped me off at the cottage and I let him have a good-night kiss, though I didn't want to make a habit of it . . . well, not if Caz was watching.

There was no sign of him, but that didn't mean he wasn't still lurking about somewhere.

*   *   *

Mimi and Juno got back from their coach tour late on the Saturday, then walked down next afternoon to give me my present of a pair of flower-patterned gardening gauntlets, and for Juno to show me the photographs she had taken on her digital camera.

Mimi was, as usual, not only unrepentant about her bit of petty plant-pilfering, but entirely failed to understand what the fuss was about. 'I don't suppose they will take, because it is the wrong time of year, but anyway, gardeners should share things,' she said.

'It might have been politer to ask first,' Juno said patiently.

'Oh, they didn't really mind,' Mimi said. 'I promised them some cuttings from my rare lavender when it's the right time to take them—and then perhaps Tom could drop them off next time he is heading in that direction.'

'Tom's dead, Mimi,' I said gently.

289

'Oh, is he? Then perhaps if I wrap them in wet kitchen towel and a plastic bag and post them, they will be all right. Not that the postal service is all it used to be,' she added.

*   *   *

We had to have the next CPC meeting at Marian's, because she had boxes and boxes of big green apples a friend in the WI had given her and she was desperate to get rid of them.

'Maggie said they were eaters, but they cook well too, and it was such a bumper crop this year that she didn't know what to do with them,' she explained. 'So I said I was sure we could divide them up among our group.'

'There are an awful lot of them,' Fay said, 'and I've got more than enough of my own to be going on with.'

'Me too,' I agreed, but since there were loads left even after the others had all taken some, I ended up with the lion's share, simply because I couldn't bear to see them go to waste. I couldn't imagine what I was going to do with them.

*   *   *

I spent a large part of that Tuesday filling the freezer with apple pies, purée and crumble, yet had hardly made a dent in the apple mountain . . .

And Nick was not at the Mystery Play rehearsal, because he'd gone off on his travels yet again, according to Mimi, who'd come down to the village hall with Juno, being in one of her restless phases. Then she added meaningfully that he was catching up on things he should have done before, only he hadn't wanted to leave Middlemoss, so I expect he'd finally just got bored and restless.

'Oh, it's the nativity, my favourite bit!' Juno said, as the vicar called, 'Shepherds and angels to the crib, please!'

As they gathered round, I noticed for the first time that the Nine Angels of the Annunciation all had bright white patches on their wings where they had repaired them with fresh sturdy new feathers.

'See yonder breet light shining on t'owd stable?' said the First Shepherd, adjusting his tea-towel headdress.

'Aye, I do that, and a right bobby dazzler it is an' all!' replied the Second Shepherd, then nudged his friend as the Three Wise Men appeared. 'Hey up, we've got company.'

'Why wasn't there a Wise Woman too?' Mimi asked in a penetrating whisper.

'I don't know—perhaps they didn't fancy riding a camel all that way?' suggested Juno.

*   *   *

By the end of a very hectic week, the larder shelves were groaning with apple-based jams and jellies, apple sauce, apple chutney, apples in wine and spiced apple . . . you name it, and I'd made it.

Of course I'd had to keep up with the pet-sitting and gardening too, but apart from escaping to Butterflake's for an hour or so again one evening with Ritch, the days passed in a sticky haze.

Then suddenly I was down to the last few apples in the bottom of a box, and made a batch of fritters with them, which I ate sifted with brown sugar,

291

drizzled with honey and blobbed with thick cream. After that I felt completely appled out and never wanted to see another one again, unless, of course, it was as apple wine.

I ceded the apple pie prize to Nick in perpetuity. And speaking of Nick, I'd heard nothing from him for days and then suddenly had a spate of postcards all at once—every single one bearing some kind of tart recipe! Perhaps that was what his next article would be about?

*   *   *

I gave all my CPC friends a jar of apple chutney at the next meeting, but I had a feeling I'd still be trying to offload the remainder next autumn.

Nick was back next day, just in time for the Mystery Play rehearsal but, like Ritch, appeared to have lost interest in going to the pub afterwards. I wasn't finding it very tempting either, because I could only take playing gooseberry to Gareth and Annie for so long, no matter how kindly they went out of their way to include me in their conversation.

As we came out of the village hall, I thanked Nick for all the postcards, then asked curiously, 'But why are all the recipes for tarts?'

'I thought you deserved them,' he said shortly and then strode off into the night, looking distinctly Mr Rochester again.

I don't know what was biting him, unless he'd heard about my occasional friendly drink at Butterflake's Bar with Ritch, and misconstrued it?

*   *   *

I spent the rest of the evening catching up with the next *Perseverance Chronicle*, having not had time to keep up with it while so preoccupied with apples—and apples formed the basis of most of what I wrote! I also made a few more notes for *Just Desserts*, because I needed to get going with that soon, before Senga started snapping at my ankles.

If Nick hadn't been sulking I could have asked him for some ideas, but at least he'd provided the inspiration for a whole chapter devoted to tarts . . .

CHAPTER 23: PUT OUT

The vicar is delighted to announce that due to an anonymous benefactor, this year's Senior Citizens' Christmas dinner (to take place on 1 December) will be roast goose with all the trimmings! As usual it will be cooked by Mrs Eva Gumball up at the Hall, most kindly assisted by Mrs Lizzy Pharamond and also, adding that touch of cordon bleu, *Mr Nick Pharamond! It will be delivered piping hot to the village hall, courtesy of our friendly local Meals on Wheels volunteers.*

Mosses Messenger

The dankness of early November set in and the children had been collecting firewood for Friday's Bonfire Night for the last week or so. I thought Jasper might come home for that, but he said he was too busy, though busy with *what*, he didn't inform me, and it was probably better not to ask.

Still, he seemed to have settled down very happily at university and was enjoying his lectures. He told me what had been discovered about the Vikings' dietary habits, from excavating their cesspits at York, at more length than I really wanted to know. It's quite amazing what passes through the digestive tract more or less whole, isn't it?

Marian brought the latest issue of the *Mosses Messenger* and pointed out the announcement about my involvement in cooking the Senior Citizens' Christmas dinner. It was a *fait accompli*, because once it had been proclaimed in the parish magazine, there was no getting out of it . . . unless they were to forget about my helping by then? It *was* almost a month away.

Saying I never wanted to see another apple again was obviously tempting fate, for Marian then asked me to make toffee apples for Bonfire Night—she runs a little refreshment table with the proceeds going to charity. As usual, Miss Pym would provide a tray of treacle toffee, Annie gingerbread pigs for the children and Faye would bake parkin. There was usually someone roasting chestnuts too and I absolutely adored those.

Marian had yet *more* apples in her car to give me, but I didn't mind really, especially after I thought up a variant, Treacle Toffee Apples, and added it to my *Just Desserts* collection. Then it occurred to me that the Bonfire Night celebrations in Middlemoss would make a whole chapter of the next *Chronicles*, if I included a few other interesting snippets of information, like the fact that we always burned an effigy of Oliver Cromwell, warts and all, and *not* Guy Fawkes like everyone else.

It was not so much that the villagers were all staunch Royalists in the Mosses, just that they knew how to enjoy themselves and deeply resented the Puritans, or anyone else, trying to put a damper on their fun, and especially the Mystery Play.

And speaking of the Mystery Play, the Tuesday rehearsal went very well . . . and in my experience, if the November rehearsals go well, then the final dress rehearsal is a total disaster! But the performance itself on Boxing Day would go down wonderfully, whatever happens, because everyone would be well oiled with mulled wine and marinated in anticipation by then.

But on Tuesday even Nick had cut out the innuendo from his interpretation of Adam and played it straight. Sombrely, even. He appeared to be still sulking, though I wasn't sure what about, and he went off again straight afterwards. There was no Ritch in the pub, either, so I played gooseberry with Annie and Gareth for a while, then went back home, where I ate two toffee apples. Just as well I'd made a lot.

I sent Jasper some of the treacle toffee left over from the apples, which I'd moulded into a square and then broken up, plus a rawhide bone for Ginny—might as well blunt her teeth before he brought her back for Christmas. I was missing him so much. It seemed to hurt more as time went on, though part of me was also, of course, happy that he was having a good time at university.

*   *   *

The toffee and treacle-toffee apples were all wrapped in circles of Cellophane and piled back into the empty apple box by Thursday, when Marian collected them after the second Mystery Play rehearsal of the week. Apparently that one had also gone swimmingly, so we were both now convinced that the dress rehearsals were doomed to some kind of disaster.

Bonfire Night, the following day, was likely to be freezing, and I felt increasingly sure my guess about another cold, snowy winter would be right: the amazing number of berries on everything was a dead giveaway.

*   *   *

Annie never went out on Bonfire Night, staying in to comfort Trinny, who clearly associated loud firework bangs with some unimaginable terror from her past and became a shivering heap. She said Gareth would show his face at the event, before joining her to roast chestnuts over the fire and watch the home videos Annie's parents had sent her of their VSO work in Africa.

I expect there will be at least a chaste foot of sofa between them.

Unks was away and Juno wouldn't bring Mimi down for the bonfire, since she got much too excited, but instead would treat her to a short private display of Emerald Cascades and Glittering Fountains in the walled garden before cocoa and an early night.

What Nick was doing I had no idea, and nor was I even remotely interested, so I set out on my own at seven, torch in hand, my innards warmed by a strong slug—or maybe two—of Miss Pym's rightly famed damson gin: last year's had been an excellent vintage, but I was down to the last couple of bottles.

The fire was well alight when I got there and the first of the fireworks were going off, under the direction of Clive Potter. There was quite a crowd about and the refreshment table was doing a roaring trade. I didn't buy one of my own toffee apples, but I did purchase a plastic cup of mulled wine.

Looking round the faces brightly lit by the fire I spotted many familiar ones, though some, like Polly Darke and her friends, were not so welcome. On the other side of the bonfire I could see Jojo, Mick, and almost the entire Mysteries cast. In fact, most of the Mosses residents had turned out as always, though I expect the event wasn't sophisticated enough for Ritch and his crowd.

From time to time, one or two of the more rebellious teenagers sneaked off into the darkness outside the firelight to set off explosive fireworks, and were yelled at for their trouble: it was all much as usual.

I sat on a log and peeled hot chestnuts out of a paper cup, then got another tumbler of punch and began to feel a lot happier. 'This is fun, isn't it?' I said, finding myself standing next to Ophelia, who was swathed head to foot in a Tolkien-style woollen cloak with a tasselled hood. It looked pretty weird by firelight, but probably not as odd as the full-length knitted coat that I was wearing, a labour of love presented to me by Annie last Christmas. It had lots of little hanging daggy bits like a raddled sheep, and the strident colour combination meant I could only wear it in the dark.

Ophelia's white face was upturned and rapt, watching a sunburst of stars. 'Oh . . . it's sooo beautiful!' she sighed rapturously. 'Beautiful, beautiful stars. Stars . . .'

Then as the firework flickered and went out she turned to me and said excitedly, '*Star!* Of course! I'll call the baby Star!'

'Star Locke?' I said doubtfully, though of course it might by then be a Star Naylor. 'If it's a boy, it might sound a bit odd.'

'No, no . . . beautiful!' she murmured, and another firework shot up into the sky and exploded into a galaxy of pinprick lights. 'Better than Rambo . . .'

'That's very true,' I agreed, beginning to feel a bit muzzy and wondering if my earlier shots of damson gin hadn't been such a good idea. Or perhaps the punch was stronger than usual. Whichever it was, I had the feeling the chestnuts were sloshing about in an awful lot of liquid, and it was probably about time to call it a day and go home . . . especially since Nick had suddenly materialised out of the shadows nearby like the Prince of Darkness.

He was looking at me with what appeared to be acute disapproval: so nothing new there, then.

'Must find Caz and tell him about stars,' Ophelia said, looking around her vaguely, though you'd need ESP to find our chameleon of Middlemoss if he didn't want to be found.

She wandered off and I too turned to go, but had only taken a step or two away from the firelight when something landed with a thud just where we'd been standing and immediately exploded with a horrendous bang and a shower of bright sparks.

I put my hands over my ears and staggered, almost falling—and then was suddenly knocked flat by someone large and heavy. He landed on top of me and rolled me over and over and even winded, shocked and with my face pressed into icy mud, I somehow *knew* it was Nick. After what seemed like ages his weight was removed and urgent hands ripped my woolly coat off.

There was a smell of singed wool, and also, possibly, singed me.

I turned over slowly, dazed and winded, then sat up in time to watch him jumping up and down on my coat. I knew it was ghastly, but it didn't quite merit *that* treatment.

'Lizzy, are you all right?' Marian cried, running

over and trying to haul me to my feet, only my knees seemed to have given up and I was a dead weight.

'I'm fine,' I gasped, reinflating my lungs and trying to wipe the mud and grass from my face.

Clive appeared out of the darkness and declared vengefully, 'I don't know who threw that firework, but if I find him, he'll wish he hadn't!'

'No one would be stupid enough to throw it in this direction on purpose. It must have been an accident, Clive,' Marian said. 'Those boys just wouldn't be told!'

I looked around suddenly. 'Ophelia? Is *she* all right? Only we were talking together just before the firework went off.'

'Don't you worry about her, she was well out of range and that Caz's with her,' Marian said soothingly. 'You were closest: did it burn you anywhere?'

Nick picked up my mangled coat and examined the limp and ruined remains with satisfaction. 'There, that's out. Only just caught it, though.' Then he bent down and hauled me effortlessly to my feet, though he had to keep one arm around me to stop me falling over again.

When he realised I was trembling violently from a mixture of shock and cold, he shrugged out of his leather jacket and wrapped it around me, the silk lining warm and slithery.

'I think Lizzy may have singed the back of her legs a bit, Nick,' Marian pointed out worriedly. 'Her jeans are charred in a couple of places.'

'Yes, and I can't seem to stand up,' I said weakly.

'Shock,' Marian said. 'Stand back, everyone, and let her get some air!'

Until that moment I hadn't even realised that the ring of spectators was pressing close, watching avidly, including Polly Darke, a half-smile on her lips like a slightly warped Mona Lisa. Then her eyes shifted sideways to Nick and she slowly took first one step back, then another, until she vanished into the darkness.

I blinked. Maybe I'd imagined her . . .

'Drink's more likely than shock, the way she was knocking the punch back,' Nick was saying unsympathetically. 'I don't think there's much harm done, but I'll take her home.'

'Perhaps you should bring her to the post office first and Marian can see if she's burned?' suggested Clive. 'It might be bad enough for Accident and Emergency.'

'I don't think so,' Nick said, 'but if it looks worse than I think it is when I've got her home, I'll phone the doctor.'

'You do that,' Marian agreed.

'Your voices sound strange,' I commented, and so did my voice, too—frail and far away. And then everything seemed to be shifting dizzyingly . . .

'I expect the blast deafened you a bit,' Clive suggested.

'No, I think I'm going to—' I began, and then the darkness closed over my head like water.

*   *   *

I woke in Perseverance Cottage lying on my own sofa in front of the glowing fire, with Nick wiping the mud from my face with a wet flannel. A *cold* wet flannel: I expect that's what brought me round.

His face, concerned and intent, was very close to

301

mine. 'At last!' he said with relief when he saw my eyes open muzzily. 'I was starting to get worried.'

'What . . . happened?'

'You fainted.'

'I *never* faint!'

'Then maybe my first guess was right, and you passed out from all that punch you were knocking back, then,' he said.

'I didn't have that much, and there's usually very little alcohol in it,' I said, attempting to sit up and feeling strangely disconnected.

'How do you feel now?'

'All right—a bit shaky.'

'I expect that'll go off. There are two small burns on your leg. I've put some antiseptic and dressings on them, but I don't think they're much to worry about.'

Actually, I was more worried by the sudden realisation that he'd removed my jeans! Under a concealing blanket, all I was wearing on my lower half were my sensible cotton pants.

My face burned and I sat up straighter and primly tucked the blanket around my legs. 'I think I ought to thank you for—well, for putting me out. That's why you threw yourself on top of me, wasn't it?'

'Yes, and I'm sorry about that, but I could see your coat was catching and it was the quickest way of smothering the flames.' He got up and came back holding the sad remains of my coat. 'I'm afraid I've made a bit of a mess of it.'

'You certainly have—and Annie knitted it for me. Now I expect she'll make me another even more hideous one, because I told her I loved it.'

Then I had an evil thought: perhaps I should tell

her he jumped on it because he was jealous, and then she might knit *him* one, too? She whips them up in no time, on giant needles.

'You ought to go to bed. Do you want me to carry you up?' he offered.

'No, I don't,' I said firmly, shivering again. 'But I'd like you to fetch the bottle of damson gin from the kitchen and then lock the door behind you when you go.'

'I don't think you should drink any more alcohol! You're in shock and would be better trying to go to sleep, and you don't have to be nervous, because I'll stay here tonight on the sofa. Go to bed and I'll make you some cocoa.'

'I'm not nervous, I don't need you to stay here with me, and I don't want cocoa—I want gin. And if you aren't going to get it for me, then I'll get it myself,' I said, attempting to rise from a tangle of blanket on slightly wobbly legs.

Nick sighed and got up. 'OK, but don't blame me if you feel terrible in the morning.'

My hand trembled so much that the glass rattled against my teeth, so he had to sit down with his arm around me and hold it. But it did the trick and I soon began to stop shaking and calm down—or maybe 'go comatose' is a better description. The warmth of the fire and the soft pink light from the table lamp were very soothing . . .

'I think Polly might have thrown the firework,' I said drowsily, relaxing against his broad chest, which was invitingly close. Anyway, it was that or fall over sideways.

He'd put the empty glass down, but hadn't removed his arm from around my shoulders and now he rested his chin on top of my head. 'I was looking at you so I didn't see where it came from. Polly *was* there, but the chances are she wouldn't do something that stupid. It was just boys messing about, and you were unlucky.'

'Perhaps you're right, but she looked so . . . so pleased afterwards . . .' I yawned hugely.

'Come on—you're all in, so I'll carry you up to bed.' He gathered me up as though I was a loose-limbed doll, but before he could rise to his feet, some compulsion made me slide my arms around his neck.

He went quite still and our eyes met and held, his like unfathomably deep, dark pools in the lamplight. Then he gave a resigned sort of sigh, tightened his grip and kissed me.

His lips tasted of inevitability: there was never anything of the minty mouthwash about Nick Pharamond.

CHAPTER 24: FLAMBÉ

I don't know why, but whenever I need a little comfort I find myself mixing up a batch of the quick and easy confection I call Choconut Consolations. They couldn't be easier to make: simply melt some good-quality chocolate (milk or plain, according to your preference) and stir in unsalted peanuts until it is a thick, lumpy mixture. (Those nuts that have been roasted in their shells give the best flavour, I've found—but remove the shells and then rub the red skins off before using, of course!) Spoon into petits fours *cases, or onto a tray covered in baking parchment and leave to go hard in a cool place, though not in the fridge.*

The Perseverance Chronicles: A Life in Recipes

Next morning I awoke slowly, with that languorous, totally sated and exquisitely guilty feeling you get after a really *bad* chocolate binge—blissed out.

But when I opened my eyes to find I was not lying in my bed but on the sofa, I instantly remembered it wasn't chocolate I'd pigged out on last night. In fact, I recollected every single moment only too clearly, right the way from Nick knocking me flat and battering me into the mud, to our kiss and *more* than make up . . . though I suppose that at least had the advantage of *not* involving icy wet earth.

For a woman whose memory span was normally similar to that of a goldfish, this was quite something, though the action replay going on in my

305

head could have done with some soft-focused editing around the edges to hide all that urgent hunger—which surely hadn't been all on my side, even if I'd started it, had it?

The curtains were still drawn and the lights were off, though the fire was burning brightly enough behind the brass firescreen for me to see that I was alone. But that was no surprise, for I'd instantly sensed on waking that the cottage was empty apart from me—long empty. Slowly I heaved myself to my feet and, clutching my blanket, tottered into the kitchen on my singed legs, wincing at every step.

Propped against the kettle was a brief note in Nick's distinctive handwriting:

Lizzy, it's six and I'm supposed to be in London at ten for the shortlist photoshoot for Cookery Writer of the Year. I'll phone you later. Mud brown suits you, by the way—you should always wear it.
Nick

And that was it! I read through it twice, as though some hidden message might reveal itself, then crumpled it into a ball and threw it with some force at the wall opposite. It bounced off and fell behind the fridge.

Then I slumped down on the chair, feeling humiliated and angry. This was worse—*much* worse—than when I confided in him at the hospital, because this time I gave him more than my secrets and Spudge recipe—and all *he* could think about was some stupid cookery award!

But so be it, I resolved: from now on, let him eat cake. I know what *I'll* be eating—Humble (or

306

should that be Humiliation?) Pie. Here's one I prepared earlier:

> Mix just enough alcohol with a bad shock and a dash of unadulterated essence of lust.
> Put in a warm, dark place.
> Remove any inhibitions and stir a little.
> The leftovers can taste bitter if eaten cold next day.

I've changed my mind about Nick being like spicy curry. Now I think he's more like that rich, dark chocolate that's been spiked with extra-hot red chillies, and one chunk is *definitely* enough.

*   *   *

Annie, receiving news from the milkman at the crack of dawn about those parts of my sizzling evening that were common knowledge, hotfooted it round the second she'd finished the first dog-walking session.

She found me slumped in the kitchen in my dressing gown over a plate of Choconut Consolations, though I'd roused myself enough earlier to stagger out into the painful daylight and let out the disgruntled hens, before showering off the last traces of mud and Nick's subtly intrusive aftershave, while singing 'I'm Gonna Wash That Man Right Outta My Hair' through gritted teeth.

While she was applying some of her Girl Guide first-aid skills to re-dressing my singed leg, I confessed to her that the most sizzling part of the evening *hadn't* been the firework-throwing incident.

She stopped heartily slapping on the Savlon,

which was a relief, and stared up at me, blue-grey eyes round and startled. 'You don't mean you and *Nick* . . .?'

'Yes, me and Nick!' I confirmed gloomily. 'I can't *imagine* what got into me, apart from a little too much of Miss Pym's damson gin. Perhaps the shock of nearly being blown up sent me temporarily insane?'

'There you are,' she beamed, ignoring this suggestion, 'I knew you were in love with each other all the time!'

'Love had *nothing* to do with it,' I said tartly. 'I don't know what it was—shock, gin, propinquity, comfort, hormones, a substitute for chocolate . . . whatever.'

'Oh, no, Lizzy!' she protested. 'I'm sure Nick—'

'Nick was gone long before I woke up, so I don't know what *his* excuse was, but he kindly left me a note making it plain some trashy award is far more important than I am. Read this!'

She finished pressing a huge Elastoplast into place and I handed her Nick's terse little note, now crumpled and looking slightly the worse for wear.

'Why's it got cobwebs on it?'

'Because it's been behind the fridge. Read it and tell me if it sounds even remotely lover-like to you.'

She did, lips silently moving, then looked up uncertainly. 'Well, I suppose he *had* to go to the photoshoot if he's been shortlisted for Cookery Writer of the Year, Lizzy.'

'Big deal,' I said sourly. 'But never mind, at least he makes it clear that food is still much more important to him than I am, just in case I was harbouring any illusions.'

'Yes, but food is pretty important to you, too.'

'Maybe, but I still put relationships first.'

She sighed. 'Then perhaps men see things differently and he thought you'd understand.'

'He was wrong, then, wasn't he?'

She pored over the note again. 'It's *very* Nick, isn't it? You couldn't describe it as romantic.'

'Not by any stretch of the imagination, and it's short to the point of being terse,' I agreed.

Annie was still trying to find excuses for him. 'I expect he was in a rush, but you'll be able to see him at the award ceremony on the telly on Monday.'

'No I won't, because I've sold Tom's and the one in here is on the blink.'

'You can come and watch mine, then.'

'Thanks, but I think I'll stay home for a couple of days. My leg is very sore and I'm covered in bruises from Nick throwing himself on top of me. I had to hobble out in my dressing gown to let the hens out and I'm going stiffer by the minute.'

She went pink. '*Lizzy!* Too much information!'

'When he was putting the *flames* out,' I explained patiently. 'He rolled me in the mud.'

'Oh, how quick-witted and brave of him! He's a *hero*!'

'Don't start going all dewy-eyed and romantic again: it's pointless. I only wish I never had to see him again, because it'll be even worse than when I babbled my entire life history to him at the hospital, while Jasper was ill.'

'You'll feel differently after he's talked to you,' she suggested, ever the optimist. 'And he *will* phone you up—look, he says here in the note that he's going to—and then you'll see he really cares about you.'

'He'll find that difficult, since I don't intend answering the phone. I'll let the machine take the messages.'

'Come on, you know you won't be able to resist answering, in case it's Jasper.'

She's quite right, I do tend to snatch it up at the first ring—and it rang right then. We both froze and stared at it.

At the sixth ring she gave in and lunged for the kitchen extension that hung on the wall by the fridge. 'Hello? Oh, Nick, it's you! Yes, Annie . . . No, I've just put a fresh dressing on it. It's not too bad, but it'll be sore for a couple of days . . . I'll ask her.' She covered the phone and held it out towards me enquiringly.

'Tell him I've got much more important things to do than talk to *him*,' I said loudly, and started hobbling round the kitchen, opening the cupboard doors and slamming things about.

'I'm afraid she can't come to the phone at the moment . . . Oh, you heard?' She looked up. 'He says, what's more important than talking to him?'

'Food, of course—*he* should understand that,' I said pointedly. 'I'm making some giant rum truffles to send to Jasper. They're one of his favourites.'

After a moment she put the phone down. 'He says he's sorry he had to dash off, but he'll come and see you when he gets back, and to be careful. Careful of what?'

'I suppose he means careful in case the thrown firework wasn't some stupid adolescent prank last night, but Polly stepping up her campaign.'

'Oh, no, I'm sure even Polly wouldn't do anything so dangerous.'

'No . . . perhaps not. She's only done petty,

310

spiteful things so far.'

'I still find it hard to believe anyone could be so nasty. Couldn't it all just be coincidence, after all?'

'The ARG stuff was certainly her idea and, besides, when I told her I knew what she was up to, she didn't deny it.'

'Then I expect she's stopped now and the firework *was* an accident,' Annie said.

'Speaking of accidents, I'm afraid I was wearing that lovely coat you knitted for me last night, and by the time Nick had finished trampling it into the mud, it was beyond repair.'

'Never mind the coat, at least *you're* OK, that's the main thing. I can always knit you another.'

'That would be lovely,' I agreed, then added, lying through my teeth, 'Nick said it was such a shame it was spoiled because it was wonderful, and he wished he had one just like it.'

'Did he? Then I'll knit him one, too,' she said kindly. 'Well, I'd better be off—take it easy for a day or two, won't you? I can manage all the pet-sitting until you're fit again.'

'I'm just a bit stiff really, there's nothing wrong with me.' To prove it I got up again to see her out.

'When I arrived, Caz was in the barn doing exercises and Ophelia was sitting on a bale of straw watching him,' she said, pausing on the doorstep to look across the courtyard. 'But it looks like they've gone now, doesn't it?'

'It's a pity he wasn't here early enough to let the hens out. You know, I'm beginning to think I might as well convert all the outbuilding into accommodation, so everyone can just move in with me,' I said a little sourly.

*   *   *

Despite what I'd said earlier, I walked down to the village later, thinking the exercise might help loosen me up a bit. I still felt as though I'd gone three rounds with a gorilla.

I went into the post office to mail Jasper the box of giant rum truffles I'd made that morning, and an Advent calendar with a chocolate behind every window. I only hope he doesn't get zits. The post office was busy and everyone in the queue was still talking about my near-roasting, though the news of Nick's TV appearance had also got out and was causing much excitement. I said I expected it would all come down to a brief glimpse of him among the also-rans, then realised how sour grapes that sounded and shut up.

Of *course* I wanted him to win it, since clearly it meant so much to him. Of course I did . . .

On the way back home I noticed that Gareth's car was parked outside the vicarage and, on impulse, paid him a visit.

He gave me tea and I got right down to brass tacks.

'Look, Gareth, I hope you don't mind my speaking frankly, but Annie is my oldest friend and all this dithering about is making her miserable. So I want to know whether your intentions towards her are honourable. *Is* Barkis willing?'

He choked on his arrowroot biscuit, but when I could get any sense out of him it was just as I thought: they were both pussy-footing around, each thinking the other one only wanted to be friends.

'She loves you, you dimwit, she told me so,' I said plainly, but he was so modest it took a while to

312

convince him. When it finally did, he stared at me with dawning hope in his blue eyes.

'She'll be at home now, having lunch,' I said casually. 'I know she's got a busy afternoon, because she's covering my pet-sitting jobs as well as her own today, but I'll be fit to work again tomorrow. I'm . . .'

But I was talking to myself, because he'd gone without so much as grabbing his coat or saying goodbye. As I let myself out, I only hoped he had a key. We didn't want our vicar arrested for breaking into his own home, did we?

*　　　*　　　*

Annie phoned me up between pet-sitting jobs, almost incoherent with happiness, to announce that Gareth had proposed and they were now engaged. They're trying to get through to her parents to give them the glad tidings, but communication with that remote area of Africa is a little difficult at present.

But I'm sure when they do hear they'll be very happy and, if anyone deserves wedded bliss, I'm sure Annie does.

As for me, I remembered a recipe in one of my books for rabbit with chilli-chocolate sauce—and it was definitely different.

313

CHAPTER 25: CRÈME DE COEUR

Sunday started bright, crisp and frosty, so I really threw myself into tidying up the garden, raking up dead leaves for compost and clearing the annual herb beds, accompanied by a lot of hopeful hens.

In the afternoon, I covered my own Christmas cake and the six individual ones I'd made for the WI hampers with marzipan. Then, having some left, I made petits fours *by sandwiching marzipan between two walnut halves and put them in paper cases.*

The Perseverance Chronicles: A Life in Recipes

I found it hard to sleep on Saturday night, despite having spent the entire evening making yet more rum truffles—this time little ones for the WI hamper goody bags.

Every time I closed my eyes, lowlights of the night before kept running on a loop through my head and I became conscious of all the aches and pains of my poor bruised, singed and battered body.

There was little work to do in the garden now that winter had arrived, but on Sunday I still found enough both there and in the kitchen to keep myself occupied. That night I did finally fall asleep, exhausted and still smelling of the rum truffles I'd been putting into little Cellophane bags tied up with silver ribbon.

*   *   *

Monday's post brought me a card depicting the Tower of London with a *Crème de Coeur* recipe scribbled on the back, but I decided Nick could keep his heart to himself—if he'd got one.

At the CPC meeting I handed over all the little bags of truffles to Marian, another task done. I'd gone braced for lots of discussion of my Bonfire Night mishap, but luckily the news of Annie's engagement and Nick's forthcoming TV appearance were much more exciting.

We toasted the bride-to-be with the bottle of elderflower champagne I'd taken with me for the purpose, though of course she hadn't yet got a ring to show off.

'But I gave Gareth my little silver dolphin ring for size, and he was going to buy one today,' she said, looking rosy-cheeked and very pretty, though I think the latter partly attributable to her having finally listened to my advice about growing out her fringe and abandoning the pudding-bowl haircut.

'Do you trust him to get something you'll have to wear for the rest of your life?' asked Faye.

'Oh, yes,' she said simply. 'I'm sure it will be lovely.'

We discussed the wedding pretty exhaustively and also the impossibility of Gareth marrying himself, though of course if Annie's parents got back in time her father could perform the ceremony.

'I'd really love that,' she said wistfully. 'To be married by daddy in his old parish—that would be so special!'

'Well, I don't see why not, if that's what you want,' Miss Pym said.

We had a second elderflower champagne toast

and then, since we were once again at Faye's, we had another ice-cream tasting. The rum and raisin had the edge on the toffee apple, but they were both good.

Faye said my champagne had given her an idea and next year she might try concocting an elderflower ice cream, which she thought would have a delicate but interesting flavour.

*   *   *

I hadn't been home for long when Unks rang up and absolutely insisted I go up to the Hall to watch the awards ceremony on TV with him, Mimi and Juno that evening so, rather than upset him, in the end I agreed.

We all crowded round the big set in his den, which is decorated with a mixture of old racing prints and early Pharamond's Butterflake Biscuit posters, reflecting the varied strands that make up the family character.

The Cookery Writer of the Year award was just one among many, so we had to sit through Sport, Fashion and goodness knows what, before we got to it. It was just as well I'd taken up some of the walnut *petits fours* I'd made on Sunday evening and a big slab of very gingery parkin.

The cameras kept panning around the room and I caught a brief glimpse of Nick at one of the tables. I'd seen him in a dinner jacket before, of course, but never at a distance. It was like looking at a stranger . . . and I had a better chance to examine the effect when he went up to collect his award. Yes, he won the thing.

'I knew he would,' Mimi said complacently,

316

through a mouthful of parkin.

'You can't have known,' Juno said. 'He's not the only good cookery writer around.'

'He's in a league of his own,' she said loyally. 'And don't you think he looks handsome in his dinner jacket, Lizzy? He's the best-looking man in the room.'

He was certainly the tallest and though with those strongly marked features you couldn't in all fairness call him handsome, he was possibly the most attractive-looking man there. I realised I was sitting forward and leaned back again, casually.

'He scrubs up well,' I agreed grudgingly.

'He's coming home in a couple of days and bringing some people with him,' Unks told me. 'He asked me if I would mind if they decorated the hall, kitchen and dining room up as if it was already Christmas, so they could photograph it for an article.'

'Isn't it a bit late for that? I thought magazines did everything well in advance.'

'It's for the Sunday magazine he writes for and they were ready to feature some footballer or other; only now he's involved in a big sex scandal and his wife and children have left him, so they asked Nick instead.'

'It will be *such* fun, like having two Christmases,' Mimi said rapturously. 'Will we have presents too, Roly?'

'No, it's all fake. Don't get your hopes up. They'll bring everything they need to decorate the place with them, including a pretend Christmas dinner. Lizzy, Nick said to ask you if you would come, because they need extra guests for the photographs. And perhaps Annie and the vicar, too?'

317

'Kind of him,' I said drily.

'We'll all be in the magazine,' Mimi said, 'pulling crackers and opening parcels.'

I seemed to have already pulled a cracker and I hadn't recovered from the big bang yet.

Unks may have detected a certain lack of enthusiasm, because he asked anxiously, 'You will come, won't you, Lizzy? And Jasper too, of course, if he's home.'

'I shouldn't think he will be, though he'll be back for the real Christmas, of course.'

'I'm going to wear my blue lace dress,' Mimi announced.

'You'll have to: it's the only decent dinner dress you've got left,' Juno pointed out. 'I keep telling you not to garden in them.'

'Well, you've only got that black thing. Unless we buy new ones? What about you, Lizzy?'

'I don't have anything suitable at all, so I'd better not come,' I said quickly. 'I'm sure Nick won't want me there, anyway.'

'He said to ask you *specially*,' Unks said and they all seemed to be looking at me meaningfully . . . though, of course, they knew about the accident, for news travels fast round here.

'He was so brave at the bonfire, wasn't he, Lizzy? If he hadn't been so quick-witted you might have been badly burned,' Mimi said, reading my thoughts.

'Then he carried you back to your cottage after you fainted,' Juno sighed. She clearly has a much more romantic streak than her bluff exterior would lead you to believe.

'Yes, he's a real hero. He even spent the night on the sofa afterwards, in case I was suffering from

318

shock and needed anything,' I added pointedly. This was quite true, though of course I didn't mention that I had spent the night there too and, unfortunately, had needed something . . . or someone.

Mimi looked very thoughtful, but before she could say anything else I said quickly, 'Did you all know about Annie's engagement to the vicar?'

This proved distraction enough to keep them going until I went home.

*   *   *

I'd put the phone down on Nick twice since he'd left. When I heard his voice I couldn't think of a thing I wanted to say to him—or nothing polite, anyway. He got the message eventually and stopped phoning. Good.

He missed yet another Mystery Play rehearsal, though we were all word- and position-perfect, and into sorting out the costumes and props, ready for our final dress rehearsal before Christmas. This we always do up at the Hall, in two sessions in random order, as ordained by Clive and Marian, and Adam and Eve are sometimes excused from wearing their skimpy outfits on this occasion, because of the cold. (I was *so* hoping it would be cold! The less exposure in my new Spandex outfit, the better.)

Mimi and Juno must have been at a loose end, because they came down to watch the rehearsals again and Juno kindly read Nick's part in her big, deep voice.

'Might as well come along to the pub with you afterwards for a quick snifter,' she said heartily when we'd all finished.

'Actually, I'm going to the Butterflakes café-bar with Ritch, tonight,' I said, slightly self-consciously, though there's nothing particularly secret about our occasional friendly drinks. And I certainly didn't want Nick thinking that there weren't lots of other men interested in me, even if he wasn't . . .

'Oh, that sounds such fun!' Mimi said. 'I've never been to the Butterflakes bar. Why don't we go too, Juno?'

'Oh, we couldn't possibly intrude on Lizzy's evening,' Juno said, and Mimi's face fell.

Ritch was awaiting me outside, but when I turned round to introduce Mimi and Juno they'd vanished. Somehow I wasn't completely surprised to find them already ensconced at a corner table at the café-bar when we went in. They smiled and waved.

'Friends of yours?' asked Ritch.

'Roly Pharamond's sister, Mimi, is the one with silver curly hair. Juno is her companion—and I'm starting to suspect they're here tonight to keep an eye on me.'

'Do you need keeping an eye on?' he asked, brightening. 'Got anything interesting planned for later tonight?'

'No, just a drink, a chat and then home—alone,' I said pointedly.

'Oh, well, worth a go. Dora told me Nick Pharamond was the hero of the hour at the bonfire and you and he are, as she put it, only waiting for your six months' mourning to elapse before naming the day.'

'*Dora* said that?' I gasped, because if so, then the whole of Middlemoss probably thought the same! How on earth did these rumours get about?

320

'Yes. Sounds like something straight out of *Cotton Common*, doesn't it, though you should be wearing widow's weeds to look the part.' He glanced at me curiously. 'So, are you and the Young Master going to get hitched, then?'

'No!' I said forcefully.

'Well, you needn't bite my head off, I didn't suggest it! Though come to think of it, he does give me jealous looks whenever he sees me talking to you!'

'That's just a sort of general disapproval,' I explained. 'He thinks of me as part of the estate's goods and chattels.'

When we left, Mimi and Juno followed us out, though they could hardly hitch a lift in Ritch's sports car.

Juno stooped and said to me through the window, 'Might just call in on the way home, Lizzy. Roly wanted some more of that lemon marmalade and it slipped my mind earlier.'

So I was definitely being chaperoned! But I was sure it was entirely their own idea, and they couldn't keep it up twenty-four hours a day. It did the trick tonight, though, because Ritch dropped me off and left immediately. I think he found Juno rather alarming.

When the terrible twosome turned up ten minutes later, Mimi had a miniature paper umbrella behind one ear and was full of exotic cocktails, giggly and overexcited, but I thought she'd go out like a light once her head hit the pillow.

I should be so lucky.

*   *   *

321

There didn't seem any way of getting out of the photoshoot, especially since Annie and Gareth were very excited about it, but I had no idea what to wear and neither did Annie.

None of our clothes looked smart enough, especially if Juno and Mimi were getting dressed up in their best. In the end we thought we'd better buy something new, and I drove us both over to Southport in the Land Rover.

Annie wanted to look in bridal shops anyway, because she and Gareth hoped to get married in January, if Annie's parents could get back for it, and that didn't leave a lot of time for the preparations. She wanted me to be chief matron of honour and the rest of the CPC to form her bridal retinue, preferably dressed in pink, like a posy of slightly passé flowers. But her thrifty little soul was shocked by the high prices so we gave up after a while and searched out our dinner outfits instead.

Annie chose a midnight-blue chiffon tunic top with matching palazzo trousers, cinched in around her narrow waist (her shape is a *very* curvy hourglass) with a gold chain belt. Mine was a dark, clingy dress in a holly-leaf colour that made my eyes look very green. It had interestingly draped bits and looked like nothing on the hanger, but it certainly made the most of what assets I possessed when it was on.

In fact, it was dead sexy, and not at all the sort of thing I would normally wear, but in it I felt armoured for any eventuality.

*   *   *

When Nick came back very early on the Thursday morning, he instantly threw the Hall into a flurry of preparation for the Christmas photoshoot, though they didn't have to put any decorations or a tree up, because everything was supplied and the house was to be professionally 'dressed'.

Mrs Gumball had sent Joe down for some eggs, which is how I knew Nick was back, and after a few hours he finally managed to tear himself away and walked into my house without a by-your-leave.

I gave him one glance, as he lounged in the doorway in dark thundercloud mode, and then concentrated on beating my fruitcake mix to death: when he was wearing his Mr Rochester expression it was never a good sign.

'Why did you keep putting the phone down on me, Lizzy? Don't we have something to talk about?'

'We have *nothing* to talk about, Nick,' I said firmly.

'Yes we have! The other night—'

'Shouldn't have happened, and as far as I'm concerned it *never* happened,' I interrupted firmly. My arm was starting to ache by now, so I stopped beating and began buttering the cake tin instead.

'But, Lizzy—'

'Look, I don't want to think about it, let alone talk about it!' I snapped, crashing the tin back down on the tiled worksurface and glaring at him.

'Why? What was so wrong about—'

'I'm not discussing it,' I said. 'Just forget it, OK?'

He gazed at me, black eyebrows drawn together in a ferocious frown. '*Forget* it? Come on, Lizzy, it must have meant something to you!'

'Shock makes people do the strangest things, Nick. But if you like, you can put it down to an excess of gratitude that you saved me from serious burns,' I suggested.

'I don't want your damn gratitude,' he snarled, and then slammed out, making everything on the dresser rattle.

After putting the cake in the oven I sat down and scraped the mixing bowl clean. It tasted salty—but that was probably all the angry tears dripping into it.

CHAPTER 26: CRACKERS

It's best to leave a few days between covering your cake in marzipan and icing it, but it works perfectly well even if you don't. Mince pies freeze very well and defrost quickly, so I usually start to bake batches of them around mid-November. I've heard some people put sugar in their shortcrust pastry, but that sounds too sickly for words: the sweetness should come from the mincemeat filling. Nor do I dredge the tops of mine in yet more sugar . . . The whole world seems to have gone sugar-crazy!
The Perseverance Chronicles: A Life in Recipes

In the morning I had just begun icing the Christmas cakes when Mimi and Juno popped round to describe how the family had been banished to the kitchen and small morning room, while the hallway, staircase, drawing room, dining room and family silver were all being buffed up to a high polish.

'Only there isn't much family silver,' Mimi said, 'unless we drink out of Roly's racing trophies.'

She was more than a little overexcited, so I suspected that Juno's main reason in bringing her was to get her away from the Hall for a little while.

'You've never seen anything like it!' Juno said. 'Mrs Gumball is in high dudgeon and says if people wanted to see their faces in the furniture, they should have let her know years ago.'

'Yes, and Juno slipped and nearly fell in the hall, because they had polished under the rug,' Mimi said, helping herself to a scrap of fondant icing.

'She might have broken her leg all over again!'

She didn't sound terribly regretful about this, but I think she'd relished the unusual amount of freedom she'd enjoyed while Juno had been laid up.

'Stupid thing to do,' Juno agreed. 'But it's all nearly ready for tomorrow now.' Then she added, casually, 'Nick's been very bad-tempered today.'

'Isn't he always?' I asked.

'Oh, no, he only looks gloomy most of the time, he isn't really,' Mimi said. 'But since he said he was going to visit you yesterday, he's been really ratty. Did you fall out?'

'None of your business, Mimi!' Juno said reprovingly.

'We may have had . . . just a little misunderstanding,' I confessed. 'But we know where we both stand, now.'

'Where's that?' Mimi asked irrepressibly, but was frowned down by Juno.

'Are all these little cakes the ones for the WI hampers?' she said, tactfully changing the subject.

'Yes, we've done six each but we decorate them all the same, so no one knows who baked which.' I opened the old biscuit tin in which I kept the cake decorations and laid out half a dozen plastic sprigs of holly, robins sitting on logs and gold Merry Christmas plaques. 'Perhaps you could put one each of those on the tops for me, Mimi, while I look out the cake bands?'

I also got out the fruitcake I made yesterday, and neither of them complained about the taste, so perhaps I only imagined the mix tasted salty.

When they'd gone I put the small cakes away in the larder, ready to deliver to Marian at some point, then turned to our own, decorating it exactly the same way I do every year, with Santa emerging from a little forest with his reindeer sleigh. The bristly fir trees were firmly stuck together in the tin like an early form of Velcro, and had to be prised apart.

*   *   *

Annie and Gareth collected me in her car next day and we all agreed that it seemed very odd to be getting glammed up for a smart dinner before it was even lunchtime. Mind you, I dress up smartly so infrequently that it would have felt odd at *any* time.

They were looking forward to it, but I would have cried off, even at this late stage, if I could have done it without upsetting Unks. I mean, it wasn't even as if we could *eat* the damned food, since it was all going to be either fake and glazed with something to make it photograph prettily, or sit under the lights for so long it would be rife with three strains of salmonella.

Mimi had already rung me to describe how Christmas had arrived at Pharamond Hall very early that morning in a large van, along with a miscellaneous assortment of photographers, food technicians and the like, plus a snootily elegant grey-haired woman, whose job was to 'dress' the rooms they were to use: deck the Hall with boughs of holly.

Mrs Gumball let us in at the kitchen door and said that they'd already photographed in there and the hallway with its garlanded oak banister, until she was fit to scream, and she'd be glad when they were done. Then she took our coats and sent us

327

through into the dining room, which looked strangely unfamiliar.

Although it was barely midday, the crimson curtains were shut and the only light came from thousands of candles glittering off the polished dark panelling. Very realistic swags of festive foliage studded with gilded baubles were draped everywhere, in a colour scheme of crimson, gold and an ecclesiastical deep purple that must have made Gareth feel quite at home.

There were a lot of strangers milling about with cameras and lights and things near the dining table, on which gleamed an unfamiliar silver candelabra and a lot of sparkling cut glass, but the family were all gathered round the fire next to a large fake Christmas tree, among a litter of discarded festive giftwrap.

Nick, looking darkly morose and Mr Rochester in an immaculate dinner jacket, leaned on the mantelpiece with his foot on the fender, gazing into the flames and barely acknowledging our entrance.

Unks made up for this, however, by saying jovially, 'Come in! What excellent timing, because they're almost ready for us to do the Christmas dinner scene. Annie, my dear, you look lovely,' he added, kissing her. 'Being engaged suits you! You're a very lucky man indeed, Gareth.'

'I certainly am,' the vicar agreed, looking devotedly at Annie, and she blushed.

'Lizzy looks pretty too,' Mimi commented brightly, 'don't *you* think so, Nick?'

'She certainly looks different,' he said, actually looking at me properly for the first time and taking in the figure-enhancing effect of my new dress with a raised eyebrow. I suddenly wished I hadn't

328

bothered dressing up, but come in the dungarees I wear when I whitewash the henhouse.

'We've been opening presents,' Mimi said. 'They were all empty, but we are having real crackers.'

'And real wine,' Unks added. 'Need something to keep us going!'

'The Christmas tree pops up, decorations and all, like magic,' Mimi confided to us. 'Roly, can *we* have one of those?'

'No, I like the real thing, smelling of pine,' Roly said. 'And you like decorating it, don't you, m'dear?'

'Oh, yes, I hadn't thought of that,' she agreed.

'Can you take your places at the table, please?' someone called, and we went where we were directed, which in my case was between Juno and Nick.

People darted in to tweak, dab and twitch everything to perfection as we posed, slightly self-consciously, as directed. I was already aware that my new green dress fitted where it touched—and it touched almost everywhere—but when the photographer kept zooming in on my cleavage I began to wonder if it might be a bit over the top in more ways than one. Then Nick glared at him and he backed off a bit.

'Can we pull the crackers now?' Mimi asked plaintively. 'Haven't they finished yet?'

'OK . . . go ahead,' a man's voice said from the dark shadows.

They were certainly big, expensive-looking crackers, with equally pricey-looking novelties inside. Mine, which I pulled with Nick, contained a gold-plated pen, a gilt cardboard crown and a tightly rolled piece of paper.

'Does your motto make sense?' Juno asked, puzzling over hers. 'I think mine is supposed to be a joke, but I'm not sure. I mean, how *could* you cross an elephant with a mouse? That's not physically possible!'

'Read yours aloud, Lizzy!' ordered Mimi gaily. She was becoming flushed and excited.

I unrolled the long, thin strip of paper and found it entirely covered in Nick's instantly familiar spiky handwriting. 'Mine doesn't make sense either,' I said quickly, crumpling it into my hand. 'Do you want my pen to go with your little photo frame and gold dice, Mimi? They seem to match, don't they?'

'Oh, yes, please!' she said, but just as I was handing it over, there was the sound of a loud altercation outside the door and a bit of scuffling.

Then Mrs Gumball lumbered in, with a small, rotund and apoplectic man hard on her heels. She jerked a thumb over her shoulder in his direction. 'It's that little twerp Lionel Cripchet, from over Rivington way.'

'*Sir* Lionel,' he snapped, bobbing up in front of her and glaring generally round, but though we must have presented a very *Night Watch* sort of tableau, the strangeness of it escaped him under the urgency of his anger: 'I'm here for an explanation!'

'Are you?' Unks said mildly, taking another sip of wine. 'Well, now you *are* here, I wouldn't mind an explanation myself about that supposedly sound horse you sold me a couple of years back. Remember? The one that mysteriously went permanently lame the day after I bought it?'

'I'm not here to talk about horses, but squirrels! Yes, that's taken you by surprise, hasn't it? I

330

suppose you thought I wouldn't find out!'

'Is the man mad?' Juno asked. 'Why is he blethering on about squirrels?'

'Yes, spit it out, Cripchet,' Roly said amiably. 'Why are you blethering on about squirrels?'

'You know very well,' he exclaimed slightly wildly, looking at the vicar and Annie as if he expected them to come out in support, despite their baffled expressions. 'I've been overrun with the little grey bastards these last two years and now—last night—I finally caught him in the act!'

'Who?' asked Nick, then added, after a moment's thought, 'And what?'

'Your gamekeeper, Caz Naylor. His Land Rover was parked up a track next to my estate at one this morning! Now, what do you say about *that*?' Sir Lionel demanded triumphantly.

'Is Caz still around?' Roly asked Mrs Gumball.

'In the kitchen. Shall I send him in?'

'Do,' he agreed. 'I am quite sure he has a perfectly innocent explanation.'

'Ha!' said Sir Lionel, moustache bristling.

Caz slid silently into the room a moment or two later, but no further than the dark shadows just beyond the reach of the candlelight.

'Ah, Caz, Sir Lionel wants to know what your Land Rover was doing parked up a track next to his estate in the early hours of the morning,' Roly said. 'Were you indeed there?'

Caz nodded, almost imperceptibly.

'And I'm sure you had a very good reason?' prompted Unks.

'Of course he had a damn good reason!' yelled Cripchet, going puce and practically dancing up and down on the spot. 'He was releasing hordes of

331

flaming grey squirrels onto my land, that's what he was doing! There's standing room only and they're fighting for territory. It's like World War Three out there!'

'What do you say to that, Caz? What *were* you doing?'

'Courtin',' he said laconically.

'Courting?' demanded the infuriated baronet. *'Courting?* You can't expect me to believe that, Caz Naylor!'

'Actually,' the vicar interjected quietly, 'Caz and his fiancée, Ophelia Locke, have just asked me to put up the banns, so I see no reason to doubt him.'

'That's right,' agreed Caz, and then, clearly feeling that enough had been said, sidled back out of the door again.

'But the squirrels . . .' began Sir Lionel, baffled and furious.

'You know, Caz said he'd found a lot of the traps sprung but empty lately,' Unks said, with an air of sudden illumination. 'And that animal rights group, ARG, *are* very active around here, so I dare say they've been releasing them onto your land, that's what it is.'

Cripchet's lips worked silently and his skin went an even more ominous shade of puce.

'A drink before you go?' suggested Nick hospitably.

Sir Lionel looked from one to the other of us and said slowly, 'It's a damned conspiracy! You're all in league together!' and then he slammed out.

The magazine crew, who'd been watching with silent appreciation, broke into a spatter of polite applause. Roly bowed.

'There, all's well that ends well, isn't it?' he said

happily. 'And if you have finished with us, too, ladies and gentlemen, then I suggest we adjourn to the kitchen for something real to eat and leave you to pack everything up.'

When I got to my feet I discovered I still had the curl of paper from the cracker clenched in my hand and, for want of a handbag, shoved it down the front of my dress when no one was looking.

Mrs Gumball had hot soup and sandwiches ready, and by the time we'd finished those, Christmas had been dismantled, packed away and driven off again. Evidently it took much less time to do that, than set it all up.

Annie and Gareth were giving me a lift home and as we left, Nick called out to me, 'Lizzy, I'll have to go away tomorrow, but I'll be back by the end of the month, so I'll see you up here bright and early on the first of December.'

I stopped dead. 'You *will*?'

'Yes, it's the Senior Citizens' Christmas dinner, remember? Mrs Gumball is expecting us to both help cook it.'

'That's right,' she agreed.

'But surely, if Nick's helping, you won't want me under your feet, too?' I suggested hopefully.

'Many hands make light work,' she said firmly. 'And I've three geese to cook!'

*   *   *

The note in the cracker was Nick's recipe for prize-winning apple pie and I instantly saw that there was no startling difference between his and my own. So if his really *was* better, then it must mean that he had a lighter hand with the pastry, which was even

333

more unforgivable.

If he wanted a motto for his cracker, 'I shot myself in the foot' would do admirably.

CHAPTER 27: CHARMED

We had the first snowfall of winter last night and I awoke to find everything fuzzily flocked in white and looking Christmas-card pretty. This is when the birds are glad of the bright-berried bushes like pyracantha, holly and viburnum— but it's still only mid-November, so let's hope there are still lots of holly berries left for the Christmas decorations!
The Perseverance Chronicles: A Life in Recipes

Jasper and Ginny arrived unexpectedly next afternoon, dropped off for a couple of hours by his friend Stu, who had bought a car.

I wished he could have given me warning, so I could have cooked him something he loved, but it was wonderful to see him. I know we've talked over the phone a lot, but it wasn't the same as actually being able to put my arms around him and give him a hug. He looked sort of subtly grown-up too . . . and even Ginny refrained from trying to bite my ankles, so perhaps absence made the heart grow fonder. I told him about the photoshoot and what a hollow mockery of a real Christmas it had been, then after a while, he popped up to the Hall to see the family and came back later with the news that Nick was off travelling abroad for the next couple of weeks, which is something he does do from time to time, filing his copy from wherever he is. But yesterday he didn't say a word about where he was going!

Mind you, he hardly said a word to me at all . . .

Mrs Gumball had given Jasper half a cold roast chicken and an apple turnover to take back to university with him, Unks a fifty-pound note (I didn't even remember seeing one of those before) and Mimi, not to be outdone, presented him with the gold crown from yesterday's cracker. I'd already packed up a moveable feast as my contribution to the student larder, so they would none of them starve before the end of term.

When Stu came to pick Jasper and Ginny up again I heroically refrained from quizzing him about how good his car brakes were, or telling him to drive carefully. I think I deserved a medal for that.

*　　　*　　　*

At the CPC meeting I gave Marian the mini Christmas cakes and so did one or two of the others. 'Oh great,' she said, 'the hampers are coming along really well, I just need to bulk buy the boxes of mince pies nearer the delivery date.'

Of course we would have happily made those, too, but when surveyed the majority of the Senior Citizens preferred shop ones, though I've no idea why.

We were all crammed into Annie's tiny cottage and once she had poured the coffee and passed the Fondant Fancies, she tipped a big bag of pine cones onto the newspaper she had spread over the table and showed us how to turn them into Christmas tree decorations.

'I got the idea from a magazine and tried it with the Brownies last year, and they looked lovely,' she said, 'though I didn't let them loose with the

336

Superglue, of course.'

She demonstrated how to glue on a ribbon loop to the top, then dabbed a little gold paint around the cone, sprinkled it with glitter, and shook off the excess, before placing it in an old egg box to finish drying.

I'd wondered why she'd asked us to bring old egg boxes with us! And come to think of it, they would be perfect for storing any breakable tree ornaments too.

That evening the Mummers were in the workshop, practising the songs they would play in the intervals of the Mystery Play, and afterwards Ritch came over to the cottage and said he thought Ophelia was imminently going to give birth to a chest of drawers.

'She *has* suddenly grown a big bump, all out at the front,' I agreed. 'Though I suppose those smocks she wears have been hiding it for months and so it's only just become noticeable. She's no idea when it's due. You'd think she was living in the Middle Ages, the way she avoids modern medicine. Did you know she and Caz are going to get married?'

'Are they?' He looked at me over a table spread with home-made goodies (I'd half-expected him to come tonight) and unleashed his glowingly attractive smile. He appeared so blondly wholesome that I admit my heart gave a bit of a thump . . . Then I reminded myself that even if he *had* given up one of his dubious habits there was still the philandering and the healthy sex rota.

'Yes, they've put the banns up already. And Annie's parents are delighted about her engagement, too—they're flying back in the New

337

Year on leave for the wedding.'

Annie, now sporting a modest sapphire ring, was going about in a permanent glow of happiness.

'She and the vicar seem perfectly matched,' Ritch said. 'Maybe *I* should try it?'

'What, marriage?' I said, startled.

'Why not?' He gestured at the table. 'A woman who can cook like this is worth hanging on to!'

'Don't be daft,' I said, though rather flattered. 'Monogamy isn't in you!'

*　　　*　　　*

The *Cotton Common* cast were kept hard at it this week, so Annie and I were also kept busy dogwalking: I was becoming very fond of Flo, and also of Delphine Lake's little dogs.

Nick was not at the Mystery Play rehearsal that evening, of course, and it was all a bit unexciting. But then, it was mainly costume adjustments and props, for there were only a couple more rehearsals before the final dress one up at the Hall, so that was only to be expected.

Marian and Clive were also very involved in the annual Mosses Christmas Show, which was to take place in early December, so naturally they liked to have the Mystery Play well in hand in order to concentrate on that at the end of November instead.

I did go to the pub for a bit with the others, where Annie and Gareth revealed to me that they've decided that spending a fortune on a big wedding was immoral, so instead they were going to have a thrifty one and make a large donation to charity.

'Luckily I'm the same size as Mummy was when she got married, so she suggested I wear her lovely wedding dress,' Annie said on the Thursday, when I called in after taking Flo for a walk. 'I took it out of storage this morning, with the veil and everything, and it was *perfect*. It's hung up in my bedroom now. And dear Miss Pym says she'll try and find four bridesmaids' outfits in shades of pink on eBay, which she can alter to fit. She makes almost all her own clothes.'

'I'd never have guessed,' I said untruthfully. 'But what about a reception? It's a pity I got rid of the big glasshouse really, though I suppose it would have been too cold in January.'

'Oh, we'll have it in the village hall, with a simple buffet: perhaps all the guests could bring a contribution.'

'I'll make the wedding cake, that can be mine,' I offered. 'And do you know, I think getting married this way is going to be much more fun!'

'Yes, that's what I think, too,' Annie said, her eyes shining. 'And it will make our special day even more wonderful, knowing that we'll be helping others.'

'Spread the love,' I agreed, giving her a hug. 'Now, show me this beautiful wedding dress!'

*   *   *

It was Stir-Up Sunday, and the day when the church service traditionally included the prayer beginning with the words, 'Stir up, O Lord, the wills of your

339

faithful people', which always used to be the signal for the Christmas puddings to be made.

My own huge, round one was long since made, but I spent most of that day cooking the ones for the Senior Citizens' Christmas lunch. Mrs Gumball does all the rest of it, but I rather like making the puddings.

We'd stopped putting charms in them after a minor disaster when one of the Senior Citizens broke his dentures on a Bachelor's Button: in any case, they always refused to give them back, and it got expensive buying new ones every year.

I felt the first twinge or two of excitement that Christmas always gave me: dim but happy memories of those spent with my parents and more recent ones with the Vanes. And whatever difficulties I'd had with Tom, I'd always tried to make sure that Jasper, too, would have a hoard of joyous treasured memories of Christmas.

* * *

It had been ages since Nick had gone abroad, but not a single postcard, with or without tart recipe, had arrived. Meanwhile the CPC had become more of a Wedding Circle, since we spent almost the whole time discussing Annie and Gareth's big day!

Miss Pym put in low eBay bids on bridesmaids' dresses and had already secured two, which were on the way.

'And there does not seem to be much interest in bidding on the others, so I will know by this evening whether we have those as well,' she said. 'They are all in shades of pink, so though we won't match, we will have a theme.'

'Lovely,' I said resignedly, though pink is definitely not my colour and, to be honest, it's not going to do a lot for Faye's ruddy complexion, either. 'Though let's hope it doesn't snow, or we will freeze to death!'

'What about if we all get an ivory-coloured pashmina or wrap?' suggested Marian.

'Good idea,' I said, for at least a pashmina is likely to be useful later.

'The meeting had better be at my house again next week, so we can have the first fitting,' Miss Pym suggested, but by then we had completely lost the thread of our rota, as usual, so it might have been her turn anyway.

*   *   *

Although Ritch still often called in at the cottage after the Mummers sessions, we hadn't been to Butterflake's for a drink for ages, probably because he has another woman—or even two or three—on the go. Caz was still hanging around the cottage just as much as usual, though, but since he'd staked his claim on Ophelia, I supposed he would want to keep an even closer eye on her.

I finally got a postcard from Nick, with a Turkish delight recipe on the back. I wondered if that was an improvement on tarts . . .

*   *   *

We all had a mince pie tasting at the CPC over at Miss Pym's neat bungalow in Mossedge. We had to wait until we'd had our bridesmaids' dresses fitted first, though, so they didn't get marked.

The four of them varied from baby pink to a deep rose (mine) and are all the traditional tight-bodiced, full-skirted type, with big, puffed sleeves. There was much pinning and tacking, then we had our mince pies and a modest sherry, since most of us were driving.

Miss Pym had also found some cheap pashminas on the internet and we gave her the go-ahead to buy them.

'And Roly is providing all the flowers, including decorating the church and my bouquet,' Annie said gratefully. 'It is so kind of him. In fact, everyone is being wonderful.'

'That's because we all love you, dear,' Marian said. 'You will have a splendid day, just you wait and see!'

What with organising the Christmas Show, Senior Citizens' Christmas hampers and lunch, *and* directing the Mystery Play (among other things too numerous to list), Marian was, by the end of November, starting to look even thinner, her huge dark eyes sunken and her cropped silver hair bristling with electricity. But she and Clive always insisted they loved to keep busy: and they must have done or they wouldn't have volunteered for everything!

Luckily for their peace of mind, Nick returned just in time for the next Mystery Play rehearsal, albeit bleary-eyed, unshaven and very, very grumpy. He snapped out his lines with barely a look at me, which boded well for the next day's early morning start helping Mrs Gumball to cook the Senior Citizens' Christmas Lunch.

I can't describe to you how much I *wasn't* looking forward to that.

CHAPTER 28: COLD SNAP

I make my own version of those fat balls for wild birds that you can buy, mixing birdseed, dried fruits, nuts, bacon rinds and crumbs with some melted dripping or lard. You can either put blocks of it on the bird table or refill those coconut shells that are pierced for hanging up. The cold weather seemed to be set to continue into December and though the child in me found pleasure in the idea of a White Christmas, it would be hard on the birds and other small creatures.

The Perseverance Chronicles: A Life in Recipes

I was up at the Hall before dawn, carrying two baskets containing the big Christmas puddings, along with some brandy butter I'd whipped up the night before. It's not far, especially if you take the shortcut through the woods and the walled garden, but by halfway I'd begun to wish I'd taken the Land Rover.

Mrs Gumball and Nick were already hard at work by the time I arrived, and had divided the cooking between them, leaving me the role of skivvy. I quickly discovered that Nick is hell on wheels in a kitchen, too, and takes no prisoners. Had it not been for such a good cause I wouldn't have stood it for a second—but never again! The moment when it was all packed into the Meals on Wheels van and trundled down the drive was wonderful—as was the stiff drink and long soak in the bath I had as soon as I got home, despite it

343

being only lunchtime. Nick had offered to drive me back, but by then I wasn't speaking to him—if I had been in the first place, which was a moot point.

Annie, who had also risen early that morning to help put the Christmas decorations up in the village hall and then stayed to serve dinner, popped in to Perseverance Cottage later to report that it had all been a great success: the geese were delicious, and we'd all got a vote of thanks for our labours at the end.

Clive was going to write it all up for the *Mosses Messenger*, with photos . . . and come to think of it, I *did* vaguely recall that he'd been up in the Hall kitchen earlier and a flashbulb had gone off right in my eyes . . .

*   *   *

Marian and Clive rushed out the first December issue of the *Mosses Messenger* at record speed, and it was as I feared: there was a photograph of me looking hot, cross, shiny and dishevelled in the Hall kitchen, flanked by Nick, in gleaming chef's whites and Mrs Gumball, wearing a crisp, frill-edged pinny and with not a hair on her head out of place.

However, there was a lovely picture of the Senior Citizens toasting Annie and Gareth's engagement in dandelion and burdock, sherry, beer or Pinot Grigio, according to their tastes.

*   *   *

Once I'd recovered from that, I threw myself into giving the cottage its annual big Christmas clean, from the attic downwards. Unfortunately, when I went up to the attic I found I hadn't fully secured the bottom section of the loft ladder, so that it slid up when I was near the top. I clung to it, swinging to and fro over the stairwell like Tarzana of the Apes but, luckily, finally dropped off when over the landing. I lay there on my back for a few minutes, winded and giggling slightly hysterically, but after that I double-checked the ladder before trusting my weight to it.

I didn't do much up there anyway, other than sweep away the cobwebs and collect the boxes of Christmas decorations . . . especially after I discovered a few more forgotten odds and ends of Tom's. And I don't know why, but they made me burst into tears. I didn't *miss* him—in fact, there was a sense of relief that he wasn't ever going to be coming home again—but I think that made me feel even guiltier.

Perhaps there was added guilt, too, about what happened with Nick on Bonfire Night—but of course that was just a combination of alcohol, shock and a need for comfort, not love. Nick may be attractive (even when he's at his worst, barking orders at me in the Hall kitchen), but he's also exasperating, and that's twice he's dropped me like a hot potato and gone off doing something food-related and therefore *far* more important.

In between all my cleaning, I baked some Christmas tree gingerbread shapes for the next CPC, though wedding mania was still holding sway. Miss Pym intended making more adjustments to our dresses, since Marian was losing weight, while I was putting it on. I blame it on being unable to do much in the garden, which lately is either frozen hard, covered in snow, or both.

I couldn't believe that already it was the last Mystery Play rehearsal in the village hall, and really we didn't need it, we were all word-perfect. So after a quick run-through, we all turned to helping Marian and Clive set the hall up ready for the village Christmas Show the following evening. I was looking forward to that, since I never got involved, so all I was expected to do was buy a ticket and go to watch it.

It was late and bitterly cold when we went out, so most of us headed straight for home. Nick silently fell into step beside me, but instead of seeing me to my door he strode off at the turn from the drive up to the Hall with a brusque 'Good night!', leaving me to it.

*   *   *

Everyone goes to the Christmas Show, including Roly, Mimi and Juno. Even Nick came this year, but when Juno offered to change places so I could sit by him, I said quickly that I was quite happy next to Roly, and Nick glowered at me.

The evening followed its usual pattern: Ted the gardener gloomily produced rabbits out of a battered top hat and silk scarves out of the ears of members of the audience. He was followed by the infants singing carols, which always reduced most of the audience to tears, and Dave Naylor singing 'O Sole Mio', which didn't.

The Senior Citizens' Tea Dance Club's display of salsa dancing was particularly memorable. Some of

346

the others may have been more technically perfect, but the fire and liveliness of Mrs Gumball's performance more than made up for any little mistakes.

* * *

On the Friday I went to Liverpool to fetch Jasper, dog and baggage home for the Christmas holidays, though I took a wrong turning and circled one of the two cathedrals twice, before charging off in what luckily turned out to be the right direction.

It was lovely to see him again, but Ginny was still about as attractive as a hairball, and gave an experimental nip or two at my ankles as I hugged Jasper.

His belongings seemed to have doubled since I left him there in October, and we had a job getting them into the Land Rover. I treated that like a sort of three-dimensional jigsaw puzzle, which is something most women are good at since *life* is a three-dimensional jigsaw puzzle containing several trick two-sided pieces. (I'm sure Nick is one of those, from an entirely different puzzle.)

All the way home Jasper was silently texting messages on his phone and when I asked who to, he said his girlfriend! He didn't expand on this interesting remark but I expect he'll reveal all eventually.

* * *

The day after Jasper came home Nick slammed in through the kitchen door like a whirlwind and demanded, 'Why didn't you *tell* me Ophelia Locke

347

was the ARG supporter who was targeting you—
and at Polly Darke's instigation?'

'How did you find that out?' I blurted, taken off
guard.

'Caz just told me, among several things he
suddenly decided I ought to know—and I might
have taken the other incidents more seriously if I'd
known about it.'

Jasper, who'd been sitting at the table finishing
off a late, late breakfast, looked up. 'Ophelia was?
What, with those animal rights people?'

'You mean, you didn't know about it either?'
Nick said in a quieter voice, seeming slightly
mollified.

'I didn't tell him—or about the other incidents,' I
said, 'because I didn't want to worry him.'

'Which other incidents?' asked Jasper.

Nick gave him a quick résumé of what had been
happening and then added, *'And* there was a
firework thrown at her at the bonfire, did she tell
you about that?'

'We don't know that was Polly,' I said, going pink
as usual when anyone mentioned Bonfire Night.

'Actually, we do, because Caz spotted her doing
it.'

'He did? Then why on earth didn't he say so?'

'You know how he feels about the police. It took
him long enough to tell me.'

'You won't tell Unks about Ophelia being in
ARG, will you?' I asked anxiously. 'Only they've
thrown her out now, and since she and Caz are
getting married it would be a pity to spoil
everything.'

'You are the strangest woman!' Nick exclaimed,
looking exasperated.

'She certainly is,' Jasper traitorously agreed. 'Do you know, I found her crying over her postcard album when I came downstairs earlier and when I asked her why, she said there was something terribly sad about *Crème de Coeur*!'

Nick seemed strangely cheered by the thought of my misery. 'She did? Well, well!'

'Shouldn't we do something about this woman, if she's playing nasty tricks on Mum?' suggested Jasper.

'Something *is* going to be done,' Nick assured him. 'Leave it to me.'

'Oh, right,' Jasper said, looking relieved. 'Well, come on, Ginny. Mum, can I borrow the car, if you don't need it today?'

'Why, where are you going?' I asked automatically.

'Meeting Stu and some other friends, and maybe going to see a film and have a pizza, but I won't be late. And I won't drink and drive,' he added patiently.

I handed him the keys to the Land Rover. 'Are you meeting your girlfriend?'

Jasper tapped the side of his nose infuriatingly, which was all the reply I got. Nick followed him out and I saw them talking together before I closed the door against the icy wind.

When I looked out again, the yard was deserted and the hens had retired to huddle somewhere warmer. The very last Honey, her thick brown feather bloomers blown up like an inside-out umbrella, was running up the ramp into the henhouse.

CHAPTER 29: CLUELESS

Today's meeting of the CPC was our Christmas party, because instead of the next one we were all going to help pack and distribute the WI Senior Citizens hampers. Everyone came to Perseverance Cottage bearing food—little triangular sandwiches, quiche, individual cream-topped sherry trifles decorated with green diamonds of angelica and, of course, Christmas cake. We ate our slices at the end with a chunk of crumbly Lancashire cheese on the side.

We had a lovely time, but after they'd gone and I was clearing the table, I couldn't help remembering back to when my son was taken ill on the same occasion, five years earlier . . .

The Perseverance Chronicles: A Life in Recipes

I scribbled a heartfelt 'but thank goodness he pulled through!' to end the paragraph, thinking how lovely it was to have him home again, even if he did seem to be out of the house most of the time. There was certainly nothing wrong with his appetite: food vanished from the fridge and cake tins overnight, and I was making mincemeat flapjacks on a daily basis.

His Christmas present wish list seemed to consist almost entirely of books and CDs, although I'd already collected a few bits and pieces, including a spectacular Swiss army knife with millions of gadgets, which I rather coveted myself. I was sure it would come in handy.

I had an awful lot of handwritten pages of notes

350

for my next *Chronicle* and the *Just Desserts* book to type up, which would keep me occupied between all the Christmas stuff. But then, I'd already made the Christmas cake and pudding, and I didn't need to think about Christmas dinner itself, because we always had it up at the Hall with the family. It will be yet another goose . . . but then, it usually was.

*   *   *

The first Mystery Play dress rehearsal (for which I wasn't needed) took place up at the Hall, and apparently went quite well, with only one or two minor mishaps. Clive and Marian randomly mix up the various acts of the play for the two dress rehearsals because there's a feeling that it would be unlucky to do the complete thing right through before the actual performance. I could only hope that the snow had thawed and it was not quite so bitterly cold when I came to rehearse in my Eve costume the following Tuesday.

While I was out on pet-sitting duty, Caz dropped a freshly cut Christmas tree off at the cottage, and by the time I returned Jasper had set it up in its stand in the sitting room and was opening the boxes of decorations we'd collected over the years, along with some old family ones I could remember my mother hanging up. Out came the fragile glass violins, trumpets and bells; the bright birds with purple and pink feather tails and the gaudy strings of slightly balding tinsel.

We don't have lights because I'm convinced they will set the house on fire. I don't know why, though perhaps distant memories of the way the bulbs used to pop when my father turned them on might have had something to do with it. I expect that's where I get my uselessness with electricity from.

Later, while Jasper finished the decorating, including hanging a stocking for Ginny from the mantelpiece, along with his own, I baked thin, crispy star-shaped spice biscuits to hang on the tree with ribbon, the finishing touch.

While I did this, the sound of carols on the CD player, the mingled smell of spices and pine . . . the memory of the cold, crisp air outside—all these seasonal elements combined until the magic of Christmas, as always, had me in its thrall.

*   *   *

Unfortunately, next morning I found PC Perkins standing on my doorstep, her dark uniform lightly frosted with snowflakes like a rather odd Christmas card. She very politely suggested that we go and look in the outbuilding where I kept my gardening tools, because she'd received an anonymous tip-off.

She didn't say a tip-off about what, but I said she was welcome to go and look, and I would follow her over once I'd put my wellies and anorak on.

When I got there, having waded through an audience of interested hens, she was standing staring up at the wall rack where my tools hung fairly neatly—and there, hooked among them, my blue steel cross-shaped wheel brace.

'Is that the one you used to change your tyre, on the day your husband took your car?' she enquired.

'It certainly looks like it,' I began, reaching up for it, but she put her hand on my arm to stop me.

'Please don't touch it, Mrs Pharamond.'

I let my hand fall to my side. 'But . . . I'm sure it

wasn't there before! I'd have noticed it when I was hanging up the tools, because it doesn't live there. I always kept it in the car.'

'So when did you last see it?'

I frowned, trying to remember, though the events of the summer seemed an awfully long time ago now. 'I'm pretty sure that when I'd finished changing the wheel, I slung it in the footwell behind the driver's seat,' I said slowly. 'Didn't I already give you a statement about that? But of course Jasper checked the wheel too, while I was in the cottage, and I can't recall what he said he did with it. He's gone up to the Hall, but I'll ask him when he gets home, shall I?'

'If you don't mind,' PC Perkins said, unfolding a large plastic envelope and inserting the wheel brace into it. 'And I'll just take this and check it for fingerprints, if you have no objection?'

'Not at all,' I said politely, 'but you'll only find mine and Jasper's, won't you?'

'Just routine. We like to tie up all the loose ends,' she said, giving me that 'I'll get you yet, you murderess' smile. After such a long silence, I'd convinced myself that I'd only *imagined* the police were suspicious of me, but clearly I'd been quite right all along!

*   *   *

When he came in, Jasper said he thought he might just have propped the wheel brace up against the barn wall when he'd finished tightening the nuts, but he couldn't be sure. He could equally well have tossed it into the back of the car, where it usually lived.

353

'But whichever way, someone must have put it with the gardening tools recently and then told the police,' I said, puzzled, 'because I'd definitely have noticed it if it had been there all this time, since I'm constantly taking tools out and putting them back—*and* it was hung on top of my favourite spade. But what's the point, when finding it won't tell the police anything they didn't already know?'

'I wouldn't worry about it, Mum. I expect she really meant it, about tying up loose ends. And you *are* vague sometimes, so you might have moved it to get at the spade, and not noticed it was there.'

'I'm not *that* vague. And who tipped them off about it, and why?'

'It's a mystery, but not one that's important. I'd forget it,' he advised. 'Or you could tell Uncle Nick about it and see what he thinks.'

'No, thanks,' I said crisply. 'He'd probably just accuse me of losing my marbles, like you.'

*　　*　　*

Jasper had now become even more antagonistic towards poor Ritch, if that were possible, and warned me that if he became his stepfather he would leave home! I assured him that even if I had been tempted to remarry, which was the last thing on my mind, I would certainly not replace one chronic philanderer with another.

I expected it was all because he overheard Ritch jokingly asking me to marry him again, when he caught us having a Christmas kiss under the mistletoe I'd suspended from the drying rack. (I hang mistletoe up every year, but that was the first time I'd struck lucky.)

Ritch and I had already exchanged presents. He gave me a delightful little sparkly crystal snowman brooch and I gave him a box of home-made Turkish Delight (from the postcard recipe sent to me by Nick) and a large rawhide bone for poor old Flo, about to be immured in kennels while her master flew off to stay with friends in the Caribbean over Christmas.

I might have felt compelled to offer to have Flo myself if it hadn't been for Ginny: one snap of Flo's powerful jaws and Ginny would be only a lingering memory. However, Flo was booked into the local luxury Dogtel, with heated beds and her own run, so I didn't suppose she'd find it too traumatic.

Jasper didn't, however, extend his antagonism towards *all* my male visitors, even on one occasion helpfully pointing out the mistletoe to Nick before he went out, though luckily I don't think he heard him.

But at least Nick now seemed to have finally accepted that I simply wanted to forget what happened on the night of the bonfire and continue as we were before, so we were back on our old, slightly argumentative but fairly amicable terms, and he was helping me with recipes for *Just Desserts*.

He began bringing down bundles of his old notebooks for me to copy things out of, though his idea of what was suitable and what wasn't didn't exactly coincide with mine.

It was no wonder I was putting on weight, because I'd adjusted my chocolate intake to compensate for . . . well, I didn't really *know* what for, but it was very comforting. Have you ever tried hot chocolate custard?

Jasper and I went up to the Hall for Sunday lunch and Roly had the newspaper magazine with the Christmas photoshoot article in it. And actually, it all looked really magical, lush and quite swish, in a slightly medieval sort of way, not fake at all.

Mimi said she thought Juno looked just like Edith Sitwell, but luckily Juno mixed her up with Edith Cavell and was vaguely flattered, saying she knew she was a heroine putting up with Mimi but that might be going a bit *too* far.

I'd taken up a box of the spice biscuits, all ready threaded with ribbon for hanging, and we decorated their big Christmas tree in the hallway after lunch, with Nick leaning over the banister to place a porcelain-faced angel on the very top.

I was convinced that their Christmas tree lights were made of Bakelite! I only hoped they'd had an electrician check them in the last fifty years.

I was so glad I'd got a Land Rover, because I used to be very nervous about driving on snowy roads and now I wasn't in the least. We had another light snowfall on top of the last lot, which had half-thawed on the roads and then refrozen, making it pretty treacherous, but I made it easily down to the village hall to help with the hampers.

Each recipient had ticked boxes on a form giving their likes, dislikes and preferences (Marian was nothing if not organised) so we just had to select from the list and assemble each box, which were the cardboard sort printed with a green holly pattern, with pop-up handles.

Several of the WI members had four-wheel-drive vehicles, so were going to deliver the hampers that afternoon, when the roads had been gritted.

'Another job done,' Marian announced with satisfaction as the last of them drove away. 'There's just the final Mystery Play dress rehearsal tomorrow, and then we can all relax and just enjoy ourselves over Christmas.'

'Except we actually have to *do* the play on Boxing Day,' I pointed out, and the thought of shivering in the snow in my new Eve outfit was not an enticing prospect.

'But that's the fun bit,' Annie said, then sighed. 'I will miss our CPC meetings until we start again in summer, though.'

'This year I think we need to start again right after Christmas,' I said, 'only as Wedding Organisers instead!'

CHAPTER 30: UNSCHEDULED APPEARANCES

The snow lingers and, though the local farmers have kept the roads around the village open, more is forecast. It won't stop the Mystery Play, though—nothing has ever done that, not even Cromwell!
The Perseverance Chronicles: A Life in Recipes

On Tuesday afternoon I walked up to the Hall after lunch for the second of the Mystery Play dress rehearsals. I left Jasper typing up some of my latest *Chronicle* onto my new laptop. He was much faster than me, so that was a big help.

He said Unks wanted him to go up to the house later in the afternoon, so he would see me there.

The cobbled courtyard of Pharamond Hall where the audience stand to watch is bound on one side by the kitchen wing and on the others by stables and outbuildings, making it very sheltered. The entrance is through a large arched gateway with, directly facing it, a second arched doorway to the coach house, which forms the stage for the performance.

Marian, Clive and most of the cast for the rehearsal scenes were already there, milling about, while the Mummers of Invention (minus Ritch, of course, who was on his way to the Caribbean) stood in one corner, running through the song for the first interval. Ophelia was wearing a knitted poncho in three shades of mud brown and it was stretched to the limit over her now enormous baby bump.

Various bits of scenery and old props had been dragged out of storage and the loose boxes on either side set up as changing rooms. I knew Joe Gumball had already hung up the stiff, heavy canvas curtains in the entrance to the coach house, because Jasper and Nick had helped him, and now he was checking that the star lantern slid easily across the wire behind it.

There was a chilly wind blowing, and since the courtyard was not warmed by braziers and a massed audience, as it would be on the night, we ran through our scenes pretty briskly. Clive was reading the Voice of God today and started with Lucifer being cast out of Heaven. The silent angels, with their freshly flighted wings, trooped on and off on cue, but when Moses did his scene he interjected more than a little acerbity into his lines: his rheumatism was clearly still playing him up.

I was on next, but luckily, due to the extreme cold, Clive kindly excused Adam and Eve from having to change into costume, which was a relief. I didn't know about Nick, but I was having serious doubts about the decency of my new Spandex outfit. Still, at least we were back on reasonably good terms again and from the tone of our voices you would have thought we were discussing the price of fish, not contemplating any kind of temptation.

After that, Miss Pym and some of the parents brought the infants up from school in an orderly but excited crocodile, carrying their animal masks, to practise the Ark scene.

'And all the animals came into t'ark out of the rain, and, by heck, it were pouring down,' Noah said, standing next to Mrs Noah, who was seated on

359

a bucket. The children started to march past two by two, growling, roaring, hissing and generally sounding like a zoo at feeding time. Last of all came a solitary unicorn.

'There's two of every darn thing—except t'unicorn. Yon's not going to breed on its own, Wife.'

'Well,' said Mrs Noah, reluctantly looking up from her knitting, which was presumably a late Christmas present she was keen to finish, 'there's no more of 'em. Reckon that's the end o' the line for t'poor little beast. I never did see much use for it, though it's proper bonny.'

'It attracts virgins, so they say,' said Noah.

'Well, it's just thee and me now, chuck, so I reckon them have died out an' all,' said Mrs Noah. 'Knit one, purl two!'

After the Ark scene we always have a break before the Nativity, so all the little animals can see Father Christmas before going home. By now Annie and Gareth had arrived together and helped Miss Pym shepherd the excited children through the arched gateway to be lined up again, *sans* masks, outside the front door of Pharamond Hall.

The rest of us went through the kitchens the back way to the cavernous hallway, where a log fire roared and the fairy lights flickered on the huge tree like so many weak fireflies (and I am sure they are not supposed to do that). Roly was sitting in an ancient carved chair next to it, dressed in the red, fur-edged hooded suit and black boots traditional on these occasions, and puffing at a cheroot, which was not. Over the years his wig and beard had yellowed with nicotine, so that I'm sure the scent of tobacco would forever remind successive generations of local children of Christmas.

In the shadows just behind the chair lurked Caz Naylor, the largest elf you ever saw, wearing pointed Spock ears and with his hat jammed down hard over his eyebrows, waiting to hand the presents to Father Christmas. What always surprised me was the way he could move so silently when his outfit was entirely covered in little bells. Perhaps he'd stuffed them with something?

The fire glowed in the huge hearth, and the candle bulbs in the cartwheel of evergreen foliage that was suspended from the ceiling were dimmed. The house smelled of cinnamon and burning fir cones, hot mince pies and spiced punch from the bowl on the trestle table laid out ready.

From beyond the great oak front doors came the sound of a lot of reedy young voices belting out 'Good King Wenceslas' at the top of their lungs: distillation of pure Christmas magic, again.

'Here we go,' Unks said, regretfully removing the stub of cheroot from his mouth and tossing it accurately into the fire. 'Let the little blighters in.'

Nick swung the door open and a tide of children rushed forward, only to be halted in their tracks by Miss Pym, who has a presence and voice that could command armies.

'*Stop!*' she commanded.

'Ho, ho, ho,' Unks said benevolently. 'Come in, one and all!'

Joe Gumball activated the CD player and 'White Christmas' began to chirrup merrily in the background.

There was a gift for every child, and while Miss Pym orchestrated the queue, the adults fell on the food and drink. A few older children appeared as parents began to turn up to collect their offspring, but there was a bag of extra gifts for this contingency, so no one went away empty-handed.

By now Jasper had arrived too, and was talking very seriously to the vicar in the corner. At a rough guess, I'd say they were discussing the eating habits of Biblical folk or something like that, unless Gareth had a personal hobby horse and a stronger will than Jasper's. Annie had gravitated across to join them, and Trinny, wearing a collar of tinsel, was circling Ginny in a vaguely menacing manner, probably trying to decide which end was which.

Jasper picked Ginny up and Trinny immediately lost interest and wandered off under the table, where there were rich pickings in crumbs and discarded pastry. Mrs Gumball's idea of children's party food ran to miniature pork pies, tiny triangular sandwiches, and little jellies in paper cases with a blob of cream and a diamond of angelica on top of each. The hot mince pies and punch were strictly for the adults.

Eventually Santa announced that the reindeer were getting restless and he had to leave, which was the cue for the last of the tired but happy children to be taken home. As the final car vanished down the drive, Clive Potter firmly rounded the cast up for the final part of today's rehearsal: the Nativity, and another song or two from the Mummers.

Jasper had already gone home and Nick was helping Roly out of his robe, boots and wig, but the rest of us trooped out again into the growing dusk, warm, full and a bit reluctant. Marian and Kylie made for the loose box changing room to adjust her Mary costume, while our Joseph, Dave Naylor, leaned against a wall in his striped robe, smoking a cigarette.

'Where's Ophelia?' Jojo asked, looking around him vaguely. 'We're supposed to be playing "While Shepherds Watched" before the next scene starts.'

'Dunno. Haven't seen her for ages,' Mick said, then cupped his hands round his mouth and bellowed, 'Ophelia!'

'That's funny,' I said. 'Now I come to think of it, I don't remember seeing her in the Hall, either. Has she gone home? I hope she's feeling all right.'

Caz appeared, without his elf ears.

'Caz,' I called, 'do you know where Ophelia is? Only no one seems to have see—'

I faltered as a piercing howl of anguish echoed from the stables we used as dressing rooms. Then Marian Potter's cropped, silvery head appeared over the half-door and she cried wildly, 'Help! Is there a doctor in the house?' before bobbing down again, more Punch and Judy than Mystery Play.

Unfortunately Dr Patel had rehearsed his scenes the previous week so he wasn't present. There was a second's breathless hush, then we all rushed across the yard. Caz beat Annie and me to it, but it was a close-run thing and the others crowded up behind.

Inside the dimly lit stable, with no more ado than a couple of pangs and an animal urge to be alone, Ophelia had chosen to give birth, if not *in* the manger, certainly right *next* to it.

She lay pale, spent and panting slightly on the straw, her big eyelids closed, while Kylie, clearly revolted, was holding a messy and screaming baby at arm's length.

It was amazing! I'd never seen an infant that so closely resembled a fox cub, and there could be absolutely no doubt that it was Caz's.

'Something to wrap him in,' Marian ordered distractedly, but Joseph was already passing his voluminous striped towelling headdress over. Caz slipped through the door, removed his child from Kylie's uncertain grasp and enfolded it in the warm material. Then he sat down on an upturned bucket. The baby, as if by magic, stopped bawling and stared up at him.

Gareth, who was still leaning over the half-door between Annie and me, now said slightly uncertainly, 'Bless you, my child!' like an aged bishop. Still, I don't expect this is a situation he's ever had to contend with before.

Clive, efficient as ever, had already trotted back to the house to tell Unks and call an ambulance. He said the horse might have bolted, but a check-up of mother and baby was clearly indicated.

*   *   *

There was a feeling of anticlimax about the rest of the rehearsals once Ophelia, the infant and Caz had been whisked away to hospital. Ophelia hadn't wanted to go, and Caz had almost balked at the sight of the ambulance's brightly lit and clinical interior, but Nick had reappeared by then and firmly shoved him in and closed the door.

'I wonder if she's actually got anything ready in her cottage for the baby's arrival,' I mused.

'Oh, yes. Dave says all the Naylors have rallied round with baby clothes and equipment,' Annie assured me.

'I think their wedding had better be postponed until after the christening,' Gareth remarked thoughtfully. 'Or perhaps we can do both on the same occasion? I'll have to consult the bishop.'

'If they can decide on a name,' I said. 'Star and Rambo seemed to be frontrunners last time I talked to Ophelia.'

Gareth gave me a doubtful smile: I expect he thought I was joking.

We rushed through the Annunciation, Nativity and Flight into Egypt at breakneck speed. Kylie was distinctly huffy, and clearly felt she had been upstaged, though Joseph, bare-headed, performed his part with perfect sang-froid.

Afterwards, most of the cast set off for the New Mystery, and I bagged a lift with Gareth and Annie. Nick followed us down in the estate pick-up, with nine angels crammed in the back and Lucifer sitting beside him.

When we got there I took our usual corner seat with Gareth and Annie, but it was only when we sat down that I realised Nick hadn't followed us but was smiling and talking with Polly Darke over near the bar. He's so tall he must have had a bird's-eye view down her cleavage: her twin prows were jutting out like the front of a catamaran.

She noticed I was watching and flashed a triumphant look in my direction as he steered her away to a darker corner, one hand under her elbow and his glossy dark head bent towards hers.

My mouth must have been hanging open, because Annie nudged me with her elbow and asked anxiously, 'Are you all right, Lizzy? You look a bit odd.'

'I'm fine,' I said with an effort, 'just a bit tired, suddenly.'

'Yes, me too. Where's Nick? I thought he

followed us in.'

'He decided to go for a bit of a tramp,' I explained.

'I expect he needed some fresh air,' Gareth said vaguely, as if we hadn't already spent most of the day out in the cold, freezing our socks off.

'If you don't mind, perhaps I'll just get off home, after all,' I said. 'I feel a bit tired, and there's such a crowd it'll take her ages to come for our orders anyway.'

'Don't you want to wait and we'll drive you back?' asked Annie. 'We won't be long, because Trinny's in the car, and she'll get cold.'

'No, that's all right,' I said, getting up. 'It's only five minutes away and Jasper will be there. I'll let you know if I hear any more about how Ophelia and the baby are doing.'

On my way out I sneaked a glance at the corner where Nick and Polly were still sitting, their heads close together.

*   *   *

'Come on, Mum, obviously he's doing it for a reason,' Jasper said, when I told him about Nick's betrayal—which I did about five seconds after arriving home. It was that or burst.

'Oh, yes, I could see that,' I said shortly. Ginny, not liking the tone of my voice, ran her teeth thoughtfully up and down my ankle.

'No, Mum, I meant it must be part of some plan he has, because he said he would deal with her, don't you remember?'

'Then he's going about it in a strange way! And if you're right, why didn't he tell *me* what he was going to do?'

'You kept everything a secret from him, didn't you? He only found out from Caz and Leila what was going on. And I expect if he'd told you, your reaction when you saw them together wouldn't have looked half as authentic. Now she'll think she's putting one over on you.'

'Maybe she is: he wouldn't be the first man unable to see past a pair of pneumatic boobs.'

'Not Uncle Nick,' he said stoutly. 'Really, Mum, you can't possibly believe that—she's a complete dog.'

'Bitch,' I said, absently, because I was wondering if he could be right. Then I realised what he'd said. 'That was a bit rude, Jasper!'

'I suppose it was—but I only meant that she's no competition, so you don't need to worry about Uncle Nick falling for her.'

'I'm not worried in the least, he can fall for anyone he likes,' I assured him, then rather spoiled the effect by adding, 'but while we're speaking of bitches, Jasper, do you think you could teach yours not to nip my ankles?'

'She's just being friendly,' he said fondly, bending down and giving her a pat. 'By the way, Unks rang and told me about the nativity at the Nativity—sorry I missed it!'

'Just don't expect a repeat performance on Boxing Day,' I warned him. 'I think we'd all better stick to the script from now on.'

CHAPTER 31: MIDDLEMOSS MARCHPANE

I just made a chocolate, fruit and nut Christmas wreath, by packing melted chocolate mixed with puffed rice breakfast cereal into a ring mould, then studding the surface with whole nuts of various kinds, crystallised cherries and other candied fruits, glued on by half-dipping them in more melted chocolate. I'm going to have it as our table centrepiece on Christmas Eve, with a red candle in the middle.
The Perseverance Chronicles: A Life in Recipes

Word had it that Ophelia discharged herself from hospital almost as soon as she had been checked over, but the Naylor clan were rallying round.

I spent the next couple of days doing Christmas baking, including the fine ham that Roly had sent down for me (he does this every year), and making a big trifle and a Middlemoss Marchpane.

I put the recipe for the latter, with one or two small adjustments, into *Just Desserts*. I was going to save it to take up to the Hall with us on Christmas Eve, for we always went to listen to the carol singers, whose first call it traditionally always was. But then Jasper's friend Stu came over to stay the night and they demolished it, so I had to set to and make another.

I drove up to the Hall, since as well as the Marchpane I had my contribution to tomorrow's Christmas dinner with me: a vat of mulligatawny soup and the giant round Christmas pudding. There was also a box of presents to put under the tree, most of them home-made and edible.

We've always had Christmas dinner up at the Hall: Mrs Gumball would go in early to cook breakfast and put the goose into the oven, then I would finish the cooking and serve it. But this year Nick was here, so apart from my soup and pudding contributions (and some brandy butter ice cream I'd got from Faye), he was doing it solo. He'd have to, because after my previous experience as chef's skivvy, I'd no intention of ever letting myself in for that again.

In fact, I was now trying to avoid him altogether, since every time I looked at him a nasty picture of his and Polly's heads, flirtatiously close together, slid into my mind. I might have agreed with Jasper that it was all just a cunning ploy to get information out of her, but I wasn't a hundred per cent convinced . . .

Joining in with the carol singers round a roaring fire up at the Hall always seemed a significant moment and by the time they'd all trooped off again, full of sherry and mince pies, I felt as full of anticipation as a child.

Back home once more, we had our usual Christmas Eve supper of thick slices of the Christmas ham with egg and chips, followed by first go at the big sherry trifle I'd made. Then we watched an old film in the sitting room on Jasper's little TV, which he'd brought back with him, along with all his other stuff. He'd fixed the kitchen one, too, by the simple expedient of changing the plug.

Jasper's stocking, which had been knitted for him by Annie when he was a toddler, hung next to Ginny's at one end of the mantelpiece. Mother Claus would fill it and hook it over the handle of his bedroom door later, as she always did . . . and I suspect she'd better hang Ginny's there too, or there would be trouble.

There was quite a heap of gifts under our tree. I couldn't resist fingering the ones from the family we had brought back with us, but of course I couldn't open them until next day, or it would spoil the surprise . . .

*   *   *

We had an orgy of unwrapping next morning while Ginny chewed noisily on a rawhide version of a candy cane and, although I'm sure we both *thought* of Tom while dividing up the presents into two piles, rather than three, neither of us mentioned his name. He'd hardly been around much for the last four or five years anyway, spending as little time in our company as possible, so the spirit of Christmas past didn't really haunt us, even if we were briefly saddened by the ghost of what might have been.

Jasper gave me a pen, the kind with liquid inside that you tilted so an Egyptian sarcophagus lid slid open to reveal a mummy's mask. There was a mummy-shaped biscuit tin too, so he'd obviously found a good museum shop somewhere. I had soaps, bath oils and gardener's handcream from Mimi and Juno, an antique-looking ring from Roly—and a new postcard album, bound in soft blue leather, from Nick. He must have noticed my old one was full up to overflowing . . . *and* he must also intend sending me a lot more, too, so I expected I was right about him soon tiring of staying in one place and he'd soon be off on his travels again.

370

Jasper retired to his room, wearing the long Dr Who scarf Annie had knitted for him, to have a private conversation on his mobile phone with his girlfriend—about whom I still know practically nothing, except that her name is Kelly—while I tidied up the discarded wrapping paper and ribbons.

Then I put on my new slinky green dress (why should all the honours go to Polly?) and we went up to the Hall for Christmas dinner.

Annie and Gareth had been invited too, and it all felt a bit like *déjà vu* after the photoshoot one, except we actually got to eat the food, and Lionel Cripchet didn't burst in and start going on about squirrels. And Jasper was there too . . . *and* Ginny, who was sick behind the door from Mimi feeding her too many titbits, so that was different from last time.

I was wearing the old and valuable-looking ring that had been Unks' gift to me, but with the large, oval emerald turned inwards so it didn't catch the light. I felt increasingly sure it was a family heirloom, in which case I really had no right to it. So, as soon as I got the chance for a quiet word, while we were going into the drawing room for coffee, I asked him if he was sure I should have it.

'Yes, my dear, it's quite fitting,' he assured me. 'Don't you like it? Would you have preferred a modern one?'

'Oh, no, I love it! Only I'm sure I've seen it in one of the portraits in the gallery, so it must be a family piece.'

'It's the betroth—' began Mimi, who'd caught up with us, spotting it for the first time, but a glance from Unks silenced her and she wandered off again

371

with a giggle.

'I want you to have it,' Roly said firmly. 'Humour an old man, m'dear?'

I thanked him, but thought that the first opportunity I got I'd check out the portraits in the gallery and see if I could spot it, because if I was right, Nick might not be so happy about having part of his inheritance given away. Meanwhile, I'd have to remember not to wear it when gardening, or it would go the way of my wedding ring, back into the earth, never to be seen again.

CHAPTER 32: HOAR FROST

The annual Middlemoss Mystery Play on Boxing Day marks the end of the old year and the start of the new and I expect the Mystery Play replaced some much older, pagan ritual that would have taken place at about the same time.
The Perseverance Chronicles: A Life in Recipes

They say the sun shines on the godly, and certainly just as I arrived there on the morning of the Mystery Play with Jasper a weak, golden light began to spread over the courtyard of Pharamond Hall.

The farmers had cleared the local roads of the last fall of snow and, though icy in places, they were passable with care. In any case, many of the audience preferred to walk there.

The Mosses Women's Institute was setting up the refreshment stand near the kitchen door (the money raised goes to local charities), and I handed over my contribution of ginger parkin, fruitcake and bags of vanilla candyfloss. I managed to restrain myself from suggesting they make themselves Santa beards out of it, because this is quite a serious occasion, really.

Jasper went off to help Caz and Joe Gumball with the myriad last-minute jobs: lighting the charcoal braziers that were set around the courtyard, testing the microphone in Unks' little striped tent, from where he would speak as Voice of God, and moving scenery. I stored my Eve costume, wig and figleaves (which are threaded onto elastic, so they are quick and easy to put on for the Expulsion) in one of the loose boxes used for changing rooms: men to the left of the coach house, women to the right.

When I came out again the audience had started to arrive, bearing picnics, folding chairs and rugs, and Jojo and Mick were warming their hands at one of the charcoal braziers. I hadn't thought how depleted the Mummers would be, since Ritch was still away basking in the Caribbean, and Ophelia, of course, had just given birth; but when I spoke to them they told me that actually Ophelia and the baby were in the kitchen with Mrs Gumball, who would mind the infant while she popped out and performed as usual.

'Is that a good idea, so soon?' I asked doubtfully.

'Yeah, she's fine, she wants to do it,' Jojo assured me, but I imagine the poor girl's performance will be even limper than usual.

'Have they decided on a name for the baby yet?'

'Sylvester Star, according to Ophelia,' Mick said, 'but I heard Caz Naylor calling it Sly.'

'That's got to be better than Rambo, though,' I said, and they agreed.

Although there was an old outside toilet behind the stables (Victorian vintage, with shiny mahogany seating), in recent years Roly has also arranged for a portable toilet block to be set up next to it, which saves much queuing during the breaks. I sensibly repaired there before putting on my Eve costume under my clothes: it would certainly be impossible to go again in that outfit. Makes you wonder how Spiderman and other superheroes manage, doesn't it?

The Spandex felt odd under my jeans, but quite warm. I left my wig hanging on the post outside the

374

loosebox, together with my figleaves, and went outside again. The courtyard was now quite full and noisy, and the WI ladies were doing a roaring trade in hot drinks. The air was cold and smelled of spices and roasting chestnuts—or, if you suddenly and unexpectedly found yourself in the vicinity of Polly Darke and her little circle of friends, as I did, civet cats.

'You've been making candyfloss again, I see,' Nick said, doing his silently materialising act right next to me.

'I call it Hoar Frost and I'm dedicating the recipe to Polly,' I said tartly. 'What is *she* doing here? And why hasn't anyone run her off the premises?'

'She's here because I invited her specially and told her it just wouldn't be the same without her,' he said, with an enigmatic smile. 'I suppose you feel much the same about Ritch Rainford. Poor Lizzy—didn't he invite you to go to the Caribbean with him?'

I felt myself blush, because actually Ritch *had*, though I knew he was only flirting, as usual.

'Yes,' I said shortly and ambiguously. 'It's a pity he isn't here for the play,' I added, fingering my sparkling little snowman brooch rather ostentatiously. 'Several of the other *Cotton Common* cast members are, though I don't know if they'll have the stamina to stay for the whole thing.'

Nick's hand captured mine and he stared at the ring on my finger. 'I didn't get a good look at that last night,' he said thoughtfully. The flat green stone gleamed with restrained opulence in its heavy, antique gold setting.

'I hope you don't mind Unks giving it to me? I suspect it's a family heirloom, but I did ask him if he was *sure* he wanted me to have it.'

'Well, then, I suppose you could say he's given you the family seal of approval,' he said blandly. 'And look, he's arrived, so we must be about to start. Who's that with him?'

'Delphine Lake, one of the actresses in *Cotton Common.*'

Pretty as a picture from silver curls to tiny, pointed blue shoes, Delphine had somehow managed to insinuate herself into Roly's royal pavilion, but then, he always did have an eye for an attractive woman. There was just enough room for another folding canvas chair, and their heads were close together in earnest conversation.

Clive Potter came out and stood in front of the canvas curtains, holding up his hands for silence, and then bid everyone welcome to the Middlemoss Mysteries.

'Now let our play begin!' he said dramatically, bowed and walked off.

A small silence ensued, then there was a squeak as Nick leaned in and switched on Unks' microphone before his voice could be heard, confiding to Delphine, '. . . and then blow me if it didn't pick itself up at the fifth, overtake the field and gallop home by a head!'

'Voice of God!' Nick whispered urgently.

'Ah, yes—excuse me, my dear . . .' There was a rustling noise, as of paper being picked up. 'I AM GOD, THE ALL-POWERFUL, ALL-KNOWING,' he declaimed loudly, then lowering his voice to a more normal level, continued, 'Listen to my words—take heed of the mysteries that will unfold before your dazzled eyes.'

The curtain was pulled back to reveal Lucifer

and nine angels against a gilded cloudy backdrop and the Mysteries were well and truly up and running. (Or *bicycling*, as would be the case during Mary and Joseph's journey to Bethlehem and subsequent flight into Egypt.)

Various interesting noise effects accompanied God's description of the Creation, which I could hear as I shrugged off my clothes in the changing room and concealed as much of myself as possible with the long, blond wig.

Then we were on.

If you've ever tried to remember your lines while inches away from a tall and attractive man dressed in little more than ballet tights, you'll understand why I found it hard to keep my eyes on the apple. He was carrying a small sheaf of hay, which may have preserved his modesty from the audience, but was not much help to me. I expect ballerinas quickly get blasé about this kind of thing.

Of course, it might have helped if he'd stuck to the text when I offered him the apple, like he's done at all the recent rehearsals, instead of soulfully telling the audience in the most *hammy* way that I'd already had his heart and he didn't think a piece of fruit was much of an exchange.

They loved it, but I was tempted to elope with the snake.

Then he took a bite, tossed it over his shoulder into the wings and led me offstage to cover my modesty with figleaves.

'Nice costume,' he said, casting away his sheaf of hay and adjusting his figleaves like a hula skirt. The effect was interesting. 'Need any help with yours?'

'No, thanks,' I said primly. Whoever plays Eve next year will need new elastic: the twang had quite gone out of mine.

We quickly took our places behind the painted bushes and the Voice of God demanded why we had eaten the forbidden fruit? I only wished I knew.

'The woman tempted me,' Nick said, passing the buck, just as men have done from time immemorial, and we were expelled from Eden.

The curtain came down and the Mummers began to play something lilting while the scene was changed for Noah's Ark.

Nick dashed off for his changing room and I headed for my own warm outfit, shivering. I quickly dressed and then went out into the courtyard through the back doorway, avoiding the scurrying animal-headed infants and a harassed-looking Miss Pym.

Nick was already in the courtyard, talking to Polly. I elected to watch Noah's Flood from the *other* side, with Annie and Gareth.

'What's Polly doing here?' Annie whispered to me worriedly, when Gareth had kindly gone to get me a hot drink (I was still freezing). 'And why is Nick chatting to her like that, and laughing and . . . well, *flirting*?'

'Search me! He said he'd invited her, so perhaps he's fallen prey to her fatal beauty.'

'No, I'm sure he hasn't, because he was flirting with *you* in the Adam and Eve scene, Lizzy, and he couldn't take his eyes off you! He must have an ulterior motive for making up to Polly.'

'That's what Jasper says,' I agreed grudgingly, 'but *I* think he seems to be enjoying himself too much.'

The curtains closed on Noah's Ark and the animals, and then reopened revealing a tetchy-

378

looking Moses seated on a mountain.

'Here are my commandments, writ on tablets of stone,' said the Voice of God.

'Could thee not find something lighter? I'm no spring chicken, that knows!' grumbled Moses.

'There are ten of them—see thee obey the rules,' ordered God, while Moses hobbled about collecting them up in his teatowel headscarf.

'I'll give it me best shot, Lord, and I can't say fairer than that.'

Ignoring this sally, God ran briskly down the list then demanded finally, *'Dost thou understand?'*

'Yea, Lord,' Moses said obediently, though with an evil look in his rheumy blue eyes. 'I'm not deaf, tha knows! I'm going back down t'mountain as fast as me legs can carry me, and I'll be straight on t'case. Idol worshipping and other ungodly goings-on will be reet out t'window.'

'Good, good—for I see everything, you know, I am omnipresent,' God added conversationally.

Then the mike squeaked and his voice suddenly boomed, 'IN FACT, POLLY DARKE, I KNOW WHAT YOU DID LAST SUMMER! I KNOW IT WAS YOU WHO LOOSENED THE WHEEL NUTS ON LIZZY PHARAMOND'S CAR, CAUSING THE DEATH OF HER HUSBAND.'

Everyone, including me and a flummoxed Moses, turned to stare at Polly Darke. Nick let go of her arm and stepped away, but I could see from his face that this was no surprise to him: God's accusation had been prearranged.

She found herself the centre of a staring, whispering circle of shocked faces: even her friends were wide-eyed.

'*Polly* did?' I exclaimed. 'But—'

379

'No, no, I didn't!' Polly yelped, looking from face to face for some sympathy. 'Why on earth would I do that? I loved him!'

'Because you expected Lizzy to drive the car, not Tom,' Nick said clearly and coldly. 'It was just one of a series of little spiteful accidents you arranged for her, because you were eaten up with jealousy.'

'No! No, I didn't! I haven't—'

'Good heavens! Surely she wouldn't do something so evil?' gasped Annie, shocked to her soft-centred core, and Gareth put his arm around her consolingly. I wished someone would put their arm around *me*: I was shaking even more now, and not from the cold.

I didn't notice PC Perkins and her youthful associate until she was actually putting handcuffs on Polly, just like in a film, and saying clear enough for everyone to hear, 'Polly Darke, you are under arrest . . .' and proceeding to give her the official caution.

Polly stared around like a hunted animal, but there was no escape: I could see the flashing lights of police cars beyond the archway, and other officers. Then her eyes fixed on me.

'It was her—her!' she cried. 'I've said so all along . . . you've no proof!'

'It was not!' boomed God into his microphone. 'And there was a witness to your wrongdoing.'

'That's right,' Caz agreed loudly from the shadows. 'I seen her doing it.'

'EVIL WOMAN, BEGONE!' God added, with finality. I think the excitement of the moment had quite rushed to his head.

There was a buzz of excitement as she was escorted out and we all listened until the scrunch of gravel under tyres vanished into the distance.

I was struggling to take it all in, but when I saw Nick talking to Caz, I suddenly realised who must have hidden the wheel brace with Polly's fingerprints on it among my gardening tools, and then tipped off the police!

Would Polly have had the strength, once Jasper had tightened the nuts, I wondered—then remembered what Ritch and Dora Tombs had said about her working out. And really, anyone can change a wheel with one of those cross-brace things, it's not that difficult.

But it had been *my* car, *me* she wanted to hurt, not Tom. Not kill me—none of her little tricks had been intended to go quite that far; though I expect she would have looked on my death as a bonus.

And in the end Caz must have told Nick everything he knew, and so they had set this very public accounting up—as revenge? I didn't suppose Polly could be charged with anything terribly serious.

The courtyard was still buzzing, but then Moses suddenly awoke as if from a trance, and banged his shepherd's crook on the floor a couple of times to regain the audience's attention.

Slowly they quietened and turned back to the stage.

'If that's all, Lord, I'll be getting off, then,' Moses said, back to the script.

'Aye, go with my blessing upon you,' God said, sounding exhausted, and invisible hands began to draw the canvas curtains across the front of the arched doorway.

'A hot rum toddy, that's what I need,' Roly added, forgetting to switch off the microphone.

'Delphine, my dear, you'll join me, won't you? There's a short break before the next acts for refreshments, and I'm sure we all need them.'

Jojo and Mick picked up their instruments and began to play, and Ophelia, looking harassed and frightened, ran out of the house, fiddle in hand.

Nick forged his way through the crowd and handed me a plastic tumbler of hot toddy, which I took automatically and drained in one: I needed it.

'Well,' he said thoughtfully, 'I don't know how we'll be able to follow that next year.'

I turned on him accusingly. 'You knew that was going to happen—you, Caz and Uncle Roly set that up. How long have you known it was Polly who sabotaged the car?'

'Not long at all. I thought that, at least, was an accident, until Caz told me what he'd seen. He'd been watching from the woods that day and saw Polly come out of Tom's workshop and look at the car, then pick up the wheel brace (which Jasper must have left leaning against the wall, by the way) and start unscrewing the nuts—by sheer coincidence on the same wheel you'd changed earlier. Then she put the wheel brace back where she found it and left. Caz was going to go down and see what she'd been up to when the coast was clear, but Tom drove off in your car before he had the chance. So Caz wrapped the wheel brace in sacking and put it behind the freezer you let him use.'

'Why? And why didn't he say anything?'

He shrugged. 'Well, you know Caz. He said he thought at first it was something to do with ARG and he didn't want to get Ophelia into trouble. It was before he knew that Polly wasn't a member of the group, just forcing Ophelia to target you.'

'He's not keen on the police anyway. But he confided in *you*.'

'Yes, he finally told me the whole thing, because he was so angry that Polly was prepared to harm Ophelia, even when she was pregnant. I negotiated with the police and they're going to forget that Ophelia was ever a member of ARG in return for Caz's statement.'

He seemed to feel this was worthy of praise, for he paused expectantly.

'Oh, well done, Nick!' Annie, who had been listening admiringly, exclaimed. 'You are clever!'

I gave her a withering look. 'I think you might have let me in on what was happening, Nick!'

'Why? You didn't tell *me* anything! I found it all out for myself.'

'Yes, but Lizzy was upset when you were flirting with Polly, Nick,' Annie said traitorously.

'No I wasn't!' I exclaimed indignantly. 'I—'

'Ssh . . . afterwards,' Nick said, a gleam in his slaty dark eyes, 'they're starting again.'

I gave him a glare and moved away, avoiding him for the rest of the entertainment, which isn't easy when you're enclosed in a small courtyard. I can't say my mind was completely on the play either—or even on the refreshments, which just goes to show how churned-up and confused I felt.

But eventually I began to be caught up in the Mysteries again, just as I was every year.

Kylie was a subdued and modest Mary, with only one or two wisps of violently pink hair escaping from her hooded robe, and her fingernails unpainted. The huge rock that sparkled in the muted light on her engagement finger was not quite in role, though: Kylie had clearly got her man.

*   *   *

There were the usual moments of light relief during the Miracles: it didn't matter that the audience had heard the lines before.

'Get up, thou great lazy lummock,' Jesus told the Lame Man forthrightly. 'Pick up thy pallet and walk.'

'I'll be reet glad to, lad, 'tis no life for a man, this. What did tha say thy name wor?' asked the Lame Man, getting up.

'Jesus of Nazareth.'

'Is that ower near Burnley?'

'Nay,' said Jesus, moving on to the next supplicant. 'What's t'matter wi' him?' he asked one of the disciples.

'He can't see owt, master.'

'That's reet,' agreed the Blind Man. 'But I believe thee can cure me and so my friends hath brought me here.'

'I'll touch thy eyes, and if thee believe, then thee will see. How many fingers am I holding up?'

'All of 'em, Lord.'

The audience cheered, then sobered for the final darker scenes before the second interval. But once the curtain was drawn across the crucifixion scene (excellently performed by Gary Naylor) the holiday spirit returned and everyone headed for the refreshments to fortify themselves for the resurrection and the grand finale.

CHAPTER 33: WELL STIRRED

'We're happy, Lord, to see thee again,' Faye said stolidly, in her role as Mary Magdalen. 'Thee said that thee would come back and thou were right. Wilt thou stay awhile?'

'Nay, I must get home to my Heavenly Father.'

'Well, I reckon he'll be reet glad t'see thee, and thou art done thy bit for mankind.'

'My father hath many mansions, Mary, and all who believe in him will be welcome in t'Kingdom of Heaven.'

'That'll be proper champion, that will,' Mary said gratefully.

'I'll be off then,' Jesus said, suiting the action to the words, and Mary followed him behind the drawn curtain.

An angel appeared, the new white goose-feather patches on his wings glistening, and stood with one hand cupped to his ear, as if listening intently.

'Here is my judgement, and the pure of heart need fear nowt,' said Roly as Voice of God, refreshed and speeding up considerably now the finishing post was in sight.

'What is thy wish, Lord?' asked the angel.

'That retribution shall visit the wrongdoers.'

'Lord, it shall be done.'

'Let it be so, for as the old year dies, another, Lazarus-like, rises anew. Our play is played out, our Mysteries unfolded,' said God.

The angel, who'd been gazing vaguely up into the rafters, now turned to look directly at the audience and said weightily, 'Look into t'mirror of thy heart

385

and, if thou like not what thou see, then freshly start again, fer Christ died fer thee.'

God, as always, got the last word. 'Heed my commandments. Keep thy conscience clear. Remember, I'll see thee agin, this time next year!'

Going by the wild applause it was certainly another Middlemoss Mystery success, but more than one mystery had been enacted, revealed and resolved today. It had been a cathartic and exhausting experience, and the audience was subdued as they slowly began to leave, while *I* felt like a well-wrung-out dishrag.

'Everyone involved in organising the play has been invited to the house for a hot toddy before we go home,' Annie said, taking my arm and giving it a squeeze. 'You're coming too, aren't you, Lizzy? Look, there's Jasper going in. And I want to know all the details about Polly, too—did you really not know *any* of that was going to happen?'

'No, of course I didn't!' I snapped, finding myself being swept through the kitchen and along the passage to the Great Hall, where the steaming silver punch bowl and a tray of sandwiches were laid out before a blazing log fire. 'I'd have told you.'

Roly beckoned me across to where he was sitting with Delphine. 'Well, my dear,' he said, 'that seems to have worked out for the best, doesn't it? Justice for poor Tom has been served, and everything is sorted out satisfactorily.'

'Is it?' I said, slightly sourly.

'You were very good as Eve,' Delphine said kindly. 'Quite beautiful in that costume.'

'Yes, you're much better with Nick as Adam,' agreed Roly. 'But if he isn't playing it next year, he can take over as Voice of God.'

'That was Lizzy's last turn in the role, wasn't it?' Nick said, having come up behind me unobserved. 'I'm not playing Adam to anyone else's Eve.'

Roly looked from one to the other of us and, beaming, took our hands and clasped them together in his. (Theatricality also runs in the Pharamond bloodline.) 'Let it be a New Year, a new beginning for both of you!' he said sentimentally.

'I don't know what you mean, Unks,' I said, trying and failing to loosen my hand from Nick's strong grip. 'And I'm afraid I'll have to be going home now. Jasper?'

'I'm going out again, to help clear up,' Jasper said quickly. 'I'll see you later.'

'I'll walk you home, Lizzy,' Nick said, 'but first there's something I want to show you.'

I couldn't imagine what he'd got that I hadn't already seen. But I let him lead me upstairs to the long gallery, switching on the wall lights as we went. He came to a stop in front of the portrait of an eighteenth-century Pharamond bride, who posed with one slender hand resting on a book—and on her finger, my ring. I just *knew* it was an old family piece.

'There—you see?' he said.

'Nick, I can't possibly keep a family heirloom, whatever Unks says. Please take it back!' I protested, tugging it off my finger and handing it to him. He accepted it, then calmly took hold of my other hand and shoved it over the knuckle of my ring finger instead.

'What on earth are you doing?' I said, trying to pull away.

'It's the betrothal ring of the Pharamonds.'

'I dare say it is, but we're not betrothed—'

'I think we are, and Unks thinks we are—so you're outnumbered. Just as well he would never let Leila have the ring, because I'd never have got it back.'

I glared at him. 'This isn't the Middle Ages, so I do have a say in all this, Nick Pharamond—and I'm not engaged to you! You are an underhand, devious—'

'Yes, I know,' he said soothingly, pulling me close, 'but I do love you. I think, deep down, I always did.'

'You have a damned strange way of showing it!'

'There wasn't much point, when we were both married to other people . . . but the postcards showed I was always thinking of you. I never wanted quite to let go of you. *And* you kept them all.'

'Only for the recipes,' I said quickly, fighting a rear-guard action, for close proximity was scrambling my brain cells and weakening my knees, just as it so disastrously had on Bonfire Night. 'Besides, we argue all the time and you despise my cooking!'

'No I don't, I just like to wind you up. You should know that by now.'

'You think *your* cooking is more important than I am!' I accused him.

He grinned. 'No, I think it's a pretty even match, actually. I don't see why I can't have my cake and eat it.'

'I do. And anyway, we're just too different—it'd never work,' I said firmly, then ruined the effect by smiling back at him.

'If mayonnaise works, I don't see why mixing the

two of *us* together shouldn't—if we do it slowly and very carefully.' His lips moved over my face and then lingered on my mouth before I could point out that curdled mayonnaise was a lot easier to rescue than a curdled marriage.

Oh, hot chilli chocolate sauce! I thought, but more in resignation than revolt. *He* was the one who broke that clinch: I couldn't have, even if you'd waved a giant Mars bar in front of me.

'And I've had a great idea! Once you've finished *Just Desserts*, we'll collaborate on a joint recipe book of all the postcards. We'll call it *A Feast of Romance*,' he added soulfully.

I laughed. Senga was going to absolutely love it—and him. 'That is a totally corny idea! And what's more, I'm not cooking anything with you, because I always end up doing all the donkey wo—'

I stopped dead as I spotted Caz silently slinking out of the dark shadows at the end of the gallery. Downstairs someone had turned up the music so that the heavenly sound of a choir singing Silent Night drifted down the long, dark gallery, while over our heads a mistletoe ball rotated in the slight draught from the open door. Caz jerked his head back in the direction of the stairs. 'Mr Roly says t'champagne's open. You two done, yet?'

'Rising nicely,' Nick said, glancing up at the mistletoe ball thoughtfully, then reaching for me again.

'Half-baked!' I amended, giving him a quelling look. 'Caz, tell him we'll be down in a minute—and perhaps you ought to cork up the champagne again, because there are just a *few* rules of engagement I need to thrash out first, before I even *consider* this insane idea.'

'Like what?' Nick asked suspiciously.

'Separate kitchens,' I said, smiling sweetly. 'And that's just for starters!'

Loved the seasonal treats in this book? Then why not try and make them yourself?

1) Mincemeat Flapjacks
These are very easy to make!

Ingredients:
4 oz butter
2 tablespoons of golden syrup
2 oz Demerara sugar (or a soft, dark brown sugar, if you want a slightly 'treacly' taste)
5 heaped tablespoons of mincemeat, either bought or home-made
5 oz rolled oats

Method:
Preheat oven to gas mark 3, 160°C, 325°F and grease a seven-inch baking tin. If using a cake tin instead, then I would line the base with baking paper, too.

Melt together the sugar and syrup in a pan over a low heat, then stir in the mincemeat and, once warmed through, the oats.

Remove from heat and mix well, then spoon into the baking tin and spread it out, flattening the top.

Put into the oven for about half an hour: it should be slightly golden brown. Remove and leave to cool for fifteen minutes before marking into squares or slices.

When cool, store in an airtight container.

2) Christmas Mincemeat Spudge
(Mashed potato fudge)

Ingredients:
5 oz of mashed potato
1 oz butter
1 lb icing sugar (and some extra, in case it is needed)
4 tablespoons mincemeat, either bought or home-made
A few drops of almond essence

Method:
Grease a small baking tray or pie dish.

Mash the potato with the butter and, while still warm, stir in the icing sugar. When smooth, mix in the mincemeat and the almond essence to taste.

Depending on the runniness of the mincemeat used, you may need to add extra icing sugar—you are aiming for a very stiff consistency that has to be spread into the tray. (The first time I tried this variation I didn't put quite enough sugar in, so it didn't set hard, but it made a lovely fudge topping for vanilla ice cream!)

When cold it will be firm and can be cut into pieces and stored in an airtight box in the fridge.

Variations:
You can make plain Spudge by omitting the mincemeat. Instead try adding vanilla essence and/ or two tablespoons of desiccated coconut. When cold, cover with a layer of melted chocolate.